MERCURY INK

SIMON PULSE

MICHAEL VEY
THE PRISONER OF CELL 25

RICHARD PAUL EVANS

MERCURY INK

SIMON PULSE

NEW YORK   LONDON   TORONTO   SYDNEY

This book is a work of fiction. Any references to historical events, real people, or real locales are used fictitiously. Other names, characters, places, and incidents are the product of the author's imagination, and any resemblance to actual events or locales or persons, living or dead, is entirely coincidental.

SIMON PULSE / MERCURY INK

An imprint of Simon & Schuster Children's Publishing Division

1230 Avenue of the Americas, New York, NY 10020

First Simon Pulse/Mercury Ink hardcover edition August 2011

For information about special discounts for bulk purchases, please contact Simon & Schuster Special Sales at 1-866-506-1949 or business@simonandschuster.com.

The Simon & Schuster Speakers Bureau can bring authors to your live event. For more information or to book an event contact the Simon & Schuster Speakers Bureau at 1-866-248-3049 or visit our website at www.simonspeakers.com.

The text of this book was set in Berling LT Std.

Manufactured in the United States of America

10 9

This book has been cataloged with the Library of Congress.

ISBN 978-1-4516-5650-3

ISBN 978-1-4516-5822-4 (eBook)

To Michael

PART ONE

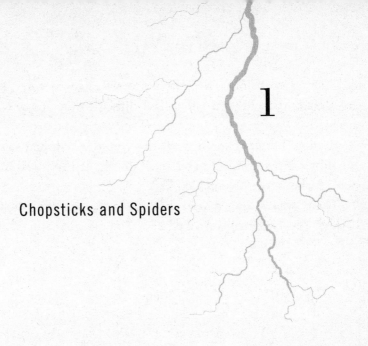

1

Chopsticks and Spiders

"**H**ave you found the last two?" The voice on the phone was angry and coarse, like the sound of car tires over broken glass.

"Not yet," the well-dressed man on the other end of the phone replied. "Not yet. But we believe we're close—and they still don't know that we're hunting them."

"You *believe* you're close?"

"They're two children among a billion—finding them is like finding a lost chopstick in China."

"Is that what you want me to tell the board?"

"*Remind* the board that I've already found fifteen of the seventeen children. I've put out a million-dollar bounty on the last two, we've got spiders crawling the Web, and we have a whole team of investigators scanning global records for their whereabouts. It's just a matter of time before we find them—or they step into one of our traps."

"*Time* isn't on our side," the voice returned sharply. "Those kids are already too old. You know how difficult they are to turn at this age."

"I know better than anyone," the well-dressed man said, tapping his ruby-capped pen on his desk. "But I have my ways. And if they don't turn, there's always Cell 25."

There was a long pause, then the voice on the phone replied darkly, "Yes. There's always Cell 25."

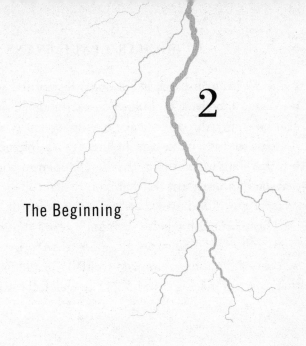

2

The Beginning

It's not like I was looking for trouble. I didn't have to. At my height it just always found me.

My name is Michael Vey, and the story I'm about to tell you is strange. Very strange. It's my story.

If you passed me walking home from school you probably wouldn't even notice me. That's because I'm just a kid like you. I go to school like you. I get bullied like you. Unlike you, I live in Idaho. Don't ask me what state Idaho is in—news flash—Idaho *is* a state. The fact that most people don't know where Idaho is, is exactly why my mother and I moved here—so people wouldn't find us. But that's part of my story.

Besides living in Idaho, I'm different from you in other ways. For one, I have Tourette's syndrome. You probably know less about Tourette's syndrome than you do Idaho. Usually when you see someone on TV pretending to have Tourette's syndrome, they're shouting swear words or barking like a dog. Most of us with Tourette's don't do that. I mostly just blink my eyes a lot. If I'm really anxious, I'll also clear my throat or make a gulping noise. Sometimes it hurts. Sometimes kids make fun of me. It's no picnic having Tourette's, but there are worse things that can happen to you—like having your dad die of a heart attack when you're eight. Believe me, that's much worse. I'm still not over that. Maybe I never will be.

There's something else you don't know about me. It's my secret. Something that scares people more than you would believe. That secret is the reason we moved to Idaho in the first place. But, again, that's part of my story. So I might as well tell it to you.

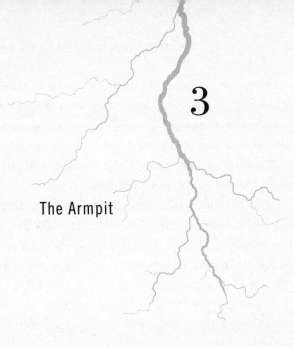

3

The Armpit

Mr. Dallstrom's office is as good a place to begin as any. Or as bad a place. Mr. Dallstrom is the principal of Meridian High School, where I go to school. If you ask me, ninth grade is the armpit of life. And there I was in the very stinkiest part of that armpit—the principal's office. I was sitting in Mr. Dallstrom's office, blinking like crazy.

You could guess that I'm not fond of Mr. Dallstrom, which would be stating the obvious, like saying, "Breathing is important" or "Rice Krispies squares are the greatest food ever invented." No one at Meridian was fond of Mr. Dallstrom except Ms. Duncan, who directed the Glee Club. She had a picture of Mr. Dallstrom on her desk, which she sometimes stared at with soft, googly eyes. Every time Mr. Dallstrom came over the PA system, she would furiously whack her baton on a music stand to quiet us. Then, after he'd said his piece, she would get all red-faced and sweaty, and remind us of how lucky we were to be led through the treacherous wilderness of high school by such a manly and steadfast defender of public education.

Mr. Dallstrom is a bald, thin scarecrow of a man with a poochy stomach. Think of a pregnant Abraham Lincoln with no beard and a yellow toupee instead of a top hat and you get the picture. He also looks like he's a hundred years old. At least.

When I was in fifth grade our teacher told us that "the easiest way to remember the difference between PRINCI*PLE* (an underlying law or ethic), and PRINCI*PAL* (the chief administrator of a school), is that the principal is your PAL." Believe me, Mr. Dallstrom did not put the PAL in principal.

It was the second time that month I'd been called to his office for something someone else did to me. Mr. Dallstrom was big on punishing the victim.

"I believe this is the second time you've been in my office this month," Mr. Dallstrom said to me, his eyes half closed. "Is that right, Mr. Vey?"

That was the other thing about Mr. Dallstrom—he liked to ask questions that he already knew the answer to. I was never sure if I was supposed to answer him or not. I mean, he knew the answer, and I knew the answer, so what was the point? Bottom line, it was the second time I'd been locked in my locker by Jack Vranes and his friends that month. This time they put me in upside down and I nearly passed out before the custodian unlocked my locker and dragged me down to Mr. Dallstrom's office.

Jack Vranes was, like, seventeen and still in ninth grade. He'd been held back so many times, he had a driver's license, a car, a mustache, and a tattoo. He sometimes called himself Jackal, which is a pretty accurate description, since both he and the animal prey on smaller mammals. Jack had biceps the size of ripe Florida oranges and wasn't afraid to use them. Actually, he loved to use them. He and his gang, Mitchell and Wade, watched ultimate fighting, and Jack took Brazilian jujitsu lessons at a gym not far from the school. His dream in life was to fight in the Octagon, where he could pound people and get paid for it.

"Is that right?" Dallstrom repeated, still staring at me. I ticked almost a dozen times, then said, "But, sir, it wasn't my fault. They shoved me inside my locker upside down." He wasn't looking very moved by my plight, so I continued. "There were three of them and they're a lot bigger than me. A *lot* bigger."

My hope for sympathy was met by Mr. Dallstrom's infamous "stare o' death." Really, you'd have to see it to understand. Last quarter, when we were studying Greek mythology and we got to the part about Medusa—a Gorgon woman who could turn people to stone by looking into their eyes—I figured out where Mr. Dallstrom had come from. Maybe it had something to do with my Tourette's, but I blurted out, "That must be Mr. Dallstrom's great-great-great-great-grandmother."

Everyone had laughed. Everyone except for Mr. Dallstrom, who had picked that precise moment to slip into our class. I spent a week in after-school detention, which wasn't all bad because at least I was safe from Jack and his posse, who somehow never got sent to detention no matter how many kids they stuffed into the lunchroom garbage cans or locked in their lockers. Anyway, that had officially put me on Mr. Dallstrom's troublemaker list.

"Mr. Vey, you cannot be stuffed into a locker without your consent," Mr. Dallstrom said, which may be the dumbest thing ever said in a school. "You should have resisted." That's like blaming someone who was struck by lightning for getting in the way.

"But I tried, sir."

"Obviously not hard enough." He took out a pen. "Who are these boys who allegedly stuffed you into your locker?" Mr. Dallstrom cocked his head to one side, his pen wagging impatiently in front of him. I stared at the pen in its hypnotic trajectory.

"I'm waiting, Mr. Vey. Their names?"

There was no way I was going to tell him. First, he already knew who had done it. Everyone knew Jack had put more kids than textbooks into lockers. Second, ratting out Jack was the shortest route to death. I just looked at Mr. Dallstrom, my eyes blinking like crazy.

"Stop twitching and answer my question."

"I can't tell you," I finally said.

"Can't or won't?"

Pick one, I thought. "I forgot who did it."

Mr. Dallstrom continued staring at me through those half-closed eyes of his. "Did you now?" He stopped wagging his pen and set it on the desk. "I'm sorry to hear that, Mr. Vey. Now you'll have to take their punishment as well. Four weeks in after-school detention. I believe you know where detention is held."

"Yes, sir. It's in the lunchroom."

"Good. Then you'll have no trouble finding your way there."

Like I said, Mr. Dallstrom excelled at punishing the victim. He signed a tardy excuse note and handed it to me. "Give that to your teacher. You can go back to your class now, Mr. Vey."

"Thank you, sir," I said, not entirely certain what I was thanking him for. I walked out of his office and slowly down the long, empty corridor to biology. The hallway was lined with posters made by the Basketball Boosters' Club with messages like GO WARRIORS, SINK THE VIKINGS—that sort of thing—rendered in bright poster paints.

I got my backpack from my locker, then went to class.

My biology teacher, Mr. Poulsen, a short, balding man with thick eyebrows and a massive comb-over, was in the middle of lecturing and stopped mid-sentence at my entrance. "Glad you decided to join us, Mr. Vey."

"Sorry. I was at the principal's office. Mr. Dallstrom said to give this to you." I handed him my note. He took the paper without looking at it. "Sit down. We're reviewing for tomorrow's test."

Every eye in the class followed me as I walked to my desk. I sat in the second row from the back, just behind my best friend, Ostin Liss, who is one of the smartest kids in the universe. Ostin's name looks European or something, but it isn't. His mother named him that because he was born in Austin, Texas. It was his private curse that she had spelled it wrong. I suspect that Ostin was adopted, because I couldn't figure out how someone that smart could come from someone who couldn't spell the name of the city she lived in. But even if Ostin's mom wasn't the brightest crayon in the box, I liked her a lot. She spoke with a Texan accent and called everyone "honey," which may sound annoying but it wasn't. She was always nice and kept a supply of red licorice in their pantry just because she knew I liked it and my mother didn't buy candy.

Ostin never got shoved into his locker, probably because he was wider than it—not that Jack and his friends left him alone. They didn't. In fact he had suffered the ultimate humiliation from Jack and his friends. He'd been pantsed in public.

"How'd it go with Dallstrom?" Ostin whispered.

I shook my head. "Brutal."

As I sat down, Taylor Ridley, who sat in the desk to my left, turned and smiled at me. Taylor is a cheerleader and one of the prettiest girls at Meridian. Heck, she's one of the prettiest girls in any high school anywhere in the world. She has a face that could be on the cover of a beauty magazine, long, light brown hair and big brown eyes the color of maple syrup. Since I'm being completely honest here, I'll admit that I had a crush on her from the second I first saw her. It took me less than a day to realize that so did everyone else at Meridian.

Taylor was always nice to me. At first I hoped she was nice because she liked me, but really she's just one of those people who is nice to everyone. Nice or not, it didn't matter. She was way out of my league. Like a thousand miles out of my league. So I never told anyone about my secret crush—not even Ostin, who I told everything. Some dreams are just too embarrassing to share.

Anyway, whenever Taylor looked at me, it made my tics go wild. Stress does that to people with Tourette's. I forced myself not to blink as I sat down and pulled my biology book out of my backpack. That's the thing about my tics. If I try real hard, I can delay them, but I can't make them go away. It's like having a bad itch. You can ignore it for a little while, but it's going to build up until you scratch. I've learned tricks to hide my tics. Like sometimes I'll drop a pencil on the ground, then when I bend down to get it, I'll blink or grimace like crazy. I'm sure the kids around me think I'm really clumsy because sometimes I'll drop my pencil four or five times in one class. Anyway, between Mr. Dallstrom and Jack and Taylor, I was blinking like an old neon sign.

Poulsen started up again. "Okay, class, we were talking about electricity and the body. 'I sing the body electric,' said the poet Whitman. Who, pray tell, can explain what role electricity plays in the body?"

He panned the room with his dusty gaze, clearly disappointed with the lack of participation. "You better know this, people. It's on your test tomorrow."

"Electricity runs our heart," the girl with massive braces in the front row said.

"Cor-rect," he said. "And what else?"

Taylor raised her hand. "It signals all of our nerves and thoughts."

"That's right, Miss Ridley. And where does this electricity come from?" He looked around the room. "Where does the electricity come from? Come on, people." It was dangerous when no one was answering because that's when he started hunting out those least likely to answer correctly. "How about you, Mr. Morris?"

"Uh, batteries?"

The class laughed.

"Brilliant," Poulsen said, shaking his head. "Batteries. Okay, Mr. Morris, perhaps it's time you changed your batteries, because clearly they are running down. Where does electricity come from, Mr. Vey?"

I swallowed. "Electrolytes?" I said.

"That would be true, Mr. Vey, if you were an electric eel."

Everyone laughed again. Taylor glanced over at me sympathetically. I dropped my pencil on the floor.

Ostin raised his hand.

"Mr. Liss," Poulsen said. "Enlighten us."

Ostin straightened himself up in his chair like he was about to deliver a lecture, which he was.

"The human body generates an electrical current through chemical concentrations in the nerves in a process called bioelectrogenesis. Whenever a nerve signal is sent, potassium ions flood out of nerve cells and sodium ions flood in. Both of these ions have slightly different charges and so the difference in ionic concentrations inside and outside the nerve cell creates a charge which our bodies process as electricity."

"Bravo, Mr. Liss. Harvard awaits. For those of you who have no idea what Mr. Liss just said, I'll write it on the board. Bio-elec-tro-gen-e-sis."

When Poulsen's back was turned, Ostin turned around and whispered, "What happened with Dallstrom? Did Jack get detention?"

I shook my head. "No, I got detention."

His eyebrows rose. "For getting shoved into your own locker?"

"Yeah."

"Dallstrom's a tool."

"*That* I know."

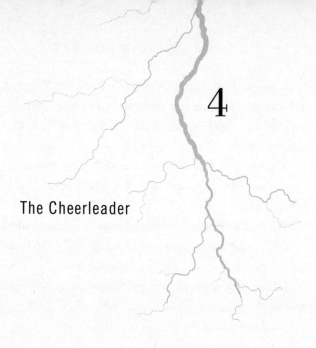

4

The Cheerleader

That Wednesday felt like one of the longest days in school ever. I had no idea that it wasn't even close to being over. After the final bell rang, Ostin and I walked to our lockers, which were next to each other.

"Want to come over and play Halo?" Ostin asked.

"Can't. I've got detention, remember?"

"Oh, yeah."

"I'll knock on your door when I get home."

Ostin and I lived just two doors from each other in the same apartment building.

"I won't be home. I have clogging lessons at four."

"Ugh," I said. It was hard to imagine Ostin doing any physical activity, but dancing with a bunch of seven-year-old girls wearing black patent leather tap shoes was like a bad car wreck—gross, but you just have to look. "You've got to get out of that, man. If anyone here finds out, you're ruined for life."

"I know. But the clogging teacher's my mom's cousin and Mom says she needs the money and I need the exercise."

"It's still cruel," I said, shutting my locker. "I'll see you tomorrow."

He put out his fist. "Bones."

"Bones," I said, bumping his fist even though I was sick of doing it—I mean, it was okay the first *million* times.

The hallways were crowded with students as I walked with my backpack down to the lunchroom. Ms. Johnson, a young, new English teacher, had just been assigned to supervise detention, which I thought was a good thing. She was reputed to be cool and nice, which, I hoped, meant she might let us out early.

I walked up to her. I had to force myself not to tic. "I'm Michael Vey. I'm here for detention."

She smiled at me like I'd just arrived at a dinner party. "Hi, Michael. Welcome." She looked down at her clipboard and marked my name on her roll. "Go ahead and pick a table."

The smell of lunch still lingered in the air (which was a punishment of its own), and I could hear the lunch workers behind the metal window screens preparing for tomorrow's disaster.

There were three other students in detention: two boys and one girl. I was smaller than all of them and the only one who didn't look like a homicidal psychopath. As I looked around the room for a place to sit, the girl looked at me and scowled, warning me away from her table. I found a vacant table in the corner and sat down.

I hated being in detention, but at least today it wouldn't be a complete waste of time. I needed to study for Poulsen's test. As I got my books from my pack, I noticed that my shoulder still hurt a little from being crammed into my locker. I tugged on my collar and exposed a bright red scrape. Fortunately, I had gotten my fingers out of the way just in time to not have the door slammed on them. I wondered if anyone would call my mom about the incident. I hoped not. She had a stupid job she didn't like and I didn't want to make her day any worse than it already was.

Just twenty minutes into detention, Ms. Johnson said, "All right, that's enough. Time to go."

I scooped my books into my pack and threw it over my shoulder. "See you tomorrow," I said to Ms. Johnson.

"See you tomorrow, Michael," she said pleasantly.

Outside the cafeteria, the halls were now empty except for the janitorial crew that had moved in and were pushing wide brooms up and down the tiled corridors. I stopped at my locker and grabbed the licorice I'd stowed in there after lunch and had looked forward to all day. I peeled back its wrapper and took a delicious chewy bite. Whoever invented licorice was a genius. I loved licorice almost as much as Rice Krispies squares. I swung my pack over my shoulder, then walked out the south door, glad to finally be going home.

I had just come around the corner of the school when Jack and his posse, Mitchell and Wade, emerged from between two Dumpsters. Jack grabbed me by the front of my shirt. I dropped my licorice.

"You ratted us out to Dallstrom, didn't you?" Jack said.

I looked up at him, my eyes twitching like crazy. "I didn't tell him."

"Yeah, right, you little chicken." Jack shoved me backward into a pyracantha bush. Sharp thorns pricked my neck, arms, and legs. The only place that wasn't stinging was where my backpack protected me.

"You're going to pay," Jack said, pointing at me, "big-time." He turned to Mitchell, who was almost as tall as Jack but not as broad-shouldered or muscular. "Show him what we do to snitchers."

"I didn't tell on you," I said again. "I promise."

Before I could climb out of the bush, Mitchell pulled me up and thumped me hard on the eye. I saw a bright flash and felt my eye immediately begin to swell. I put my hand over it, trying not to lose my balance.

"Hit him again," Jack said.

The next fist landed on my nose. It hurt like crazy. I could feel blood running down my lips and chin. My eyes watered. Then Jack walked up and punched me right in the gut. I fell to my knees, unable to breathe. When I could finally fill my lungs with air, I began to groan. I couldn't stop blinking.

"He's crying like a baby," Mitchell said joyfully. "Cry, baby, cry."

Then came Wade. Wade West had yellow hair and a crooked nose. He was the smallest and ugliest of the three, which is probably why he was the meanest since he had the most to prove. "I say we pants him." This was a specialty of Wade's. By "pants" he meant to pull off my pants—the ultimate act of humiliation. Last year in eighth grade, Wade had pantsed Ostin behind the school, pulling off his pants and underwear in front of a couple dozen classmates. Ostin had to run home naked from the waist down, something he had never lived down.

"Yeah," Mitchell agreed, "that'll teach him for ratting us out."

"No!" I shouted, struggling to my feet. "I didn't tell on you."

Just then someone shouted, "Leave him alone!"

Taylor Ridley was standing alone near the school door, dressed in her purple-and-gold cheerleading outfit.

"Hey, check out the cheerleader," Wade said.

"You're just in time to watch us pants this guy," Mitchell said.

"Yeah, shake those pom-poms for us," Jack said, laughing like a maniac. Then he made up his own cheer, which was surprisingly clever for Jack. "Two, four, six, eight, who we gonna cremate?" He laughed again. "Grab him."

Before I could even try to get away, all three of them grabbed me. Despite the fact that my nose was still bleeding and I could barely see out of one eye, I went wild, squirming against their clamplike grips. I got one hand loose and hit Jack in the neck, scoring only a dull thud. He responded by thumping me on the ear.

"Come on, you wimps!" he shouted at Mitchell and Wade. "You can't hold this runt?" They pinned me facedown on the ground, the weight of all three of them crushing me into the grass.

"Stupid little nerd," Mitchell said. "You think you can rat on us and not pay?"

I tried to curl up so they couldn't take my clothes, but they were too strong. Jack pulled on my shirt until it began to tear.

"You leave him alone or I'll get Mrs. Shaw!" Taylor shouted. "She's right inside." Mrs. Shaw was the cheerleaders' adviser and taught home economics. She was a soft-spoken, matronly woman and about as scary as a throw pillow. I think we all knew that she wasn't actually inside or Taylor would have just gotten her in the first place.

"Shut your mouth," Jack said.

Hearing him talk that way to Taylor infuriated me. "You shut your mouth, you loser," I said to Jack.

"You need to learn manners, blinky boy."

"You need mouthwash," I said.

Jack grabbed me by the hair and pulled my head around. "You're going to be wishing you'd kept your mouth shut." He smacked me again on the nose, which sent a shock of pain through my body. At that moment something snapped. I knew I couldn't hold back much longer.

"Let me go!" I shouted. "I'm warning you."

"Ooh," Wade said. "He's warning us."

"Yeah, whatcha gonna do?" Mitchell said. "Cry on us?"

"No, he's gonna wipe his nose on us," Wade laughed. He pulled off my shoes while Mitchell grabbed my waistband and started tugging at my pants. I was still trying to curl up.

"Stop struggling," Jack said. "Or we're going to take everything you got and make you streak home."

"Leave him alone!" Taylor yelled again.

"Mitch, hurry and pull his pants off," Wade said.

A surge of anger ran through my body so powerful I couldn't control it. Suddenly a sharp, electric ZAP! pierced the air, like the sound of ice being dropped onto a hot griddle. Electricity flashed and Jack and his posse screamed out as they all fell to their backs and flopped about on the grass like fish on land.

I rolled over to my side and wiped the blood from my nose with the back of my hand. I pushed myself up, red-faced and angry. I stood above Jack, who was frothing at the mouth. "I told you to leave me alone. If you ever touch me again, I'll do worse. Do you understand? Or do you want more?" I lifted my hand.

Terror was evident in his eyes. "No. Please don't."

I turned and looked at his posse. Both of them were on the ground, quivering and whimpering. In fact, Wade was bawling like a baby and moaning, "It hurts . . . it hurts so bad."

I walked over to him. "You bet it hurts. And that was just a little one. Next time you bully me, or any of my friends, I'll triple it."

As the three of them lay there groaning and quivering, I sat back on the ground, pulled on my shoes, and tied them. Then I remembered Taylor.

I looked back over at the door, hoping she had gone inside. She hadn't. And from the expression on her face, I could tell she had seen everything. Bad, bad news. My mother was going to kill me. But there was nothing I could do about that now. I grabbed my backpack and ran home.

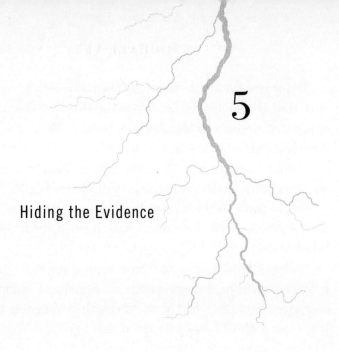

5

Hiding the Evidence

By the time I got home, my left eye was nearly swollen shut. I set my backpack on the kitchen table, then went into the bathroom and looked at myself in the mirror. My eye looked like a ripe plum. There was no way of hiding it from my mother. I got a washcloth and wiped the blood off my nose and chin.

My mother usually got home around six thirty, so I heated up a can of SpaghettiOs for dinner, grabbed the blue ice pack she kept in the freezer for her occasional headaches, then held the ice against my eye while I played video games with one hand. I know I should have been studying for my biology test, but after a day like this one, I just didn't have it in me.

I really didn't want to talk to my mom about my day, so when I heard her key in the door, I ran to my room, shut the door, turned out the lights, threw off my shirt, and crawled into bed.

She called for me from the front room. "Michael?" Twenty seconds later she knocked on my door, then opened it. I pretended to be sleeping, but she didn't fall for it.

"Hey, pal, what are you doing in bed?"

"I don't feel well," I said. I pulled the covers over my head.

"What's wrong?"

She turned on my bedroom light and immediately saw my torn shirt on the floor and the blood on it. "Michael, what happened?" She walked over to my bed. "Michael, look at me."

"I don't want to."

"Michael."

Reluctantly, I pulled the covers down. Her mouth opened a little when she saw my face. "Oh my . . . what happened?"

A lump came to my throat. "Jack and his friends wouldn't leave me alone."

"Oh, honey," she said. She sat down on the side of my bed. After a minute she asked, "Did it . . . happen?"

I didn't want to tell her. I didn't want to upset her more than she already was. "I'm sorry, Mom. I tried not to. But they wouldn't leave me alone. They were trying to pull my pants off."

She gently brushed the hair back from my face. "Stupid boys," she said softly. I could see the worry on her face. "Well, they had it coming, didn't they?" A moment later she said, "I'm sorry, Michael. I wish I knew what to do."

"Why won't they just leave me alone?"

My cheek was twitching and she gently ran her thumb over it. Then she leaned forward and kissed my forehead. "I wish I knew, son. I wish I knew."

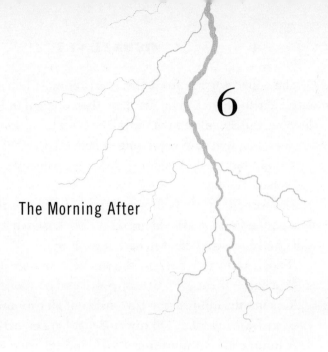

6

The Morning After

My radio alarm clock went off at the usual time: 7:11. I had my radio set to the *Morning Zoo* show. The hosts, Frankie and Danger Boy, were talking about people who suffered from bananaphobia—the intense fear of bananas.

I gently touched my eye. The swelling had gone down some, but it still ached. So did my heart. I felt like I had betrayed my mom and I worried that we'd have to move. Again. The thought of starting over filled me with dread. I couldn't imagine how hard it would be for her. I went into the bathroom and looked in the mirror. *You look pretty sorry*, I thought. I showered and got dressed, then walked out to the kitchen.

My mother was standing next to the refrigerator dressed in her orange work smock. She was a checker at the local Smith's Food Mart. She was making waffles with strawberry jam and whipped cream. I was glad, not just because I loved waffles, but because it meant she wasn't mad at me.

"How's your eye?" she asked.

"It's okay."

"Come here, let me see." I walked over to her, and she leaned forward to examine it. "That's quite a shiner." She pulled a waffle from the iron. "I made you waffles."

"Thanks."

I sat down at the table, and she brought over a plate. "Would you like orange juice or milk to drink?"

"Can I have chocolate milk?"

"Sure." She went back to the kitchen counter and poured me a glass of milk, then got a can of powdered chocolate from the cupboard and stirred some in. The sound of the spoon clinking against the glass filled the room. She brought the glass over to the table, then sat down next to me.

"So these boys who were picking on you . . ."

"Jack and his friends."

"Do I need to call their parents?"

"I don't think Jack has parents. I think he was spawned."

She grinned. "What about the other boys?"

"They crawled out of the sewer."

"So would it help if I called these sewer creatures' parents?"

I cut a piece of waffle and took a bite. "No. It would just make things worse. Besides, I don't think they'll be messing with me anymore."

"Do you think they'll tell anyone what happened?"

"No one would believe them anyway."

"I hope you're right." She looked across the table. "How are the waffles?"

"Good, thanks." I took another bite.

"You're welcome." Her voice was pitched with concern. "Did anyone else see what happened?"

"A girl."

"What girl?"

"She's in one of my classes. She was telling them to leave me alone when it happened."

The look of anxiety on her face made my stomach hurt. After a moment, she stood. "Well, I guess we'll just cross that bridge when we get to it." She kissed me on the forehead. "I better go. Want a ride to school?"

"No, I'm okay."

Just then there was a knock. My mom answered the door. Ostin stood in the hallway. "Hello, Mrs. Vey."

"Good morning, Ostin. You're looking sharp today."

Ostin pulled in his stomach. He thought my mother was a "babe," which made me crazy. Ostin was fifteen years old and girl crazy, which was unfortunate because he was short, chubby, and a geek, which is pretty much all you need to scare girls our age away. I have no doubt that someday he'll be the CEO of some Fortune 500 company and drive a Ferrari and have girls falling all over themselves to get to him. But he sure didn't now.

"Thank you, Mrs. Vey," he said. "Is Michael ready?"

"Just about. Come on in."

He stepped inside, dwarfed by the size of his backpack.

"Hey, Ostin," I said.

He looked at my black eye. "Dude, what happened?"

"Jack and his friends jumped me."

His eyes widened. "Did they pants you?"

"They tried."

"High school," my mother said. "You couldn't pay me a million dollars to go back." She grabbed her keys and purse. "All right. You boys have a good day. Stay out of trouble."

"Thank you, Mrs. Vey."

"See ya, Mom."

She stopped at the doorway. "Oh, Michael, we're doing inventory at the store today, so I'll be late tonight. I'll probably be home around eight. Just make yourself some mac 'n' cheese."

"No problem."

"You sure you don't want a ride?"

Ostin almost said something, but I spoke first. "We're fine," I said.

"Okay, see you later." She walked out.

"Your mom is so hot," Ostin said as he sat down at the table.

"Dude, shut up. She's my mom."

He pointed to my face. "So what happened?"

"Jack thought I ratted him out to Dallstrom. So he and his posse jumped me behind the school."

"Wade," Ostin said bitterly. "You should have just zapped him."

I put my hand over his mouth. "Shut up. You know you're not supposed to know."

"I know. Sorry." He looked over at the door. "She's gone anyway," he said. His face brightened. "Hey, I got the multimeter from my uncle so we can test you." Ostin had this idea about measuring how many volts of electricity I could generate, which frankly I was curious about too.

"Cool."

"Seriously, dude, I don't know why you hide your power. It's like having a race car you have to leave parked in the garage all the time. Why even have it? You could be the most powerful kid at school. Instead you get beat up."

"Well, Jack and his friends won't be bothering us anymore."

Ostin looked at me in surprise. "Did you do it?"

"Yeah."

"Cool! Man, I wish I had been there to see you hand down the righteous judgment."

I took another bite. "If you were there, you'd have a black eye too. If Wade didn't pants you first."

He frowned at the thought of it. "So does your mom know you used it?"

"Yeah."

"Did she freak?"

"Yeah. But she was cool about it. She's worried that someone might find out, but she doesn't want me to get beat up either. They started it. I just finished it."

"Speaking of, are you going to finish those waffles?"

"There's extra in the kitchen."

"Cool. My mom made gruel for breakfast."

"What's gruel?"

"It's punishment. Really, dude, it tastes like wallpaper paste. I think they feed it to prisoners in Siberian gulags."

"Why does she make it?"

"Because she ate it when she was a kid. But your mom's waffles . . . oh, baby. The only thing better than how she looks is her cooking."

"Dude, just stop it."

Ostin shook his head. "I was born in the wrong house." He threw two waffles on a plate and brought them over to the table, where he drowned them in a sea of syrup. "Did anyone else see you do it?"

"Taylor."

"Taylor Ridley? The cheerleader?"

"Yeah."

"What did she do?"

"She just stared."

"Wow. I wish I had been there." He took a massive bite of waffle, the syrup dribbling down his chin. "Did you study for our biology test?"

"A little. In detention. How about you?"

"Don't need to. It's all right here." He pointed to his head. Ostin had a 4.0 grade point average only because the scale didn't go higher. If his body matched his brain, he'd be Mr. Universe. "Do you have detention today?"

"I have detention for the next four weeks unless you can figure out a way to get me out of it."

"Maybe you should just shock Dallstrom."

"Only in my dreams."

Just then the front door opened and my mom leaned in. "Michael, can you give me a hand?"

"Sure. What's up?"

"Just come outside."

"Need some help, Mrs. Vey?" Ostin asked.

"You stay put, Ostin. I need to talk to Michael alone."

Ostin frowned. I got up and walked outside, shutting the door behind me. "What's wrong?"

"I left the car's dome light on all night and the battery's dead. Can you give me a jump?"

"Sure."

I followed her out of the building and across the parking lot to our car, a ten-year-old Toyota Corolla. She looked around to make sure no one was watching, then she climbed inside and popped the hood. I lifted it the rest of the way up, then grabbed the car battery's terminals. "Go ahead," I said.

The starter motor clicked until I pulsed (which is what I call what I do, pulse or surge) and the engine fired up. I let go of the battery. Mom raced the engine for a moment, then she stuck her head out the window. "Thanks, honey."

I shut the hood. "Sure."

"Have a good day."

She pulled out of the parking lot as I went back inside. Ostin was still at the table finishing his waffles.

"What was that about?" he asked, his mouth full.

"Car battery was dead."

"And you started it up?"

"Yeah."

"That is so cool."

"At least my electricity's good for something."

"It's good as Jack-repellant," Ostin said cheerfully.

I looked at him and frowned. "Stop eating. We're going to be late."

He quickly shoved in two more bites, then stood. I threw my pack over my shoulder, then Ostin and I walked the five blocks to school.

Meridian High School was the fourth school I had been to since we moved to Idaho five years earlier. On the first day of high school, my mother had said to me, "Don't get in trouble—and don't hurt anyone," which I'm sure would have sounded ridiculous to anyone who didn't know my secret. I mean, I'm shorter than almost everyone at school, including the girls, and I never started problems, except by being small and looking vulnerable.

When I was in the sixth grade at Churchill Junior High, a bunch of wrestlers put me in the lunchroom garbage can and rolled me across the cafeteria. It was chicken à la king day and I was covered with rice and yellow gravy with carrots and peas. It took five minutes before I couldn't take it anymore and I "went off," as my mother calls it.

I wasn't as good at controlling it back then, and one of the boys was taken to the hospital. The faculty and administration went nuts. Teachers questioned me, and the principal and the school police officer searched me. They thought I had a stun gun or Taser or something. They went through my coat and pants pockets, and even the garbage can, but, of course, they found nothing. They ended their investigation by concluding that the boys had touched a power cord or something. None of the wrestlers got in trouble for what they had done and all was forgotten. A few months later my mom and I moved again.

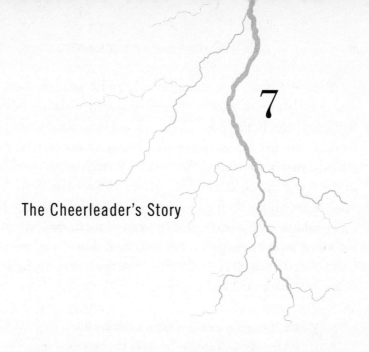

7

The Cheerleader's Story

If you've ever had a black eye, you'll know what my day was like. Everyone just stared at me like I was a freak or something. By the end of the day I was walking with my head down and my eyes partially covered by a copy of the school paper—the *Meridian Warwhoop*. Still, the day wasn't all bad. I didn't see Mr. Dallstrom once, and there was no sign of Jack or his friends. I figured I had probably scared them off for at least a few days.

As I walked into biology, my last class of the day, I noticed Taylor Ridley staring at me. I ignored her gaze and sat down.

"Hey," she said. "Are you okay?"

I didn't look at her. As usual my tics started.

She leaned toward me. "Michael."

I didn't even know that she knew my name.

The tardy bell rang and Mr. Poulsen began walking up and down the rows of desks, handing out our tests.

"People, today's test comprises one-fifth of your final grade, so you don't want to rush it. I want complete silence. N'er a word. You know the penalty for cheating, so I won't elaborate, except to remind you that it's an automatic F and an unpleasant visit to Mr. Dallstrom." (*Is there any other kind?* I thought.) Mr. Poulsen walked to the front of the classroom. "When you're done with your tests, bring them to me, then go back to your desks and sit quietly."

I could see Ostin squirming in front of me, happy as a pig in mud. He loved tests. Sometimes, for fun, he'd download them from the Internet and quiz himself. Clearly something was wrong with him. I pulled out my pencil and began.

1. Which definition best describes a chromatid?
    a. Protein/DNA complex making the chromosome
    b. Molecules of DNA with specific proteins responsible in eukaryotes for storage and transmission of genetic information
    c. Five kinds of proteins forming complexes with eukaryotic DNA
    d. Each of a pair of identical DNA molecules after DNA replication, joined at the centromere

D, I thought. *D? Or is it A?* I was mulling over my answer when a folded piece of paper landed on my desk. I unfolded it.

How did you do that?

I glanced around to see who had thrown it. Taylor was looking at me.

I wrote back, *Do what?*

I looked up at Poulsen, who was at his desk reading a book, then threw the note back. Within seconds the note was on my desk again.

You know. I saw you do something to those boys.

I sent her another note.

I didn't do anything.

Taylor wrote back.

You can trust me.

I was writing another denial when I heard Mr. Poulsen clear his throat. I looked up. He was standing at the top of my row, staring at me.

"Mr. Vey. Those notes wouldn't have something to do with the test we're working on?"

I swallowed. "No, sir."

"Then you picked the wrong time to share your feelings with Miss Ridley."

I blushed while the class laughed. He walked toward me. I was blinking like crazy. "I think I was quite explicit about the rules. Hand me that note." I looked down at the paper. I couldn't give it to him. If he read it aloud everyone would know.

"Wait," Taylor said. "He didn't do anything. I was the one passing notes."

He looked at Taylor and his expression changed from stern disciplinarian to gentle educator. I think even he had a crush on her. "What did you say, Miss Ridley?"

"I wrote the notes, not Michael."

He looked at Taylor in disbelief. She was the model student, incapable of such a shameful act. Then, while he was looking at her, Taylor did the strangest thing. She smiled at Mr. Poulsen with a confident smile, then cocked her head to one side and narrowed her eyes. Suddenly Mr. Poulsen looked confused, like a man who had just been awakened from a nap. He blinked several times, then looked at Taylor and smiled. "Excuse me, what was I saying?"

"You said we have forty minutes left on our tests," Taylor said.

He rubbed his forehead. "Right. Thank you, Taylor." He turned back toward the class. "Everyone keep at it. You have forty minutes left." He walked back to his desk while everyone in our class looked back and forth at each other in amazement. I couldn't believe what had just happened. I looked back at Taylor.

"You can trust me," she mouthed.

It took me the whole class to finish the test. In fact, I ran out of time on the last three questions and just randomly circled letters. Ostin had finished the whole thing in less than fifteen minutes and strutted to the front of the room to turn in his test, unaware that the rest of the class was staring daggers at his back. For the rest of the period I could hear him sneaking cheese puffs from his backpack.

After the bell rang, Ostin and I walked out to our lockers.

"Man, that test was cake," Ostin said. "I can't wait for the next one."

"You're a freak," I said.

Suddenly Taylor grabbed my arm. "Michael, we need to talk."

"No we don't," I said. I kept walking, leaving her standing there.

Ostin looked at me in amazement. "Dude, that was Taylor Ridley you just brushed off."

I looked at him. "So?"

He smiled. "That was so cool."

Taylor ran in front of me and stopped. She looked at Ostin. "Excuse us, please."

"Sure," Ostin said, looking thrilled that Taylor had spoken to him.

After he'd taken a few steps back, she turned to me. "Please."

"I can't," I replied.

"I need to know," Taylor said. "I really, really need to know."

I just looked at her. "What did you do to Mr. Poulsen?"

"I don't know what you're talking about," she said, mimicking what I'd written to her on the note.

"You did *something*," I said. "I saw it."

"Really? Well, so did you."

"Nothing I can tell you about."

"Michael, please. It's important." She grimaced. "I'm begging."

"Dude, she's begging," Ostin said, forgetting that he wasn't supposed to be listening.

Taylor turned to him. "Excuse me," she said sharply.

Ostin wilted beneath her gaze. "Sorry." This time he crossed to the opposite side of the hall.

I looked at her for a moment, then said, "I'd get killed for telling you."

"No one will ever know. I promise." She crossed her chest with her finger. "Cross my heart."

I looked over at Ostin, who was still pretending not to listen. He shook his head.

Taylor looked at him, then back at me and sighed. "Michael, I *really* need to know. I promise, I'll never tell anyone." She leaned in closer. "I'll even tell you *my secret*." She just stood there, staring at me the way Ostin stared at jelly doughnuts. Then she put her hand on my arm. "Please, Michael. It's more important than you can possibly imagine."

She looked so desperate I wasn't sure what to do. Finally I said, "I couldn't tell you here anyway."

"We can go to my place," she said quickly. "I live just down the street. No one's home."

Ostin looked at me in amazement. I could guess what he was thinking. *Dude, Taylor Ridley just invited you to her house!*

"I can't," I said. "I have after-school detention."

"That's okay, I'll wait for you," she said eagerly.

"Don't you have cheerleading or something?"

"Only on Mondays and Wednesdays. And Fridays if there's a game." She looked deeply into my eyes. "Please."

Saying no to the girl you have a crush on is hard enough, especially when she's begging, but I had also run out of excuses. I exhaled loudly in surrender. "Where do you want to meet?"

Taylor smiled. "I'll just go with you."

"To detention?"

"I don't think they'll try to keep me out, do you?"

"I don't know. No one ever tries to get *into* detention. It's like breaking into jail."

Taylor smiled. "Then I guess we'll find out."

"Hey," said Ostin, who had inched his way back into our conversation. "What about me?"

Taylor looked at him. "What about you?"

"I'm Michael's best friend. Ostin," he said, eagerly putting out his hand. Taylor just looked at him.

"He's my friend," I said.

"What do you want?" she asked.

"I want to come with you guys."

"We can trust him," I said.

She looked him over, then turned back to me. "Sorry, but I can't."

I looked at Ostin and shrugged. "Sorry, man."

He frowned. "All right. See you guys later."

As Ostin walked away, Taylor turned to me. "Let's go, you delinquent."

We walked down the hall together, something I never thought would happen in a million years. I wondered if Taylor might be afraid to be seen walking with me—like her popularity quotient might fall a point or two (I wasn't sure how that worked), but she didn't seem to care. She must have said "Hi" about a hundred times between my locker and detention. As usual I felt invisible.

As we walked into the lunchroom Ms. Johnson looked at Taylor quizzically. Taylor was one of those students who was always the teacher's pet: perfect citizenship, always got her homework done, raised her hand to speak, never a cause of trouble. I once overheard a teacher say, "If only I could have a classroom of Taylors."

"Do you need something, Taylor?" Ms. Johnson asked.

"No, Ms. Johnson. I'm here for detention."

"I'm surprised to hear that." Ms. Johnson looked down at her clipboard. "I don't have you on my list."

"I know. I didn't get in trouble or anything. I'm just waiting for my friend Michael."

Ms. Johnson nodded. "That's very kind of you, being supportive of a friend, but detention isn't a place to hang out."

Taylor just looked at her with her big, soft brown eyes. "Please? I really think I can help him change his ways."

I turned and looked at her.

Ms. Johnson smiled. "Well, if you really want to help, I don't see why not. But you can't sit together. We can't have talking."

Taylor flashed a smile. "That's okay, Ms. Johnson. I've got a lot of homework to catch up on." She waved to me. "Be good." She sat down at Ms. Johnson's table, grinning at me.

I'm pretty sure that Taylor was the happiest person to ever go to detention. Frankly, I wasn't hating it too much myself. I couldn't believe that the best-looking girl at school was in detention waiting for me. The lunchroom was at least ten times more crowded than the day before, which meant that there was either a sudden outbreak of misbehaving, or Mr. Dallstrom had had a bad day. I was about to sit at the end of a long table near the back wall of the cafeteria when someone said, "Not there, tickerhead."

I looked up. Cody Applebaum, a six-foot ninth grader, was walking toward the table, sneering at me. "That's my side of the table."

I had no idea what a tickerhead was. "Whatever," I said. I walked to the opposite end of the table and sat down. I opened my algebra book, unfolded the day's worksheet, and began doing my homework. About five minutes into my studying something hard hit me in the head. I looked up at Cody, who was laughing. He had a handful of marbles.

"Knock it off," I said, rubbing my head.

"Knock it off," he mimicked. "Puny wimp. Go tell your mama."

Sometimes I felt like I was wearing a sign that said PICK ON ME.

I went back to my book. A few seconds later another marble hit me in the head. I looked up. Cody was now leaning against the wall on the back two legs of his chair. He raised his fist and bared his teeth like an angry baboon.

"Stop it," I said.

"Make me."

I went back to my studying. Less than a minute later another marble hit me in the head. As I looked up, I noticed a metal trim that ran along the wall where Cody was leaning.

I don't know why I did it—maybe I was still feeling great from finally putting Jack in his place, maybe it was the obnoxious smirk on Applebaum's face, or maybe it was that I was showing off for Taylor. But, most likely, it was the culmination of too many years of being bullied. Whatever the reason, I was done with playing the victim. I slowly reached back and touched the trim behind me and pulsed. Cody let out a loud yelp and fell back off his chair, smacking his head against the wall, then the floor. When Ms. Johnson stood up to see what had happened, Applebaum was lying on his back rubbing the back of his head.

"Cody! Quit screwing around."

He looked up from the ground. "Something shocked me."

"Right, Cody. I saw you leaning back on your chair," Ms. Johnson said. "One more outburst like that and I'm adding two days to your detention."

Cody climbed back into his chair. "Sorry, Ms. Johnson."

I looked over at Taylor. She was looking at me, slowly shaking her head. I shrugged.

Ms. Johnson let us out early again. On the way out of the cafeteria, Taylor said, "Nice spending time with you, Ms. Johnson."

"You too, Taylor." Ms. Johnson glanced over at me. "Hopefully your behavior will rub off on some of the other students."

"I hope so," she said.

Taylor laughed when we were out of the cafeteria. "Stick with me, Vey, maybe my behavior will rub off on you."

"Thanks," I said sarcastically. Actually I was happy to stick with her, but for other reasons.

As we walked down the hall, Taylor asked, "What did you do to Cody?"

"Nothing," I said.

"Same 'nothing' you did to Jack and his gang?"

I grinned. "Maybe."

"Whatever you're doing, you shouldn't do it in public like that."

"You should talk. Besides, Cody started it."

"It doesn't matter," Taylor said.

I turned to her. "It does to me. I'm sick of being picked on and doing nothing about it." I opened the door for her, and we walked out of the school.

"I know. But if you keep doing it, someone's going to figure it out."

"Maybe. Maybe not."

We walked toward the back of the schoolyard. "Where do you live?" I asked.

"It's just through that fence over there and two houses down. So, tell me about the other day when Jack was picking on you."

"You have to first tell me what you did to Mr. Poulsen."

Taylor nodded. "Okay. I'll tell you when we get to my house."

Taylor's house was a tan rambler with plastic pink flamingoes in the front yard and a small grove of aspens on the side. She took a key from her pocket and unlocked the door.

"No one's home," she said. She stepped inside, and I followed her. The house was tidy and nice, bigger than our apartment, but not by much. There was a large wood-framed picture of her family above the living room fireplace. She had two older brothers. Everyone in Taylor's family had blond hair and blue eyes except Taylor.

"Where's your family?"

"My parents are at work. My brothers are in college. I usually only see them on weekends."

"Where do your parents work?"

"My mom works for a travel agency that does educational tours for high school students. My father's a police officer." Taylor turned on the lights and led me to the kitchen. "Want some juice or something?"

"No thanks."

"Go ahead and sit down."

I sat down at the kitchen bar while she looked inside the fridge. I put my hand over my right eye, which was fluttering like a moth's wing.

"How about some lemonade?" she asked.

"Sure."

She poured us both a glass then sat down next to me. "Can I ask you something?"

"Sure."

"Why do you blink like that?"

I flushed. "I have Tourette's syndrome."

"Tourette's syndrome? You mean, like those people who shout out swear words for no reason?"

"That's Tourette's, but I don't do that. I do other things."

"Like blinking?"

"Blinking. Sometimes I make gulping noises. Sometimes I make faces."

"Why?"

I shrugged. "No one really knows why. Tourette's is a neurological thing, so it can affect any part of my body."

"Does it hurt?"

"Sometimes."

She thought it over. "Is it okay that I'm asking you about this? I'm not trying to embarrass you. I just thought, if we're going to be friends, I should know."

What she said made me happy. *If we're going to be friends . . .* "Yeah. It's okay."

Taylor stood. "Let's sit in the family room. You can bring your drink." We walked into the next room, then sat down next to each other on the sofa. I took a drink of lemonade and puckered. "Wow. That's sour."

"My mom must have made it. She makes it really tart." Taylor took a sip. "Yep, Mom."

I set down my glass.

"So," she said, lacing her fingers together, "are you going to tell me what you did to those boys?"

"You said you'd tell me your secret first."

Taylor smiled nervously. "I know I did, it's just . . ." She looked at me with her beautiful brown eyes. "Please. I promise I'll tell you. It's just easier if you go first."

There was something about Taylor that made me feel like I could trust her. "Okay," I said. "What did you see?"

"I heard a loud zap. Then I saw Jack and his friends rolling on the ground like they had been tased."

I shook my head. "That's pretty much what happened."

"How did you tase them?"

As I thought over how much I wanted to share, Taylor said, "My dad has a Taser. He also has a stun gun. He showed me how they work."

My mother had made me promise to never tell anyone about my electricity, but we had never talked about what to do if someone already knew. Or at least thought they did. "I don't know if I should say," I said.

Taylor leaned closer and touched my arm. "Michael, I understand. I really do. I've never told anyone my secret. But I'm tired of keeping this to myself. Aren't you?" Her eyes were wide with sincerity.

I slowly nodded. Ostin was the only person I'd ever told about my electricity, and telling him had been an incredible relief—like a hundred pounds falling off my shoulders. I slowly breathed out. "You know when people rub their feet on the carpet and build up electricity, then touch someone to shock them?"

"Static electricity," she said.

"Right. When I was little I would touch people and it would shock them like that. Except I didn't have to be on carpet. I could be on anything, and I didn't have to rub my feet. Only the shock was much worse. Sometimes people screamed. It got so bad that my mom made me wear rubber gloves. As I got older, it got more powerful. What I did to those boys was nothing compared to what I could have done."

Taylor set down her lemonade. "So you can control it?"

"Mostly. Sometimes it's hard."

"What does it feel like when you shock?"

"To me or them?"

She grinned. "You. I can guess how it feels to them."

"It's like a sneeze. It just kind of builds up, then blows."

"Can you do it more than once?"

"Yes. But I can only do it so many times before I start to lose energy. It takes a few minutes to build it up again."

"Do you have to touch someone to shock them?"

"Yes. Unless they're touching metal, like Cody was today."

She nodded. "That was actually pretty cool. Do you ever shock yourself?"

"No."

"How come?"

"I don't know. Electric eels don't shock themselves." I took another small sip of the lemonade and puckered.

"You don't have to drink it," Taylor said. "I won't be offended or anything."

"It's okay." I set the glass down. "Your turn. What did you do to Mr. Poulsen?"

A wide smile crossed her lips. "I rebooted him."

"You what?"

"You know, like rebooting a computer. I reboot people. I think it's an electric thing, too. The brain is just a bunch of electrical signals. I can somehow scramble them."

"That's weird."

"You're calling *me* weird?"

"I didn't mean it like that. I'm not saying you're weird."

"Well, I am. And so are you. I don't think there's anyone else in the world like us."

"Unless they're hiding it like us. I mean, I sat next to you in class and I never knew."

"That's true."

"When did you first notice that you were different?" I asked.

"I think I was around seven. I was lying in bed one night under the covers when I noticed that there was a bluish-greenish glow coming from my body."

"You have a glow?" I asked.

"Yeah. It's just faint. You can only see it in the dark and if you look closely."

"I glow too," I said. Hearing that she had the same glow made me feel good—like I wasn't so different. Or alone.

"That summer I was playing wizard with some friends and I cast a spell, only they fell to the ground and started to cry. At first I thought they were just pretending. But they weren't. They couldn't remember what they were doing."

"That's why Mr. Poulsen couldn't remember what he was doing," I said.

She smiled. "Yeah. It comes in handy sometimes."

"Does it hurt the person you reboot?"

She seemed embarrassed. "I don't know. It's not like I do it all the time. Want me to do it to you?"

"No. Do you want me to shock you?"

"No." She looked at me seriously. "You know, Michael, my parents don't even know about this. Do you have any idea how good it feels to finally tell someone?"

I nodded. "Yes."

She smiled. "Yeah, I guess you would." She lay back into the cushion. "So your parents know?"

"My mother does. My father passed away when I was eight."

"I'm sorry." Her expression grew more serious. "So what does your mother think of it?"

"I think it scares her. If she knew I was talking to you about it she'd be really upset."

"She won't hear it from me," Taylor said. "I wish I could tell my parents. I've tried a few times, but whenever I ask to talk to them they get nervous, like I'm going to tell them I've done something wrong. I guess I'm just afraid of how they'll react."

"You should tell them," I said.

"I know. Someday I will."

Taylor leaned forward and said in a softer but more excited tone, "There's something else I can do. Want to see it?"

"Sure."

She patted the sofa cushion next to her. "Come closer."

I scooted closer until our bodies nearly touched. I started gulping but stopped myself. "This isn't going to hurt, right?"

"No." She leaned toward me until we were touching. "Now think of a number between one and a million."

"One and a million? Okay." I thought of the last four digits of my phone number.

"Just keep thinking of the number." She reached over and took my hand. Suddenly a big smile came across her face. "Think of the number, silly, not me."

"What, you're reading my mind?" I asked jokingly. It wouldn't take a mind reader to know what I was thinking—the most beautiful girl at school was holding my hand. I focused on my number again.

"Three thousand, nine hundred, and eighty-nine," she said.

I looked at her in astonishment. "How did you do that?"

"I don't know. But I'm pretty sure that it's part of the same rebooting thing. I mean, it's all about electricity, right? Our thoughts are just electricity firing, so when I touch you, your thoughts show up in my brain as well—same projector, different screen."

Her explanation made sense. "So you can really read minds?"

"Yes, but not without touching. If I were to put my forehead against yours I could see even better."

I wouldn't mind that, I thought, forgetting that we were still holding hands. A big smile came across her face. I blushed and let go of her hand. "So all you need to do is touch someone?"

She nodded. "I've even been able to read people's minds if they're touching metal—like the way you shocked Cody." She leaned back again. "So what do we do now?"

"First, we need to promise never to reveal each other's power."

"We already did that," she said.

"Right. Second, I think we need to stick together."

She looked at me with a funny expression. I'm glad she wasn't touching me. After a moment she said, "That's a good idea. We should start a club."

"A club? With just the two of us?"

"Unless you know someone else like us."

"Ostin should be in our club. He could come in handy."

"Who's Ostin?"

"He's my friend. You just met him at my locker. He sits in front of me in biology."

"The know-it-all kid."

I nodded. "He's my best friend."

"Does he have powers?"

"No. But he knows a lot about science and electricity. He's really smart. Like mad scientist smart. His mother told me when he was only six years old, their DVD player broke. Before his father could take it in for repair, Ostin had taken it apart and fixed it."

"He's not too smart socially," Taylor observed.

"That's a different kind of smart."

"But can he keep a secret? Because no one can know about this."

"He's kept my secret since I told him."

"How long ago was that?"

"Almost three years. Besides, who is he going to tell? I'm his only friend."

Taylor didn't look completely convinced, but she nodded anyway. "All right, he can be in our club."

"We'll need to come up with a name," I said. "Every club has a name."

"You're right. How about . . . the Power Team."

I frowned. "No, too boring. How about, the Electric Eels."

"Yuck," she said. "Have you ever seen one of those? They look like fat snakes with acne. Besides, shocking people is your thing. You could call yourself Eel Man."

I didn't really care for the name, though I did like that she referred to me as a man. "And you could call yourself the Human Reset Button."

She shook her head. "Let's just stick with our real names."

"Okay. Besides, we don't have to come up with something right now. Ostin's good at this kind of thing. He'll have some good ideas."

We sat a moment in silence.

Taylor stood. "Would you like some more lemonade?"

"No, I'm good."

She looked at the clock above the television set and groaned. "My mom will be home in another half hour. You better go. My parents are kind of strict. I'm not allowed to have boys over when they're not here."

I stood. "I need to get home anyway."

She walked me to the door. "Thanks for coming over."

"You're welcome. When should we get together again?" I tried not to sound too eager. "For our club."

"When's good for you?"

"How about tomorrow night?"

"I can't, there's a basketball game. Aren't you going?"

"Right. I forgot." The truth was, I hadn't ever gone to a school game.

"How could you forget? It's the regional championship."

"I've just had a lot going on lately."

"How about Saturday?"

"Saturday's good during the day. But at night my mom and I are kind of celebrating my birthday."

"Saturday's your birthday?"

I nodded. "But we're really celebrating on Monday, since my mom has to work all day Saturday."

Taylor said, "My birthday is Sunday."

"Really? That's a coincidence."

Her brow furrowed. "Maybe it's not. We were born on nearly the same day and we both have electrical powers. Think about it. Maybe it had something to do with the stars being in alignment or something."

It may sound strange, but I had never considered why I had electrical powers any more than I had wondered why I had Tourette's. "If that's the case, then there would be tens of thousands of people like us," I said.

Taylor shrugged. "Maybe there are."

"I doubt it," I said. "Or we would have at least heard of a few of them. I mean, someone pops a zit and it ends up on the Internet."

"You're right." She thought some more. "Were you born here?"

I shook my head. "I was born in Pasadena, California. How about you?"

"I don't know. I was adopted."

Now I understood why Taylor looked so different from the rest of her family. "So, we'll get together Saturday?" I asked.

"Sure. But first I need to make sure my parents don't have plans. They've been on my back lately for being gone too much. I'll let you know."

"Great."

She opened the door for me. "Bye, Michael."

"See ya, Taylor. Thanks for the lemonade."

"You're welcome. Talk to you tomorrow."

After she shut the door, I took off running. I had just formed an exclusive club with Taylor Ridley. I didn't need to run. I could have floated the whole way home.

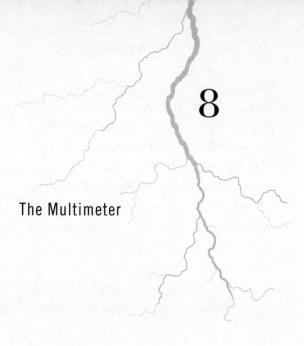

8

The Multimeter

As soon as I got inside the apartment building, I knocked on Ostin's door. He opened it, his face bent in disapproval. "So how's the cheerleader?" he asked snidely.

"I know you're mad you got left out."

"What did you do, make out?"

"Shut up, Ostin. Do you want to come over or not?"

It took him two seconds to get over it. "Yeah, wait." He ran back into his apartment, then returned carrying a small yellow-and-black device and a notepad and pen. "Let's start our tests."

As he was shutting his door, Ostin's mom shouted, "Where you going, Ostin?"

"I'm going to Michael's."

"Be careful," she said.

Ostin looked at me and shrugged. His mom was a little protective. Actually she was a lot protective. I'm surprised she didn't make him wear a helmet to clogging.

"We're having dinner soon. Ask Michael if he wants to eat with us."

He looked at me. "Want to eat with us? We're having fish sticks."

"No thanks." I hate fish sticks.

He turned back. "He's not going to eat with us."

"Dinner will be ready by seven. Don't be late."

"Okay."

He shut his door while I walked down the hall and unlocked my apartment. As soon as we were inside, Ostin opened his notebook and clicked his pen. "All right," he said, using the tone of voice he used when he was doing something scientific. "First things first. Today is Thursday, the fourteenth of April. How are you feeling?"

"Why are you asking me that?"

"I want our experiment to be accurate, so try to be as specific as possible. Are you feeling more or less electric than usual?"

"I don't ever feel electric," I said.

"Okay. Usual," he said, scribbling in his notebook. "Weather is fair. I checked the barometer earlier and it's one thousand seventeen millibars and humidity is negligible." He brought the multimeter over to me, which looked a little like a fat calculator with cables attached. "Okay, clamp these on your fingers."

I looked at the clamps. "I'm not going to put those on my fingers. They're sharp."

"Do you want this to be accurate or not?"

I rolled my eyes. "Okay." I clamped the copper leads around my fingers. They bit into my skin.

"Now, don't do anything until I tell you."

"Just hurry. These things hurt."

"When I say 'go,' I want you to pulse with all your power. Five, four, three, two . . . wait."

"What?"

"I don't know. The screen on this thing just went blank." He pushed some buttons. "Okay. Four, three, two, one, *go!*"

I surged as hard as I could. The snap and crackle of electricity filled the room and there was a spark from my fingers to the clamps.

"Holy moley," Ostin said. He set down the multimeter and began writing in his notebook. "You produced eight hundred and sixty-four volts."

"That sounds like a lot."

"Dude, that's more than a full-grown electric eel. You could paralyze a crocodile with that." His eyes narrowed. "You could kill someone."

The way he said that bothered me. "I'm done," I said. I was taking the clips off my fingers when the front door opened and my mother stepped in. Ostin quickly hid the machine behind his back. I looked at her in surprise. "Mom. What are you doing here?"

"I live here," she said, looking at us suspiciously.

"But you said you were working late."

"You sound disappointed."

"No, I . . . I'm just surprised."

"I had a headache, so they let me come home early." Her eyes darted back and forth between us. "What's going on?"

"Nothing," I said.

"You were doing something. What do you have behind your back, Ostin?"

Ostin froze. "Nothing." His "nothing" sounded more like a question than a statement.

My mother walked up to him and put out her hand. "Let's see it."

He slowly took the multimeter from behind his back and handed it to my mom. She examined the device, then looked up at him.

"What does it do?"

He swallowed. I was hoping he'd make something up—calculate algorithms or something.

"It measures voltage."

"Voltage? You mean electricity?" She looked perplexed. "Why would you . . ." She stopped and looked at me. I could see anger change her countenance. "How long has Ostin known?"

I swallowed. "I don't know. A while."

"Thirty-four months and nine days," Ostin said.

Shut up, I thought.

My mother handed the multimeter back to Ostin. "You need to go home now, Ostin," she said. "I need to speak to Michael."

"Okay, Mrs. Vey," he said, eager to get out of our house. "Have a good night."

Run, you wuss, I thought.

After the door shut, my mother looked at me for what seemed like a year. Then she said, "Come here." I followed her over to the couch. "Sit."

I sat and she sat next to me. For a moment she just held her head in her hands. The silence was excruciating. Finally she looked up. "Michael, I don't know what to say to you. Do you know how hard this has been, moving away from our home and everyone we know in California, to come to a new city just so that no one would find out about you? I gave up a good-paying job at a law firm to be a checker at a supermarket."

I lowered my head. "I'm sorry, Mom."

"No, sorry doesn't cut it. Who else knows about this?"

"The boys yesterday. And Taylor."

"Who's Taylor?"

"The cheerleader who saw me."

"Did you see her at school today?"

"Yes."

"Did she ask you about what happened?"

I swallowed. "I went to her house."

My mother's eyes widened. "Please don't tell me that you talked to her about what happened."

I slowly nodded.

She threw up her hands. "Michael, what were you thinking? Now we may have to pick up and start over again. I am so tired, I don't know if I can do it."

My eyes welled up. "I'm sorry, Mom. I didn't mean to . . ."

"Michael, it doesn't always matter what you mean to do, it

matters what you do. Please, explain to me, why would you risk everything and tell them?"

For a few moments I just sat there silently. Then, suddenly, it all came out. "I'm sick of having everyone at school think I'm just some wimpy kid who makes funny faces and noises. I'm sick of being bullied all the time. And I'm sick of hiding who I am.

"Ostin is the only friend I have. He doesn't care about my Tourette's or my electricity. He just likes me for me." I looked up into her eyes. "I just want someone to know the truth about me and still be my friend."

She put her head down. Then she took my hand. "Michael, I know it's not easy being different. I don't blame you for feeling this way. It's just that most people can't understand your special gift."

"You think this is a gift, Mom? It's not. It's just another reminder that I'm a freak."

"Michael, don't say that."

"Why? That's what they call me."

"Who calls you that?"

"The kids at summer camp last June. They surrounded me and said, 'Let's see what the freak does next.' And they don't even know about my electricity, they were just talking about all my ticking and blinking."

Her eyes welled up with tears. After a moment she asked softly, "Why didn't you tell me?"

"Because you have enough to worry about."

She looked like she didn't know what to say.

"I'm just tired of everyone picking on me all the time for no reason except they think they can. I'm tired of knowing I could stop them and I don't. You know who I hate more than them for picking on me? I hate myself for letting them. I'm tired of being a nobody."

My mother wiped her eyes. "You're not a nobody, Michael. You're a great kid with a big heart." She kissed my forehead, then said, "I owe you an apology. I was wrong when I said that it doesn't matter what you meant to do. Sometimes we can't know what's right. We can only know that we meant to do the right thing—and that we had the right reason."

"How do we know if it's the right reason?"

My mother looked into my eyes, then said, "If love is our reason we may veer off course sometimes, but we'll never be lost." She put her arm around me. "Michael, I'm sorry for getting mad at you. I was just scared. Ostin's been a good friend, hasn't he?"

I nodded. "The best."

"And he's kept your secret?"

"Yes."

"Then I'm glad you told him. It's best to not keep secrets from our best friends." She crossed her arms at her chest. "Now tell me about this cheerleader."

"I think she's like me."

She smiled. "She likes you?"

"No, Mom, she's *like* me."

"What do you mean?"

"She has powers too."

My mom's expression changed. "What?"

"She showed me. It's been her secret too. She even glows like me."

"She can . . . shock?"

"Sort of. It's like she can shock people's brains. And she can read minds."

"Are you sure?"

I nodded. "She showed me."

She looked down for a moment, then softly said, "He said there might be others . . ."

"What?" I asked.

She shook her head. "Nothing. It's nothing. So, is she cute?"

"She's the cutest girl in the whole school."

"Work that." She smiled at me. "Why don't you go see if Ostin wants to go to Baskin-Robbins with us."

I smiled. "Okay, Mom." I stood and started toward the door.

"Michael."

I turned back.

"When I start thinking about all the hard things in my life, I think of you and I feel lucky to be me. I could not be more proud of you. And I know your father would be just as proud."

I walked back and hugged her. "I love you, Mom."

Her eyes moistened. "I love you more every day. Never forget that."

That night I had a double-decker ice cream at Baskin-Robbins—Bubble Gum and Pralines and Cream. Ostin had a triple-decker. My mother didn't have anything. She just kept looking at me and smiling.

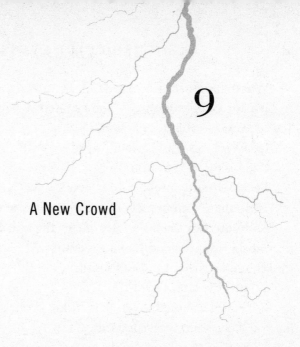

9

A New Crowd

The next day I didn't see Ostin until lunch. I found him sitting where we always sat, at a small round table near the vending machines. It was pizza day and he'd gotten an extra slice. He waved to me. "Michael." I sat down at the table.

"Your eye's looking a lot better," he said.

"Thanks. Where were you this morning?"

"I had a dentist appointment."

"How'd it go?"

"It was just a checkup. Two cavities."

"Probably all the ice cream you ate last night," I joked. "At my last appointment I had three. I can only chew sugarless gum now." I opened my carton of milk. "So we're starting a club."

"Who?"

"Us. You, me, and Taylor."

"What kind of club?"

"It's for people with . . ." I hesitated. I hadn't told him about Taylor. "Unique abilities like mine."

"Excellent. So why Taylor?"

"I don't know. Why you?"

"Because of my intellect, of course."

"Well, there's more to Taylor than meets the eye."

"And with her there's a lot to meet the eye. Her superpower can be that she's super good-looking," Ostin said.

"That's not what I meant," I said.

"What's the club called?"

"We haven't named it yet. Something about electricity. I was hoping you'd come up with something."

"I'll put my computer on it," he said, tapping the side of his head. He took a bite of pizza. Before he'd finished chewing he said, "Hey, we get our tests back in biology today."

"Can't wait," I said sarcastically.

"How'd you do?"

"I don't know. B maybe. If I'm lucky." I didn't have to ask him what he was getting. We both knew he got an A. He could teach the class.

Just then one of the cheerleaders walked up to our table. There was a basketball game today and the cheerleaders always wore their outfits on game day. "Is this seat taken?"

Ostin's eyes were as wide as glazed doughnuts. "No."

"Good." She dragged the chair off to a nearby table.

"Any time, babe!" Ostin shouted after her. "Come back if you need another one. Got plenty of 'em. I'm your chair connection." He turned to me. "Did you see that? She spoke to me."

I nodded. "Yeah, I think that's going somewhere."

He took another couple of bites of pizza. "So what happened with your mom last night? First she's mad as a hornet and then she's taking us out to ice cream."

"She's just afraid that someone will find out about me. That's why we moved from California, you know. And our last apartment."

"Yeah."

"You haven't told anyone, have you?"

"Never."

"Good. Because I'd have to shock you if you did."

He looked at me anxiously. "You're kidding, right?"

"Like an electric eel."

He stopped chewing.

I punched his arm. "Relax, I'm kidding." Then I added, "Sort of."

Just then Taylor walked up to our table. She was also wearing her cheerleader outfit. She looked as pretty as ever. I could feel my tongue knot up, and I started blinking like crazy.

"Hi, Michael. Is this seat taken?"

"No, you can take it," Ostin said eagerly. "I'll even carry it for you."

She looked at him. "No, I mean, may I sit here?"

"Sure," I said. I couldn't believe she wanted to sit by us. She turned to Ostin, who looked like he might hyperventilate with excitement. "Dallas, isn't it?"

"Ostin."

"Right. I knew it was a Texas thing."

"I was just telling Ostin about our club," I said.

Taylor suddenly looked nervous. "Did you tell him anything else?"

"No," I said.

Ostin looked at us curiously. "Tell me what?"

"Nothing," I said.

"Nothing," Taylor said. She turned to me. "Remember when you asked me where I was born? You'll never believe what I found out."

Before she could tell me, two guys walked up to our table wearing letterman jackets. Spencer and Drew. They both played on the basketball team. They were two of the coolest guys at Meridian. "Hey, Taylor," Spencer said. "Whassup?"

She smiled. "Hi, guys."

They sat down at our table.

"This is my friend Michael," Taylor said. The taller of the two reached out his hand. "Hey, I'm Spencer."

The other guy just bobbed his head. "Drew."

"Hi," I said. Ostin looked starstruck.

"So are you guys nervous for the game?" Taylor asked.

"Nah," Spencer said. "It's just another game."

"Not hardly," she said to me. "It's the regional championship. The winner of this game goes to State."

Drew said, "Cottonwood's won their last three games. They have this forward who's on fire."

Ostin looked at him quizzically. "Literally?"

"What?"

"He's literally on fire?"

I kicked Ostin under the table.

Drew looked at me. "Where'd you get the shiner?"

"I got in a fight."

He turned to Taylor. "Hey, this isn't the kid you told us about who kicked Jack's butt?"

"That's him," Taylor said. "I watched him beat up Jack and two other guys. He has a black belt."

"You gotta be kidding me." Drew looked at me in awe. "Dude, you're legend."

I wasn't sure what to say. "Thanks."

"I'm Ostin," Ostin said.

Drew said to Ostin, "You gonna eat both those pieces of pizza?"

"Uh . . ."

"Great." Drew reached over and took one, shoving half of it into his mouth.

Then two more cheerleaders walked up to our table. "Hey, guys. Hi, Tay."

Taylor said, "Hi, Dom. Hi, Maddie."

"Hello, girls," Drew said. "Move over, Houston."

"Ostin," Ostin said.

The girls sat down between Drew and Ostin. Ostin had a blissful look on his face, like he was in heaven—a nervous heaven—but heaven all the same. I was anxious too. I kept turning away to blink, hoping no one would notice.

"We're having a party at Maddie's house after the game," Dominique said. "Are you all coming?"

"Yeah," Spencer said. "We'll be there."

"Can you come, Tay?"

"Yes." She turned to me. "Michael, you're coming to the game, aren't you?"

Her question caught me off guard. "Uh, yeah. Of course," I said. "Wouldn't miss it."

Ostin looked at me like I'd lost my mind.

"Great. You guys want to come to the party after?" Taylor asked.

"Sure," I said.

Taylor turned to the cheerleaders. "Guys, this is my friend Michael."

"Hi, Michael," Dominique said.

"Hi," Maddie said.

"That's Houston," Drew said, pointing at Ostin.

"Nice to meet you," Ostin said.

"Do you have something in your eye?" Maddie asked me.

I turned red. "Uh, no."

"You were just blinking kind of funny."

I wanted to crawl under the table.

"Michael has Tourette's syndrome," Taylor said.

"Oh, I thought you were, like, winking at me," Drew said.

"No. I can't help it."

"Is it, like, contagious?" Drew asked.

"Duh," Taylor said. "Is stupidity contagious?"

Drew looked genuinely baffled. "I don't know, is it?"

Spencer laughed. "You're such an idiot, dude."

"Sorry," Drew said to me.

"It's okay. I was born with it. It makes me blink and stuff."

Dominique said, "I have a cousin with—how do you say it?"

"Tourette's."

"Yeah, Tourette's. His name is Richard, but everyone in his neighborhood calls him King Richard, because he's, like, totally amazing on any board. Skateboard, snowboard, wakeboard—if it's a board, he can rule it."

"That's nothing," Drew said. "Mike here is a little Chuck Norris. The other day he beat up three guys twice his size. You should have seen it. It was awesome."

"That's so cool," Dominique said.

I glanced at Taylor. She grinned.

Ostin just sat and listened, so excited that he didn't seem to notice the loss of his pizza. When the second lunch bell rang, he popped up like a toaster pastry. "Gotta go," he said. "Lovely hangin' with you ladies."

No one at the table acted like they'd heard him.

"Hold on," I said, standing. "I need to go too."

"Hey, stay cool, man," Spencer said to me. "See you tonight?"

"Yeah. Good luck with your game."

"Spencer's made All-State," Taylor said. "He already has college scouts checking him out."

"That's really cool," I said.

He shrugged. "I throw a ball through a hoop. Nothing to it. See ya around, man."

Taylor stood up with me. She put her hand on my arm as we walked away from the table. "Sorry we crashed your table. I didn't plan on that happening."

"No, it's cool. I'm just not used to hanging out with those guys."

"What guys? Spencer and Drew?"

"Yeah. And the cheerleaders."

Taylor nodded. "You mean the popular kids."

"Yeah."

"They're no different than anyone else. Besides, they like you."

"Really?"

"Couldn't you tell?"

"No." I looked at her. "So why did you lie to them?"

"I didn't lie."

"You told them I'm a black belt."

"I told them you *have* a black belt. What's that around your waist?"

I grinned. "That's not what they thought you meant."

"Look, word's gotten out about what you did to Jack. I mean, you took out three kids twice your size. You think that's going to go unnoticed? I was just protecting your secret."

Another bell rang. Taylor sighed. "I've got to go. Can't be late to class. Look, I found out something I need to tell you, but I've got to run. We can talk at the party tonight."

"Okay," I said. "Wait, I don't know where your friend lives."

"You can go with me. Just meet me after the game."

"Where will you be?"

"Cheering." She lightly punched my arm. "See ya."

"Bye."

Ostin was waiting for me outside the cafeteria doors. "Dude, that was epic. Bones." He put out his fist.

I bumped it. "What was epic?"

"Our table became the cool table."

"Yeah. That was weird."

"And they love you. You're in with the in crowd. I can't believe Taylor is, like, all over you."

"No she's not."

"Are you blind? That hottie's got the hots for you, and she is H-O-T, hot."

"We're just friends," I said.

"Whatever, dude. Whatever. So are we really going to the game?"

"And the party after," I said.

"Wow," Ostin said with a broad smile. "What a day."

After school I walked down to the cafeteria but Ms. Johnson had canceled detention because of the game, so I headed home alone.

As I walked out the doors Jack, Mitchell, and Wade were standing there. My first thought was that they were waiting for me, but the surprise on their faces convinced me otherwise. My stomach churned with fear and anger.

Jack threw down the cigarette he was smoking. "What's up, man?"

he said. His tone was different from before—like we were now buddies or something.

I didn't say anything, but kept on walking.

"How did you do that?" he shouted after me.

I spun around. "Do what?"

"Electrocute us."

"You want another demonstration?"

Jack raised his hands. "We don't want any trouble," he said. "We're good, right?"

Wade took a slight step back, and Mitchell looked like he'd wet his pants if I said "Boo!"

"No, we're not good. I'm still on detention because I wouldn't tell on you guys. You need to talk to Mr. Dallstrom and fix that." I stepped toward them, suddenly feeling the liberation of having nothing to hide. I don't know if it was old anger or new confidence, but I said to Jack, "If I have to spend another week in detention . . . " I poked him on his chest and he jumped back, probably anticipating another shock.

"Okay. I'll tell Dallstrom it's my fault."

"Good, because if I have another week of detention, I'm coming after you." I turned to Mitchell. "And you." Then I turned my whole body toward Wade. "And especially you. And if you think it hurt last time, next time you're going to think you were struck by lightning. You understand?"

"Hey, no prob, man," Wade said, his voice quivering.

"We're cool," Mitchell said.

"We better be," I said, turning from them. As I walked away, a large smile crossed my face. I just couldn't help it. I couldn't remember the last time I'd felt that good.

Ten minutes later I knocked on Ostin's door and he answered. "Hey, you're back early."

"They canceled detention. So, can you go to the game?"

"Yeah. My mom was so excited she almost fainted. She said, 'Finally you're doing something normal.'"

"Just be sure to wear your clogging shoes," I said.

"They're tap shoes."

I hit him on the arm. "Just kidding. I'm going home. I still haven't asked my mom. I'll call you in a couple hours."

When my mother got home from work, she hung her sweater in her room, then started boiling water for spaghetti. "So what do you want to do tonight?"

I had been excited to tell her about the game, but now that she was home I was afraid to ask her. I suppose I felt a little like I was letting her down. "I thought maybe I'd go to the school basketball game," I said uneasily. "If it's okay with you."

She turned to me and smiled. "That sounds fun."

"But then you'll be alone."

"I think I can handle that. Do you want me to pick you up when the game's over?"

"Well, we've been invited to a party afterward. It's at one of the cheerleaders' houses."

She looked at me. "So, last night you had no friends, and today you're getting invited to cheerleader parties. What was in that ice cream?"

"It's Taylor."

"She's the cheerleader?"

"Yeah. She's kind of becoming a friend."

I don't know the last time I saw my mother smile that wide. "Is she nice?"

"She's really great." I looked at my mom. We had spent every Friday night together since we moved to Idaho. "You sure you're okay alone?"

She dropped the pasta into the pot. "Are you kidding?" she said, winking at me. "I'm just glad to finally get you out of my hair. Do you know how many books I have to catch up on? Just call when you're ready to leave the party, and let me know where to pick you up."

I smiled. "Thanks, Mom." I gave her a hug. I love my mother.

Neither Ostin nor I had ever been to a school basketball game before. We sat near the floor at one end of the gymnasium. Ostin looked as out of place as a Twinkie in a salad bar. I panned the floor for Taylor, but I couldn't see her.

"These metal bleachers are bruising my butt," Ostin said. "How long do these things last?"

"You're too soft," I said, still looking for Taylor.

"Your girlfriend's over there," Ostin said, pointing to a flock of cheerleaders on the other side of the floor.

"She's not my girlfriend."

"Yeah, right," Ostin said.

I waved to Taylor several times, but she didn't see me. Or at least she didn't act like she did.

The game was close. At halftime, Meridian was down by five points. The drill team had come out to do their thing when I saw Taylor walk over to our side of the gym.

"Taylor!" I shouted.

She didn't even look up. Then she walked up to the end of our bench, where Tim Wadsworth was sitting. Tim Wadsworth was the guy every girl at Meridian dreamed of. He had perfect skin, golden hair with a soft curl, straight teeth, and a body that would make a Greek Olympic statue envious. Mr. Perfection was flirting with Taylor or vice versa. I couldn't tell. As I watched her I got madder and madder. He was holding a Coke and talking to her. Then she took a drink from his cup.

Without even thinking about it I surged.

There were at least twenty people on the bench and they all jumped up at once, like they were doing the wave. Tim also jumped, spilling his Coke all over himself. At first Taylor just looked confused, then she looked down the bench and saw me. She glared.

"Why'd you do that?" Ostin asked, rubbing his butt. "That really hurt."

"Let's get out of here," I said.

We walked down to the floor and started to leave the auditorium when Taylor shouted, "Michael!" I turned around. She stormed up to me, her eyes snapping. She glared at Ostin. "Texas boy, leave."

"Okay," Ostin said, quickly walking away.

She turned back to me. "What was that?"

I was twitching like crazy. "None of your business."

"It is my business when you act stupid and start drawing attention to yourself."

"You're one to talk. You're always the center of attention."

"I'm talking about drawing attention to your power."

"Is it really that you're worried about or is it Tim Wadsworth?"

"Tim Wadsworth?" Her expression softened. "Oh, I get it. You're jealous that I was talking to him."

"No, I'm not."

"Yes, you are."

"No, I'm not."

She smiled. "Hey," she said sweetly, putting her arms out. "Come here." I couldn't believe she had gone so quickly from wanting to hit me to wanting to hug me, but I didn't really understand girls at all. I just went along with it. "You know, Michael . . ."

Touching her felt really wonderful. "Yes?"

Suddenly she pushed me back. "Ha, you are jealous."

She had hugged me just to read my mind. "You tricked me."

"Yeah, well, you just shocked a whole row of people. The custodian is under the bleachers looking to see if there's a loose wire or something."

"Well . . ."

"That's all you have to say?"

Frankly, I didn't know what to say. Suddenly she started to laugh. She was soon laughing so hard she was crying. I just watched her. I was totally confused. "This is so crazy," she said. "Could you imagine if these people around here could hear what we're saying?"

"They'd think we're nuts."

"You should have seen Tim's face when you shocked him. He had Coke dripping from his hair." She looked into my eyes. "I don't remember the last time I had this much fun. I'm so glad I've gotten to know you."

"Me too," I said.

She exhaled. "Well, I've got to get back to cheering or Mrs. Shaw will have my head. But you and Dallas are still coming to the party with me, right?"

"Ostin," I corrected.

"Sorry, I keep getting that wrong."

"Yeah, we'll come. If you still want us."

"Of course I do. It will be fun. Besides, I really have to talk to you about what I found out."

"Great. Where should we meet?"

"Just come down to the floor after the game. See ya." She took a few steps and then stopped. "By the way, you're a lot cuter than Tim Wadsworth."

She spun around and ran back to the floor. I don't know. It may have been the greatest moment of my life.

10

A Suspicious Coincidence

The end of the game was pretty exciting. Meridian was ahead by just one point with three seconds left on the clock when they fouled Cottonwood's best player, sending him to the line to shoot free throws. He must have been pretty nervous because he missed both of his shots badly—one of them by at least ten feet.

Everyone went wild. After the game Ostin and I walked down to the floor. Taylor was surrounded by a couple dozen friends, but she smiled when she saw me. "Ready to go?"

I nodded.

"Angel's dad is going to give us a ride to Maddie's."

"Me too?" Ostin asked.

"Of course."

The four of us walked out to the parking lot. Angel was a pretty Asian girl, and Ostin just stared at her until it was embarrassing.

Finally she stopped and turned to him. "What?"

"Ostin," he said, putting out his hand to shake.

She looked at his hand, then slowly put out her own. "I'm Angel."

"Are you Chinese or Japanese?"

Her brow furrowed. "Chinese."

"Were you born in China?"

"Yes."

He nodded. "What brought your parents to America? Opportunity? Freedom of speech?"

"My parents are American," she said. "I was adopted."

"Oh, you're adopted."

I wanted to smack him.

"Sorry, Angel," I said. "Ostin doesn't get out much."

"Hardly ever," he said.

She shook her head. "It's okay."

"And I think you're the prettiest girl in the world," Ostin blurted out.

"Enough," I said to him.

Angel smiled.

Maddie's home was the last on a long, tree-lined street called Walker Lane, where the rich kids in our school lived. I think her home could have fit our entire apartment building in it and still have had room for an indoor swimming pool, which, by the way, it had. It was the first party I'd been invited to since we moved to Idaho, unless you count Ostin's last birthday party, which was only me and his obnoxious cousin, Brent, who only came because his aunt made him. Brent broke a beaker in Ostin's new chemistry set within five minutes of Ostin opening the box. I thought Ostin would have a mental breakdown.

Angel's dad drove a nice car, a BMW with leather seats the texture and color of footballs. I knew it meant nothing to these kids to ride in a car like that, but I thought it was really cool. So did Ostin. He was grinning like a Cheshire cat, though it also may have been because he was sitting next to Angel. When Mr. Smith dropped us off, I said, "Thank you, sir."

He smiled. "It's nice to see that not everyone's lost their manners. You're welcome, son."

As we walked up to the house Taylor took my arm. "Well played."

"What do you mean?" I asked.

"Nothing," she said. "You're a real gentleman."

The stairway to the house was lined with little pointy trees growing in ceramic pots. I stopped at the door. I don't always notice my vocal tics, but I was gulping loud enough to get Taylor's attention.

Taylor looked at me. "You okay?"

I stopped gulping. "Yeah. I guess I'm just a little nervous."

"It's cool. Don't worry about it. We're just here to have fun."

I took a deep breath. "All right."

She opened the door and we were met by a rush of music and light. The house was filled with kids. Maddie, one of the cheerleaders we'd met at lunch, was standing by the door talking to several basketball players. The only one I knew was Spencer.

"Hey, Tay!" Maddie shouted. The girls hugged. They did a lot of that.

Spencer looked over. "Hi, Taylor."

"You were awesome tonight, Spence!" she said.

"Yeah," I said. "You were awesome."

"Thanks, little dude."

Maddie looked at me and cocked her head. "What's your name again? Trent? Trett?" I suddenly realized that she was thinking Tourette's.

"No. It's Michael."

"Michael. I wonder why I thought it was Trett."

"And I'm Ostin," Ostin said.

She didn't even look at him.

"You have a nice house," I said.

"Yeah." She patted my arm. "Well, have fun." She flitted off.

Ostin was clinging to me like lint to a belly button—at least until he spotted the food table. "Hey, hold the phone, I'll be right back."

Taylor turned to me. "Hold whose phone?"

"It's just a saying. He found the food."

"Good. They'll be happy together."

A moment later Ostin returned carrying a plate brimming with potato chips and brownies. "This stuff is great."

"I see you've made yourself at home," Taylor said.

"My home is nothing like this."

"Would you like a drink?" I asked Taylor, surprising myself at how formal I sounded.

She reciprocated my tone. "Why yes, kind sir. Thank you."

"Come on, Ostin," I said.

On the way to get a soda, Ostin said to me, "I never thought I'd be invited to a party at a place like this."

"I never thought I'd be invited to a party," I said.

The food table was in the middle of a luxurious dining room where lit wall insets held porcelain statues spaced evenly between large, original oil paintings mostly of fruit bowls. In the center of the food-laden table was a large tub of ice, packed with bottled water and cans of soda. Drew walked up to me.

"Hey, it's little Chuck Norris. Give me some," he said, raising his hand.

"Hey, Drew," I said. I set down the cup and we high-fived, clasping hands as we did. He fell to one knee pretending I had him in some kind of kung fu grip. "Don't hurt me, man," he laughed. "Don't hurt me."

I chuckled nervously. "Hey, congrats on the game. You guys played really well."

"We dodged a bullet, man. Cooper is their best free-throw shooter and he tossed two bricks in the last three seconds. We were lucky."

Living alone with Mom, I had never engaged in small talk about sports, so I wasn't sure if I was doing it right. "Well, you know what they say about being lucky . . ."

Drew looked stumped. "No. What do they say?"

"It's better to be lucky than good."

He looked at me for a moment, then laughed. "You're all right, little dude."

"Hi," Ostin said.

"Hey, what's up, Houston?"

"Nothing," Ostin said, trying to sound cool. "Just hanging."

"Houston, we have a problem," Drew said, then burst out laughing at himself.

Just then a mountain of flesh named Corky walked up behind Drew. Corky was the size of a small planet and had an entourage of girls who moved around him like satellites. I knew who Corky was only because he was always being called up onstage at the school assemblies for winning some award or another. The last thing he'd won was the State Heavyweight Wrestling Championship. He took Drew in a choke hold, then released him. "Drew-meister, what gives?"

"Just hanging around the oasis with my little black-belt friend."

Corky looked me over. My head barely came to his chest. "This isn't the guy you were talking about."

"He's the man," Drew said. "Little Chuck Norris."

"He's a shrimp."

"Only on the outside," Drew said. "On the inside he's a powder keg of pain, just waiting to explode on someone."

Corky laughed. "You're pulling my leg, aren't you? I could crush him like a bug."

"I'd like to see that," said Drew. "Battle of the Titans."

Corky pointed a massive finger at me. "You're talking about the little guy?"

Drew put his arm around me. "This is exactly who I am talking about."

He looked at me incredulously. "C'mon, little guy," he said, gesturing for me to follow him. "Let's go outside and spar a little. I want to see what you got."

Drew laughed. "He'll mess you up, dude. I'm not kidding."

"I've got to see this," one of the girls said.

"I really can't. I've got to get Taylor a drink," I said.

"She won't die of thirst," Corky said. "C'mon, I won't hurt you. We're just playing around."

Just then Taylor walked up. "Hi, guys. Hi, Cork." She looked around. "What's going on?"

"Corky wants to engage the little dude in hand-to-hand," Drew said. "Called him out."

Taylor looked at me, then back at Drew. "What?"

Ostin translated. "He heard about Michael's fight with Jack and he wants to see what Michael can do."

"Black belt or not, I'm going to crush him," Corky said.

Taylor glanced over at me with a look that said: *How do you get yourself into these things?* Then, to my surprise, she said, "Awesome. Let's do it." She looked around, then shouted, "Everyone outside! Michael's going to take down Corky!"

I couldn't believe what she was saying. As we walked out amid the river of bodies, I whispered, "Are you trying to get me killed?"

"Trust me."

"That you will get me killed?"

"No, I'm trying to get you out of this mess."

The house emptied as everyone poured out of the house into the backyard. Corky started cracking his knuckles. Ostin grabbed my shoulder. "Dude, you know you can't use your power."

"I know."

"He's going to kill you."

"I know."

Taylor walked to the front of the crowd as if she were the master of ceremonies. "Okay, so here's the deal. First one knocked to the ground loses. Fair enough?"

"Fair enough," Corky said, bobbing a little.

"Taylor . . . ," I said.

She reached into her pocket. "And here's a twenty-dollar bill that says Michael's going to put Corky on his back. Any takers?"

Everyone looked at each other, but to my surprise, no one was willing to bet against her. I mean, the guy could wad me up like a piece of paper and shoot me out a straw. Taylor looked at Corky. "C'mon, Corky. You're going to crush him, right? Where's your money?"

He looked at her hesitantly. "I don't have my wallet . . ."

"In fact, let's make it sweeter. The loser has to wear my skirt to school on Monday."

I looked at her. Now I was sure she was trying to get back at me for shocking Tim at the game.

". . . All day," she continued. "And, he has to carry the other's books and tie his shoes."

To my surprise Corky was suddenly looking very nervous.

"Come on, Corky," Taylor said. "He's half your size. On the other hand, there's only one of you. The last time I saw him, he had three guys on their backs begging for mercy. It was the most amazing thing I've ever seen." Taylor turned back to face the crowd, who had formed a half circle around them. "Who wants to see Corky wearing my skirt on Monday?"

A large cheer went up. I noticed that Corky was sweating. "Hey, I was just kidding around. I don't want to hurt the little guy. Cool?"

I breathed out a sigh of relief. "Cool."

Just then Drew stepped in. "Arrgh," he said in his best pirate, "them be fightin' wards, matie. Wards yu'll be a regrettin'. Li'l Norris be so tough he can kick the back side 'a yar face."

Everyone laughed, which started a barrage of Chuck Norris jokes.

"Little Norris is so tough, when he does push-ups he doesn't push himself up. He pushes the earth down."

"Little Norris is so tough, he can lead a horse to water *and* make it drink."

"Spiderman owns a pair of Little Norris pajamas."

"Little Norris is so tough he can make onions cry."

"What's the matter, Corky?" someone shouted. "Chicken?" Then someone started a chant: "Vey, Vey, Vey."

Now Corky couldn't back out—he'd never live it down. There was no way around it; we were going to spar. It was a classic David and Goliath scenario, except I couldn't use my slingshot. I was going to get killed.

Taylor sidled up to me. "That didn't go the way I thought it would."

"Really?" I said.

"It's not so bad."

"How is this 'not so bad'?"

"Well, no one expects you to beat him. So if you lose, you'll look brave for fighting a monster. And if you somehow win, you'll be a legend."

"I feel much better now," I said sarcastically.

She looked at Corky, then back at me. "Wait. I've got another idea."

"I can't wait to hear it."

"When I say 'go,' run into him as hard as you can and try to knock him down."

"Are you kidding me? He's a freakin' brick wall."

"Trust me."

"I did."

"Trust me again."

"Let's go!" Corky shouted impatiently. "Let's get this going."

"All right," Taylor said, stepping away from me. "When I say 'go,' come out fighting. Ready . . ."

Corky's eyes narrowed into small slits as he leaned forward on the balls of his feet, squaring off the way he did before a wrestling match. After the razzing Taylor gave him, I don't think he was going to hold back.

"Get set . . ."

His fists balled up. I swallowed and tried not to look overly terrified—just a little terrified. I was certain he could smell my fear.

Don't panic, I told myself.

"Go!"

I took off running at him, feeling like a pitched baseball about to be smacked out of the park. Shouting like a madman, I slammed into him with everything I had, my face buried into his very solid abs. To my amazement he stumbled backward and fell, crashing to the ground in an azalea bush.

"Yeah!" shouted Drew, running to Corky. "I told you, man! Little Norris rules."

I lifted myself up. Corky was still on his back, covered in white flower petals and looking dazed. Drew pointed his finger in Corky's face. "I warned you, don't mess with the little Norris. The kid's got sweet moves."

The truth is, I was more surprised than anyone, including Corky. I put my hand out to lift him up, which he fortunately ignored, since I'd need a car jack to lift him. He slowly climbed to his feet, wiping off his backside. "Good job, kid."

Taylor walked up to him. "I'm not letting you wear my skirt," she said. "You'll stretch it. But it looks like you'll be carrying Michael's books."

I waved it off. "No," I said, "we were just messing around. He could have crushed me like a bug. Thanks for taking it easy on me."

Corky, still confused about what had happened, looked at me and nodded. "Hey, no problem. I don't know where you learned that junk, but you're pretty good."

Drew put his arm around me. "He's the man. You gotta start hanging out with us, Little Norris."

The crowd gathered around me. A pretty girl with long black curly hair walked up to me. I knew her from math class but she had never acknowledged my existence. "Hi, Michael. I'm Chantel. That was so cool," she said, her brown eyes locked on mine.

"Thanks."

"What school do you go to?"

"Meridian. I'm in your math class."

"Really? I've never seen you."

"I sit right behind you."

"Oh," she said, blushing a little. "Lucky me."

Taylor grabbed my arm. "Come on, Michael."

"We'll catch up later," I said to her.

She smiled and waved. "See you in math."

Everyone was giving me high-fives and patting me on the back as Taylor dragged me off.

"Why do I have to go?" I asked.

"So you don't get a big head," Taylor said.

"Where are we going?"

"Where no one will hear us. Come on, Ostin."

"You got my name right," he said.

We went back inside. Ostin grabbed another brownie from the table and the three of us went upstairs to a bedroom. Inside, Taylor locked the door behind us.

"Where'd you learn that move?" Ostin asked. "That was awesome. You took down gorilla-man without your powers."

"It wasn't me," I said. I looked at Taylor. "Was it?"

She sat down on the bed. "It was sort of you. You did knock him down."

Ostin's eyes darted back and forth between us. "What did she do?"

"The same thing she did to Mr. Poulsen. She rebooted him. Didn't you?"

"What?" Ostin said.

I looked at Taylor. "Can I tell him?"

She rolled her eyes. "You just did."

"Well, you showed him first."

"What are you talking about?" Ostin said, looking back and forth between us.

"Taylor has powers like mine," I said.

Ostin's jaw dropped. "She can shock like you?"

"Not exactly. She can shock people's brains."

"What?"

"She can reboot people."

I didn't have to explain "reboot" to Ostin—he was all about computers. "Ah," he said, a large smile crossing his face. "Like pressing the reset button. I get it. That's why Poulsen looked like he'd been sucker-punched. I just thought he had a brain tumor or something. Then how did you knock Corky over?"

"I didn't, Michael did. I just rebooted him a second before Michael crashed into him. He didn't even know where he was."

"That's awesome!" Ostin said.

"No, it's not," I said. "She shouldn't be using her powers in public like that. Someone will figure it out."

"I know." She looked down, covering her eyes with her hands.

"I need to confess something." She looked up at me. "But first, you need to promise me that you won't get mad, okay? I feel bad enough about it."

"What did you do?" I asked.

"Promise me."

"All right. I promise."

"I won the basketball game for us. At least I might have."

"What do you mean?"

"I rebooted that guy as he was shooting his free throws. That's why he missed so badly."

"That's just wrong," Ostin said.

I looked at her in disbelief. "After what you said to me at the game? What happened to not using our powers in public?"

"I know. I just didn't want to lose. I'm such a hypocrite. I, like, ruined that guy's life."

Ostin started pacing. "People, we need to keep this under control. That's why we need the club, to set standards." His mouth spread in a broad smile. "And I have a name for our club. The Electroclan."

"What's an Electroclan?" I asked.

"It's just a name," Ostin said. "The electro part is self-evident. A clan is a group of people who all have the same . . ."

"I like it," Taylor said before he finished. "It's catchy."

"I told you he was good at this," I said.

I could tell by his crooked smile that Ostin was feeling pretty good about himself. First Taylor had remembered his name, now she liked the name he'd come up with for the club. "Now we need bylaws and a mission statement."

"What kind of bylaws?" Taylor asked.

"Like, for instance, who we can tell about our powers," Ostin said.

"Which would be *no one*," I said.

"And when we can use our powers," Ostin said.

"That's easy for you," Taylor said. "You don't have powers."

"Yes I do. Advanced intellectual powers."

"They're not electric."

"You're wrong. Technically, all thinking is electric. The brain consists of about a hundred billion cells, most of which are neurons whose primary job is shooting electrical impulses down an axon, and—"

"All right," I said, "we get it."

"So, I'm just as powerful as . . ." He suddenly looked down, then over at me. "What was I saying?"

I looked at Taylor and she grinned.

Ostin turned red. "You rebooted me, didn't you?"

"Well, you're just so powerful."

"You can't do that," he said. "You don't know if that damages someone's brain. It could burn brain cells."

"Relax, Ostin," I said. "You've got plenty to burn." I turned to Taylor. "He's right, you know. We shouldn't be using our powers on each other."

"I was just fooling around."

"All right," I said. "Rule number one: No using powers against each other."

"And we need a mission statement," Ostin said, though this time not quite as confidently.

"We need a mission," I said.

"I think I have one," Taylor said, moving closer to me. "To find out why you and I have powers. I've discovered something that might be important."

I sat down on the bed next to her. "What?"

"Okay, you were born in California, right?"

"Pasadena."

"Get this . . . so was I."

"Really?"

"I asked my parents. I was born at Pasadena General Hospital. So I went online and tried to find our birth records. They have the records of births for the last forty-two years. In all that time just eleven days are missing. Guess which days."

"Our birthdays?" I ventured.

"Exactly," Taylor said.

"That's weird," I said.

"Statistically, an improbability," Ostin said. "You two born at the same hospital nearly the same day with the similar mutant variation."

"Mutant variation?" I said.

"For lack of a better term."

"Find a better term," Taylor said. "I like power."

"Clearly," Ostin said, loud enough for us to hear.

"I mean the word *power*. We have similar powers." She looked at Ostin. "I'm not a mutant."

"Technically," Ostin said, "you are."

"Yeah, well, you're a geek."

"Doesn't change the fact that you're a mutant."

"If you say that again I'm going to reboot you."

I stood up. "Stop it, you two. Ostin, quit calling us mutants or I'll shock you."

He blanched.

"Why would the records be hidden?" I asked.

"Same reason I hide my diary from my mother," Taylor said.

"Because you'd get in trouble if she found it," I said. I smiled at Taylor. "I think you're onto something."

"Except we've hit a dead end," she said. "The records are gone."

"There's more than one way to skin the proverbial cat," Ostin said, still sounding a little abused. "The county recorder's office will have vital statistics for . . ."

"Can you even speak English?" Taylor said.

"Excuse me. The government has records of all the deaths and births during that time period even if the hospital doesn't."

"Excellent," I said. "So we just look up those births and see where they lead."

"I'll do it," Ostin said. "I'll look them up and analyze them for our next club meeting. When should we meet again?"

"You have your birthday party tomorrow," Taylor said, "and I have mine on Sunday. Monday I have cheerleading practice. How about Tuesday?"

"Works for me," Ostin said. The only thing Ostin ever had on his calendar was clogging and the Discovery Channel.

"Good with me," I said. "Then the first meeting of the Electroclan is hereby adjourned until next Tuesday."

"Good," Ostin said. "I hope there's some of those brownies left."

The three of us walked back downstairs. I glanced at my watch. It was around ten thirty. I said to Taylor, "I need to call my mom for a ride home."

"Don't you have a phone?" she asked.

I felt embarrassed. "No. Things are kind of tight right now."

"You can use my cell phone," she said. She flipped it open and handed it to me. I pushed the buttons, but the screen kept dissolving into static. "What's wrong with your phone?"

She looked at it. "I don't know, nothing was wrong with it earlier. Let me try it." I handed it back. She pushed a few buttons. "It's fine. Maybe it's you."

"Maybe you better dial."

"What's your number?"

"Two-zero-eight, five-five-five, three-nine-eight-nine."

She dialed the number. After a moment she said, "Hello, Mrs. Vey, this is Taylor Ridley. I'm calling for Michael." I put my hand out for the phone, but she didn't surrender it. "Thanks, we're having a good time." Long pause. "That sounds really fun. When are you doing it? Okay. I think that will be fine. I look forward to meeting you too. Here's Michael." She handed me the phone with her hand over the mouthpiece. "Your mom invited me over tomorrow night for cake and ice cream."

"You're coming?"

"If it's okay with you."

"Sure." I put the phone to my ear. "Hi, Mom. Yeah, that's okay. Sorry, I just have a bad connection. Well, it's just me, okay. We're over on Walker Lane. Walker Lane. It's the last house. You can't miss it, the house is huge. Okay. Bye."

I handed Taylor her phone. "That's so weird," I said. "I've never had that problem before."

"Maybe your electricity is increasing," Taylor said.

"Tomorrow, we'll check your voltage again," Ostin said.

I felt like an old car battery when he said that.

Ostin said to Taylor, "Hey, if you're coming over to Michael's, we can have another meeting."

I looked at Taylor.

"Fine with me," she said.

"Fine with me," I said.

Ostin smiled. "Great. Bones." He put out his fist.

I put out my fist.

"I don't do that," Taylor said.

I admired how easily she'd gotten out of that. I'd have to remember to do that next time.

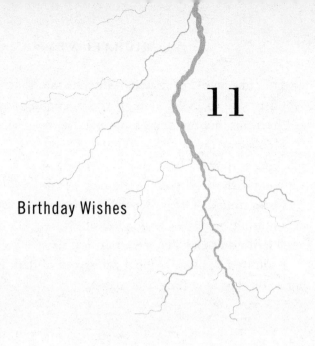

11

Birthday Wishes

Saturday morning my mother got up early and made my second favorite breakfast: hot chocolate and crepes, both of them topped with whipped cream and chocolate syrup. My birthday was the one time of year that my mother said nothing when I filled my plate with more whipped cream than crepe.

She made herself a simple crepe with butter and powdered sugar then sat down next to me. "I'm sorry I have to work today. Are you sure you're okay with celebrating after school on Monday?"

"I don't care what day we celebrate," I said with my mouth full.

"And we'll have cake and ice cream tonight. Do you and Ostin still want to go to the new aquarium on Monday?"

"Yeah. And can we go to PizzaMax for dinner?"

"Whatever you want. It's your day." She smiled at me and her eyes got all sparkly. "I can't believe you're fifteen. Another year and you'll be driving. You've grown into such a fine young man. I am so proud of you."

My mom always got emotional on my birthdays. "Watermark moments," she called them. Whatever that means.

"Thanks," I said.

"Wait, I have a present." She ran out of the room and came back a moment later carrying a small rectangular box wrapped in tissue paper. "I know we usually wait until we have cake to open presents, but I wanted to give this to you now. It's special."

I pulled off the wrapping to expose a dark blue velvet box. I opened it. Inside was a man's watch.

"Wow."

"It was your father's," she said.

I lifted it out of the box, admiring it.

"Do you like it?" she asked.

"A lot. It's cool."

"Well, you're a man now, so I wanted to give you something special. Turn it over; there's something on the back."

I turned the watch around. It read, I LOVE YOU FOREVER—MOM.

"I had it engraved," she said.

I hugged her. "Thanks, Mom."

"You're welcome."

I couldn't imagine a better gift. I wanted to tell her that she was the best mother in the world. I didn't. I should have.

12

The First Meeting

About an hour after my mother left for work, Ostin knocked on my door. He was carrying the multimeter and his notebook. He noticed the can of whipped cream on the counter. "Dude, did you have crepes?"

"Yes."

"Any left?"

"In the fridge. You can microwave them."

He heated up the remaining crepes, then piled them high with powdered sugar and whipped cream while I played a video game.

"That was a cool party last night," he said.

I nodded, intent on my game. "Yeah, it was."

"Especially when you knocked Corky over."

I didn't say anything.

"Taylor's really a babe. You know she likes you."

"She likes everyone."

"I don't mean it like that. I mean she *likes* you. I read this book on body language. And I was watching her body."

"Yeah, I bet you were."

"No, for scientific purposes."

"I bet," I said.

When he'd finished eating the last of the crepes, he came over to the table. "Okay, let's see if there's been a change in your electrical status."

I paused the game. After the cell phone incident I was curious to find out myself. "Let's do it."

"Wait, what's that?" he said, pointing to my new watch.

I held up my arm. "It's a watch my mom gave me this morning for my birthday."

"What's it made of?"

"I think silver."

"Hmm," he said. "Silver has high conductivity, even more than copper. That's why they use it in satellites and computer keyboards." Ostin always vomited up everything he knew about a subject.

"So?"

"Well, you should probably take it off. It might throw off our readings."

"All right." I unclasped it and laid it across the kitchen counter. Then I clipped the multimeter's cables to the ends of my fingers.

Ostin looked down at the machine. "Ready? Three, two, one, go!"

I surged.

Electricity sparked from the copper ends. "Whoa!" Ostin cried. He set down the machine and began scribbling in his notebook.

I unhooked the clips. "What was I?"

"Dude, you're not going to believe it."

"What?"

"This thing goes to a thousand volts and it's saying ERROR. You're definitely becoming more electric."

I sat down on one of the kitchen bar stools and put my watch back on. I wondered what that meant: more electric. "Do you think it will stop?"

"I don't know. No wonder Taylor's cell phone didn't work." He set down his notebook. "So is Taylor really coming over for cake and ice cream?"

"She said she was. Then afterward we can have our first official meeting of the Electroclan."

"That's sick," Ostin said. "Real sick."

Ostin and I played video games most of the day except when we took a break and walked to the 7-Eleven for Slurpees.

Around five o'clock Ostin's dad came and got him for dinner. After he left I made myself macaroni and cheese again, then lay on the couch and read from one of the books I'd been assigned in my English class—*Lord of the Flies*. I read until Ostin came back an hour later. We still had time for a few games of Halo before my mother got home.

Mom got home at the usual time, a little after six thirty. I could tell from her eyes that it had been a hard day. Still, she smiled when she saw me. She was carrying a chocolate butter-cream cake from the supermarket's bakery. "I got your favorite cake," she said as she walked in. "Hi, Ostin."

"Hi, Mrs. Vey. How was work?"

"It was work," she replied. She set the cake down on the counter. She looked at the multimeter but didn't say anything about it.

"Did you boys get some dinner?" She spotted the dishes in the sink and the pan still on stove. "Oh, you did. Mac and cheese."

"Sorry, I didn't do the dishes," I said. "I got distracted with the game."

"That's okay, it's your birthday."

While my mother was changing her clothes, the doorbell rang.

"Michael, would you get that?" she shouted from her room.

"Got it, Mom."

I paused the game, then opened the door. Taylor stood in the hallway holding a wrapped package. I immediately started blinking.

"Happy birthday," Taylor said. She held out the present. "This is for you."

"Wow. Thank you." I felt dumb that I hadn't gotten her anything. "Come in."

"Thanks."

Ostin stared in awe, as if we'd just received an angelic visitation, which wasn't far from the truth.

"Hi, Tex," she said.

I knew she was kidding, but I don't think Ostin did. He was a genius about everything but girls.

"Hey, Taylor," he said. He'd pretty much given up on correcting everyone. As he was fond of saying, "I don't care what you call me as long as it's not late to dinner." I think he meant it.

My mother walked out from her room. She smiled when she saw Taylor. "You must be Taylor," she said.

"Hello," Taylor said. She walked up and shook my mother's hand. "It's so nice to meet you."

"It's nice to meet you, too." My mom glanced over at me standing there, holding the wrapped package.

"Taylor brought me a present," I said.

"How thoughtful. Michael, will you get the ice cream from the freezer?"

"Sure."

My mom led Taylor over to the table. I hoped she wouldn't interrogate her, but, of course, she did.

"So Ridley's an interesting name. Is it Scottish?"

"No, it means 'cleared woods' in Old English. So I'm like a vacant lot."

My mother laughed. "Have you lived around here for a while?"

"I've lived in the same house my whole life."

"Do you have any brothers or sisters?"

"I have two older brothers. They both go to college. So it's kind of like being an only child."

"Well, we're happy you could come tonight. Just go ahead and sit down, and I'll get the cake."

"Thank you, Mrs. Vey."

My mother walked back into the kitchen, where I was scooping ice cream into bowls. "What a cute girl," she whispered to me. "Well done."

"C'mon, Mom. She's just a friend."

My mom just smiled. She put sixteen candles on the cake—one extra for good luck—lit them, and carried the cake to the table.

The three of them sang "Happy Birthday" to me, and we sat around the table for the next hour and talked and laughed. Taylor and my mother really seemed to hit it off.

I was surprised at how talkative Taylor was. She even told us her favorite birthday story. "When I was five, my mom made this *Beauty and the Beast* cake with all these plastic trees and they caught on fire so we had a big forest fire on our kitchen table until my dad blew it out with the fire extinguisher. He's a little extreme that way. It put out the fire but ruined the cake, so my mom ended up putting candles on Twinkies."

We all laughed except for Ostin, who, no doubt, would have done the exact same thing as Taylor's dad.

"When is your birthday, Taylor?" my mom asked.

"Sunday."

She turned to me. "Michael, why didn't you tell me? This should have been a joint party."

"It's just cake," I said.

Taylor said, "So, Michael, are you going to open my gift?"

"Yes." I peeled the paper back, then opened the box. Inside was a black hoodie with our school's name printed on the front.

"Do you like it?" Taylor asked. "I thought you could, like, wear it to the games."

I held it up. "It's awesome. Thanks."

"Cool," Ostin said. "My birthday is in October."

My mother smiled. "That's a very sweet gift."

Taylor grinned happily. "It's nothing."

We sat around and talked until nine, when my mother started gathering up the dishes. "I think I'm going to call it a night. Taylor, do you have a ride home?"

"My dad's going to pick me up."

"Well, it was very nice meeting you. I hope we'll be seeing you again."

She smiled. "Thank you, Mrs. Vey. I'm glad you invited me."

"You're very welcome. Good night, Ostin."

"Good night, Mrs. Vey. Thanks for the cake."

My mom walked over to me and kissed my forehead. "I love you. Happy birthday."

"Thanks, Mom. I love you too."

She walked off to her bedroom.

When she was gone, Taylor said, "Your mom is really nice."

"She's a babe," Ostin said.

"Dude, she's my mother. You've got to stop saying that."

"Sorry."

Taylor laughed. "Well, she is. I hope I'm that hot when I'm a mom."

I wished my mother had heard what Taylor said. Lately she had been saying that she thought she looked old.

Ostin said, "So, let's get our meeting started. Who's going to call it to order?"

I looked at Taylor.

"I think you should be the president," she said to me.

"Why me?"

"Because I said so."

"I second that," Ostin said.

Somehow her reasoning seemed a little ironic, but I wasn't about to fight her on it. "Okay, I call the first meeting of the Electroclan to order." I looked at Taylor. "Now what?"

"We need to follow up on our last meeting."

"We need minutes," Ostin said.

"No more than thirty," Taylor said. "My dad's coming to pick me up."

"No, minutes is what they call the notes from the last meeting," I said.

Ostin rolled his eyes.

"Sorry," she said.

Ostin started. "In our last meeting Taylor shared her discovery that you were both born in the same hospital in Pasadena, California, a very unlikely coincidence. Then Ostin pointed out that the fact that both of you having this mutan—"

Taylor looked at him and he stopped.

". . . power is a statistical improbability. And third, the hospital records of said hospital, for the eleven days around your birth dates beginning April sixteenth, appear to have been conveniently expunged."

Taylor looked at me. "Does he always talk like this?"

"Pretty much," I said. "*Expunged* means erased." I only knew because Ostin loved using that word. "Thanks, Ostin."

"I have something very important to add to the record," Ostin said.

"Go ahead," I said.

"I discovered something very disturbing. During those eleven days there were two hundred and eighty-seven births in Pasadena County."

"What's so disturbing about that?" Taylor said.

Ostin looked at her. "May I continue?"

"Sorry."

"Fifty-nine of those babies were born at Pasadena General Hospital, where you two were born. As I looked over the records, I came across something very, very peculiar." He paused just to make sure he had our attention. "Forty-two of the children born during that time didn't live more than two days."

"What?" Taylor and I said almost in unison.

"I checked the same time period the month before and there was *only one* baby that didn't live."

"Forty times the number of . . . ?" I couldn't say it.

"That is so sad," Taylor said. "Did it say what happened to them?"

"Unknown causes." Ostin scratched his head. "But it gets stranger. Only seventeen of the babies born at Pasadena General lived, and that includes you two."

I leaned forward on my chair. "You're saying that out of fifty-nine births only seventeen babies survived?"

"Precisely." Ostin knit his fingers together. "It couldn't be a coincidence. A forty-two-hundred-percent increase in death in an eleven-day period and the records of those eleven days disappear. I'm guessing that whatever caused those deaths has something to do with whoever destroyed the records."

"We need to find out what was different about those eleven days," Taylor said.

"My thinking exactly," Ostin said. "Just give me a few days to get to the bottom of it."

Ostin told Taylor about my most recent voltage test and a few minutes later we adjourned our meeting. A little after nine thirty, Taylor's dad called from our parking lot and I walked her out. Her father was driving his police cruiser, which seemed to me kind of strange, as I always just thought that police cars were for picking up bad guys, not your kid. I guess I had never known anyone who had a police officer for a parent.

Taylor's dad looked pretty tough. His window was down and his arm was hanging out of it. He smacked the side of the car as we approached.

"Dad, this is Michael."

"The birthday boy," he said. "Why aren't you in your birthday suit?"

Taylor rolled her eyes. "Dad, why do you try to embarrass every boy I'm with?"

He leaned back into the car. "It's my job."

"Sorry about that," Taylor said. "He loves to harass boys. When I'm old enough to date he's going to be a nightmare."

"It's okay," I said. "Thanks for coming over. And for the gift. It was really cool."

"Thank you for inviting me." She smiled. "Actually, I guess I should thank your mom."

"She's braver than I am," I said. "Hey, we're going to have my real birthday party Monday after school. We're going downtown to the aquarium and then out for pizza. Want to come?" Somehow the invitation sounded dumb as it left my mouth.

"I'd love to."

"Really?" I guess I was still getting used to the idea that she liked being with me. "We're leaving around four thirty."

She frowned. "I'm sorry, that won't work. I have cheerleading until five."

"We can wait," I said.

"Are you sure?"

"We could even pick you up at school."

"That sounds good. You sure it's okay with your mom?"

"She'll be thrilled. I can tell she likes you."

Taylor smiled. "Okay. I'll see you at school." She climbed into the patrol car. "Thanks again."

"Have a happy birthday tomorrow," I said.

"Thank you. Good night."

"Good night, Mr. Ridley," I said.

"Night, Michael."

Her father drove off. The police car's siren chirped, then its lights flashed for just a second. Taylor waved to me from the back window. Hands down it was my best birthday ever.

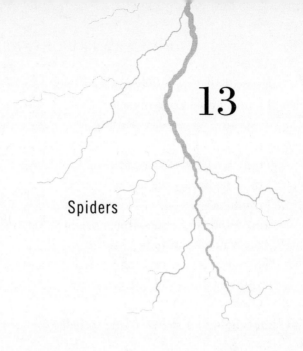

13

Spiders

I've never cared much for Mondays. If I were the king of the world, I'd have Mondays removed from the calendar. Of course the problem in that is that Tuesday would become the new Monday, which would defeat the purpose. Then again, if I were king of the world I probably wouldn't hate Mondays. Notwithstanding, this was one Monday I was looking forward to. I was celebrating my birthday with my mom, Ostin, and Taylor at PizzaMax. What could be better than that?

As I suspected, my mother was thrilled to hear I had invited Taylor, though I'm not sure if she was more excited that Taylor was coming, or that I had actually gotten up the courage to ask her. We were eating breakfast when I said, "So we need to pick Taylor up at the school, okay?"

My mother smiled. "No problem."

"I was thinking I should get her a present. Do you know what girls like?"

She smiled at me wryly. "I should hope so, I'm a girl."

"I know. I mean one my age."

"Trust me, we're all the same. We like clothes and jewelry. And flowers."

"I only have twenty-six dollars," I said.

"Does she have an iPod?"

"I think so."

"You could get her an iTunes gift card. We have them at the store."

"That's a cool present," I said.

"That way every time she listens to a song she bought with it she'll think of you."

"Mom."

She laughed. "I'm just trying to help."

Ostin had another dentist appointment that morning, so after breakfast my mom dropped me off at school. I can't believe the difference a weekend can make. Somehow I went from zero to hero. People I didn't even know said hi to me in the hall, and the basketball team, who previously didn't know I existed, had taken to calling me "Little Norris." I'd be lying if I said I didn't like it.

That afternoon I was standing in line for hot lunch when Ostin marched up to me. "Dude, we need to talk."

"Hold on, I'm getting my lunch."

"This is more important than food."

Those were words I never thought I'd hear from Ostin's mouth. "You're serious."

"As a heart attack, dude. And we need Taylor."

I looked around. "I don't know where she is."

"She's over there," he said, pointing across the crowded lunchroom. That's when I first realized Ostin had Tay-dar. I don't know why he was so much better at finding her than I was, but he definitely was. Taylor was sitting at a table with five other girls. "You need to get her. Now."

"You go get her," I said.

"She won't come with me. She doesn't even remember my name."

"Yes she does. She's just teasing you."

"You're the president of the Electroclan," he said. "It's your responsibility."

I wondered what good it was being president of something if you're always being told what to do by the members. I relented. "All right."

"I'll meet you in the courtyard."

I left the lunch line and walked up to her table. Taylor was in the middle of telling a story, and one of the girls nudged her when she saw me approach. Taylor looked up at me. "Hi, Michael."

I felt awkward with all the girls looking at me. I did my best not to twitch. "Uh, can I talk to you?" I fumbled for an excuse. "About biology."

She looked at me quizzically. "Sure. What's up?"

"Can I talk to you in private?"

"Wooo," one of the girls said.

"Shut up, Katie," Taylor said, standing. "I'll be right back." We stepped away from the table.

"What's going on?"

"Ostin says he needs to talk to us. He says it's important."

"Important?"

"He skipped lunch to talk to us."

"It must be important. Where is he?"

"He's in the courtyard."

We walked together to the school's outer courtyard. Ostin was sitting alone on a bench, a little hunched over as if hiding. He stood when he saw us. He was clutching a piece of paper.

"Hi, Ostin," Taylor said. "What's up?" Had he not been so grim I think he would have been overjoyed that she got his name right.

"Everyone sit down," he said gravely.

We sat on both sides of him.

"Remember our last meeting? We were wondering about what might have happened around those days you were born."

"The eleven days," I said. "When all the babies died."

"Exactly. What I did was look through the newspaper for anything out of the ordinary that began the day or week before April six-teenth. Everything looked pretty usual until I found this." He held up a sheet of paper. "It's a newspaper article from the *Los Angeles Times.*"

He read it out loud.

> PASADENA—Scientists from Elgen Inc., an international medical equipment provider, announced today the discovery of a new method of body imaging, which they claimed will "render current MRI (Magnetic Resonance Imagery) technology obsolete."
>
> The new machine, called the MEI (Magnetic Electron Induction), was created at a cost of more than $2 billion and, according to its developers, "has the potential to deliver benefits of diagnosis and treatment once considered an impossibility." Dr. C. James Hatch, Elgen Inc.'s CEO, said, "This new technology will have the same effect on current medical technology that the X-ray machine had at the turn of the 19th century."
>
> Current MRI technology uses radio waves to generate images of organs and tissues. In closely guarded technology, the MEI creates electrically charged molecules that are 1,200 to 1,500 times more visible than current MRI readings. This method is the first of its kind to employ electrons to create an enhanced view of the body.
>
> "This new technology will benefit every known discipline of medicine and possibly many that have not yet been pioneered," said Dr. John Smart, one of the machine's inventors and professor emeritus at Harvard Medical School. "This technology may very well pave the way to new disciplines in health studies."
>
> The MEI technology has received FDA approval for limited human testing and is currently being installed in Pasadena General Hospital. Human testing is planned to begin April 16 of this year.

Ostin set down his paper. "Now here's the clincher. Twelve days later a small article ran in the *Times* saying that the MEI experiment had been temporarily suspended due to some minor technical malfunction."

"Hmm," I said. "What are the odds that all those babies started dying the day the machine was turned on and ended the exact same day they turned it off?"

"Impossible odds," Ostin said. "Crazy impossible. The machine must have something to do with it."

"You mean they put all those babies through the machine?" Taylor asked

"No, they wouldn't do that. I'm guessing that something went wrong and the machine's waves traveled through the walls."

"And if the machine was somehow responsible for those deaths," Taylor said, "the people who owned the machine wouldn't want others to find out about what happened to all those babies or they could be sued for millions."

"Hundreds of millions," Ostin said.

"Wow," Taylor said. "Think about it, they've been hiding this from the public for fifteen years. If they knew that we knew . . ."

"That," Ostin said, looking even more worried, "is why I needed to talk to you." He turned to Taylor. "How did you look up those first hospital records?"

"On the Internet."

"Where?"

"On my computer," Taylor said.

"At home?"

"Yes. Why?"

He combed his fingers back through his hair. "I was afraid of that."

"What's wrong with that?" I asked.

"Hopefully, nothing. But they might have set up spiders."

Taylor asked, "What's that?"

"Spiders comb the Web looking for references to certain topics or inquiries. They could have programmed their computer to alert them whenever someone looks up a certain topic."

"Such as birth records at Pasadena General during those eleven days," I said.

Ostin nodded. "Exactly," he said breathlessly. "You need to clear off anything on your computer connected to that search, cookies and everything. If they track you down . . ."

"What would they do?" Taylor asked.

"They've already killed forty people. With more than two billion dollars of research at stake, who knows?"

Taylor suddenly blanched. "Oh no."

"What?"

"Something happened Saturday while I was at your party. What was the name of that company again?"

"Elgen Inc."

Taylor suddenly looked pale. "Meet me at my locker." She sprinted off toward the building. She had already opened her locker by the time we caught up to her. She pulled out a glossy, trifold brochure and handed it to me. The piece looked like a recruitment brochure for some kind of fancy school. The cover of the brochure had a picture of well-dressed, smiling students walking in front of a beautiful building.

Taylor said in a hushed voice, "This guy came over Saturday night and met with my parents. He said he was from a very special school in Pasadena, California. He told my parents that nationally this school only selects seventeen students a year and that I had been recommended by an anonymous source for entry. They said it was the most prestigious boarding school in the country and those who attended were guaranteed a full-ride scholarship to the university of their choice: Harvard, Yale, anywhere.

"My parents were way excited, but told him that they could never afford the tuition. The man said not to worry about it, that they were offering me a full scholarship, including books, room, and board. All I had to do was show up."

Ostin looked jealous. "But you're only in ninth grade."

"That's what my parents said, but the man claimed that starting their students young is one of the reasons their students are so successful and that any student enrolled in their school could pretty much name their college and salary. My parents told him they needed to think about it, because they didn't want me to be away."

"What's the name of the school?" I asked.

"The Elgen Academy of Pasadena."

"Elgen?" I looked again at the brochure.

Taylor looked afraid. "What have I gotten myself into?"

"You've got to erase everything off your computer as soon as you can," Ostin said.

I shook my head. "If it's them it's already too late for that. You better tell your mom and dad."

"Tell them what? That their daughter has superpowers and some big corporation is hunting her down?"

"If that's what it takes," I said.

She leaned back against her locker and slid down until she was sitting on the ground. Her eyes began to fill with tears. I sat down next to her. Without looking at me she said, "I'm scared."

"Listen," I said. "My mother has been in tough spots before. She'll know what to do. We'll pick you up from cheerleading and we'll figure it out tonight."

Taylor wiped her eyes. "Okay. That's a good plan."

"Trust me, it will be okay." I looked at the brochure again. "May I keep this?"

She nodded. I folded it up and put it in my pants pocket.

Just then a voice came over the PA system. "Michael Vey to the front office. Michael Vey."

Taylor looked at me with wide eyes.

"What's that about?" Ostin asked.

"I have no idea."

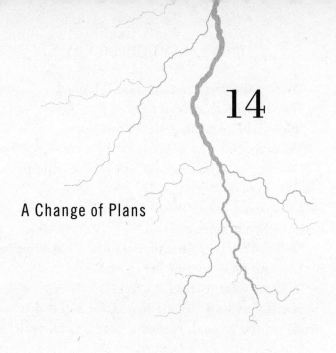

14

A Change of Plans

I walked to the front office about as enthusiastically as a man on his way to the electric chair—and with about as much hope. I was ticking like mad—blinking and gulping. As I stood in the waiting room, the school secretary, Mrs. Hancock, walked out of Mr. Dallstrom's office. She greeted me with a smile. "Hello, Michael," she said. "Mr. Dallstrom will be right with you."

I swallowed. I was afraid that was the reason they were calling me. I had no idea why Mr. Dallstrom wanted to see me—I hadn't been shoved in a locker for days.

A moment later he came to his door. He was smiling, which looked frighteningly out of place, like lipstick on a pig.

"Michael, come in."

"Yes, sir." I followed him inside his office. He sat back in his chair and smiled again.

"Have a seat," he said, gesturing to the chair in front of his desk. "How's school going?"

I looked at him, wondering if some alien being had taken over his body. I slowly sat down. "It's fine."

"Great. I just wanted to tell you that your detention has been canceled. I'm sorry about that little misunderstanding. And Mr. Vranes and his cohorts will be doing their time. I guarantee they won't be bothering you anymore."

"Oh." It was all I could think to say. "Thank you."

He stood and walked around his desk to me, putting his hand on my shoulder. "Michael, we're proud that you're a member of our student body."

Now I was certain I was being punked. "You are?"

"Absolutely we are." Mr. Dallstrom leaned back against his desk. "Michael, I have some terrific news. Two of Meridian's pupils have been awarded the prestigious C. J. Hatch Scholarship to the acclaimed Elgen Academy in Pasadena, California. And you are one of them." He stuck out his hand. "Congratulations."

I gulped. How had they found both of us? I timidly offered my hand. When I could speak I asked, "Why me?"

"Why not you?" Mr. Dallstrom said. "Elgen Academy selects their elite student body using a closely guarded process that involves scholarship, citizenship, and character. I am told that this is the first time in the academy's illustrious history that two students have been invited to the academy from the same city—let alone the same school. We are very proud indeed."

"I don't know what to say."

"Say hurray!" he said. "This is the chance of a lifetime! The academy's board will be contacting your parents directly and extending the offer. I'm certain that they'll be as proud and excited as we are."

"It's just my mom," I said. I was suddenly very afraid for her.

"And, Michael, the best part is that your good fortune is shared by the entire student body of Meridian High. If you and the other student accept this remarkable offer, our school will be given a two-hundred-thousand-dollar grant to use however we best see fit. We could restock our library, refinish the basketball court floor, procure new music stands, buy new wrestling mats, and still have plenty to go around." He leaned forward. "This is the biggest thing ever to happen to Meridian High. Your picture will hang proudly on our Hall of Fame."

"What if I can't go?" I said.

His expression fell. "And pass up this incredible, once-in-a-lifetime opportunity?" He leaned forward, looking at me with an expression that was oddly both friendly and threatening. "I'm sure we can count on you to do the right thing."

I swallowed. "Yes, sir."

"I better let you get back to class. Don't want to stand in the way of our greatest student. Do you need a tardy slip?"

"Uh, no. I don't think the bell's rung yet."

"Right you are. You can go. Have a great day."

I walked out of his office more terrified than I had gone in.

Ostin and Taylor were waiting for me outside fifth-period biology. Taylor didn't look like she felt well.

"Are you okay?" I asked.

She had a hand on her right temple. "I'm just upset."

"What happened?" Ostin asked. "Why did they call you down to the office?"

I was still processing everything, and I didn't want to upset Taylor any more than she already was. "I'll tell you later."

Ostin's brow furrowed. "Did you get in trouble?"

"I'll tell you later," I repeated.

"Let's just go to class," Taylor said. "I need to get my mind off of this."

"Good idea," I said.

Taylor didn't say much during biology. Actually she didn't say anything. She looked like it was all she could do to not go running out. More than anything I wanted to reach over and hold her hand. I didn't blame her for being afraid. I was afraid. Actually, I was terrified.

I had no idea who those people were and what they would do.

I met Taylor in the hallway after class. "Are you all right?"

She nodded but said nothing. Ostin walked up. He looked as nervous as we were.

"You remember the plan?" I asked Taylor.

She nodded again.

"Okay," I said. "We'll pick you up at five."

"I'll meet you at the front of the school," she said.

"Are your parents home?" I asked.

"They don't get home today until after five. Why?"

"Just in case my mother needs to talk to them."

"I hope not." She sighed. "I'll see you later."

"See you."

She turned and walked off to the gymnasium.

Ostin and I walked in the opposite direction out of the school. We hadn't even left the schoolyard when I said to him, "I don't feel right about this. Maybe we should stay with her."

"That would seem weird."

"So?"

"If she'd wanted us to stay she would have asked."

"Yeah," I said. "You're probably right."

"So what did Dallstrom want?"

"I've been offered a scholarship to Elgen Academy."

Ostin blanched. "Oh no."

"It gets worse. They've bribed Mr. Dallstrom. They've offered the school two hundred thousand dollars if Taylor and I go."

"You'll have to change schools—Dallstrom will make your life miserable if you don't go."

"I know."

"When are you going to tell your mom about all this?"

"I'm more worried about *what* to tell her. What if she wants me to go?"

"This is bad," Ostin said, shaking his head. "Really bad."

We walked the rest of the way home in silence.

* * *

My mother got home from work later than she had planned—just a few minutes before five. She called as she opened the door, "Michael, Ostin, you guys ready?"

"We're over here, Mom." We were sitting in front of the television watching the Discovery Channel. It was Shark Week.

"When is Taylor done?"

"She has cheerleading until five."

"It's almost five now," she said. "We better hurry."

Mom, Ostin, and I climbed into the Toyota and drove over to the school. My mom pulled up to the school's front steps and put the car in park.

"Where are we meeting her?" my mom asked.

"She said she'd be in front," I said.

"Maybe they're running late," Ostin said. "Or she went back inside."

My mother said, "You two run in and see what's up."

I opened my door. "C'mon, Ostin."

We ran up the stairs into the school's main lobby but Taylor wasn't there. We walked down to the gym. Inside, groups of cheerleaders were practicing stunts. I looked around but I couldn't see Taylor. "Where is she, Ostin? Use your Tay-dar."

"She's not here," he said.

"She has to be."

"She's not."

Mrs. Shaw, the cheerleader adviser, was on the other side of the gym. I walked over to her. "Excuse me, Mrs. Shaw. Do you know where Taylor Ridley is?"

She looked up from her clipboard. "Taylor said she wasn't feeling well, so she left early."

"She walked home?"

"I don't know. She might have called her parents."

"Thank you," I said.

Ostin and I walked out of the gym.

"That doesn't make any sense," Ostin said. "Why didn't she call?"

Just then I spotted Taylor's friend Maddie. She was wearing

gym clothes and walking down the hall texting. I called out to her. "Maddie!"

She looked up and smiled. "Hi, Michael. How are you?"

"Fine. Have you seen Taylor? It's really important that I find her."

"She left practice early. She had a really bad headache."

"Did you see her leave?"

"Yeah."

"How was she acting?"

"Well, she was upset because of her headache."

"Was she alone?"

She looked at me with an idiotic grin. "I'm not telling on her."

"This isn't a *thing*," I said. I looked at her phone. "Look, will you call her? Please."

"She never answers her phone. I'll text her."

"Great. Just ask her where she is."

"Sure." She thumb-typed a message. Less than a minute passed before her phone buzzed. "She's at home."

I felt some relief. "Tell her I'm here to get her and ask if I should come over."

She began typing. Her phone buzzed again. "She says she's sorry she forgot to call. She's not feeling well and will have to pass on tonight, but happy birthday." She looked at me. "I didn't know it was your birthday. Happy birthday."

"Thanks." I turned to Ostin. "At least she's okay," I said.

We walked back to the car and climbed in. My mom looked confused. "Where's Taylor?"

"She went home early," I said. "She had a headache."

She looked as disappointed as I felt. "That's too bad. Maybe next time."

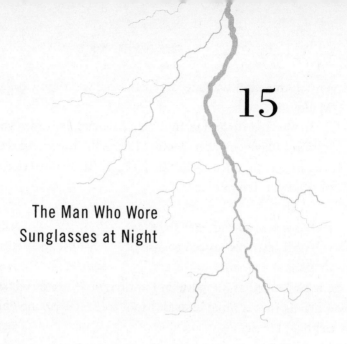

15

The Man Who Wore Sunglasses at Night

None of us spoke much as we drove downtown. I have to admit that Taylor's absence had dulled my excitement. I think even Ostin was upset.

When we got to the aquarium, my mother looked at me and smiled sadly. "Let's have a good time, okay?"

"Okay," I said.

Even though it was a weekday, the aquarium was running a Family Night Special so the place was crowded. The busiest exhibit by far was the sharks, with their cold, unblinking eyes and their teeth bared beneath them, gliding through the water just inches from the tank's glass, as if death were only a few inches away from you. I suppose that's how I felt about everything right now, as if something bad were circling me, just waiting to bite. I soon discovered that Ostin was feeling the same way.

"Do you think Taylor's safe?" he asked me.

"I don't know."

"Do you think we are?"

"Not if she isn't."

It was hard keeping my mind on the exhibits. The three of us wandered over by the electric eels. *Electrophorus electricus* are ugly creatures with pocked skin as if they'd all grown up with a bad case of acne.

There were three eels in the tank, and the largest was about six feet long with a dark gray back and an orange underbelly. There was a voltage meter connected to the outside of the tank with a red needle that occasionally bounced around as the eels sent out surges. Out of curiosity I slid my hand over the metal corner of the tank and pulsed a little. The voltage meter jumped with my charge. Then, to my surprise, the eels in the tank all swam to me as if I had summoned them. Maybe I had. I turned back to see if my mother had seen this but she was looking through her purse. As I looked at her I wondered if I should tell her about my invitation to the academy. I wanted to but I wasn't even sure where to start. A few minutes later I walked over to her.

Before I could say anything, Ostin said to my mother, "Did you know that electric eels are not really eels?"

"Really," she replied, no doubt prepared for Ostin's upcoming monologue. My mother always looked genuinely interested in what Ostin had to say, which was probably one of the reasons he had a crush on her—which, by the way, still grossed me out.

"They're a species of gymnotiformes, also known as knife fish. Biologically, they're closer to the carp or catfish than the eel. And they breathe air, so they have to come to the surface every ten minutes."

"I didn't know that," my mother said.

"They are at the top of the food chain, which means they have no natural predators. In fact, even a baby electric eel can paralyze an alligator with its shock."

I knew most of this already. For obvious reasons, I had always taken great interest in electric eels. When I was nine I used to write "EEM"—secret for "Electric Eel Man"—on the corners of my papers, as if it were my secret identity. Still, I let Ostin talk. I think he would explode if he didn't.

"They're basically a living battery. Four fifths of their body is used in generating or storing electricity. They can produce a charge upward of six hundred volts and five hundred watts, which is powerful enough to be deadly to a human. Though some experts claim they've produced up to eight hundred volts."

"I'd hate to take a bath with one," she said, smiling.

"Or give a bath to one," I said.

She looked at me and grinned. When I was three years old, I accidentally gave her a shock while she was bathing me. It knocked her over. It was pretty much showers after that.

"Eels use their electric shock to stun or kill their prey, but they can also use low voltage like radar to see in murky waters. It's called electrolocation. It's how they find food."

"Speaking of eating," my mother said, "is anyone getting hungry?"

That was one way of shutting Ostin up. "Is that a trick question?" he asked.

"I'm hungry," I said.

"Good," she said. "I'm starving. Off to PizzaMax."

The pizzeria wasn't actually called PizzaMax. Its real name was Mac's Purple Pig Pizza Parlor and Piano Pantry, which is as dumb as it is long, but they have awesome pizza. My mother and I ate there the first week we lived in Idaho, and a few weeks later when she asked me where I wanted to eat, I only remembered the Mac's part. The name stuck.

We ordered six pieces of cheesy garlic bread, an extra-large Mac's Kitchen Sink pizza, which has everything you could imagine on it (except anchovies—gross!), and a cold pitcher of root beer.

While we were eating, my mom asked me, "What do Taylor's parents do?"

"Her dad is a police officer. Her mom works at a travel agency."

My mom nodded. "She's a really nice girl. I hope she comes around again soon."

"I hope she does too," I said.

"Still like your watch?" my mother asked. I think she just wanted to see me smile again.

I held up my arm so she could see that I was wearing it. "Love it."

I could tell this made her happy. She looked into my eyes. "Are you feeling okay?"

"Yeah," I said.

"You're kind of quiet tonight."

I was never very good at hiding things from my mother. "I guess I just have a lot on my mind."

"Are you still upset about Taylor?"

I shrugged. "A little."

She put her hand on my shoulder. "Things don't always go as planned, do they? But in the end they seem to work out."

"I suppose so," I said. I hoped so.

We had been at PizzaMax for nearly an hour when Ostin excused himself to go to the bathroom. My mother smiled at me, then slid around the vinyl seat of our booth to get closer.

"Honey, what's wrong? You're really ticking."

I slowly looked up at her. "Mr. Dallstrom called me down to his office today."

Her brow fell. "Oh. What happened?"

"Nothing happened. I got offered a scholarship."

A smile crossed her face. "What kind of scholarship?"

"It's to this really prestigious school in California."

Her smile grew even larger. "Michael, that's wonderful. What's the name of the school?"

I was relieved to see her happy. "The Elgen Academy."

Her smile immediately vanished into a look of fear. "Did you say Elgen?"

Her expression frightened me. "Yeah."

"In Pasadena?"

"How did you know that?" I asked.

She turned pale, like she was going to be sick.

"Mom, what is it?"

"We need to go," she said, her voice quivering. "We need to get Ostin and leave now."

"Mom, what's wrong?"

"I can't tell you here . . ." She looked at me intensely, her eyes dark with fear. "Michael, there's more to this than you know. Your father . . ."

Just then Ostin returned. "I'm ready for another frosty mug of root beer," he said.

I looked up at him. "We've got to go," I said.

"Right now?"

"Right now," my mother said. "Something's come up."

It was dark outside when my mother paid the bill. We were walking out to the car when Ostin said, "Wait. I forgot my jacket."

"Hurry," my mom said to him as he turned to run back inside. We continued walking to the car.

My mother was unlocking our car door when a man appeared between our car and the truck next to it. His clothes were dirty and worn and his face was partially cloaked in a dark gray hoodie. He said to my mother, "Excuse me, do you have a dollar?"

My mother looked at him, then said, "Of course." My mother always helped others. She lifted her purse.

When my mom's head was down, the man pulled a gun from the hoodie's pouch. "Just give me the purse."

My mother dropped her keys on the ground.

"Okay," she said, her voice pitched. "You can have it. You don't need the gun."

"Shut up!" he said. "Just give it to me and shut your mouth. If anyone screams, I shoot."

"Don't talk to my mother like that," I said.

He pointed the gun at me. He looked nervous and was shaking. "I'll shoot you first."

"Please," my mother said, "just take the money." She handed her purse to him. "Just take it. There's credit cards and cash, you can have it all."

He cautiously reached out and took the purse from her, the gun still shaking in his hand. He backed off again. "I want the car too," he said. "Give me your keys and back away."

"I dropped the keys," my mother said. "They're right there. I'm going to pick them up."

"You don't move," he said, pointing the gun at my mother's chest. "You," he said to me, "give me the keys."

I looked at him, then my mother.

"Bring them to me now and I won't shoot your mother."

"Okay," I said. I crouched down and lifted the keys, then slowly walked toward him. About a yard away from him, I turned back and looked at my mother.

"What are you doing?" he said angrily. "Give me the keys."

My mother guessed what I was thinking. She shook her head.

I looked back at the man. Maybe I had watched too many super-hero movies, but if ever there was a moment to use my power it was now. I could stop him from taking our car and my mother's purse. I was handing him a ring of metal. All I had to do was surge.

I took another step forward, then slowly reached out with the keys. His hand shot out and grabbed them. The instant he touched the key ring there was a loud snap and a yellow spark that briefly lit up everything around us. The man screamed out as he collapsed to the ground. I had never shocked anyone so hard before, and there was a pale mist of smoke in the air.

The man wasn't moving, and for a moment I wondered if I had killed him. It seemed that time stood still. I looked at my mother, wondering how she'd react. She was staring at the man on the ground. The silence was broken by a deep voice.

"Well done, Michael."

I quickly turned around. I have no idea where he came from, but a man was now standing just a few yards from us. He was sharply dressed in a tan suit with an orange silk tie. Even though it was dark, he wore thick-framed sunglasses. His hair, dark brown with sideburns, was nicely styled. He looked at the mugger, then back up at me, and lightly clapped. "Really, that was impressive.

What was that—nine hundred, a thousand volts?"

I looked at my mother, then back at him anxiously.

"Who are you?" my mother asked.

"A friend, Sharon. A friend and an admirer of Michael's. And his gift."
My mother and I exchanged glances. "Yes," he said, smiling, "I know all
about it. As a matter of fact, I know more about it than you do."

Just then the thief groaned, and I looked down at him. He was
struggling just to lift his head. As I watched him anger flooded
through my body. If I had ever wondered if my electrical powers
were somehow connected to my emotions, there was no doubt of it
now as I felt power surging through me like I had never felt before.
I looked down at my hands. Electricity was sparking in blue arcs
between my fingers, something I'd never before experienced.

"It's an emotional reaction," the man said. "Fear, anger, hate—the
powerful stuff causes your nervous system to react. It's peculiar isn't
it? Normal people respond with adrenaline—but special people like
you react electrically."

My mother put her hand on my arm. "Michael, we need to go."

I didn't move. "How do you know all this?" I asked.

The man took a step forward. "Michael, we've been looking for
you for a long, long time . . . almost since you were born."

"Michael," my mom said.

"Why?" I asked.

"To reunite you with the others."

"Others?"

"You're not alone, Michael. There's more of your kind than you
think. More than just your friend Taylor."

His mention of Taylor startled me.

"I'd like to introduce you to some of them right now. Behind you
is Zeus."

Suddenly a young man was standing next to my mother. He was
good-looking but unkempt. He had long, greasy, blond hair and wore
a Levi's jacket with the sleeves cut off and no shirt underneath. Even
though he was only my age he had a tattoo on his chest of a lightning
bolt. My mother looked at him anxiously.

"And this is Nichelle."

A young woman stepped up behind the man. She wore black clothing and dark, thick makeup, mostly black or dark purple, the way the Goth kids do. Both kids looked about my age, though Zeus was taller than me.

"Zeus, show Mrs. Vey what you can do."

He smiled darkly. "Glad to." He lifted his hands, and electricity flew from his fingers to my mother in blue-white strikes. My mother screamed and collapsed just like the man I had just shocked.

"Mom!" I dropped to the ground next to her, cradling her head in my arms. "Why did you do that?" I shouted.

"She'll be okay," the man said. "It just took the wind out of her."

My eyes darted back and forth between the three of them. "Who are you?"

"I'm your friend," the man said softly. "Nichelle?"

The girl started toward me. As she approached I noticed that the Zeus guy took a few steps back, as if he were afraid of her.

As the girl neared me I started to feel different. Everything was out of place, the man, the two kids, my mother on the ground, it was all like a bad dream. I felt weaker. The electricity stopped arcing between my fingers. Then I began to feel dizzy. I looked at the girl, and she looked into my eyes with a strange, emotionless stare. I couldn't make sense of any of it—who these people were and why they were there. More importantly, what they wanted with us.

With each step the girl took toward me, my dizziness increased. Then my head began to pound like a bass drum. I put my hand on my forehead as my vision began to blur.

"Take it easy on him, Nichelle," I heard the man say. "He's not used to it."

Suddenly I heard Ostin's voice, blending into what seemed like a collage of other sounds. I looked down at my mother. She was still, but gazing at me. I saw her lips move but I couldn't hear her. I couldn't hear anything other than the loud buzzing in my ears. I think she said *I love you*. It seems like that's what she said. It's the last thing I remember before passing out.

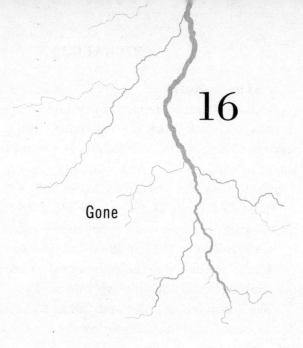

16

Gone

When I woke, I was in a bed with aluminum side rails. I was lying beneath clean, white sheets and there was an IV taped to my arm. I felt as if I had been drained of all my energy and every joint of my body ached, throbbing like a bad toothache. It took a moment for my eyes to adjust to the light above me. I groaned out, as if expulsing a nightmare. Ostin appeared at my side.

"Michael?"

I turned my head toward him. He was standing in front of closed blinds that glowed from the daylight behind them. Next to him were his mother and father. Ostin's father was in charge of maintenance for the county's parks and recreation, so he was rarely home. I was surprised to also see him in the room. I looked around for my mother but didn't see her.

"Where am I?" My tongue stuck to my dry mouth and it was difficult to speak.

"Honey, you're in the hospital," Mrs. Liss said. Her face was pinched with concern.

"How did I get here?"

"Paramedics," Ostin said.

"You passed out," Mrs. Liss said. "The doctors were afraid you had a stroke."

"Where's my mother?"

"Do you remember what happened?" Mr. Liss asked.

It hurt my head to think about it. "There was a guy with a gun. Then this man with two kids. One of them shocked my mother."

"Shocked?" Mr. Liss said. "What do you mean?"

I looked at Ostin. "Did I dream that?"

He shrugged. "I only saw the gunman."

"Is my mother okay?"

Ostin didn't answer.

I turned to Mr. and Mrs. Liss. "She's okay, isn't she?"

Mrs. Liss walked closer and put her hand on mine. Her eyes were filled with tears. "I have some bad news, honey. Your mother's gone."

I looked at her blankly. "What do you mean?"

"The police believe she's been kidnapped," Mr. Liss said.

My heart froze. *Kidnapped?* "Why would someone kidnap her?"

"We don't know."

My body's pain was nothing compared to the agony I now felt. Tears filled my eyes. How could this have happened? My mother had spent her life protecting and caring for me, and now I had failed to protect her. I had let her down. Why couldn't they have just taken me? I wanted to fall asleep and wake up again in my own house, talking to my own mother. I wanted something to make sense. I wanted the nightmare to end.

17

Lieutenant Lloyd

That afternoon the police came to interview me. Mr. Liss had gone to work, leaving Ostin and his mother still with me. There were two policemen, both in uniform. The officer who did most of the talking was older, with gray hair.

"Michael, I'm Lieutenant Lloyd of the Boise Police Department. This is Detective Steve Pearson."

Detective Pearson waved from behind. "Hello, Michael."

"Hey," I said.

Lieutenant Lloyd said to Ostin and his mother, "We have some questions for Michael. Would you mind waiting outside for a few minutes?"

"Of course," Mrs. Liss said, putting her hand on Ostin's back. "Let's go, Ostin."

Ostin looked at me sympathetically. "See ya, buddy."

After we were alone, Lieutenant Lloyd walked to the side of my bed. He must have noticed my ticking because he said, "Don't worry. We're here to help."

He grabbed my bed's railing with one hand. "I'm really sorry about what's happened to your mother, son. The good news is we have the man who held you up in custody. We're just trying to put the pieces together. I need you to tell me everything you remember about what happened."

I closed my eyes. Remembering what had happened was like pulling a Band-Aid off a bad cut. "I remember some," I said.

"Please tell us what you remember."

I rolled my tongue around inside my mouth. It felt thick and heavy. I was blinking pretty hard. "My mom had taken us out for pizza for my birthday. We had just finished eating and were walking out to our car . . ."

"You and your mother?" Detective Pearson asked.

I nodded. "Yeah. My friend Ostin was with us, but he went back inside to get his jacket."

"Go on," Lieutenant Lloyd said.

"My mom was unlocking the car when this guy was there."

"The guy with the gun?"

I nodded.

"Clyde Stuart," Detective Pearson said. "His name is Clyde Stuart. Where did he come from?"

"I don't know. He was just between the cars. Neither of us saw him at first."

"What did he do?" Lieutenant Lloyd asked.

"He asked for some money. When my mom went for her wallet, he pulled out a gun and asked for her purse."

"Then what?"

"He told us to give him our car keys. I handed them to him."

"Anything else?"

I shook my head. "That's it."

Lieutenant Lloyd looked at me with a perplexed expression, then turned back to his partner. Detective Pearson said, "What we can't figure out is what happened to the suspect."

I realized the gap in my story. My eyes darted nervously between them. "What do you mean?"

"He was incapacitated when we arrived on the scene," Pearson said. "He claims the keys shocked him."

I blinked several times. "I don't remember."

"Stuart was acting like he'd been hit by a Taser," Lieutenant Lloyd said. "We had to carry him into the police cruiser."

"Taser?" Pearson said. "It was more like he was struck by a bolt of lightning."

"Maybe he was," I said.

Lieutenant Lloyd wrote something on his pad. Then he said, "We're wondering if the gunman had an accomplice. Was there anyone with him?"

"No."

"Did you see anyone else around?"

"There was a man."

Lieutenant Lloyd looked up from his pad. "What man?"

"I don't know. Just a man. He was dressed in a suit. And he had a boy and a girl with him about my age."

"Did he come from the pizza place?"

"Maybe. I'm not sure."

"What did he look like? His face?"

"I'm not sure about that either. He was wearing sunglasses."

"At night?" Pearson asked.

"Yeah. I thought it was weird."

"What else do you remember about him?" Lloyd asked.

"He had short, dark brown hair. He looked . . . rich."

"Definitely didn't look like Stuart," Lloyd said, jotting down more notes in his pad. "Did you see them take your mother?"

"No. I fainted or something."

"Fear will do that," Pearson said.

I didn't think it had anything to do with fear, but I said nothing.

"Do you have any idea why someone would want to kidnap your mother?"

I shook my head. "No. Why don't you ask Stuart?"

"We've interrogated him but he's tight as a clam. We know he's hiding something, but whomever or whatever he's protecting has got a real hold on him. Apparently he's a lot more afraid of them than he is of us."

"Will you find her?"

Lieutenant Lloyd looked at me sympathetically. "We'll do our best. I promise." He saw the anguish on my face and added, "We're not done with Stuart yet. I've still got a few tricks up my sleeve." He took a card from his front pocket. "Take this. It has my office and cell phone number. If you think of anything else just call me." The two policemen started to leave the room. Lieutenant Lloyd stopped by the door. "Oh, by the way, the gun Stuart had was empty."

"Empty?"

"No bullets. I thought it might make you feel a little better to know that he wasn't intending to shoot you."

He might as well have, I thought.

The policemen walked out. Ostin rushed in as soon as they left. "Do they know where your mother is?"

"No." I lay back in bed. "What did you see?"

"Hardly anything. When I got to your car, you and that man were lying on the ground and your mom was gone. I didn't see anyone else. I ran back to the restaurant and told them to call the police."

"There were three people besides the gunman," I said. "A man in sunglasses and two kids our age. The man knew my name. He knew my mom's and Taylor's names. He knew about my power."

Ostin scratched his head. "How could he have known all that?"

"I don't know."

"He brought his kids?"

"I don't think they were his. And they had electrical powers. At least one of them did. The man called him Zeus. He's the one who shocked my mom."

"He could shock like you?"

"Sort of. Except his electricity left his body. Like lightning." I leaned forward. "There's something else I remember. He seemed afraid of the girl."

"What did she do?"

"I don't know. But the closer she got to me the dizzier I felt. Then I passed out." I combed my hair back from my face. "They're not going to find my mother."

"Don't talk that way."

"Have you heard from Taylor?"

"No, not yet."

I lay back in bed. "At least she's safe. It's a good thing she didn't come with us."

PART TWO

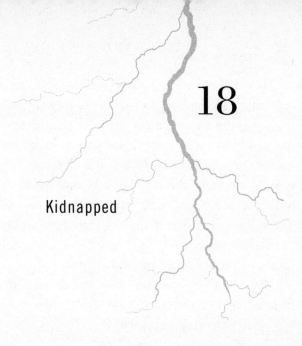

18

Kidnapped

Taylor shook with fear in the backseat of the utility van. Her head still ached, as did her hands, which were strapped in front of her with plastic ties. She felt as if she'd been drugged. A leather strap crossed at her waist, holding her tightly to the seat, and her legs were bound at her ankles with leather shackles fastened to the floor. The van appeared to have been designed for this very purpose—transporting prisoners. On top of her fear, she felt carsick and wondered if she might throw up.

It had all happened so fast. She had been at cheerleading practice for only a few minutes when she came down with an excruciating headache and had to sit down. After ten minutes Mrs. Shaw suggested she go home. That was when Taylor first noticed the scary-looking girl watching her from the gym door. At first she went outside and sat on the concrete steps waiting for Michael, hoping the pain would go away. She noticed that the scary girl followed her at a distance.

Then the pain got so severe that Taylor knew she couldn't wait any longer, so she began walking home. She was crossing the school's back parking lot when a white van pulled up beside her—the van she was held captive in. Taylor had thought the van was one of the school's food-service vehicles, and she hadn't paid much attention until it stopped, the side door swung open, and the scary-looking girl—the same girl who now sat in front of her—stepped out. Taylor's first thought was *Why is that girl wearing a dog collar?* Her headache immediately intensified until she fell first to her knees, then to all fours, dizzy and disoriented.

"Take it easy!" someone shouted. Then a man got out from the front of the van and stood next to her. "Are you okay?"

"I don't think so," Taylor said.

"Let me give you a hand."

Her head was spinning, and the buzzing in her ears was so loud that she didn't resist the two men picking her up and carrying her inside the van, blindfolding her, and strapping her down to the back-seat.

Then someone put something over her mouth and nose. That's the last thing she remembered. She wondered if anyone had seen her being kidnapped and called the police. Maybe her father was coming for her right now. She desperately hoped so, but doubted it. The whole thing had taken less than thirty seconds. She had been taken without even a scream.

Heavy rock music played from the front of the van. Earlier, when Taylor woke, her captors were arguing over whether to listen to classic rock or rap. They flipped a coin to decide. Classic rock had won out, and Aerosmith was playing, adding to her headache.

The scary-looking girl sat alone on the bench in front of her. The girl was about her age, though a little shorter. She had short black spiky hair streaked with purple, black makeup, and she wore a black leather collar around her neck, studded with what looked like real diamonds. She had earbuds in both ears, the white cord running down her neck.

For the last hour Taylor had tried to reboot the driver, even though she knew it would likely result in crashing the van. A crash would, at least, draw outside attention, and she'd rather take her chances with an accident than with these people. But her attempts to reboot him were only met with pain—a sharp prick in her temples. Taylor decided to ignore the pain and try rebooting again with all her might. She pressed the thought, but the pain just grew. It was like sticking pins into her own head. She finally groaned out and stopped.

The girl in front of her turned around and removed one of the buds from her ear. "I'd tell you to stop doing that except it feels kind of good."

"Doing what?" Taylor asked, her head still throbbing.

"Whatever it is that you do to people's brains."

Taylor looked at her. "How do you know what I'm doing?"

"I can feel it. But you're wasting your time. It doesn't hurt me and it won't get past me."

"Who are you?"

"Nichelle," she said. "I'd shake your hand, but"—she paused and smiled—"you're tied up." Her smile fell into a dark glare. "Actually, I wouldn't shake your hand anyway, and the better question is, what am I?"

"What are you?"

"I'm your worst nightmare. Just think of me as an electrical vampire. And girl, I could feed off you all day." The girl put the earbud back in and turned around.

Taylor had never before felt so helpless or afraid. She thought of Michael and his mother waiting for her; she thought of her parents. They probably hadn't noticed her absence yet, thinking that she'd gone with Michael and his mother. It wouldn't be until late that evening that they started worrying. Her mother would be a wreck and her father would be following up on every resource available to a police officer, but by then she'd be long gone, maybe even out of the state. She wanted to be home with all of her heart.

"Why does my head hurt?"

"That's me. Letting you know I'm here." She smiled. "I can increase the pressure if you like."

"No thank you."

"I thought you might say that." Nichelle turned completely around and looked into Taylor's eyes. The pain started increasing, higher, then higher.

Taylor shouted out, "Stop. Please."

The girl was enjoying herself. "Hurts, don't it."

Taylor's eyes filled with tears. "Yes."

The pain stopped. "See, I'm what an electrician would call a ground wire. I just soak up all those lovely powers of yours until we can get you to where you're going."

"Where are we going?"

"You'll see. Don't want to ruin the surprise."

"Why do I feel so sick?"

"Funny you should ask. The scientists at Elgen wondered that same thing. They think it's because your body has become so used to high levels of electricity that you don't feel normal without it. That's what makes me so darn annoying."

"Elgen? Are we going to the Elgen Academy?" Taylor asked.

"So you don't want to be surprised, eh? Okay then, we're going to the lah-bor-a-tory," she said, purposely drawing out the word like she was a mad scientist. Taylor couldn't tell if she was trying to sound comical or scary, but it didn't matter. Either way, it was scary.

"What are you going to do to me?"

"Same thing scientists always do with lab animals—poke and prod around, and when they're done, they'll dissect you like a frog in a middle school biology class."

Pure fear passed through Taylor. "Why? I haven't done anything."

Nichelle shrugged. "Why not?" She leaned back. "You ask too many questions. They're hurting my ears. Like this . . ."

Suddenly a painful, high-pitched squeal tore through Taylor's head. She started crying. "Stop it. Please, stop it."

"Say 'pretty please.'"

"Pretty please."

"'With a cherry on top.'"

Taylor sobbed. "With a cherry on top."

Nichelle smiled. "Good girl." The pain ceased. "Now, no more talking. You just be real quiet there, and in the future, should I ask you something, you will refer to me as 'Master.' You got that?"

Taylor just looked at her.

The girl's eyes narrowed. "I asked you a question."

Taylor's head started filling with the noise. "Yes, Master."

"Very good."

Nichelle gave Taylor a big grin, turned back around, replaced the earbud, and lay back. "I love the abductions," she muttered. "It's the only time I can do whatever I want without getting in trouble. It's been a long time since any fresh Glows have been brought in."

A voice up front said, "Knock it off, Nichelle."

She pulled out an earbud. "You're no fun. It's boring back here. I could make her bark like a dog or do something really embarrassing."

"Just leave her alone."

She turned around and said to Taylor, "These old dudes have no sense of humor. By the way, you should have seen what I did to that boy you led us to. Vey. He had a lot of electricity in him. Much more than usual. When I shut him down, I almost killed him. He's probably still in the hospital."

"You have Michael?"

"I can't hear you," she sang. She winked. "You didn't say 'Master.'"

"I'm sorry," Taylor said quickly, afraid she might hurt her again. "You have Michael, Master?"

Nichelle smiled. "No. The little guy's friend showed up and we had to go. But we'll have him soon enough. We took a little insurance. You and his dearest mumsy."

"You have Mrs. Vey, Master?"

"Yes, we do."

A sharp voice came from the front. "Nichelle, just shut up."

Nichelle leaned toward Taylor. "Now look what you did. You got me in trouble." She turned back to the front. "Oh, chill. It's not like she'll ever get the chance to tell anyone." She shook her head.

"Idiots," she said under her breath, once again replacing the earbud. "No more talking," she said to Taylor. She leaned her head against the interior metal wall of the van.

Taylor tried to keep from crying. She was in pain and frightened. She wondered if what the girl had told her about the laboratory was true. Would they really cut her open? As frightened as she was to find out, she had to know. She leaned her head against the van's wall to read Nichelle's mind. She saw images of the school from the brochure, she saw other youths her age, some of them well dressed and laughing, and she knew Nichelle hated these kids. She saw something she didn't understand—she saw herself at the school interacting with the other students as if it had already happened. Was she seeing the future? Then she saw other youths lying on the ground, some in pain, others crying in a dark place that looked like a dungeon. She sat back up, unable to continue. Everything she saw in Nichelle's mind terrified her.

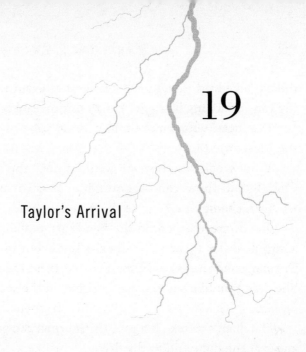

19

Taylor's Arrival

The van drove through the night, and Taylor slept for most of the ride, waking only when a voice came over the two-way radio up front or when the van stopped for gas. Taylor was given no food and only a bottle of water that Nichelle held for her to drink, purposely spilling a good portion of it down the front of Taylor's shirt and jeans.

"Gross, you wet yourself," she said.

The ride was mostly through desert until early the next morning, when they came again into city traffic.

Around 2:00 p.m. the van pulled into a driveway with a guard booth and a tall gate lined with razor wire. The driver rolled down his window and showed the guard a badge, and the gate opened. They drove around to the back of the building, where a large overhead garage door lifted, and the van pulled inside. When the overhead door had closed behind them, the men climbed out and one of them opened the side door. Nichelle stepped out, then leaned against the van, stretching her legs. "Hurry this up. I have to pee."

"Don't get your knickers in a twist," one of the men said. "Just stay close."

"What would you boys do without me?" she said. "Ain't it awful? Can't live with me, can't shoot me."

"Don't tempt me," one of them said.

One of the men undid the bands around Taylor's feet and waist and pulled her forward. Taylor ducked down as she stepped out of the van to the orange-yellow painted concrete floor of the garage. She was trembling with fear, and felt like her legs might give out on her.

"Hatch says to take her into the infirmary to get checked out," the guard at the door said to the driver.

Nichelle and one of the drivers took Taylor inside the building and down a well-lit corridor to a room at the end of the hall. The sign on the door said EXAM ROOM B. Upon their entrance, a tall woman with cropped yellow hair, thin-rimmed glasses, and wearing a white lab coat looked up from her desk.

"This is Taylor Ridley?" she asked the man.

"Yes. Sign here," he said, thrusting out a clipboard. The woman signed the document, then handed the clipboard back to the driver. "Muchas gracias," he said, and walked away.

The doctor looked up at Taylor. "So you're Taylor."

Taylor swallowed. "Yes, ma'am. Where am I?"

"I'll ask the questions," she said sharply. "You're in my office. I'm Dr. Parker, the resident physician at the Elgen Academy." The woman turned to Nichelle. "Tell Miss Ridley what will happen if she doesn't cooperate."

"She knows," Nichelle said. "Don't you?"

Taylor nodded.

The doctor walked up to Taylor and cut off her plastic cuffs with a pair of surgical scissors. Taylor rubbed her wrists.

"Thank you," Taylor said.

"Remove your clothes," the doctor said.

For a moment Taylor just stood there, then a sharp pain pierced her skull. "Stop! I'll do it," Taylor said quickly.

She undressed down to her underwear. She didn't know if they'd make her take everything off, but she wasn't going to until they made her. To her relief, they didn't.

"Lay your clothes on the chair."

"Yes, ma'am."

The doctor lifted a tablet computer from her desk. "Relax," she said in a tone that only made Taylor more uncomfortable. "We're just giving you a routine physical examination to see how healthy you are. Step onto the scale."

Taylor did as she was told. The doctor checked the number on the scale and wrote on her pad. Most of what the doctor asked Taylor to do was no different than when her mother took her to her own doctor for her annual physical, with one exception. She had Taylor stand against the wall and grasp two chrome bars. Then the doctor put on a thick pair of sunglasses. "I'm going to ask Nichelle to leave for a moment," she said. "Are you going to behave yourself? Or do I need to bring in a guard?"

"I'll behave, ma'am," Taylor said, looking at the ground.

She nodded to Nichelle. "Stay close."

"Okay." Nichelle walked out of the room.

The doctor said to Taylor, "This device tests your electrical pulse."

Taylor remained silent as the doctor attached sensors to Taylor's body. After a moment the doctor explained, "The electric children have a secondary pulse. Actually, it's more like an EKG. I made Nichelle leave because she distorts the readings."

When the doctor was done running the test, she punched a series of numbers into a machine that spit out a roll of paper. "I shouldn't be surprised by this," she said. "Your readings are identical to your sister's."

"I don't have a sister," Taylor said.

The doctor looked at her with a peculiar smile but said nothing. She walked to her desk and pushed the talk button on the intercom. "Nichelle, come in, please."

Nichelle walked back into the exam room. Taylor immediately recoiled with fear.

The woman gave Taylor a thin cloth jumpsuit. "Put this on."

Taylor stepped into it and zipped it up, noticing the plastic zipper and snaps.

"Nichelle," the doctor said, "it's time for Miss Ridley's interview. Take her to her cell."

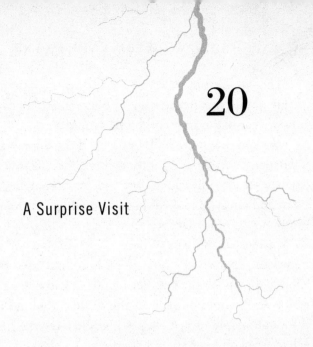

20

A Surprise Visit

I was released from the hospital around six o'clock. A social worker from the state had come to my room to talk with me, and it was agreed that for the time being I would stay with the Lisses. We stopped at McDonald's for dinner, then drove to Ostin's house.

Mrs. Liss had always been nice but tonight she was especially kind. As we walked into the apartment, Mrs. Liss said, "Michael, honey, you can get your things and bring them over. You and Ostin can share a room for the time being."

"I'd like to stay in my own room for now, if that's okay."

She thought about it. "It is just down the hall. I guess that'll be all right. Take this with you." She took a bag of red licorice from her pantry and handed it to me. "It will help."

"Thanks."

"Want me to come over with you?" Ostin asked.

"Thanks, but not now."

He patted me on the back. "I understand." He's probably the only fifteen-year-old in the world who would.

I walked down the hall. I unlocked the door, walked into the dark apartment, and flipped on the lights. Since we moved to Idaho I had spent a lot of time alone, but the apartment had never seemed so quiet and empty. I looked down at my birthday watch, then I twisted it around on my wrist.

My eyes teared up. Where was she? I went into my mother's bedroom. There was a picture on her nightstand of the two of us at Zion National Park in southern Utah. It had been a beautiful day, and Kolob Arch could be seen in the distance behind us. As I picked up the photograph I wondered if I would ever see her again. My heart ached. I lay on her bed and cried.

Sometime in the next hour there was a knock on the door. I wiped my eyes and walked out. I had assumed it was Ostin, but to my surprise Taylor's dad and a woman I guessed was her mother stood in the hallway. They looked very upset.

Officer Ridley spoke first. "Hi, Michael, we're Taylor's parents. Could we speak with you?"

I looked at them nervously, reacting with my usual tics. I assumed they were here to talk to me about my mother. "Sure," I said, stepping back from the door. "Come in."

Mrs. Ridley's eyes were puffy. Taylor's father put his arm around her, and they walked inside, shutting the door behind them.

"Is Taylor okay?" I asked.

Mrs. Ridley began to cry. Mr. Ridley said, "When was the last time you heard from Taylor?"

"Yesterday afternoon. She was going to go with us to the aquarium. But when we got to the school, she was gone."

Mrs. Ridley began to cry harder.

"What's happened?" I asked.

"You haven't heard from her?" Mr. Ridley asked.

"No, sir."

He looked at me suspiciously. "Then you didn't know that Taylor ran away?"

My heart froze. "No. Why would she do that?"

He shook his head. "You know, I'm tough on her sometimes. I just . . ." He paused, overcome by emotion. "I told her that if she didn't start spending more time at home she would have to give up cheerleading." He rubbed his palm over his eyes. "She texted her good-bye."

"We just didn't see it coming," Mrs. Ridley sobbed.

"She won't return our texts," Mr. Ridley said. He took his wife's hand. "We wanted to ask you a favor. We just want her home and safe. Will you please tell her that we love her, and we would really like to talk to her?"

"If I hear from her," I said. I felt sick but knew I couldn't show it. "But I'm sure she has a lot of other friends she'd contact first."

"Then you have no plans to see her?" Mr. Ridley asked. There was a strong inflection in his voice.

"No. I haven't heard from her since yesterday."

They were both looking at me with a peculiar gaze. Finally Mrs. Ridley said, "An hour ago she sent another text that said 'Tell Michael I'll see him soon.'"

Chills went up my spine. When I could speak I said, "I don't know what she meant by that, but if I hear from her I'll call you. I promise."

They both sat looking at me, and I guessed they were trying to decide whether I was telling the truth or not. Finally Mr. Ridley said, "Thank you, Michael." They stood and walked to the door.

Mrs. Ridley stopped in front of my door, blotting her eyes with a Kleenex. "I don't know if you know this, but Taylor was adopted."

"She told me."

"The counselors told us that sometimes adopted children can carry a sense of abandonment. We tried to fill that, but I guess we failed."

"I don't think you failed," I said. "There must be some kind of misunderstanding."

"That's kind of you to say, Michael. Taylor thinks a lot of you. I think if you told her that we love her, she'll believe you. I think she might come back."

"I don't know what's going on, but I do know that Taylor loves you both. I'll let you know if I hear from her."

"Thank you," Mrs. Ridley said. Mr. Ridley put his arm around her and led her out of my apartment.

As soon as they were gone I ran down the hall and knocked on Ostin's door. Ostin answered the door holding a half-eaten toaster strudel. He read the panic on my face.

"What's wrong?"

"They've got Taylor."

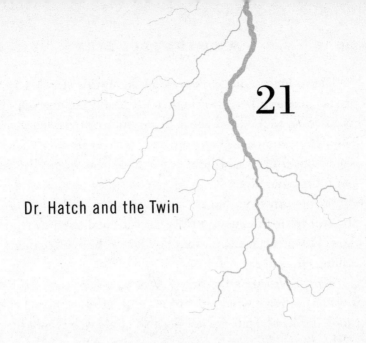

21

Dr. Hatch and the Twin

The cell Taylor was placed in was windowless and rectangular, with the walls, ceiling, and floor lined in a soft, pinkish rubber coating that resembled the material that pencil erasers are made of. Mounted to each wall were surveillance cameras, speaker boxes, and other sensors designed to monitor the cell's occupant's activities. On one wall were two chrome bars that stuck out about six inches from the wall—similar to the testing apparatus in the exam room.

In one corner of the room there was a porcelain toilet and sink. The only thing that looked normal was the bed, which was on a wood frame.

Taylor walked over to the bed. There was no metal of any kind used in its construction. The mattress was filled with down feathers. The bed had one other difference she didn't fail to notice: leather restraining straps.

The room was lit by fluorescent lighting concealed behind thick plastic plates. There was neither a thermostat nor switches in the room of any kind, and she had no control over light, heat, or air. The people watching her from the cameras would decide when she would have lights and how hot or cold she would be. She had no control over anything.

Taylor turned on the sink and was grateful that water came out. She still felt nauseous from the car ride, and she washed her face in the cold water. Then she went and lay on her bed, looking up at the ceiling.

She wasn't sure what time it was. She wasn't even sure what day it was. Mrs. Shaw would be furious with her for missing cheer. Taylor shook her head. Had she not been so afraid, she would have laughed at the thought. If only Mrs. Shaw was the worst of her worries. Besides, everyone would know by now that she had been abducted. They had to, didn't they? Her friends would be calling one another, they'd organize search parties. Wouldn't they?

She thought of how worried her parents must be. Just a few days earlier they had scolded her for being gone from home too much. The argument had ended with her slamming her bedroom door. She regretted how she had acted. She'd give up everything she had to be home right now. Even cheerleading.

As Taylor lay on top of the bed thinking, she heard a quick burst of air followed by a sharp metallic click. Her door opened. Nichelle stepped inside, followed by a tall man in a suit and tie. He wore over-sized black-rimmed glasses with dark lenses that concealed his eyes, similar to the glasses the doctor had put on during her tests.

"Sit up," Nichelle barked.

Taylor sat up on the bed. The man walked to the center of the room. "Hello, Taylor," he said. "You're a sight for sore eyes."

Taylor stared at him, her heart pounding fiercely.

"He said 'hello,'" Nichelle said. A sharp, piercing scream entered Taylor's head.

Taylor grabbed her ears and let out a small scream. "Stop!"

"Stop it," the man said sharply to Nichelle. "Go."

Nichelle frowned. "Yes, sir." She walked out of the room without looking at Taylor.

"I'm sorry about that," the man said. "Nichelle gets a bit Draconian."

"I hate her," Taylor said. She immediately regretted this, wondering if she'd be punished.

To her surprise, the man just nodded. "Be assured that you're not alone in that," he said. "Most of the students here do." He smiled warmly. "Let's start over. I'm Dr. Hatch. You are at the Elgen Academy. I hope your trip here wasn't too unpleasant."

Taylor looked at him incredulously. "Why have you kidnapped me? You can't hold me here. My father will find you and—"

He raised his hand. "Your adopted father, Dean Charles Ridley of the Boise Police Department, thinks his little girl has run away. In fact you have already texted him twice today telling him how much you dislike him, and how you never intend to go home as long as he's there."

Hearing this made her heart ache. Taylor began to cry. "Why are you doing this to me?"

"Taylor, I'm sorry it had to begin this way. I really am. But once you see things for what they really are, I promise you won't be upset anymore." He stepped toward her and crouched down to look into her face. "Do you know how long I have been looking for you? You're a very special girl. Not just because you're a Glow, but because you have something that we can't learn from the other Glows."

"What's a Glow?"

"That's our term for the electric children. You all give off that faint glow. Surely you've noticed it."

She didn't answer.

"Of course you have. Anyway, that's why I wear these glasses." He took them off and held them up so Taylor could see. "We invented them right here. They are designed to magnify that glow. I can spot one of you a mile away. Actually, one point seven miles to be exact." He rubbed his eyes, then he looked into her eyes and smiled. "Taylor, you're a very special girl, and part of something that's bigger and more exciting than you can imagine. We have a chance to change the world. I don't mean slap a Band-Aid on it; I mean throw the past out and start fresh. We could create a society where everyone has enough to eat, sufficient medical care, and housing. A world where life is about personal growth and expression, not survival. No more wars. No more hunger. A world where all your needs are met. And you can be a part of its creation."

"What are you talking about?"

"We are creating a world of people just like you—a race of superior beings." He let the statement ring off in the silence. "Taylor, do you know why you are electric?"

"Because your machine didn't work right."

He nodded. "Very good. Exactly. You see, some people, particularly some investors, saw that as a failure. But they missed the bigger vision. We discovered something much, much more valuable. You know, many of the great inventions of our day were accidents. Microwave ovens, penicillin . . ." He smiled. "Even potato chips."

Taylor said, "You killed all those babies."

Hatch stood. "I didn't," he said sharply. "The machine did. Accidentally. Accidents with machines happen every day, don't they? Let's keep things in perspective, Taylor. During that time frame, more babies died in car accidents on the California roads than were harmed by our machine. But you don't hear an outcry about that, do you? You don't accuse the car salesmen or automotive engineers of being mass murderers, do you? Of course not. Accidents are the price of civilization. Blood oils social progress. Sure, it was awful, but was it worth it? Believe me, it was." He looked carefully into her eyes to see if she was buying his argument. He decided she wasn't. "Still, it was unfortunate. And that's where you can help us—and help save the lives of future babies. Would you like to help save babies' lives, Taylor?"

Taylor swallowed.

"Would you?"

"Yes," she said softly.

"I thought so. You're a good girl. I like that about you." He leaned toward her. "We want to study you to see why you lived and they didn't. You can help us learn what the difference is between your body and theirs. If we can isolate that factor, we can create electric children without endangering their lives. And you, Taylor, hold a very special key to that discovery—something that the other Glows can't help us with. Do you want to know what that is?"

Taylor slowly nodded.

"You did well in science," Hatch said. "I've seen your transcripts. You got an A minus on Mr. Poulsen's last biology test. Not bad. So you know that one of the tools we scientists use to study genetics is identical twins. Especially those who have been separated from each other at birth. It teaches us things about genetic influences versus environmental factors—what you're born with compared to what you pick up along the way. You, Taylor, are one of those identical twins."

"I'm not a twin," Taylor said.

"*Au contraire,*" Hatch said with an amused grin. "I'd like you to meet someone." He turned back toward the door. "Nichelle, please ask Tara to come in."

At his command, a girl stepped into the room. Taylor froze. The girl looked exactly like her. Before she could say a word, Tara walked up to her and smiled. "Hi, sis."

Taylor's eyes darted back and forth between Hatch and Tara. "I don't understand."

Hatch smiled. "Ah, the learning begins. There are a lot of things you don't understand yet," Hatch said. "But you will." He smiled at Tara. "Have a seat, Tara. Just there on the bed."

"Thank you."

Hatch's voice became softer, almost gentle. "Taylor, you were born a twin. When your biological mother, a teenage girl named Gail Nash of Monrovia, California, gave you up for adoption, Tara was the first to be adopted. She went to a home right here in Pasadena just three miles from the academy—right here in our own backyard. We found her almost nine years ago."

He looked at Tara, who nodded enthusiastically. "Nine years this coming June."

Taylor just stared at the girl in astonishment. Could this be some kind of trick?

"You, Taylor, on the other hand, were adopted by a family in another state. And everyone knows how inefficient government bureaucrats can be. Your records were lost in the transfer between state agencies. You vanished like a grain of rice in a rice paddy. We might never have found you had you not come looking for your birth records."

Taylor felt sick. Ostin was right: She had exposed them.

"There were seventeen electric children. We had located them all except for two. You and Michael Vey."

Taylor jumped when he said Michael's name.

Hatch smiled. "Yes, you know Michael, don't you?"

She didn't answer.

"Don't worry. You did him a favor by leading us to him. We might never have found him without you."

She felt even worse. "He's here?"

"Not yet. But he soon will be. In fact, he doesn't know it yet, but he's about to start planning his trip to see us." He turned to Tara. "That's all for now. Why don't you come back a little later and show Taylor around."

She stood. "Okey-dokey." She smiled at Taylor. "It's so exciting to finally see you. You're going to love it here. We're contributing to the world in a way you never dreamed possible. And Dr. Hatch is the smartest man alive." Tara looked back at Hatch and he nodded his approval.

"There are some really cool benefits to being here, like, we're not treated like children. Also, we have family vacations twice a year. I've been all around the world. And we get cool presents." She flashed her diamond watch. "How many fifteen-year-olds have a twenty-three-thousand-dollar diamond Rolex watch?"

"Thank you, Tara," Hatch said. "You can tell her all about it later."

"I've gotta go. I'm so glad you found us. I've waited years for us to be together. Ciao!"

She walked out of the room.

"Beautiful girl," Hatch said. "Of course, you know that, since you're an exact replica." He leaned forward, his face taking a gentle demeanor. "So let me tell you what you can expect while you're here. Over the next few days we'll be doing some general kinds of physiological testing. Basic stuff—blood work, an electrocardiogram, and a full body scan. We also have some special tests we've designed to help understand your special gifts. Nothing painful; we just want to make sure you're healthy. The doctors out there don't understand special individuals like you, and so they miss things. We've already saved the lives of some of your colleagues."

"I just want to go home."

Hatch moved closer to her. "Taylor, I know it's hard right now. You've been plucked from all you know like a rose from a weed patch. Change is always hard, but that doesn't mean it's not good. Usually the hard things in our life lead to good."

Taylor wiped her eyes. "You're not going to let me go home?"

"Look, just five minutes ago you didn't even know that you have a sister, and now you do. And soon your friend Michael will be joining us. You need to stop thinking of this as an abduction, and think of it as a long-awaited homecoming—a family reunion, if you will. *This* is your home."

"For how long?" Taylor asked.

Hatch looked at her with a perplexed gaze. "For the rest of your life."

PART THREE

22

The Revelation

One thing I knew about Ostin, if he didn't understand something, his brain attacked it without ceasing, comparing facts and calculating figures with the intensity of a computer-processing chip. Around nine thirty at night his breakthrough came. He was lying on the couch in my front room, staring at the ceiling as I paced from one side of the room to the other like a caged leopard.

"I just don't get it," I said. "How did they know who I am? How did they know about our powers?"

Ostin was quiet for another minute, then he suddenly shouted, "That's it!"

"*What's* it?"

He jumped up from the couch. "I've been trying to figure out why they came after you at all. You weren't looking for those records." He looked at me, his eyes wide with excitement. "It's because they don't care about the records."

"What do you mean?"

"They're not trying to hide the information about what their machine did. They're looking for the survivors. And when they found Taylor, they found you!"

"I'm not following you."

"Look, these guys have all the records of every baby who survived. What if those other children all had powers like yours and Taylor's? If they discovered that their machine gave those babies special powers, that could be worth billions."

"That's a big 'if,'" I said.

"Is it? You said the other kid, Zeus, shocked your mother, right? So we know there's at least one other"—he spoke the word cautiously—"mutant.

"The only other people we know who were born at that hospital at that time have electrical powers. So, statistically, we're batting a thousand. There were seventeen children who survived. Maybe they all have powers."

He paused, waiting for the last of the puzzle pieces to come together. Then he pounded the palm of his hand with his fist. "It was a fake." Ostin looked at me the way he did when he solved a difficult math problem. "The whole thing with the gunman was fake. It was a test."

"Why would they do that?"

"Because you don't pick up an electric eel without getting shocked. They first had to see what you could do. You said the man in the sunglasses appeared after you shocked the gunman, right?"

"That's right. And he said, 'Well done, Michael.'" I stopped pacing. "You might be on to something. He knew my name and what I did. And Clyde . . ."

"Who's Clyde?"

"He's the gunman. I remember thinking that he looked really nervous, like he didn't want to be there. He was shaking like crazy. And his gun didn't even have bullets." I looked down. "But then why did they take my mom and not me?"

"Maybe they wanted to take both of you, but didn't get the chance. You said you heard me coming, right?"

"Right."

"But they were gone by the time I returned. They must have run out of time. They already had your mother, so they took her and ran."

"Which means they're probably still looking for me."

"They don't have to," Ostin said.

"What do you mean?"

"They have your mother. They know you'll come looking for them." He looked in my eyes. "Whoever took your mom took Taylor. So if we can find one of them, we can find the other."

I suddenly had a flash of inspiration. "Wait. I think I know where Taylor is."

"Where?"

"The academy."

I ran into my bedroom and found the brochure Taylor had given me from her locker. I brought it back out to the front room and spread it open on the counter. "Here. It's got to be the place. Or at least it's connected."

Ostin looked at the brochure. "Five-thirteen Allen Avenue, Pasadena, California." He looked up. "I think you're right. I'm betting that the Elgen Academy is really just for kids with electrical powers."

Ostin's logic made sense to me. Why else would they offer a scholarship to me when there were hundreds of kids with better grades? "You could be right," I said.

"Now what?" Ostin asked.

"We tell the police," I said.

Ostin shook his head. "No way. They'll never believe us."

"Why wouldn't they?"

"Think about it. Two teenagers walk into a police station and tell them that a secret agency is kidnapping mothers and cheerleaders?"

Hearing it like that did sound crazy.

"But we have proof," I said.

"No, we have a hunch and some articles on the Internet. They'll think we're crazy. And even if we somehow convinced them to look into it, this is a multibillion-dollar company. If they find anyone snooping around, they'll just move your mom and Taylor to some-place else and then we'll have nothing." Ostin stood and began to pace. "We need to know more about our enemy. But it's not like they're going to have a Facebook profile. Where do we learn more?"

"Clyde, the gunman," I said.

"But he's in jail."

"Lieutenant Lloyd could get us to him."

"Why would he do that?"

"He said their first interrogation was worthless. Maybe I can con-vince him that I might be more effective." I brought out the card Lieutenant Lloyd had given me. "I'm going to call him." I immedi-ately went to the phone and dialed Lloyd's cell phone number.

A gruff voice answered. "This is Boyd."

His full name was Boyd Lloyd? No wonder he went by Lieuten-ant. "Lieutenant Lloyd, this is Michael Vey."

"Michael. What can I do for you?"

I had been so eager to call him that I had dialed without thinking about what I was going to say. "I, uh, just had a thought. You said you had spoken to the gunman, but he didn't say much."

"No, he was as tight as pantyhose on a hippo."

"I was wondering if maybe he would talk to me."

"You want to speak with Clyde?"

"Well, maybe seeing me might make him talk."

There was a long pause. "Frankly, we couldn't do much worse than we did with his last interrogation. Hold on, I'm going to call my partner. May I call you back at this number?"

"Yes," I said. "Bye." I hung up the phone.

"What's up?" Ostin asked. "Why did you hang up?"

"He wants to talk to his partner."

About ten minutes later my phone rang. "Michael, it's Lieutenant Lloyd."

"Yes, sir."

"I spoke with my partner. He thinks there's a chance it might work—a small chance, but worth trying. So if you're willing to face Clyde, I say let's go for it."

"Thank you, sir."

"What time are you available?"

"Any time is good. I'm not back to school yet."

"Then how about I pick you up in the morning."

"Yes, sir."

"I have your address on the police report. I'll come by around ten."

"I'll be ready. Thank you."

"Thank you, Michael. We'll keep our fingers crossed. I'll see you tomorrow."

"Bye." I hung up then turned to Ostin. "We're in."

"Well done," Ostin said. "You know, you could always just shock Clyde again."

"The man helped kidnap my mother. Whatever it takes," I said. "Whatever it takes."

23

Clyde

I didn't sleep well that night. I had a nightmare about my mother sitting in a cage at the zoo surrounded by laughing hyenas and calling for me to help her. Ostin woke me when he knocked on my door at seven. I answered the door still in my pajamas. He was dressed for school.

"What's up?" I asked groggily.

"Not you," he said. "My mom told me to come get you for breakfast."

I rubbed my eyes. "Okay. I'll be right there."

I went back to my room and put on my robe, then walked down the hall to the Lisses' and let myself in. Breakfast was on the table and Ostin and his father were already eating. Mrs. Liss had made wheat toast with a fried egg in the middle.

Mr. Liss was reading the paper and dipped it a little to look at me. "Good morning, Michael."

"Good morning," I replied.

"That's your plate," Ostin said.

I sat down next to him.

At the sound of my voice, Mrs. Liss came out of the kitchen. "Good morning, honey. How did you sleep?"

"Not very well."

"That's understandable. You just make yourself right at home."

I poured myself a glass of orange juice.

"There are hash browns, too," Ostin said, pushing a plate my way. "With cheddar."

"Thanks."

"Is there anything else you want?" Mrs. Liss asked. "Do you need some ketchup or Tabasco sauce for your egg?"

"No. I'm good," I said.

Mr. Liss glanced at his watch and set down his paper. "I've got to go." He stood, looking at us. "You boys take it easy." Mr. Liss had an unusually deep voice that made everything he said sound like an order.

"Yes, sir," I said.

"See ya, Dad," Ostin said.

Mr. Liss grabbed his jacket and keys from the counter, kissed Mrs. Liss, then walked out. When he was gone Mrs. Liss said, "I forgot the salt and pepper." She walked back to the kitchen.

Ostin said in a hushed voice, "I wish I could go with you to the police station."

"Me too."

"Are you nervous to see him?"

"Yeah." I took a drink of juice.

Mrs. Liss walked back in. "Here you go, darlin'." She salt-and-peppered my egg for me even though I didn't want it. "So, Michael, do you feel up to going to school today?"

"Not yet," I said. "Lieutenant Lloyd is going to pick me up at ten. We're going down to the station to talk to the man they put in jail."

Her brow furrowed. "Oh? I didn't know that. Would you like me to go with you?"

"No, I'll be all right."

"How are you on clothes? Do you need some laundry done?"

"I'm okay for now." The truth was, I'd been wearing the same clothes for three days.

"Well, whatever you need, just ask. I'll just be your mama until your mama gets back."

"Thank you," I said, grateful for how she'd said it.

Ostin finished eating, then went and got his backpack. "I better get going." I walked to the door with him. "Good luck," he said. "Bones."

"Bones," I replied. We bumped fists and then he walked off down the hallway.

"Thank you for breakfast, Mrs. Liss."

"You're welcome. Please let me know when you get back from the police station."

"Sure thing." I went back to my apartment and showered and dressed. Then it was time to go outside to the parking lot to wait.

I was sitting on the curb when Lieutenant Lloyd pulled up in his police cruiser. He rolled down his window. "Good morning, Michael."

The morning sun was high above the mountains and I shielded my eyes with both my hands. "Hi."

"How are you?"

I shrugged. I know he was just being friendly but it was kind of a stupid question. "I've been better."

He nodded sympathetically. "Come sit in the front seat."

I climbed into the car, put on my seat belt, and we drove downtown.

The drive to the jail took about twenty minutes. I was ticking a lot. Lieutenant Lloyd didn't say anything about it, but I'm pretty sure he noticed because he asked me again if I really wanted to do this. I guess taking a minor into the jail is pretty unusual, and he was probably having second thoughts about it. I told him I was positive it was the right thing.

When we arrived at the jail, I went through all the security, metal detectors and all, then followed Lieutenant Lloyd down a long corridor, passing other police officers on the way. At the end of the hall were two doors. He led me through the door on the left into a darkened room. "This is the observation room," he explained. "This is where we watch what's going on in the interrogation room."

There was a large two-way mirror as well as two monitors mounted to a console. The gunman, Clyde, was sitting in a chair on the other side of the glass, his hands handcuffed behind his back. Seeing him filled me with anger.

"This is Detective Muir," Lieutenant Lloyd said, gesturing to a man sitting in front of the bank of monitors. He'll be recording everything."

I turned back. "You record what happens inside?"

"Every word," he said.

I hadn't thought about that. I wouldn't be able to speak freely.

Lieutenant Lloyd looked into my eyes. "You're still sure you want to do this?"

"I'm sure," I said.

"You're a brave young man," he said. "Okay, then. We have Stuart in handcuffs, but if you feel threatened at all, let me know." He patted his gun belt. "I have my Taser."

Me too, I thought. "I'm ready."

As we started to walk out I brushed by the recording console and pulsed. Suddenly all the screens in the room went blank.

"Wait," Muir said. "We just went down."

Lieutenant Lloyd groaned. "What timing."

"It's like we got a power surge or something," Detective Muir said, flipping a few switches. He spent the next five minutes trying to get the system back up.

Finally Lieutenant Lloyd asked, "Does the phone still work?"

"Yes."

"We'll use the intercom on it. We won't be able to tape it, but at least we'll hear what's going on."

We walked back out to the hallway. Lieutenant Lloyd unlocked and opened the interrogation room door, and we stepped inside. The room was rectangular with bare white cinder-block walls. Clyde sat at the opposite end of a long, wooden table. He wore an orange jail jumpsuit with the name STUART and a number printed above the left breast.

"Hello, Clyde," Lieutenant Lloyd said.

Stuart didn't look at Lieutenant Lloyd, but glared at me.

"I'm sure you remember who this is."

He said nothing.

"Let me help you remember. This is Michael Vey. He's the son of the woman you helped kidnap."

He scowled. "I know who he is."

"Good. Because you owe him an explanation."

Clyde turned his body sideways. "I don't owe him nothin'."

Lieutenant Lloyd shook his head. He whispered to me, "Like I said, he's not cooperating."

"Maybe if I talked to him alone."

He thought about it for a moment, then said, "I was afraid it might come to that." He walked up to Clyde. "I'm leaving Michael alone with you. Don't try anything crazy."

Suddenly Clyde's expression changed from anger to fear. "No! You can't leave him alone with me. I have rights against cruel and inhumane punishment. I have rights!"

Lloyd looked at him like he was crazy. "I was saying, I'm leaving him alone with you. But I'm watching you carefully through the glass so don't get any ideas. . . ." Lieutenant Lloyd turned back to me and shook his head. "Be careful," he whispered. "The man's nutty as a bag of trail mix. Good luck."

When the door shut, Clyde looked up at me and our eyes met.

"Where's my mother?"

His lips pursed. I stood up and took a few steps toward him. I knew the police were listening so I chose my words carefully. "Do you need something to jog your memory?"

"You stay away from me, electric boy."

"What did you call me?"

"I know all about your kind, you glowing freaks."

"My kind?"

He scowled. "Yes, your kind." For the first time I noticed the scars running up his arm. He followed my gaze, then looked back up at me. "Yeah, that's from one of you. You Glows are all alike."

"How many are there of us?"

"Too many. One of you is too many."

"I only did what I did because you pulled a gun on my mother. *You* made me do it."

"That's because they made me do it."

"Who made you?"

He didn't answer.

"You know, I can reach you from here," I said, which wasn't true but he didn't know it.

He sneered at me, then said, "Hatch."

"What's a hatch?"

"Hatch isn't a *what*, you idiot. He's a *who*."

"Who is Hatch?"

He didn't answer.

"Is Hatch the guy with the sunglasses?"

"They're not sunglasses. It's how he sees the Glows." He said the word as if it were bitter on his tongue.

"What's a . . . Glow?"

"You're a Glow."

"Who were those other two kids with him?"

"Glows. Zeus and Nichelle."

"I saw what Zeus does. What does Nichelle do?"

"She's Hatch's protection against Glows." His face bent in a dark grin. "Oh, you're going to like her. Trust me. She's the nastiest of the whole stinking, nasty bunch of you."

"How long have they known about me?"

"Since you were a baby. They just couldn't find you. You and the other."

I guessed he was talking about Taylor. "Where is she?"

"You'll have to ask Hatch."

"Where did they take my mother?"

"How would I know that? They left me."

"Where did they plan to take my mother?"

"You'll never find her," he said, and a dark smile crossed his face. "You have no idea what you're up against, glow worm. They have private jets and hidden compounds. They're all over the world. Your mother could be anywhere by now."

"Where is Hatch?"

He looked away.

"Where is Hatch?" I said louder. I began rubbing the table. "Do you need some persuasion?"

"What are you going to do, kill me? You'd be doing me a favor. They're going to kill me anyway. You'll see. To them we're all expendable. Even the Glows."

I decided to change my tactic. "If I can stop Hatch . . ."

He interrupted me with laughter. "You think you can stop Hatch? The U.S. Marine Corps couldn't stop Hatch."

"If I can stop Hatch, I'll be able to prove that they forced you into this. Help me find my mother and I promise I'll testify for you and get you out of here."

Clyde's laughter only increased. "You think I want to go out there with them? I'm safer in here."

I leaned forward and whispered, "Is Hatch at the school in Pasadena?"

He looked down.

"Is Hatch at the school in Pasadena?" I repeated.

Without looking up he said, "It's not a school."

"Is that where he is?"

He looked up. "You'll find out soon enough."

I looked at him for another moment, then over at the mirror. "I'm done," I said.

When I turned back, Clyde was smiling. "Hatch is waiting for you, you know. He's been waiting a long, long time. He really wants you."

Just then the door opened and Lieutenant Lloyd walked in. "All right, Clyde."

"You know who this kid is, don't you?" Clyde shouted. "He's a Glow. He can shock you worse than that Taser you're wearing. He can kill you. He can kill all of us. They're going to take over."

I looked up at Lloyd and shrugged.

"Shut up," Lieutenant Lloyd said.

"They're going to take over the entire world!"

"Save it for the judge," Lieutenant Lloyd said.

As I walked out of the room Lieutenant Lloyd put his arm on my shoulder. "Sorry, kid. That's what I was afraid of. Ever since we brought him in he's been ranting about hatches and glow worms." He shook his head. "The man's insane."

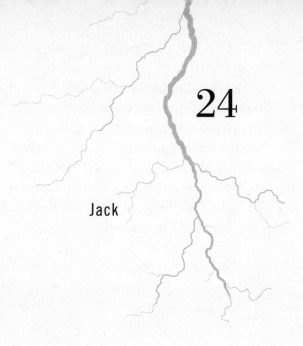

24

Jack

Ostin came to my apartment directly from school. I was on my knees filling my backpack with clothes.

"What are you doing?"

"Packing. They're in Pasadena."

"Clyde told you that?"

"Sort of. The man in the sunglasses is named Hatch."

"Hatch?"

"And you were right. There are more of us electric children."

"Did the police hear all that?"

"Yeah. But they just think Clyde's crazy."

Ostin sat on my bed. "So now what?"

"I'm going to Pasadena."

"How do we do that?"

"What do you mean, 'we'?" I said.

"You can't go alone. What if you need help?"

"This isn't a video game, Ostin. It's real danger. If something goes wrong, we can't just push a reset button."

"Which is precisely why I need to go. What good is being here without my best friend?"

I looked at him. "Thanks."

"So how do we get there?"

"Jack."

Ostin's eyes widened. "Jack the bully?"

"Yeah, he's perfect. He's got his own car."

"There's no way my mom will let me go with him driving."

"Your mom can't know."

"You're right. She'd freak no matter what." He looked down. "What makes you think Jack will drive us?"

"He owes me." I rubbed my hands together and they made the crackling sound of electricity. "I think I can persuade him."

25

Tara

Taylor was sitting on her bed eating supper when she heard her door unlock. A voice from a speaker said, "Enter."

The door opened, and Tara walked into the room. She was smiling. "You finally got some food, huh?"

Taylor looked up. In spite of her mistrust of the place, she felt a natural kinship to Tara. "Yeah. What's with all the bananas?"

"High in potassium. It's good for us." She shook her head and her smile grew. "Crazy, huh? You must feel like you fell down the rabbit hole."

"The rabbit hole?"

"You know, *Alice in Wonderland*. But really, it's not as bad as you think."

"I've been kidnapped, tied up, tortured by some deranged Goth chick, and locked in a cell, and you say it's not so bad?"

"You're right, Nichelle's pretty awful, isn't she?" She swayed a little. "As far as the cell, it's just temporary. It's just until you see that they mean you no harm. They have a lot of experience with this."

"Kidnapping?" Taylor asked.

Tara shook her head. "Look, sis, I understand why you're so upset. I really do." She walked over and sat on the bed next to her. "And I'm sorry if I don't seem more sympathetic, but I'm just so happy you're here. My own sister. I've waited for this day for so long."

"How long have you known you're a twin?" Taylor asked.

"Nine years—since Dr. Hatch found me. He promised me that someday he'd find you. And he did."

"I didn't even know I had a sister."

"It's kind of cool, isn't it?"

Taylor pushed away her tray. "I'm sorry, I'm just scared and I don't know what I'm doing here."

"I really do understand," Tara said. "But it will be okay. Trust me. They just want to know why we're so different. The research they do here will save millions of lives someday. And they take really good care of us. Really good care. We even have our own concierge service."

"What's that?"

"You know, like at fancy hotels. You can ask for pretty much anything and they'll get it for you. Clothes, front-row concert tickets and backstage passes, gadgets—almost anything, within reason. I mean, if you asked for a jet, they'd probably say no. But I asked for a diamond bracelet once and they got me one."

"Why would they do all that?"

"Because we're the special ones. Out of billions of people in this world there're only seventeen of us. Well, actually, thirteen of us now."

Taylor wondered what she had meant by that.

"We're like royalty. Try it. Just ask for anything."

"Okay. I want to go home."

Tara sighed. "Except that. Taylor, give it a couple weeks. If you are still so unhappy, then I'm sure they'll let you go."

Taylor looked at her with surprise. "Really?"

"Of course. I don't have a lock on my door. I come and go as I wish. The thing is, they have to protect themselves, too. They have a lot of money invested in all this and they're working with kids. It's a big risk. Does that make sense?"

Taylor looked down for a moment. "Yeah, I guess it does. But then why did they kidnap me?"

"They didn't want to. They invited you to come to the Elgen Academy, didn't they? And everything they promised was true, the best schooling, and the college of your choice. In fact, when you turn sixteen, you can have any car you want. A Ferrari, a Rolls-Royce, Maserati, anything. But your adopted parents wouldn't let you go, would they?"

"No."

"They don't even know about your powers, do they?"

"No."

"Exactly. They have no idea how special you are."

"How do you know all this?"

"Because you're my sister." Her eyes moistened with emotion. "I've waited a long, long time for you."

Taylor felt a little better. "So, are you . . . electric?"

She nodded. "Of course."

"What can you do?"

"Well, we're twins, so my powers are like yours, but a little more refined. I've had years to practice them here." She sat back on the bed. "Okay, want to see something?"

"Sure."

"Okay. Here goes." Tara closed her eyes.

Suddenly, Taylor felt a warm rush of happiness flow through her. Taylor laughed. "How did you do that?"

"Cool, isn't it? I've learned to stimulate the part of the brain that produces serotonin—kind of a happy drug. I can also do the opposite, but you don't want to feel that."

"What do you mean 'the opposite'?"

"I can make you feel the negative emotions. Like rage or incredible fear."

"How much fear?"

"Black-widows-crawling-all-over-your-body fear."

Taylor bristled.

"Like I said, you don't want to feel that."

Taylor shook her head. "No, I'll pass on that."

"You'll learn, too. Part of our education at the academy is working with scientists to develop our powers. They have also found that eating certain things enhances our abilities."

"Like bananas?" Taylor asked.

"Yeah. You can have all the banana shakes you want. Banana cream pie, banana smoothies, the list goes on. Also, minerals help. We take special supplements three times a day. We also avoid refined sugar. It gets in the way of things. Once I gave up soda pop for a month and I doubled my stretch."

"Stretch?"

"That's some of the jargon they use here. You'll learn it. Stretch is how far you can push your powers. One boy here has such a powerful stretch he can reach airplanes."

"What does he do to airplanes?" Taylor asked.

Tara shook her head. "Nothing," she said.

"So can you read minds?" Taylor asked.

Tara's expression fell. "No. Can you read minds?"

Her reaction worried Taylor. "Uh, no. I mean, I just thought with what you can do, you might be able to."

"No. None of us can read minds. I think Dr. Hatch would freak out if someone could. I mean, just imagine what they could do."

Taylor nodded. "What about Nichelle?"

Tara grimaced. "No one here likes Nichelle. She's a beast. Just stay close to Dr. Hatch and she'll keep her distance. She used her power on me once, and Dr. Hatch disciplined her."

"Why didn't you just do something to her?"

"Our powers don't work on her. She's like a vampire. She sucks our power."

"That's what she told me."

"Yeah, she thinks it's cool. She's such a loser. The thing is, around

us she's powerful but in the outer world she's nothing. Like Kryp-
tonite can kill Superman, but you and I could wear it for jewelry.
In the outer world she's just another Goth. Anyway, it's against the
rules to use our powers without Dr. Hatch's permission. And we're
never allowed to use our powers on each other. Just the GPs."

"What's a GP?"

"You'll find out."

"What time is it anyway?"

"It's around ten. Bedtime. So you better get some good rest. We
have a busy day tomorrow."

"Doing what?"

She stood. "I don't want to ruin the surprise, but trust me, you're
gonna love it." She leaned forward and kissed Taylor on the forehead.
"Sleep tight, don't let the bedbugs bite." She walked out and the door
clicked locked behind her.

Taylor lay back on her bed and looked up at the camera's blinking
red light. *Wasn't worried about the bedbugs*, she thought.

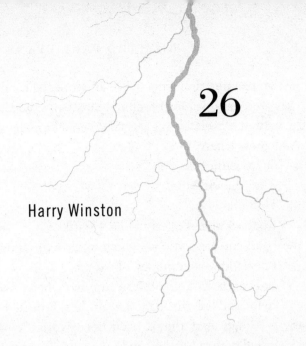

26

Harry Winston

Taylor only knew it was morn-
ing because a nasal voice over the room's speaker told her it was time
to wake up. She was still lying in bed when the lock clicked and Tara
walked in. Her arms were full of clothing. "Get up, sleepyhead."

Taylor sat up rubbing her eyes. "I didn't sleep much last night."

"Well, you'll have to nap later, because right now we have a lot of
fun to get to."

She laid the pile of clothes at the foot of Taylor's bed. "Fortunately we wear the same size in everything so you can borrow my
things for now."

Taylor looked down at her smock. "You mean I don't have to wear
this thing?"

Tara stared at her. "You're kidding me, right?"

Taylor shrugged. "I don't know."

"Wow, you've got this place all wrong. This isn't a prison. That's just an examination smock. We all wore them on our first day when they were establishing baselines. But that was yesterday. Today's your lucky day. Dr. Hatch said to take you shopping for a new wardrobe. And guess where?"

Taylor shrugged.

"The Miracle Mile."

"Huh?"

"Rodeo Drive, Beverly Hills. Heard of it? If you're anything like me—and you are—you are going to have the time of your life."

"I don't have any money," Taylor said.

Tara laughed. "You don't need money here. Now get dressed."

Taylor looked through the clothes Tara had brought. None of them looked as if they'd even been worn. "Wow. These are some expensive brands." She picked up a pair of jeans.

"You can keep whatever you like; I'll just get more. Actually, you'll get whatever you need today." Tara held up a blouse. "I love this one, it looks great with my . . . our complexion. Do you like it?"

"Yeah."

"Try it on."

Ignoring the video cameras, Taylor slipped off the smock and put on the blouse.

"You look ridiculously beautiful," Tara said. "You're the most beautiful girl in this place." She laughed. "Oh, that's kind of like complimenting myself, isn't it?"

Taylor grinned. "Yeah, it is."

After Taylor was dressed, the two girls walked outside the cell to an elevator. Tara put her finger on a fingerprint sensor pad. The screen turned green and the elevator door slid open.

"We'll stop by the cafeteria and get some breakfast on the way out," Tara said. She pushed the button for floor one, and they ascended two levels to the main floor. "This way to the cafeteria," she said.

The cafeteria looked less like a school cafeteria than a restaurant in a fancy hotel. They were met at the door by the restaurant's maître d', a short, Italian man with silver hair and a black tuxedo. "Good morning, ladies. You both look *bellissima*."

"Yes we do," Tara said. "Thank you for noticing."

"Thank you," Taylor said.

"What will it be today? Crab Benedict and banana-and-candied-walnut oatmeal are today's chef specials."

"I just want a banana smoothie," Tara said. "We're in a hurry."

"I guess, me too," Taylor said.

"Will you be having that to go, then?"

"Yes," Tara said. "And fast."

"Yes, very well." He ran back through the kitchen doors and just a few minutes later a waiter brought out their smoothies in plastic goblets with small, silver spoons. Tara took both glasses and handed one to Taylor. "Let's go, sis. We're burning daylight."

"Where are we going?"

"I already told you. Shopping."

"Outside?"

"Well, duh?"

Taylor looked around. "No one is going to stop me from leaving?"

"Why would they do that?"

"Dr. Hatch said—"

"Oh," Tara interrupted. "That reminds me. Dr. Hatch is going to meet up with us a little later. He said he has a surprise for you." Her eyebrows rose. "So get excited. His surprises are epic. He doesn't do things small."

Taylor followed her out the front door. It was the first time Taylor had seen the sun for several days. Her instinct told her to bolt, but she was still surrounded by fences, and Tara's happiness and reassurances had calmed her some. A Rolls-Royce Phantom was waiting for them at the curb. The driver stood at the back door, holding it open for them. "Good morning, ladies."

"Morning, Griff," Tara said.

"Good morning," Taylor said.

"Welcome to the academy, Taylor," the driver said. "My name is

Griffin. If I can do anything to make your day more pleasant, please let me know."

Taylor wondered how he knew her name. The two girls climbed into the backseat. Taylor had never been in such a luxurious car. The interior was all leather, glass, and highly polished burled wood. A glass partition separated them from the driver. In the center console was a telephone. Taylor's heart jumped. "Can I call my parents?"

Tara shook her head. "We'll have to ask Dr. Hatch. But it's probably too soon. There's still too much of that still in you."

"Too much of what?" Taylor asked.

Tara pointed to the world outside the compound. "That."

The drive from Pasadena to the palm-tree-lined streets of Beverly Hills was only twenty-five minutes. It was a bright day, and the sidewalks were crowded with both the glamorous and those seeking it.

Griffin parked the Rolls in a reserved spot on South Santa Monica Boulevard, then followed a few yards behind the girls as they shopped.

"Why is he following us?" Taylor asked.

"Duh," Tara said. "Someone's got to carry our bags."

Rodeo Drive started at the Beverly Hills Hotel and stretched on for nearly a mile. Tara explained that the district took up three city blocks and had over a hundred boutiques, hotels, and salons. Every fashion designer worth visiting had a shop in the neighborhood. In the first block they passed stores Taylor had only heard of: Lacoste, Juicy Couture, Chanel, Hugo Boss, and Giorgio Armani.

Tara pulled Taylor toward Juicy Couture, a tall glass store with a window display of mannequins in jewel-studded tracksuits with purses patterned with Couture's trademark crowns slung over their shoulders. Tara wanted to look at the swimsuits and pulled a floral print tankini from the rack.

"What do you think of this?"

Taylor looked at the price tag. "Two hundred and thirty dollars for a bathing suit?"

Tara shrugged. "I know. A bargain, right?"

They crossed Brighton Way and continued down Rodeo Drive. Tara pulled Taylor into Salvatore Ferragamo. At Tara's insistence, Taylor selected a pair of sunglasses in red and Tara got the same ones in purple.

Outside a store called Dolce & Gabbana, Tara squealed, "They have their new collection in! Come on!"

A woman standing near the front of the store smiled as the girls entered. "There are two of you! Which one of you lovely ladies is Tara?"

"I'm Tara," Tara said, curtseying. "This is my twin, Taylor."

"Twice the charm. It's such a pleasure meeting you, Taylor. How may we serve you ladies?"

"We're here to dress Taylor up," Tara said.

"Our pleasure." The woman snapped her fingers in the air. "Marc, bring Tara and Taylor some sparkling water." She turned back to the girls, smiling unctuously. "This way, please."

Taylor whispered to Tara, "She knows you?"

"Of course. I'm one of her best customers."

The woman led them to dressing rooms, where her staff delivered outfit after outfit of gorgeous fabrics and light dresses. They spent more than five thousand dollars and the salesladies waved happily to them as they walked out, the girls' arms heavy with shopping bags, which they surrendered to Griffin.

Taylor trailed behind Tara all morning as they walked through Tara's favorite stores: Bebe, Gucci, Chanel. Even though they were the identical age, Taylor thought Tara acted more like a twenty-one-year-old than a fifteen-year-old. She knew her way around the stores, and if they didn't already know her, all she had to do was say that she was with the Elgen Academy and the employees tripped over each other to help them.

At Tara's urging, Taylor purchased nine pairs of jeans, six skirts, four pairs of shoes, eight shirts, two leather jackets, and three bags of accessories. Just for fun, Tara picked out three identical outfits.

Taylor was nervous about all the money they were spending. She had once used her mother's credit card to download an album without asking, and she'd been grounded for a week. "Whose credit card are we using?" Taylor asked.

Tara held it up. "American Express Black card. It's mine. I just have to ask first. But they've never turned me down. I think it has like a two-hundred-thousand-dollar limit."

Taylor's jaw dropped. "You've got to be kidding."

"Nope. Far cry from Preston Street, eh?"

Taylor looked at her. "How do you know where I live?"

"I asked, of course." Tara smiled. "Sis, you just don't understand how excited I've been to have you here. You coming *home* is the greatest thing that's ever happened to me."

The way Tara said "home" scared her. Taylor wasn't sure how to respond to Tara's excitement. Finally she just said, "Thank you."

A few minutes later Taylor was looking at a diamond necklace displayed in the window of Tiffany & Company when Tara said, "Dr. Hatch said to not buy any jewelry."

"I was just looking."

"No problem," she said. "He'll be here soon anyway. He wanted to meet us around one. Which is"—she looked at her watch—"almost a half hour from now. Are you ready for a break?"

Taylor nodded.

"Good. Because I want to show you something." Tara led her to Via Rodeo, where they wandered through the cobblestone roads, pausing at the fountains and wrought-iron lamps and arches. Griffin still followed, but at a distance.

"This is so beautiful," Taylor said.

"It's European," Tara explained. "Have you ever seen the real thing? Europe?"

"No. Someday." Taylor's parents had promised to take her on a tour of Europe the summer after she graduated from high school. Something that even with her mother's professional discounts, they'd still have to save and sacrifice for. Thinking of her parents made her heart ache.

Tara touched her shoulder. "No? You will. You are going to love our vacations." They walked past a crowd of tourists posing in front of a fountain and crossed the street toward the Beverly Wilshire.

"Are you having fun?"

Taylor nodded, even though she was still afraid.

"Told you you'd like it. Only one thing I'm disappointed about. I usually see celebrities. I guess you can't have everything." Before Taylor could respond, Tara asked, "Are you hungry yet?"

Taylor figured they had spent more than ten thousand dollars on clothes. "Are you sure we're not going to get in trouble for spending so much?"

"We might get in trouble for not spending enough. This is what we're supposed to do."

"I just can't believe this," Taylor said, feeling confused.

"Believe it. It's the way it is all the time. Dr. Hatch always says special people should have special things." Her face lit. "You like sushi, don't you?"

"I'm not sure. I've never had it. But I've always wanted to try it."

"I've got a place for you."

They walked a couple of blocks to a Japanese restaurant. Urasawa. The restaurant's lobby was crowded and Tara pushed her way to the hostess counter, which embarrassed Taylor immensely.

"A table for three," Tara said.

The hostess, a middle-aged Japanese woman, looked at her dully. "Do you have reservations?"

"No," Tara said confidently. "We're with the Elgen Academy."

The woman slightly bowed. "My apologies; *gomen nasai*. Right this way." She whispered into a nearby waitress's ear, then grabbed the menus and immediately led Tara and Taylor to a table near the back of the restaurant. "We reserve this table for celebrities," the woman said. "Welcome to Urasawa."

As they sat down a kimono-clad waitress brought out a plate of *gyoza*.

"This is amazing," Taylor said. "I can't believe they just let us in."

Tara looked at the menu. "Of course they did."

Taylor looked at the empty seat. "Is Griffin going to eat with us?"

Tara crinkled her nose. "No. Why would he do that?"

"Then who's the third seat for?"

"Hopefully, that seat would be for me," Dr. Hatch said. He was standing next to the table, dressed casually in light slacks and a polo shirt.

Tara smiled. "Hello, Dr. Hatch."

Taylor bristled at the sight of him, but faked a smile.

"May I join you?" he asked.

"Of course," Tara said.

He pulled out a chair and sat down. "So how goes the shopping? Having fun?"

"We've spent about ten thousand dollars so far," Tara said.

"Only ten?" Hatch said. "Come on, girls, you need to pick up the pace. Shop like you mean it."

Taylor looked at him in wonderment. Dr. Hatch lifted a pair of chopsticks and helped himself to one of the dumplings. "Hmm," he said. "Fabulous."

The waitress returned with a large platter of sushi, tempura, and *yakiniku*. The waitress bowed to Dr. Hatch. "Dr. Hatch, *youkoso*."

"Domo arigato gozaimasu."

Tara and Dr. Hatch attacked the food while Taylor fumbled with her chopsticks.

"This is great sushi," Tara said. "Not as good as that place we ate at in Tokyo last summer . . . But it's still good."

"Kyubei," Hatch said. "Wonderful restaurant. One of the few places that still serves puffer fish."

"You went to Tokyo?" Taylor asked.

"Oh, yeah. We go everywhere. Last year the family went on a trip to Japan, Beijing, Hong Kong, and Taiwan."

"I've always wanted to travel," Taylor said.

Dr. Hatch handed Taylor a fork. "Chopsticks can be such a bother. Please, enjoy. The *unagi* is especially delicious."

Taylor speared a piece. "What's this?"

"Eel," Tara said. "It's my favorite."

Taylor took a tiny bite while Tara and Hatch watched her expectantly. "What do you think?" Hatch asked.

"It looks gross, but it's pretty good."

Hatch smiled. "Things aren't always what they seem," he said.

Taylor sensed he wasn't talking about food.

"Bet you didn't have sushi this good in Idaho," Tara said.

"I didn't have it at all. Sushi's kind of expensive."

"That's too bad," Tara said.

"It's not a big deal," Taylor said defensively. "It's just food."

"Taylor's right," Hatch said. "It is just food. And besides, want is a thing of the past." He smiled at her. "From now on you're going to experience things you've only dreamed of. And you're going to travel to places you've only imagined: Bali, Nepal, Moscow, Paris, Rome. And that's just the beginning. We have a student traveling right now from London to Dubai. It's a brave new world, Taylor. A brave new world with endless opportunities."

He gestured with his chopsticks. "Think of it. Every day billions of people wake up to lives of desperation—some just hoping to survive another miserable day. Those few with enough to eat are hoping their lives might mean something—hoping their dreams and existence won't just blow away with the sands of time. But not you. Not anymore. What we do at the academy, what you do as one of the chosen, will endure. Someday people will read books about you. You will be talked about and discussed just like the early pioneers and explorers in today's textbooks. You are Christopher Columbus, Marco Polo, and Neil Armstrong, all in one."

"Why would they talk about me?" Taylor asked.

"Because you are a pioneer in a very real sense. You are the prototype of the next great species. You will be more famous than you can possibly imagine."

Taylor didn't know what to say. She had always wanted to be famous.

After another half hour Hatch said, "Are you girls almost done eating? Because I have a surprise for Taylor."

Tara smiled. "Lucky girl. Dr. Hatch has the best surprises."

"Are you ready?" Hatch asked.

"I guess so," Taylor said.

Hatch stood and raised his hand. The waitress rushed over. "*Hai,* sir."

"Put it on our tab, thirty percent tip."

"Yes, sir. Thank you, sir."

They walked out of the restaurant. A black Cadillac Escalade with tinted windows was idling out front. Two black-suited men with ear radios and aviator sunglasses stood next to the car. Hatch waved to them. "We're just going to walk. It's only a few blocks from here."

"What's a few blocks?" Taylor asked.

"Have you ever heard of Harry Winston?" Hatch asked.

"Harry Winston the jeweler?"

"Exactly," he said, looking impressed. "How do you know Harry Winston?"

"It's in that song, 'Diamonds Are a Girl's Best Friend.' They say, 'talk to me Harry Winston.'"

Dr. Hatch laughed. "Brava! Very good, Taylor. You're much too young to know that though."

"My mom liked that song. I mean, likes that song." It bothered her that she had used the past tense.

Hatch nodded. "Did you know that Harry Winston acquired, then gave away the most famous diamond in history? It's called the Hope diamond and it's more than forty-five carats. Today it's on display at the Smithsonian Institution in Washington, D.C. What's most impressive to me is that not only did he acquire a gem once owned by King Louis the XIV, but he also had the guts to cut it. He had the courage to improve it. That's how you make history. You cut against the rough." He looked up. "And here we are," he said, raising his hands.

The store was composed of smooth gray stone. A simple brass sign out front read HW, and below that, HARRY WINSTON.

A man opened the door for them. "Hello, Dr. Hatch."

Hatch waved the girls ahead. "Ladies. After you."

Taylor had never been in such a luxurious place before. The floors were carpeted in rich chocolate hues and the walls were a dark mahogany. It was cool inside and windowless, the room lit by large wall lamps. The atmosphere was hushed, as if they'd entered a museum or library.

"This is *the* place to buy jewelry. It's where the stars come when they're up for an Oscar," Tara said.

"And you," Hatch said to Taylor, "are a star."

An older gentleman with silver hair whisked across the room to greet them. "Ah, Dr. Hatch," he said with a French accent. "It's so good to see you again. I have the necklaces you requested right over here."

"Thank you. Tara, I'm going to spend a little time with Taylor. Why don't you find yourself some earrings."

"Yes, sir."

"This way, Taylor," Hatch said.

The jeweler led them to a small private room. In the center of the room there was a round, polished marble desk with a mirror and a magnifying glass. "Shall I bring in a preliminary selection?"

"Please," Hatch said, matching the Frenchman's formal tone and winking at Taylor. The man nodded and left the room.

He returned a moment later carrying three boxes, which he laid reverently in front of Taylor, lifting the lids off one by one. "I would like to show you a sampling from our classic selection. First, the Loop Necklace." He held it out for her to examine. "This elegant piece is made up of three hundred and fifty-eight round diamonds. It is immaculate."

"It's beautiful," Taylor said.

"Would you like to see it on?" Hatch asked.

"Really? Sure." Taylor held her hair off her neck while the jeweler placed the necklace on her. He fastened the necklace, then slid a small oval mirror across the table toward her so she could look at herself.

The necklace felt heavy and cool. Each diamond glistened like it was on show.

"Wow . . ." She touched the necklace. She couldn't believe she was wearing it.

"Show her the next one," Hatch said.

"The next one?" Taylor asked.

The man nodded as he unclasped the necklace Taylor was wearing. "Certainly. The Baby Wreath Necklace consists of one hundred seventeen round and marquise-cut diamonds for a total of twenty-five carats. The pendant is set in platinum." The necklace was shorter and thicker, the diamonds set in an intricate pattern of holly-shaped links.

"Do you like it?" Hatch asked.

"It's cool," Taylor said.

"And the one I've saved for last. Nightlife. Made up of sixty round and pear-shaped diamonds for a total of thirteen carats within a platinum setting."

Taylor gasped when she saw it. The brilliant diamonds hung from a delicate-looking platinum chain, the different diamond cuts alternating in a stunning pattern.

Hatch turned to Taylor. "Anything stand out?"

Taylor smiled in spite of herself. "This one. Definitely." She touched the necklace delicately.

The jeweler nodded approvingly. "A beautiful piece," he said.

"We'd like to try it on, please," Hatch said.

The man lifted the necklace out of its case and handed it to Hatch. Hatch put it around Taylor's neck. The white diamonds glistened against her tan skin like they were alive. Taylor had never seen anything so beautiful in her life. She wondered what her friends would think if they saw her now. But rather than joy, the thought brought her sadness. She missed her friends and she felt guilty for enjoying herself.

"What do you think?" Hatch asked.

"It's the most beautiful thing I've ever seen."

"How much is this trinket?" he asked.

"Just a minute, sir." He turned over the tag. "That piece is one hundred sixty-eight."

"One hundred and sixty-eight dollars?" Taylor asked.

The jeweler almost choked.

"No," Hatch said. "One hundred sixty-eight *thousand* dollars."

Taylor suddenly felt very uncomfortable. "That's like wearing a house."

"Fortunately not quite as heavy," Hatch said, smiling. "But do you like it?"

"Of course. It's incredible."

"Good. Then it's yours."

She looked up at him in amazement. "What?"

"It's our welcome-home gift to you."

Taylor was speechless. "You're kidding."

Hatch put his hand on her arm, touching her bare skin. "I would never kid about something as important as that. We are so glad you've come home."

As he spoke his thoughts coursed through Taylor's mind. A chill rose up her spine and the depth of the darkness filled her with such terror she was suddenly nauseous. Taylor shuddered and pulled away.

Hatch looked at her curiously. "Are you okay?"

Taylor swallowed. "Sorry. I guess I'm not used to sushi."

He nodded. "Of course. It's an acquired taste."

"Would you like the necklace wrapped up or will you be wearing it out?" the jeweler asked.

Hatch looked at Taylor. "Taylor?"

Taylor unfastened the necklace. "I don't mean to sound ungrateful, sir. But you've already done enough. I'm really not used to all this."

"I understand." He turned to the man and handed back the necklace. "Put this on hold. The young lady would like to think about it."

"Very well, sir," he said, disappointment evident in his voice. He returned the jewelry to the display case.

"Can we just go back?" Taylor asked.

"Absolutely. You came in the Rolls?"

"Yes," Taylor said.

Hatch took out his phone and pushed a button on it. "Pick us up outside Harry Winston." He slid the phone back in his pocket. "Come on, Tara."

Tara took off the pearl earrings she was trying on and said to the woman helping her, "Sorry. Out of time."

The three of them walked outside, where the Rolls was waiting for them. The black Escalade was parked behind it. Griffin opened the door and Taylor climbed in first. Hatch sat down next to her. Tara sat in the front next to the driver.

Hatch said, "You know, Taylor, everyone in the family is very excited to meet you."

Taylor swallowed. Then she forced out, "I'm looking forward to meeting them as well."

"I hoped you'd say that, because I've asked the chef to prepare a special dinner in your honor—a personal favorite of mine, beef Wellington. I hope your stomach is a little more agreeable with that than the sushi."

"I was raised on casseroles and pizza. I'm afraid I'm just kind of an average girl."

Hatch frowned. "No, Taylor. You're anything but average." His expression lightened. "But don't worry, we're not all china and crystal, we eat pizza and hamburgers, too. However, tonight is a very special occasion and requires a special cuisine." He leaned back and smiled. "The lost daughter has returned."

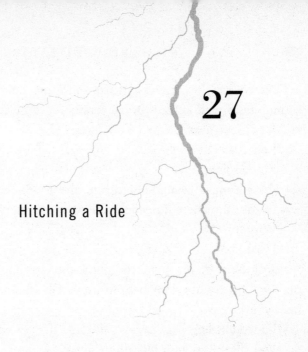

27

Hitching a Ride

Jack lived about twelve blocks from my home, in a poor neighborhood. I found his address in the school directory, then went to see him.

Jack's house was at the end of a short, dead-end road called Leslie Street: an aged box of a home with chipped aluminum siding and faded cloth awnings. The front window had been broken and was covered with cardboard that was kept in place with duct tape. The yard was overgrown with weeds and pyracantha bushes. There were at least six cars at the house, some of them parked on the grass or on the road in front, most with flat tires and rusted bodies. Only one or two of them looked like they might actually run.

I climbed three steps to the Astroturf-covered porch. The doorbell had yellowed masking tape over it with the word BROKE written in marker. I opened the rusted screen door and knocked on the wood door behind it. A minute or so later Jack answered. He was wearing a T-shirt with the sleeves cut off, exposing his muscular arms and shoulders, as well as his tattoo. I forced myself not to blink. "What do you want?" he asked.

"I need to talk to you."

"I'm listening."

The TV was blaring behind him and I wondered if someone else was inside. "Not here. I need to talk to you someplace more private."

"Why?"

"I just do."

He looked at me for a moment, then stepped out on the front porch, shutting the door behind him. "Go ahead. My old man can't hear you."

"I need a ride."

"You think I'm your chauffeur now?"

"To Pasadena."

His face looked even more distressed. "Isn't that, like, in California?"

"Yeah."

"Man, what is this, a shakedown? I went to Dallstrom like you said. I'm not going to let you keep bullying me. I'll go to the teachers and tell them what you did."

"Calm down," I said. "I'm not here to bully you. You're the only one I can go to with this."

"Why not your old man?"

"I don't have a father."

"Then your mother?"

"Don't you watch the news?"

"No."

"My mother was kidnapped. I'm pretty sure she's in Pasadena. That's why I need a ride there."

"Why don't you call the police?"

"It's complicated. They can't help."

"Dude, I'm not driving all the way to California."

I reached into my pocket and pulled out a wad of bills I had taken from mom's secret stash. "Look, I've got money. I'll pay you three hundred dollars. It's all I've got."

He eyed the money. I could tell he was wavering. "Where'd you get that kind of dough?"

"It's my mom's emergency stash."

"Three hundred bucks, huh? When do you need to go?"

"As soon as possible."

"Just us?"

"And my friend Ostin."

"What if I bring someone? To help drive."

"Who?"

"Wade."

I hated Wade even more than Mitchell, but if it got me to California sooner, I'd deal with it. "Okay."

"What do we do after we're there?"

"You drop us off and you're done. That's it."

"No ride back?"

"No. I don't know how long we'll be."

Jack looked over at his car, a restored 1980 Chevy Camaro with a navy blue body and yellow racing stripe. "And you want to leave today, huh?"

"As soon as possible. I just need to get some things from my house. And pick up Ostin."

He scratched his stomach, then slowly exhaled. "Okay. I'll call Wade. Where do you live?"

"Not far. Over by the 7-Eleven off Thirteenth East. We'll meet you in the 7-Eleven parking lot in an hour. Deal?" I reached out my hand but he just looked at it fearfully.

"I'm not going to shock you."

He took my hand and we shook. "Deal."

I walked back to the apartment and knocked on Ostin's door. "We leave in an hour."

He looked at me as if I'd spoken in Chinese. "Leave? Where?"

"California. Didn't you think I was serious?"

"With Jack?"

I nodded. "Yeah." I purposely didn't say anything about Wade.

Ostin looked anxious enough without being thrown in the car with his archenemy.

He looked back over his shoulder. "Man, my mom's going to be so chapped at me. She's going to ground me until I'm fifty."

"Ground you from what?" I asked. "Homework or clogging?" We both knew that Ostin pretty much spent all his time in his room anyway.

"From hanging out with you."

"Yeah," I said. "Well, I wish my mom was around to ground me." I slid my hands in my pockets. "Like I said, you don't have to go."

"I never said I wasn't going," he said. "Let me get a few things. I'll be right there."

About ten minutes later Ostin knocked on my apartment door, then let himself in. He had a backpack that was mostly filled with junk food like potato chips and cheese puffs.

"What did you tell your mom?"

"I told her I was going to hang out with you."

"She's going to be worried out of her skull," I said. "She'll probably call the police."

"I thought of that. I taped a note to your door. It says I went to Comic-Con with you and my uncle."

"Will she believe that?"

"I don't know, but that's where my uncle is this week. He's so hard-core he never takes his cell phone, so my mom can't check."

"Brilliant," I said. I picked up my bag. "Ready?"

"Let's do this."

I looked out to make sure no one was watching, then I locked our apartment door and we walked down the hall and out the building.

The 7-Eleven was only fifty yards from my home. Jack wasn't there yet so we went inside and got cherry cola Slurpees and sat on the curb to wait.

"What if he doesn't come?" Ostin asked.

"He'll come. Besides, I'm paying him three hundred dollars."

"Where did you get three hundred dollars?"

"My mom's emergency fund." I rubbed one foot with the other. "If there ever was an emergency, this is it."

About fifteen minutes later Jack's Camaro pulled into the parking lot and up to the gas pumps.

"There he is," I said.

Ostin squinted. "Who's that in the car with him?"

"Wade."

Ostin's eyes widened. "You didn't tell me Wade was coming."

"Sorry. It was part of the deal."

"I hate Wade."

"It's no big deal."

"You don't understand. I really, really hate Wade. Like, if he were in a shark tank and reached up to me for help, I'd throw chum in the water."

Ostin has a great imagination.

"Look," I said, "we don't have a lot of options. Wade can help drive. Besides, he's not going to do anything to you. He's afraid of me."

Ostin just shook his head. "This just keeps getting worse."

Jack and Wade both climbed out of the car. Jack walked up to me. "I need money for gas."

I took the roll of bills out of my pocket and counted out a hundred and fifty. "Here. Half now, half when we get there."

He stuck his jaw out a little. "Fair enough."

Wade looked at Ostin and smiled. "Hey, I know you. I didn't recognize you with your pants on."

"Stay away from me."

"Relax," Wade said. "That was before I found out your friend's a Taser." He smiled and went inside the store. Ostin and I carried our packs over to the car. Jack opened the trunk and we put our things inside. Jack finished filling the car with gas about the time Wade came back out. He had pork rinds, mini-doughnuts, beef jerky, and a six-pack of Red Bull. "Let's go, boys."

"Sit in back," Jack said to Wade.

"What?"

"I want to talk to Michael."

"But . . ."

"Back, now."

Wade scowled, threw Jack the bag of jerky, and climbed in the backseat. Ostin stared at me with the look of a man climbing into a snake pit, but he got in anyway.

I shut my door and Jack fired up the Camaro. I think he'd taken off the muffler to make it louder, because it roared like a jet. He looked over at me and smiled wryly. "California, here we come."

28

Road Trip

A few minutes after we were on the highway, Jack turned to me, offering his open bag of beef jerky. "Here, help yourself."

I took a piece. "Thanks."

He set the bag to his side. "If you want more, it's right here." He rubbed his chin. "So, how long have you been shocking people?"

After all the years I'd spent hiding my power, it was strange talking so openly about it. "Since I was a kid," I said. "Like two or three."

"Do you know how much it hurts?"

I shook my head. "Not really. I've never been shocked."

From the backseat came Ostin's first words since he'd climbed into the car. "You've never been shocked?"

"I don't think I can be," I said.

"So, you could like grab a power line and it wouldn't hurt you?" Wade asked.

"I don't know. But, when I was four, I chewed through the vacuum cleaner's power cord and it shorted out in my mouth. I just remember it tickled a little and afterward I felt really good."

"Wait," Ostin said. "You mean it's possible that electricity makes you stronger?"

"Like I said, I don't know. I've never tested it."

"You could, like, eat batteries," Wade said.

"No," I said. "They'd break my teeth."

Ostin looked happy again as he finally had something to think about besides Wade. "We need to test this," he said. "I'll think of a way to test this."

29

According to Plan

Hatch sat back in a tucked leather chair in his plush, mahogany-paneled office at the academy. Four flat-screen television monitors played on one wall. All were set to different channels, but all of them were covering the same story. In the past hour, two British Airways jets leaving London's Heathrow Airport had crashed shortly after takeoff, strewing wreckage across miles of coastland. He watched it all with a knowing smile.

His phone buzzed. "Sir, your phone call."

"Is the line secure?"

"Yes, sir."

"Put him through."

Hatch lifted the receiver. "Hatch."

The voice was gravelly and coarse with a slight British accent. "I just heard the news. Well done."

"Just as planned."

"BA is claiming mechanical difficulties."

"That's a little hard to swallow with two wrecks within the same hour, but not surprising. They have to tell the public something. So far there are also three terrorist groups claiming responsibility, but they're late to the party—we gave British Airways a specific schedule a week in advance. There will be another accident each day they don't meet our payment schedule."

"Has any money been transferred yet?"

"Not yet. But it will. We're offering them a bargain. Those 747-800s are going for a little over three hundred million dollars each, not to mention the lawsuits and loss of business. British Air can pay the ransom or shut down."

"Who's next?"

"Emirates airline. As soon as they saw the British Airways crash they responded to our demand. First payment is seventy-five million. With all that oil money they won't even miss it."

"Where's our boy?"

"Still in London. As soon as we get payment we'll move him to Rome."

"Very well. Take good care of him."

"We have a whole contingency with him. He's got more security than the queen."

"Too bad we don't have a few more just like him."

Hatch smiled. "We might. We found the last Glow."

"You found Michael Vey?"

"Yes. And we ran a diagnosis of Vey's E patterns. He has the strongest el-waves we've come across yet. He could be the most powerful Glow of them all."

"Promising. Where are you keeping him?"

"We don't have him yet. But we have his mother. And he's on his way to Pasadena right now. He has the idea that he's going to rescue his mother. He'll be disappointed to learn that she's not here."

"Will he cooperate?"

"You know what it's like bringing in these Glows when they're older. But he's been living just a little above poverty, and like I said, we have his mother. He'll be persuaded."

"Inform the board the moment you have him."

"Of course."

Hatch set down the phone. He loved it when a plan came together. And everything was going according to plan.

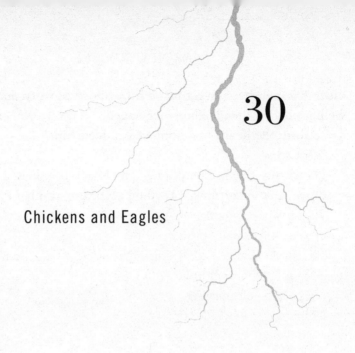

30

Chickens and Eagles

Upon their return to the academy, Tara and Griffin helped Taylor carry her purchases to her new room on the third floor of the building—a beautiful, well-lit suite across the hall from Tara's. The room had wood floors with a thick Persian rug and a two-hundred-year-old antique French armoire across the room from her four-poster bed. The room was much larger and nicer than hers at home and had its own bathroom and walk-in closet.

Taylor noticed that the windows didn't open and were made of something other than glass. Tara had assured her that it was for her protection, not to keep her in, but Taylor still had her doubts.

While she was thinking about where to put her new clothes Tara walked in. "Need any help?"

"I'm just deciding where to put it all."

Tara picked up one of Taylor's new skirts. "I think we should share clothes just for the fun of it. I've always wanted to do that but no one here is my size." She turned back to Taylor. "So are you excited about your party tonight?"

"I guess."

"You don't sound excited."

"I'm still homesick."

Tara walked over next to her. "I know. But once you get to know everyone, you'll feel a little better."

Taylor sat on her bed. "I don't know about that. I really just want to go home. Don't you miss your family?"

"What do you mean?"

"The family who adopted you."

"Oh. They're gone."

"Gone?"

Tara sat on the bed next to her. "Well, I started coming to the academy when I was six. I'd stay here all week, then sleep at home on the weekends. It was a good arrangement. Then one day there was an accident. My parents' house caught fire and they didn't get out. Fortunately I wasn't there, or I probably would have died too."

Taylor was stunned. "That's horrible. Do they know what caused the fire?"

"The fire department said it was an electrical fire. Ironic, huh?"

Taylor had a sick feeling about it. All the fun of the day drained away. She thought about the man visiting her house and talking to her parents. She hoped one day her house wouldn't catch fire too.

"What if it wasn't an accident?"

Tara squinted. "What do you mean?"

Taylor saw the look on Tara's face and decided against pursuing it. "Nothing," she said. "So the state let you stay here?"

"Fortunately, in the school contract, there was a clause that in case something happened, Hatch received guardianship. I was so young at the time I don't remember much. I've lived here most of my life. This is my family. That's why I am so excited for you to join us."

"How many live here?"

"Nine, counting you."

"Will Nichelle be there?"

"Yeah. But just ignore her. That's what we all do." Tara started counting on her fingers. "There's Quentin, he's the cute blond, you'll like him. And he's a flirt. There's Bryan, he's Puerto Rican, big muscles, but he's really immature. Kylee, who I love, she was my best friend until you came along. I think she might be a little jealous of you, so I'll give her some special attention tonight. Zeus. He's kind of cute, but I need to warn you that he kind of smells. But don't say anything to him about it."

"I don't usually tell people they stink when I first meet them," Taylor said.

Tara grinned. "It's not really his fault. Because of his electric makeup, he can't bathe without shocking himself. Anyway, he's really sensitive about it."

Taylor nodded.

"Then there's Grace. She's really shy, so it will take a while before you get to know her. And there's Tanner. He's out of the country right now on an assignment."

"How many of us are there?"

"There were seventeen of us in the beginning, but there's only thirteen of us left. And some of them aren't in the family."

"What do you mean, 'left'?"

Tara frowned. "Don't worry about it."

Taylor looked down. Hearing that four of them had disappeared scared her as much as anything else that had happened to her. "Do they all have powers?" she asked.

"Every one of them."

"What kind?"

"All sorts. We don't really talk about that. I mean, of course we know. Like Zeus can shoot electricity like lightning, Bryan can burn through things, and Kylee's like a magnet, which means you don't ever give her your credit card because she ruins them, and everyone knows what Nichelle can do. But it's more of a gossip thing. Dr. Hatch says we don't talk about it because it's like in the business world, employees don't talk about each other's paychecks because it causes problems." Tara glanced up at the clock on the wall. "Is that really the time?"

"I think so."

She grabbed Taylor's hand. "Come on. We can't be late."

The girls hurried downstairs to the main floor. The other youths had already arrived and the dining room was loud with chatter. The dining room tables had been brought together to form one long rectangle, large enough to seat the whole family. Taylor and Tara were the last to arrive and every eye followed them in.

A handsome blond boy stood as they entered and smiled at them. "Wow, I'm seeing double."

"I'm Tara," Tara said.

"And that makes you Taylor," he said, slightly bowing. "I'm Quentin. I'm the student body president. Welcome to Elgen Academy."

"Hi," Taylor replied shyly. "I mean, thank you."

"Welcome to the family." He took her arm. "Let me introduce you to the rest of the gang. That's Bryan."

"Woo hoo," Bryan said, pumping his fist in the air. "I'm number one." He punctuated his claim with a loud belch.

"Number-one dork," Quentin said.

"I told you," Tara whispered to Taylor. "Immature."

"And that's Zeus."

Zeus bobbed his head. Taylor noticed that he was seated with spaces between him and the others, and she remembered what Tara had said about his smell.

"That's Kylee and Grace."

"Hi," Kylee said tersely.

Grace looked at her but said nothing.

Quentin said to Taylor, "Don't take it personally, Grace is a little shy. She's that way to everyone at first." He looked at Nichelle, who was sitting alone at the far end of the table. "You've already met Nichelle," he said. Nichelle glared at Taylor.

"There's also Tanner, but he's out of the country. You'll meet him in a couple of weeks. Since you are the guest of honor, Dr. Hatch asked me to seat you at the head of the table. He will sit to your right. And Tara," Quentin said, "Dr. Hatch requested that you sit on Taylor's left side."

"Whatever you say, boss," Tara said.

Tara led her to the front of the table and Taylor sat down. Bryan said, "Hey, you guys look alike."

"We're twins, idiot," Tara said.

"You're such a dork," Kylee said to Bryan, rolling her eyes.

Taylor looked around. She caught Zeus staring at her. He looked away. She thought he was cute. A moment later Dr. Hatch walked into the room.

"Sorry I'm late, everyone. I was just finishing up a call." He sat down at the head of the table. "You've all met Taylor?"

"I introduced her around," Quentin said.

"Thank you, Quentin. Now I expect you all to make her feel right at home."

"Where are you from?" Kylee asked.

"Idaho."

"Where's that?"

"Kylee, don't embarrass yourself with your ignorance," Dr. Hatch said flatly.

Taylor said, "Idaho's on the other side of Washington, above Utah, west of Montana."

"Thank you, Taylor," Hatch said. "I guess I'll have to talk to Miss Marsden about her geography lessons." Hatch lifted a small brass bell next to his plate and shook it. Waiters immediately appeared with platters of food.

The chef had prepared a remarkable feast, though Taylor wasn't very hungry after the lunch they'd had. The servers brought in trays full of beef Wellington, Yorkshire pudding, and roasted lamb with vegetables and potatoes. Taylor filled her plate, but mostly just picked at it as she glanced back and forth at each of the others. Quentin was definitely in charge, and the most popular of them all. She guessed that Kylee and Tara had a crush on him, and Zeus seemed jealous of him.

"Do you find the cuisine agreeable?" Hatch asked her.

"Yes, sir. It's very good."

"It's not pizza, but hopefully it's easier on your stomach than the sushi."

"Yes, sir."

"I think you'll like the dessert as well. We're celebrating some favorable news we got out of the UK today, so everything is English. In keeping with the theme, dessert is an English trifle."

"Yum," Kylee said. "Yum, yum, yum."

"You're such an idiot," Nichelle said.

"And you're an ugly, psycho freak," Kylee said.

"Ladies," Hatch said. "Enough."

"Sorry," they both said to Hatch, but not to each other.

When they had finished their meals, the waiters brought out the trifles, as well as cake, fruit, and pudding served in tall crystal chalices that looked like parfait glasses.

"This is delicious," Taylor said.

"Overall I'm not a huge fan of English cuisine," Hatch said, "but they do some things right."

As the group was finishing dessert, Hatch looked at his watch, then again rang the brass bell. The head server immediately appeared.

"Yes, sir."

"Pour the champagne, please."

"Right away, sir."

The server walked back into the kitchen, then returned with a dark green and black teardrop-shaped bottle. He moved quickly around the table, pouring a small amount of the sparkling amber liquid into each glass. Taylor had never tasted champagne before. She watched the bubbles stream upward in clean bright lines. "You drink champagne?" she asked Tara.

Tara smiled. "Of course. We're treated like adults here." She leaned close to Taylor as if sharing a secret. "Quentin told me this champagne is more than thirty-five hundred dollars a bottle."

Taylor couldn't comprehend it. "That's like three hundred dollars a glass," she said.

Just then Hatch rose from his seat.

"Ah," he said, sniffing his drink. "What an aroma. A 1995 Clos Ambonnay. Simply divine." He extended his glass in front of him. "I'd like to raise a toast to the newest reunited member of our family, Taylor."

Everyone lifted their glasses, including Kylee, who hadn't said anything since Hatch's reprimand.

"To Taylor. May our dreams be her dreams, and may all her dreams come true."

"Here, here," said Quentin.

Everyone began tapping glasses, except Nichelle, who just took a long drink.

"In honor of this special occasion, and other good news, I have a very special treat. I have secured front-row tickets for tonight's Colby Cross concert at the Staples Center."

Everyone cheered.

"Colby Cross?" Taylor said. "She's my favorite singer."

"I know," Hatch said as he stood. "So we'd better be on our way. The limos await."

At Hatch's lead everyone stood and followed him out of the room, Zeus and Nichelle leaving last.

As they climbed into the car Taylor said to Tara, "I can't believe we have front-row seats to Colby Cross!"

"I told you Dr. Hatch would take good care of you. You have nothing to worry about."

Taylor sighed. "It's just the way everything started—being kidnapped was really scary."

"I know. I think he's trying to make up for that. Just keep an open mind, sis. You'll be glad you did."

Taylor sat back into the leather seat and for the first time since her abduction she really smiled. Maybe Tara was right. Maybe what she'd read in Dr. Hatch's mind was false. After all, he'd been nothing but generous and kind. Maybe if her parents had known how well the students were treated they would have wanted her to come. She didn't know what to believe anymore. "Front-row seats," she said again. "It's just so hard to believe."

"Believe it," Tara said. "It's your new life, Taylor. First-class, front-row everything."

A half hour later the limos pulled up to the front of the Staples Center and everyone got out. Once inside the arena an usher checked their tickets, then escorted them to the front row.

As the group was walking to their seats a large, muscular man, with his arm around a woman, bumped into Zeus.

"Hey, watch it," Zeus said.

The man looked over his shoulder and grinned. "Dude, you stink. Take a shower."

The woman laughed.

Zeus turned red. "Is that your girlfriend or is Farm Town missing a goat?"

The man stopped and turned around. "What did you say?"

"Did I stutter? I called your girlfriend a goat."

The man flushed with anger. "You're gonna die, loser." He came at Zeus, grabbing him by the arm. "I'm gonna—" Bolts of electricity shot out of Zeus's fingers. The man cried out and dropped to the ground like a bag of concrete. His girlfriend screamed.

Zeus kicked the man in the side. "Like that, loser?" Suddenly Zeus bent over in pain. "Aargh . . ."

Hatch stood above him with Nichelle at his side. Hatch's face was red with fury. "Thank you, Nichelle."

"Glad to help, sir."

Just then two security officers arrived on the scene. The larger of the two asked, "What's going on?"

The man's girlfriend pointed at Zeus. "Him!" she screamed. "He shot my boyfriend."

Hatch stepped forward. "Excuse me, officers, but I witnessed the entire exchange. The man was acting peculiar, then he just collapsed." Hatch looked at Tara and slightly nodded.

Suddenly the girlfriend began screaming at the top of her lungs "Snakes! There are snakes everywhere!" She began flailing wildly. "Get them off me! Get them off me!"

The guards looked at each other. One pulled out his radio. "Requesting backup near section AA. Also medical assistance, possible drug overdose." While one of the guards struggled to restrain the woman the other said to Hatch, "Thanks for your help."

"Don't mention it."

When the security guard had turned away, Hatch grabbed Zeus by the arm and pulled him aside. "Out to the car. Now."

"But the concert . . ." He doubled over again. "Sorry. It won't happen again."

"No, it won't. Now go."

Zeus staggered toward the exit. Hatch shook his head.

"Totally against family policy," Tara said. "Boy, he's gonna get it when we get back."

"What will Dr. Hatch do to him?" Taylor asked.

"Nichelle will punish him for a while. She just loves doing that. Then he'll lose privileges for a few weeks and probably be grounded to his room for a few days."

Hatch walked back to the group, Nichelle at his side. "Sorry about that," he said to Taylor. "Zeus knows better than to use his gift to hurt others."

Taylor looked at Nichelle, and Nichelle's eyes narrowed as she glared back at her.

"Let's not let Zeus's unfortunate decision put a damper on things. Our seats await."

Their seats were perfect, front row and center, unlike anything Taylor had ever dreamed she would experience. In spite of everything, she was giddy with excitement. When Colby came onstage, the arena erupted in smoke and pyrotechnics, and everyone jumped to their feet. Taylor couldn't believe how close she was to the singer.

Colby started the concert with one of Taylor's favorite songs, "Stay With Me." Several times the singer came to the front of the stage and reached out her hand and Taylor actually got to touch her.

After an hour and a half the stage lights darkened for intermission.

"Nichelle," Hatch said, "go get Taylor and me a couple of Cokes."

"Okay," she said, glaring at Taylor. After she left, Hatch leaned over to Taylor. She noticed he had put on his dark glasses. "Are you having a good time?"

"More than I can say. Thank you, Dr. Hatch."

"You're welcome. We're just so pleased to have you with us."

"I'm pleased to be here. I don't know how to thank you."

"It's my pleasure, really. But now that you ask, could I ask a small favor of you?"

"Of course."

"I'd like to see your gift in action. Sometime during Colby's next few songs, I want you to reboot her—when I tell you to."

Taylor looked at him. "I'm sorry. What?"

He smiled. "Just for fun. No one will know."

Taylor swallowed. "I don't know . . ."

Hatch's expression turned serious. "I'm asking you to do something for me, Taylor."

Taylor swallowed again. She felt uncomfortable with the request, but after all that Hatch had done for her, she didn't dare disobey. *It's not really that big of a deal*, she told herself. After all, hadn't she done the same thing at the basketball game? "Okay," she said hesitantly. "Just tell me when."

Hatch's expression lightened. "I'll tap you on the sleeve."

The applause was even louder when Colby came back onstage but this time, instead of excitement, Taylor felt dread. She took a deep breath. What Hatch had asked her to do was wrong, but what choice did she have?

Colby sang a few more songs and Hatch just watched quietly, smiling and even clapping. Every now and then he looked over at Taylor. Taylor began to hope that maybe he had forgotten or changed his mind. He didn't. Colby was in the middle of Taylor's favorite song, "Love My Love," when Hatch tapped Taylor's arm. Taylor looked at the singer.

"Now," Hatch said firmly.

"Yes, sir." Taylor cocked her head. It was a fast song and Colby's voice suddenly screeched, then stopped in the middle of the chorus, as if she'd forgotten what song she'd been singing. For a few seconds she just looked around, unsure of where she was, while the band kept on playing. Then she grabbed the microphone and started singing, starting again with the first verse. At the end of the song there was a strange hesitancy in the arena, followed by the usual thunderous applause.

"Wow," Colby Cross said into the microphone. "Never had that happen before. I just kind of blacked out. Early onset Alzheimer's, huh?"

"That's okay, Colby! We love you!" a boy shouted from a few rows back. Colby laughed at herself and the crowd applauded again.

Taylor looked over at Hatch. He was smiling and nodding approvingly. "Well done," he said. "Well done."

Taylor sat quietly for the rest of the concert, even when everyone stood for an encore. She felt sad. She had betrayed someone she admired.

After the concert, they returned to the limos. Dr. Hatch switched cars, presumably to talk to Zeus, so Taylor, Tara, Bryan, Kylee, and Nichelle sat in the back, Bryan switching places with Dr. Hatch.

Taylor desperately wanted to talk to Tara but didn't want to talk in front of the others, so she was silent the whole way home, even when Bryan and Kylee got in a brief argument about who was a better singer, Colby Cross or Danica Ross, and they asked her for her opinion. "They're both good," she finally said.

"Yeah?" said Kylee. "At least Danica doesn't forget the words to her own songs."

The comment made Taylor's stomach hurt. She was glad when Nichelle threatened to silence both of them if they didn't shut up.

That night, as Taylor was getting ready for bed, Tara walked into her bedroom. Tara was already in her silk pajamas.

"So, what's up?" Tara asked.

"What do you mean?"

"Do you always get depressed after seeing your favorite singer?"

"No."

"Then what's wrong?"

Taylor sat down on her bed, her hands clasped between her legs. "Do you know when Colby was singing "Love My Love" and suddenly stopped singing?"

Tara smiled. "That was you?"

She nodded. "Dr. Hatch made me do it."

Tara looked at her. "Is that all?"

"Is that all? I embarrassed her in front of thousands of people."

Tara shook her head. "C'mon, she's a celebrity. They paid her a million dollars to sing for three hours, I think she'll get over it. And besides, no one cared. You heard that guy yell from the crowd—they loved it. It made her seem more human."

Taylor sighed. "I guess you're right."

"Dr. Hatch was just seeing you in action. Think of it as a cheerleading tryout. And you passed."

"Does he do that often?"

"What?"

"Test you."

"No. Just now and then to make sure you're on board."

"What if you're not?"

Tara's expression changed. "You know, you can make this good or bad, it's up to you. It's about attitude."

"No, it's about hurting someone else."

"Dr. Hatch doesn't hurt people just to hurt people. You saw how mad he was at Zeus for shocking that guy. Dr. Hatch is just . . . careful."

"Does he ask you to do things?"

"Yeah. I mean, not much lately. More earlier."

"And it never bothered you?"

"Nope."

"Really? Never?"

She looked suddenly pained. "Once. But you get over it. At first you might hate it but before you know it, you'll volunteer to do it." She forced a smile. "Why do you care? We're better than them."

"Them?"

"You know, people."

Taylor looked at her. "We're people. My parents are people."

"Taylor, they're not your parents. And we're not people. We're special."

"Maybe you are, but I'm just a cheerleader."

"I know it's hard being different, but it's like the story Dr. Hatch tells us about the chickens and the eagle."

"What story?"

Tara's face grew animated. "Oh, you're going to like this. It goes like this: A farmer once found an abandoned eagle's nest with an egg inside. Out of curiosity he took the egg home and put it under one of his chickens. The chicken hatched the egg and took care of the eagle like it was just another chick. As the eagle grew it walked around the coop with the chickens, pecking at the ground the way chickens do.

"One day a wise man saw the eagle in the coop. 'How do you keep the eagle from flying away?' he asked the farmer. The farmer said, 'It's easy, because the eagle thinks he's a chicken.'

"The wise man said, 'But it's not. And it's wrong to keep it in this coop. Eagles are majestic birds and destined to fly.' The farmer said, 'Not this one. He's sure he's a chicken.' The wise man said, 'No, once an eagle always an eagle.'

"He then went out to the henhouse, picked up the eagle, and threw him in the air. 'Fly, eagle!' he said. But the eagle just fell to the ground. He tried it again, throwing the eagle higher. 'Fly, eagle!' but the eagle just fell again and went back to pecking in the dirt.

"Then the wise man carried the eagle to the top of the henhouse and pointed the eagle toward the sun. 'You are not a chicken, you're an eagle. You were meant to soar high above the chickens. Now fly!' and he threw the eagle up into the air. Suddenly the eagle stretched out its wings and took off into the sky."

Tara looked into Taylor's eyes. "You, me, all of us electric children are those eagles. Dr. Hatch is the wise man. If you just want to keep on pecking through life with the chickens, it's up to you, sis. So what will it be, eagle or chicken?"

"But I like the chickens," Taylor said.

Tara grinned. "Come on."

Taylor sighed. "Of course I want to be an eagle."

"Good. Then stop worrying so much about the chickens. They don't matter. Eagles eat chickens. It's not because eagles are bad, it's just how they're made." Tara stood, then kissed Taylor on the top of her head. "Have a good night."

"You too."

"Light off?" Tara asked.

"Sure."

Tara switched off the light and closed the door. Taylor lay back looking at the ceiling. "I miss the chicken coop," she said softly.

She wanted to talk to someone who would understand. She wanted to see Michael. She wondered when she would see him again.

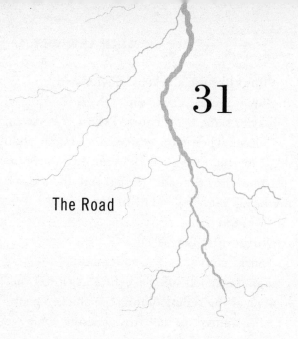

31

The Road

Ostin sat in the backseat of the Camaro, pressed up against the side, reading a book. I could tell he was still mad that I hadn't told him about Wade. For the most part Wade kept his distance, listening to his iPod and playing his DS.

A couple of hours into the drive Wade asked, "What are you reading?"

"A book," Ostin said. "Ever seen one?"

"Ever seen a fist?"

"Knock it off," Jack said.

"Porky," Wade said. "Oink, oink."

"Stop it," Ostin said.

"Never seen a hog read before. Are you gonna eat the book when you're done?"

"Shut up."

"Oink, oink."

"Hey, Wade," Jack said. "Ever wonder what a thousand volts would feel like on your tongue?"

His grin disappeared. "No."

"Then keep your mouth shut."

Wade sat back and put his earbuds back in. I looked in the rearview mirror. Ostin looked pretty miserable. I felt bad for him. For his sake, I wished he hadn't come.

I turned to Jack. "Thanks."

"Sorry about that." A few minutes later Jack asked, "You an only child?"

"Yeah. How about you?"

"I've got two brothers and a sister."

"Are you the oldest?"

"No, I'm the youngest. I'm the only one still at home. One of my brothers is in Iraq. He's a Marine." He said this with obvious pride.

"That's cool."

"Yeah, he's really cool. He even got a medal for bravery."

"How about your other brother?"

His smile fell. "He's in prison."

I wasn't sure how to respond. I didn't know anyone in prison. I wanted to ask what he'd done but it didn't feel right. I didn't have to.

"He got really messed up on drugs. He and a guy were stealing snowmobiles to get money for drugs when the owner came out. The guy with him had a gun and he shot the man. My brother didn't even know that he had a gun, but the way the laws are, he's also guilty. So he'll be in prison a long time."

"Do you see him very much?"

"Nah, he's in Colorado. I only see him once a year." His voice lifted. "My sister's doing real well, though. She married a guy who owns a chain of tanning salons. They have a real nice home and two little kids."

"Do you see much of her?"

"Nah, she doesn't have much to do with the family. She got

married young to get away. That's because my folks used to fight a lot before my mother left."

I now understood why Jack locked kids in lockers. I'd probably be doing the same if I came from a home like his.

"What about you? What happened to your dad?"

"He had a heart attack."

"Was he old?"

"No. My mom said he had a 'bad ticker.'"

"That's too bad."

I looked back. Wade's eyes were closed and he was still wearing his earbuds. I wasn't sure if he was sleeping or just listening to music, but I figured that either way he couldn't hear me.

"What's Wade's story?"

"Not good. His parents were alcoholics. His old man used to beat the tar out of him until the state took him away. He lived with foster parents until they put him with his grandma, but she don't really want him. She's not shy about telling him, either. You'd think an old lady would be nicer, but that prune could strip the bark from trees with her tongue. So he just hangs with me most the time. I'm kind of like his only family."

"He's lucky to have you," I said.

Jack looked at me with a peculiar expression. "Thanks, dude." Then he looked back to the road. I swear his eyes were moistening. I turned away so I wouldn't embarrass him.

It took us four hours to reach Winnemucca, Nevada. We stopped at a gas station to fill the Camaro's radiator with water, then we ate dinner at Chihuahua's Fiesta Restaurant. I got a burrito, Jack and Wade got two, and Ostin got the taco platter. We ate quickly, then got back on the road.

"So how do you do it?" Jack asked me.

"Do what?"

"Shock people."

I shrugged. "I don't know. It's like asking how you sneeze. It just happens."

"But you can control it . . ."

"Yeah. Usually."

"Why didn't you shock us when we shoved you in the locker the first time?"

"Because I'm not supposed to use my power. My mother didn't want anyone to find out. She was afraid something might happen."

"Like what?"

"Like what did. That's why they took her."

"I didn't tell anyone," Jack said.

"I know. It wasn't you."

"So you know who took her?"

"Some corporation."

"This is like a James Bond movie," Jack said. "What are you going to do when you get there?"

"I'm going to find my mother."

"Hate to say it, but even if she's there, it's not like they're going to just let you in. If they kidnapped her, she's going to be guarded."

"I know. I'm making this up as I go."

"I get it," Jack said. He took a drink from his Red Bull and looked back at his watch. "We've got another ten hours. If we drive through the night we'll be there by morning."

"Then let's drive through the night."

"I need to pick up some more Red Bulls." He reached in back and thumped Wade on the head, waking him.

He pulled his earbuds out. "What?!"

"Get some sleep. You're driving from Bishop to Pasadena."

32

Another Simple Request

That night Taylor had a dream. She was down on a football field cheering while her parents were in the stands looking for her. She kept shouting, "I'm down here!" But they couldn't hear her for all the noise. She awoke crying.

A half hour later someone knocked on her door. One of the servants, a young, dark-haired woman who spoke broken English, handed her an envelope.

"Excuse me I bother you," she said. "Bless you."

Taylor opened the envelope.

Family Meeting
Library. 9:00 a.m. sharp. Attendance mandatory.
Be dressed casually, we will be leaving the academy.
—Dr. Hatch

Now what? she thought.

Taylor got dressed, then crossed the hall to find Tara, but she had already left her room. Taylor didn't know where the library was but saw Quentin waiting for the elevator.

"Hey, Quentin."

He turned, his usual smile on his face. "Hey, Tara."

"I'm Taylor."

He stopped and looked at her. "Of course you are. Sorry. I'll figure it out eventually." He put his hand on her back. "Do you have any birthmarks or anything I should look for?"

"Afraid not."

"It shouldn't be too hard. You're prettier than she is."

Taylor rolled her eyes. "Yeah, right. We're identical."

They stepped into the elevator and Quentin pushed the button for the first floor.

"No, there's something different about you. I swear it."

Taylor ignored the comment. "Are we going to the library?"

"Yes. Just follow me."

A few seconds later the elevator door opened.

"After you," Quentin said.

"Thank you." Taylor stepped out into the hall, followed by Quentin.

"Do we have family meetings a lot?"

"No. Just on special occasions."

"So, do you know what it's about?"

"Yes. But I can't tell you. Doctor's orders." He grinned. "But you'll be glad you went."

They arrived at an open door and walked in together. "If you want, let's hang out today," Quentin said. "And by the way, you can call me Q. It's easier."

"Thanks, Q."

"Any time. Talk to you later."

Tara was already inside the library. She was standing next to Dr. Hatch and they both looked at Taylor as she entered.

Taylor was sure they had been talking about her.

Bryan was the last to arrive, his hair sticking up on the side of his head as if he'd just rolled out of bed. Tara left Hatch's side and sat down next to Taylor. "Morning, sis."

"Morning."

"Good morning, everyone," Dr. Hatch said.

"Good morning, Dr. Hatch," they said in unison.

"I have an announcement." He turned to Taylor. "Taylor, since all of you were born around the same time, having individual birthday parties got to be a little ridiculous. So we started having one large family celebration instead. Sometimes we have great activities here at the academy and sometimes we travel to other places."

"Yeah, deep sea fishing off Costa Rica, man," Bryan said.

"My favorite was riding bikes through Tuscany," Quentin said.

"That was cool," Tara said to Taylor. "That was last year."

Hatch smiled. "We've had some good times. I was thinking that since Taylor missed the family party, well, since she's missed the last fourteen, it's only fair that we have one especially for her."

Everyone cheered except Nichelle, who never looked happy. Hatch reached into his coat pocket and brought out an envelope. "So this morning we are going to the Long Beach Arena for the X Games Motocross finals."

Bryan jumped up and high-fived Quentin.

"Oh yeah, oh yeah."

Zeus sat quietly in his seat, looking angry. Taylor guessed he had been grounded from the activity.

Hatch added, "And of course, we have VIP seating. We're so close to the action you can smell the fear."

"All right," Bryan yelled. "Smell the fear, this is going to rock!"

There was a chorus of thank-yous, which Taylor joined. "Thank you, Dr. Hatch."

Hatch smiled at Taylor. "Nothing's too good for family," he said. Then he added, "For my eagles."

What he said bothered her. She knew that Tara had told him about their conversation the night before.

"You know it," Bryan said. "We're eagles! Chickens peck, eagles fly!"

"So let's fly," Hatch said. He stood and raised his hands. "The limos await. Pick up your box breakfast on the way out."

Everyone jumped up except Zeus, who was slumped back in his chair, his legs spread, and his hands clasped between them. Zeus looked up at Hatch penitently, but Hatch walked past him without a word.

On the way to the cars, Taylor asked Tara, "What are the X Games?"

"Are you kidding?" Tara said. "Don't they have television in Idaho? The X Games are only the coolest thing in the world. They've been sold out for months."

Quentin walked up behind her. "So, Taylor, you want to sit by me at the games?"

Both Tara and Kylee frowned.

"Sorry, Quentin," Dr. Hatch said. "I will have the honor of sitting next to this birthday girl."

"Sorry, sir."

The kitchen staff was waiting outside in the parking lot and handed each of them a boxed breakfast as they climbed into the limos. Inside the box was a carton of orange juice, a bagel, an egg and sausage croissant, a cup of yogurt, and, of course, a banana. Taylor spread cream cheese over the bagel, then sat back and watched the scenery. She was in such a different world—half dream, half nightmare. She was feeling more confused each day.

Her mother always told her that she was special—that she was going to leave her mark on the world. And here she was—a new life had been unfolded before her filled with opportunity, growth, wealth, power, and privilege. Just like her mother promised. So why did it all feel so wrong? She looked at Tara and Quentin. They weren't bad. Maybe Tara was right. She needed to trust more and give Dr. Hatch a chance. After all, he had gone out of his way to welcome her. Didn't all his efforts warrant a little consideration? Was he really so bad? She thought back to the time at Harry Winston's, when she saw a glimpse inside Hatch's mind. Could she have been mistaken? What if she was brainwashed?

She closed her eyes. It seemed just too much for her to figure out. Sure, she was living a dream, but if it were up to her, she'd wake from it. Deep in her heart she wanted her little home, her friends from school, and her family. And all the front-row seats, gourmet meals, and diamond necklaces in the world weren't going to change that.

The limos drove in through a special VIP entrance, and the youths walked to the stadium through a background of X Game contenders gearing up and revving their motorcycles.

Dr. Hatch showed his pass to a security guard and they were led out to the competition. Hatch was wearing his glasses again and he stood at the gate and watched as they filed past. "Nichelle, sit on the far end of the row, please."

She frowned. "Yes, sir."

"Taylor, Tara, you sit next to me."

Taylor faked a smile. "Thank you." She had been hoping he'd leave her alone. She was afraid he might ask her to do something again.

They slid down the metal bench to their seats as the sound of the motorcycles filled the air like a swarm of angry bees. "What's the X stand for?" Taylor asked.

"It's short for *extreme*," Tara said.

Taylor nodded. It certainly was. The motocross jumping competition was one of the most amazing things she had ever seen. Each of the riders took a turn following a course of jumps, hills, and ramps, performing stunts off each one. They not only jumped from ramp to ramp, but the riders would do acrobatics in the air. The first rider took her breath away. He was more than eighty feet in the air when he did a handstand on his motorcycle's handlebars.

"That's incredible," she said.

"That's for sure," Hatch said. "One mistake and you're finished."

"Watch," Tara said. "This next guy is my favorite. He's the first rider to do a double backflip on his motorcycle."

Standing right in front of them was a squad of cheerleaders, or at least an X Games version of them. They were more like beautiful dancing girls in bikinis. Still, seeing them filled Taylor with longing. She wished she were cheering.

Hatch watched Taylor watch them. "Do you miss that?"

She looked over. "Excuse me?"

"Do you miss your cheerleading?"

She nodded. "Yes."

He smiled sympathetically. "It's too bad the academy doesn't have enough students to field a team. I guess it's just one of the sacrifices of being special. We do, however, have some very interesting connections. If, in a few years, you'd like to be a cheerleader for the Dallas Cowboys football team, I could pull some strings and make it happen."

Taylor looked at him in amazement. "Really?"

"I know that's little consolation in the meantime, but still, you must admit that there are some overriding benefits to being a part of the academy."

"Yes," Taylor said.

"Indeed," Hatch said. He looked down at his watch. "It's almost lunchtime. Taylor, what will you have to eat? They have ice cream, pizza, sodas, hot dogs."

"I'd like a hot dog," Taylor said.

"Great. And you, Tara?"

"I just want an ice cream."

He handed Tara a hundred-dollar bill. "Please get us two dogs, a beer, and whatever you want."

"Yes, sir."

When Tara was gone, Hatch leaned toward Taylor. "I've been meaning to talk to you. I wanted to apologize."

"For what?"

"I'm really sorry about how all this started. I can understand why you might think we're terrible. I just hope you understand by now that our objectives are all in your best interest, as well as the world's."

"I understand. Tara's explained it," Taylor said, even though she wasn't sure how much she believed.

"Good. The truth is, if you're going to change the world, you don't always have the luxury of time or convention. You can't make omelets without breaking a few eggs, can you?"

"I guess not."

"No, you can't. Now tell me about your friend Michael."

Hearing him say Michael's name filled Taylor with dread. "What do you want to know?"

"What's he like?"

"He's nice."

"I noticed from his report that he's spent a fair amount of time in school detention. Is he a troublemaker? Rebellious?"

She didn't want to talk about Michael but she wasn't sure how to avoid it. "No. He's a good kid. I think he's just unlucky."

"Unlucky," Hatch repeated. "Well, his luck is about to change."

Taylor didn't know what to say. Just then Hatch reached into his coat pocket and pulled out his cell phone. "Hello?"

Taylor looked back out over the grounds, happy for the interruption. After a few more minutes Tara returned with the food. "There you go," she said, handing Taylor two hot dogs and a beer. "Give this to Dr. Hatch."

Taylor handed him the beer and dog. She unwrapped her own hot dog and lost herself in the competition. After a few more competitors, Taylor turned to Tara. "This is really cool!" she shouted over the noise.

Tara smiled. "The coolest. Didn't I tell you?"

Taylor was applauding an amazing jump when Hatch leaned over to her. "See that next rider? The one in the yellow jacket?"

She nodded. "He's really cool."

Hatch said, "He's currently tied for first and this is his last chance to score. I don't want him to win."

Taylor looked at him, wondering why he was telling her that.

"I don't want him to win," he repeated.

"Then hopefully he won't do his best."

"Hope isn't a plan," Hatch said. "It's blind faith in luck. It's chance. Winners don't ever leave things to chance. So when he's in the middle of his jump, I want you to reboot him."

Taylor just looked at him. "But he'll crash."

"That's a distinct possibility."

"It could kill him."

"That's also a possibility, but that's the risk you take in these types of sports. Why do you think all these people are here?"

Taylor's forehead furrowed with concern.

Hatch leaned back, his expression changing some. "I'm not asking much, Taylor. I just want to see if you have what it takes to fit in with us."

Taylor swallowed. Below her the rider rode up to the platform at the top of the ramp. He had removed his helmet and was waving to the excited crowd while cameras flashed around him. He blew a kiss to a woman holding a baby, who Taylor guessed was his wife, then he pulled his helmet back on and began revving his engine. Dr. Hatch leaned back and sipped his beer.

Tara looked at her, then leaned close. "You gotta do it, Taylor. He's not kidding."

"He's asking me to kill someone."

"He's asking you to prove your loyalty. Chicken or eagle, sis?"

"I can't do it."

Tara looked at her nervously. "You have to."

"No, I don't," Taylor said.

"You don't understand. You have to do what Dr. Hatch says."

"What if I don't?"

Tara's eyes widened with fear. "You don't want to find out."

The motorcycle took off. It dipped low, then shot off the end of the ramp, sailing sixty feet in the air. Camera flashes popped as the bike sailed through the sky. The rider twisted back and was in the middle of his second flip when suddenly the bike went awry. The crowd screamed as the bike landed sideways on the opposite ramp, flipping tail over front while the rider flopped across the ground behind it until he slammed into a retaining wall below a long row of bleachers. The rider lay motionless. The woman he had blown a kiss to was running toward him as emergency crews sprang into action, accompanied by the sound of a siren.

Hatch stood and looked at Taylor, then Tara, his face bent in anger. "We're going," he said fiercely, brushing past Taylor. "Nichelle, with me."

The entire family stood. As they slid down the bench Taylor said to Tara. "What happened? I didn't do that."

Tara was furious. "All he asked for was a show of faith. Was that too much?"

"He asked me to kill someone."

"So what."

"So what?" Taylor said. "How can you say that?"

Tara turned on her. "They're just *people*!"

The limousines were waiting where they'd been dropped off and the drivers jumped out at their approach, opening the car doors. Even though no one spoke to her, Taylor could feel everyone's anger directed at her. She wondered how they all knew. Hatch didn't say a word the whole way back.

At the academy the driver opened the door and Hatch climbed out, followed by the other three girls. "Tara, go to your room and wait for me."

Tara furtively glanced at her. There was fear in her eyes, and they began welling up with tears. "Yes, sir," Tara said, and quickly ran off. Taylor was afraid for both of them.

Hatch pointed at Taylor. "You come with me."

Nichelle looked at her, a half smile crossing her face. Taylor shivered. "Yes, sir," she said. Taylor followed Hatch to the elevator. He pushed a button marked D and they descended. When the door opened, they stepped out into a dark corridor. Taylor followed Hatch while Nichelle quietly followed a few yards behind her. They stopped in front of a heavy metal door. Hatch turned to Taylor. "Would you like to explain to me what happened?"

"Nothing, sir. I didn't do anything."

"Precisely." He shook his head. "After all I've done for you . . . all

I asked for was a simple demonstration of loyalty and gratitude and this is how you thank me."

Taylor was terrified. "But he fell . . ."

Hatch tapped his glasses. "I can see when you use your powers. Tara decided to step in for you. I will deal with her later."

"She was only trying to protect me."

"Yes. And deceive me."

"It's my fault."

"Yes, it is. If you had acted with integrity none of this would have been necessary." He opened the door to expose a large, dark room. "I'm so very disappointed in you, Taylor. I extended a hand of friendship and you bit it. I had sincerely hoped we could do this the easy way. I guess I was wrong." He grabbed her by the arm and pulled her into the room.

"You're hurting me," Taylor said.

"You have no idea what hurt is. But you will. Nichelle, Miss Ridley needs a little lesson in gratitude—about an hour's worth to begin with. Oblige me."

A sadistic smile lit Nichelle's face. "I'd be happy to."

Nichelle stepped inside the dark room and Hatch shut the door behind the girls. He could hear Taylor's screams even before he reached the other end of the corridor.

33

The Lesson

Taylor was curled up on her side, shaking with pain. Her clothes were soaked with sweat and her face was streaked with tears. "Please stop," she sobbed. "Please."

"I'll stop when Dr. Hatch tells me to stop."

"You're one of us. How could you do this to us?"

"It's what I do."

"You hurt others?"

"We all do what we were born to do. Out there, I'm no one. If it weren't for the academy I'd be flipping hamburgers somewhere. But in here, I'm a VIP."

"You're a sellout."

Nichelle sneered. "Aren't you the saint? In the end, everyone sells out. Even the saints."

"You're wrong," Taylor said, her voice strained. "Some people would rather die than hurt others."

"Well, you might just get your wish." She walked over and slapped Taylor on the head. "Did I hear you're a cheerleader?" She cleared her throat. "Were a cheerleader?"

Taylor didn't answer.

"I hate cheerleaders. Stuck-up, shallow imbeciles." She crouched down next to Taylor. "Don't you know how stupid you look out there shaking your pom-poms?"

"At least I'm not hurting anyone."

"No? How about all those girls who wanted to be cheerleaders and weren't pretty enough or popular enough? You think you're so good. It's easy to be good when everyone's kissing your feet—when you have perfect skin and teeth." She grabbed Taylor by the hair and lifted her head. "In here you're no one, cheerleader. You remember that. You can't even walk unless I say so. If they let me, I could drain you like a bathtub and watch you die. So how about a cheer for me? Because in here, I'm the star quarterback."

"Until they don't need you anymore," Taylor said. "Then you'll be thrown out with the rest of the trash."

Nichelle yanked Taylor's hair. "Don't push your luck, cheerleader," Nichelle growled. "I don't always stop when they tell me to." She let go of Taylor's hair and Taylor fell to the ground. "Oh, they'll always need me. As long as there're mutants like you out there, they'll need me." Nichelle stood up. "And our session isn't over yet. So just sit back and enjoy yourself." She smiled darkly. "I know I will."

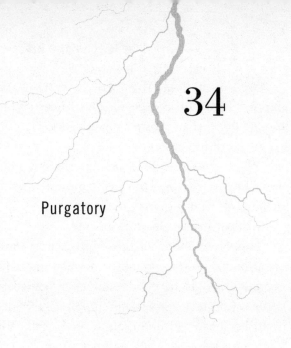

34

Purgatory

Taylor was still unconscious when she was taken by gurney from the holding room into a reinforced cell. She had no idea what time it was when she woke, or how long she'd been out. She was lying on her stomach on a vinyl mat that was too short for her. Her head was throbbing and she groaned with pain. She couldn't see much—the only light in the room was a series of small red diodes blinking from the security cameras—and she was even more afraid than before. She thought of her home, her mother and father and brothers, and began crying. "I want to go home," she said to herself.

"I know," a boy's voice said softly.

She was startled by the voice. She tried to crawl away but couldn't. She couldn't move.

"Be still. I'm not going to hurt you." He gently touched her. She could feel his skin against hers and she entered his mind. It was peaceful and soft and safe.

Taylor looked up. Her eyes had adjusted some to the darkness, and she could see kneeling next to her was an African-American boy. He appeared to be about her age, though he was much larger than her. He was kneeling next to her and gently stroking her back. She could see the pale glow of his skin. He was one of them.

"Please don't hurt me," Taylor said.

"I won't hurt you, Taylor. I'm a friend."

"You know my name."

"Yes."

"Who are you?"

"My name is Ian."

"You're one of them," she said.

"I am one of you, not them."

"Where are we?"

"We're on Level D. This is where they put the disobedient ones. We call it Purgatory."

"Who's 'we'?"

"There are three of us who won't obey Hatch. Four, counting you. So what did you do? Or I should ask, what didn't you do?"

"Hatch wanted me to cause an accident at the motorcycle show. I could have killed the rider."

"That's one of Hatch's tricks."

"Tricks?"

"First, he tries to buy you. He makes you feel obligated so he can manipulate you by guilt. If you're stronger than that he tries to get you to do something wrong. Something small at first, then he increases it. Once you cross the line, he has you. He will hold it over you forever and he keeps upping the ante. You're lucky you're down here. Because if you were still up there, you'd be a murderer."

"My sister Tara's not a murderer."

"Yes she is. Tara, Bryan, Zeus, Quentin, Grace, Kylee, Nichelle, Tanner. They've all sold out. That's why they're up there and we're down here."

"She's my sister."

"She's your twin," Ian said. "She was younger than most of us when they started with her. She couldn't fully grasp what she was being asked to do until it was too late."

Taylor tried to move but the pain made her groan out.

"Just stay still. Nichelle's drained the juice out of you. It takes a while to come back." He left her side, then returned with a cup of water. "Have something to drink. It helps."

Ian guided the cup to Taylor's lips. She drank thirstily.

When she had finished drinking she asked, "Did they do this to you?"

"Yes. Many times. But not as bad. I think they mostly keep me here because my powers aren't as aggressive, so I'm not as valuable to them. That and because I'm blind."

"You're blind?"

"My eyes are. I'm not."

"I don't understand."

"I can see, just not with my eyes. I see the same ways sharks and electric eels see: through electrolocation. Instead of using light waves to see, I use electric waves."

Taylor remembered learning about that in biology.

"Electrolocation has its advantages. Like, it doesn't matter if it's day or night, and I can see through solid objects. You can too, of course—as long as the object permits light waves to pass through them, like glass or ice; but most solids don't. I can see through any-thing electrons can pass through."

"You can see outside these walls?"

"I can see outside the school. Unless Nichelle's around. Then I'm blind."

"Can you see me?"

"Yes. You look just like Tara." Ian sat back on his haunches. "I have no way of comparing my sight to yours, since I've never seen through my eyes. But I have a pretty good idea of the difference between your sight and mine. I can also see Glows and I can see how power is used."

"Like Hatch's glasses," Taylor said.

Ian nodded. "Yeah. They studied me to learn how to make them. You know, this place is a laboratory. They're constantly doing experiments."

"Nichelle said they're going to dissect me."

"A dead Glow does them no good. She just knows how to frighten you. It's what she's good at."

"How long have you been here?"

"Three years."

Taylor began to cry. "I can't do it."

"You will. You're stronger than you think you are."

Taylor buried her head in her hands.

"I want to introduce you to the others."

"There're others here?"

"Like I said, there're three of us."

In spite of the pain, Taylor lifted her head and looked around. To her surprise there were two other girls. One was Chinese. The other was a blond with eyes blue enough that Taylor could see them in the room's lighting. Both of them were glowing.

"That's McKenna," Ian said.

The Chinese girl nodded. "Hi."

"Hi," Taylor said.

"And that's Abigail," Ian said.

"Hello," Taylor said.

Abigail knelt down next to her. "Hi, Taylor. I'm going to touch you," she said softly. "It won't hurt. I promise." Abigail gently pressed her hand against Taylor's back, and Taylor felt a light wave pass through her body, taking with it all her pain and fear.

Taylor exhaled with relief. "What are you doing to me?"

"I'm taking away your pain for a moment."

"You're healing me?"

Abigail shook her head. "No. I can't do that. I can only take away pain while I'm touching you. But when I stop it will come back."

"It feels so good right now."

"I'll do it for as long as I can," she said kindly. "It takes effort, but maybe I can hold out long enough for you to fall asleep."

"Thank you, Abigail."

"You can call me Abi."

"Thank you, Abi."

"You're welcome. Now try to get to sleep."

Taylor closed her eyes and buried her head in her arms. Before she fell asleep she said, "I love you, Abi."

Abigail smiled. "I love you too."

35

Breaking into Prison

We arrived in Pasadena a little after noon. I was asleep in the backseat of the Camaro, lying across Ostin. I woke when we stopped for gas and to change drivers. Wade's eyes were bloodshot and he looked like he was about to pass out. He stumbled into the gas station to use the bathroom.

"Where are we?" I asked Jack.

"We're in Pasadena," he said. "I need the school's address."

"I've got it." I handed Jack the brochure, then got out of the car and stretched. The California air was moist and warm and, in spite of my worries, it felt good. I looked in the back window and saw that Ostin was still snoring, so I went inside the gas station. I got two bottles of strawberry-flavored milk and a box of doughnuts. I knew Ostin would be hungry when he awoke.

By the time I returned to the car Wade had climbed in the back and already fallen asleep. I sat in the front.

"Wade was pretty tired," I said to Jack.

"Yeah, he was. We would have been here sooner but he stopped in Lancaster and slept for four hours." Jack started the car. "Are you ready?"

I was blinking pretty hard. "No. Probably never will be. Let's go."

Jack smiled. "Nice."

Pasadena was lush and green with palm trees everywhere. I was eight when my mother and I moved from California, and I hadn't been back since. The city seemed foreign to me.

"Take Colorado Boulevard to South Allen," I said. "Then turn right."

Jack followed my directions and in a few minutes we were on Allen Avenue. "That's the place," I said. "It looks just like the picture. Except for the prison fence."

Jack parked the car at a gas station about a half block from the school. "Wade, wake up," he said.

"Who . . ."

"We're here."

Ostin woke as well and started searching for his glasses. He had fallen asleep wearing them, and I had picked them up off the car floor.

"Here you go," I said, handing them to him.

"Where are we?" he asked.

"The school," I said.

Ostin looked out at the building. "That's a school?"

"Looks more like a prison than a school," Wade said groggily.

"How are we going to get inside?" Ostin asked. "The fence is at least twelve feet high and there's barbed wire."

"And the entrance is guarded," Wade added.

"Getting in is not going to be easy," Ostin said. I think he meant "possible" instead of "easy."

Jack shook his head. "He's right, man. What are you going to do?"

I looked out at the building for a few more moments, then I sighed. "Well, it's not your problem. You got us here." I reached into my pocket and took out the rest of the money. "Here's the rest."

Jack took it without counting. "Thanks. Good luck."

"C'mon, Ostin," I said.

As we were climbing out of the car, Jack said, "Look."

I turned back toward the building. A white food-service truck was passing through the gate. "Get back inside, I have an idea."

We climbed back in and Jack started up the Camaro.

"What's your idea?" I asked.

He put on his sunglasses, then pulled out into the street. "We're going to borrow that van."

"Borrow?" Ostin said.

"This is life and death, right?" Jack asked.

"Absolutely," I replied.

We followed the van at a distance for about six miles, until it pulled into a parking lot, where there was a fleet of identical vans. Two men climbed out of the van and walked to the building. As soon as the men were out of sight Jack parked a couple stalls from the van. "Wade, follow us in the car." He looked at Ostin and me. "Let's go."

Jack, Ostin, and I ran, slightly stooped, to the van. I figured we'd have to break the window to get in, but the van was unlocked and we quickly climbed in. Jack checked on top of the visor, then in the ashtray for a spare key but didn't find one. He pulled out a pocket-knife, reached under the dash, and began sorting through wires. It only took a few minutes for him to hotwire the car. "These old vans are easy picking," he said.

"Where'd you learn to do that?" I asked.

"I'm not a car thief, if you're wondering. My old man's a mechanic."

"I wasn't wondering," I said. "Just impressed."

Jack drove out of the lot without drawing any attention. There was a CB radio mounted below the dashboard. Jack reached down and switched it on. "Better keep it on," he said. "So we know when they discover the van's missing."

Ostin was sitting in the back of the van with a bunch of metal trays stacked on a trolley. He lifted a lid. "Hmm. Chicken cordon bleu," he said.

"Don't steal food," I said.

"We just stole their van," Ostin said. "I don't think they'll care about a few leftovers. Besides, it might be my last meal."

"He's got a point," Jack said. "If they don't let us in the gate, we're screwed."

"What's our story?" I asked.

"What do you mean?" Jack said.

"I doubt they're expecting the food-service people back so soon. We better have a story."

"I've got one," Ostin said. "Tell them we left a stack of trays with chicken cordon bleu in the kitchen and it will stink up the place if we don't get it back."

"Not bad," I said. "I wonder if we'll need ID." I began looking around the van for paperwork or a badge but didn't find anything. "Nothing. All we've got is the story."

"We can make it work," Jack said.

Ostin said, "Hey, look at these." In a back compartment there was a stack of white food-service smocks and a sack of paper serving hats. "Uniforms."

Ostin lifted the smocks and hats out of the drawer and handed one to Jack and me. Even the smallest smock looked like a dress on me, but I put it on anyway. We drove back to the gas station parking lot, where Wade hopped out of the Camaro. I climbed in back and Wade got into the front seat of the van.

"Put these on," Jack said, handing Wade a smock and hat.

"Sweet," Wade said.

We circled the block and headed for the school. "Ready for this?" Jack asked.

"Yeah," I said from the back.

Jack pulled into the driveway and slowly up to the guard shack. The guard, a stern, powerful-looking man in a navy blue security uniform, wore a gun at his hip. "What's up?"

Jack looked surprisingly calm. "Sorry, we left a couple trays of blue chicken in the kitchen."

The guard squinted. "What?"

"You know, blue chicken, delicious from the oven but give it an hour out of the refrigerator and it's going to be stinkin' to high heaven. Stink up the kitchen, the dining area, the whole building. That blue chicken is stinky. Whoo. Diaper stinky."

The guard looked at him for a moment, then grinned. "All right. Go get your stinky chicken."

"Thanks."

The gate opened and we drove through.

"Blue chicken?" Ostin said. "It's chicken cordon bleu."

"Whatever," Jack said. "It worked."

He drove around the side of the building. We weren't exactly sure where to go, but there was only one open garage. In the back of it there was a door guarded by a man with a gun.

"Whoa," I said. "We've got another guard."

"Worse," Ostin said. "See that plate by the door? It's a magnetic switch. It's like my dad's office: You can't get anywhere without a card. No card, no entry. You better find something."

Wade looked through the glove compartment. "Nothing," he said.

"What do I do?" Jack asked. "Pull in?"

"We have to now," I said, "or they'll know something's up."

"Maybe we could offer the guy some food," Ostin said.

"Do you ever think of anything else?" Wade asked.

"Wait," I said, "he might be onto something. We'll carry the trays in and ask the guy to open the door for us."

Ostin sneered at Wade.

"Whatever we're doing," Jack said, "we better do it fast. 'Cause we're here."

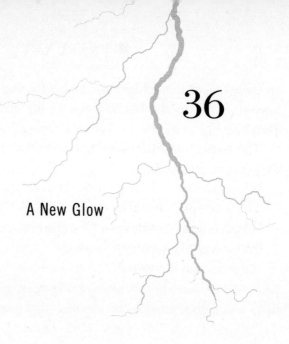

36

A New Glow

"Taylor."

Taylor slowly rolled over, again feeling the pain in her body. Ian was kneeling next to her.

"They're listening to us, so talk softly. Do you know about the last electrochild?"

"What do you mean?"

"There were seventeen of us. They found all but two, you and one other."

"Michael," she said. "His name is Michael. Why?"

"There's a new Glow outside the compound."

"What does he look like?"

"He's small, but the electricity around him is wild. Is he good or bad?"

"He's good."

Ian nodded. "Let's hope he stays that way."

"What's he doing?"

"He's with three other teenagers. I think they're trying to find a way in."

"We need to warn him that Hatch knows he's coming. Can you warn him?"

Ian shook his head. "No. I can only see."

Taylor covered her eyes. "I've failed him. I've failed everyone."

"This isn't your fault, Taylor. You're a good person."

"How do you know that?"

"Because you're down here."

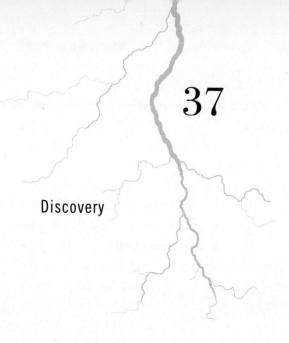

37

Discovery

Jack slowly pulled the van into the garage, put it in park, and killed the engine. The guard watched us intensely.

"Ready, Ostin?" I asked.

"Yeah," he said, looking very *unready*.

I slid open the side door and stepped out. I grabbed one of the metal containers, then started toward the building's entrance. The guard's eyes were glued to me, and his hand hovered above his gun. When I was a couple of yards from him he said, "Stop."

I stopped. "Yes, sir."

"Where's your ID?" he asked.

I struggled to control my tics. "Sorry, it's in my pocket. Would you mind getting the door for me?"

His expression didn't change. "I need to see your ID."

"You recognize me, don't you? We talked last week."

"I wasn't here last week," he said.

I gulped. "It must have been another guard. In those glasses you all look alike."

"Your ID."

I sighed. "Okay. Here, it's just in my pocket. Hold this for one second."

Jack opened his door and started to get out of the van. "Is there a problem?"

The guard turned to him, "Get back in the van. I need his ID and your ID."

"I'm getting it," I said. "Just give me a hand." I pushed the tray toward the guard. He put his hands out, pushing back against the metal tray. "I'm not going to . . ."

I surged. His mouth opened but before he could make a sound he dropped to the ground unconscious. I set the tray on the ground.

"Whoa," Jack said. "I'm glad you didn't hit us with that much juice."

"It was only half," I said. "I'm getting more electric."

Ostin jumped out of the van. "Good job, dude."

"Don't start high-fiving yet." I took the lanyard hanging from the man's neck, then looked through his pockets for anything else we could use. I pulled out a thick plastic card. "What's this?"

"That's a magnetic key," Ostin said.

I held up the lanyard. "Then what's this?"

"Either a duplicate or you need two different keys."

"Now what?" Jack asked.

"Tie him up in the van and get ready to roll. Ostin and I will go find my mom and Taylor and bring them here."

"On it," Jack said. "Good luck, dude."

"Thanks for your help."

"I wasn't going to let you have all the fun."

I took the magnetic key on the guard's lanyard and swiped it across the black pad. The red diode turned green and the lock clicked. "We're in."

I pushed open the door. Inside was a long, brightly lit corridor with surveillance cameras on both ends. Ostin and I stepped inside.

"I've got the feeling we're being watched," Ostin said.

"Just act cool," I said. "They'll just think we're food-service guys." I kept walking. "Where do you think she is?"

"Where does the dog hide the bone?" Ostin asked.

"Just talk normal," I said.

"Find an elevator."

There was an elevator at the end of the hall. Inside the buttons were. 4-3-2-1-GL-D.

"What's GL?" I asked.

"Ground level, or garden level if they're being fancy. Push D."

"What's D?"

"I have no idea. But it's below GL."

I pushed the button but nothing happened. Outside I could hear footsteps coming down the hall.

"Look, it needs a key. Try yours."

I shoved it in the slot but nothing happened. The footsteps got closer.

"Try the other key."

I switched keys and the elevator door shut. "That's it."

The elevator began moving down. It stopped just a few seconds later and the door opened. I stuck my head out. We were in another corridor. The overhead lights must have been on dimmer switches because they were barely illuminated. Also there were thick metal doors spaced every fifteen or twenty feet that looked a little like the door to the refrigerated room in the back of the grocery store where my mom worked. There were metal boxes outside each door with bright green diodes. The hall was empty but there were security cameras mounted at each end of the hall. It was eerie being in such a large building and seeing no one.

"What's with all the security cameras?" Ostin asked.

"Mr. Dallstrom would be in heaven," I said. "We better hurry. I doubt the food-service guys come down here." We crept down the hall to the first door. The doors were thick metal with dark, mirrored glass in horizontal slits about four inches wide and a foot high.

I looked through the window on the first door. It was dark inside and I couldn't see anything or anyone. I went to the next door and looked inside. It was also dark, but I thought I could see a faint glow. "I think there's someone in this one."

"Is it your mom?"

"No. Whoever it is, they're glowing."

"It could be Taylor," Ostin said. "Try your keys."

I swiped both of them over the keypad but nothing happened. "It's not opening." I looked up and down the hall, feeling more nervous by the second.

"I bet it's a magnetic lock," Ostin said, looking it over. "You might be able to counter it with your electricity." He crouched down to examine it, then nodded. "The secondary magnetic coil should be about here. Let me see your hand. Don't shock me."

I held it out. He guided it to one side of the lock and backed away. "Okay, now."

I pulsed. There was a slight crackle of electricity but nothing happened.

"Give it more," he said.

"Okay." This time I pulsed with everything. The light in the hallway flickered and there was a clicking sound followed by the hiss of escaping air. "Are you done?" Ostin asked.

"Yeah."

Ostin grabbed the door and pulled it open. "It worked."

"All right," I said. I stepped into the room. It was dark except for the dim light coming from the hallway. I looked around, waiting for my eyes to adjust.

"Michael," a voice said. "It's me."

There was a girl lying on the floor in the corner of the room. Even in the darkness I knew who she was.

"Taylor," I said. "We found you."

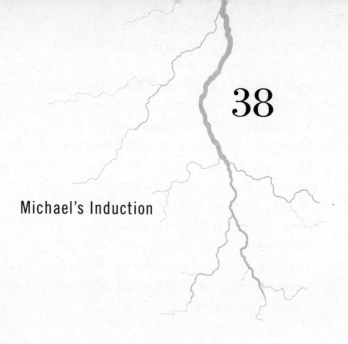

38

Michael's Induction

Taylor was barely able to move. I knelt down on the floor next to her. "What have they done to you?"

She started crying. "I'm so sorry I led them to you."

I put my hand on her shoulder. "It's going to be okay, Taylor. We're going to get you out of here. Have you seen my mother?"

"No. But they told me they have her."

"Did they say where?" Ostin asked.

"No."

"Taylor, what kind of school is this?"

"It's not a school. It's a laboratory."

"A laboratory? For what?"

Another voice came from the darkness. "To learn how to make more of us."

I spun around to see a young man standing on the other side of the cell. He looked about my age but was a full six inches taller. He was African-American and glowing. Standing behind him were two teenage girls, one Chinese, the other a tall blonde, who were both glowing as well. I'm not surprised that I hadn't seen them, as they were in the opposite corner of the cell and I was only focused on Taylor.

"I'm Ian," the boy said. "I've been watching you and your friends since you arrived this morning."

"From down here?"

"I see through electrolocation. I can see through the walls."

"Like electric eels," Ostin said. "That's cool."

"Why are you down here?" I asked.

"Around here you either do what Hatch says or you end up in the dungeon."

The two girls walked toward us. The Chinese girl said, "I'm McKenna."

"And I'm Abigail."

"I'm Michael," I said. "Do you also have powers?"

McKenna nodded. "I can make light and heat. Abigail can take away pain."

"Electric nerve stimulation," Ostin said. "Very interesting."

I turned back to Ian. "Do you know who else is down here?"

"I can see everyone in the building," he said.

"Do you know if my mother is here? They kidnapped her."

"How long ago did they take her?"

"Just a few days ago."

Ian shook his head. "The only female prisoners are on the next floor up and they've all been here for more than a year."

My heart fell.

Ian suddenly looked up toward the corner of the room. "Oh no," he said. "The two guys you came here with are being taken away by the guards." He turned back toward me. "How did you get in here? In this room?"

"Michael demagnetized the door," Ostin said. "With his electricity."

Ian shook his head. "That's impossible. The locks aren't magnetic. The sliding bolts are made of resin and work pneumatically. Everyone here has electrical gifts, so they prepared for that." Ian looked back up. "They're coming."

"Who's coming?" I said.

Ian didn't answer. He grabbed the girls and stepped away from the door, back to the corner of the room.

"If I didn't open the door," I asked, "then who did?"

A voice boomed from an unseen speaker. "That would be me, Michael. We've been expecting you. Welcome to Elgen Academy."

There was suddenly a loud screech in my head and I felt dizzy, just as I had in the parking lot when my mother was taken. I fell against the wall, covering my ears. Everyone in the room groaned except Ostin, who looked around curiously at us. "What's happening?"

"It's Nichelle," Ian said.

"What's a Nichelle?" Ostin asked.

The cell door opened. The man I had seen outside the pizza parlor was standing there next to the creepy girl.

"Hello, Michael," the man said. "I see the group has been reunited." He stepped inside the room.

"Shock him," Ostin said.

I took a step forward, then the screeching dropped me to my knees. Everyone else screamed.

Hatch turned to Ostin. "Ostin, isn't it? I thought you were supposed to be smart." He looked down at me. "What do you call yourself? The Electrokids? The Electroclub?"

"The Electroclan," Ostin said.

"Right." Hatch smiled darkly. "You don't belong here, Ostin. But here you are."

"I belong wherever Michael is," Ostin said.

Hatch smirked. "Loyalty. I like that. Even when it's misplaced, there's something endearing about it. Unfortunately, this is where your relationship ends. Michael, if you'll follow me, we'll let Ostin stay here with the others."

Ostin looked at me.

"I'm not leaving them," I said.

An even higher-pitched screeching poured through my head, followed by an increasing tightness, as if a metal band had been put around my head and cinched up. It was the same thing I had felt when my mother was taken—as if life itself were being drawn out of me through a straw. "Aargh." I fell to the ground, grabbing my temples.

"Stop it!" Taylor shouted. "Leave him alone."

"Mike knows how to stop it," Hatch said.

"Okay," I shouted. "I'll go."

Hatch nodded at Nichelle and the sound and pain stopped. "Come along, Mike. I'm a busy man."

I staggered to my feet. "My name is Michael."

"A Glow by any other name is just as electric, but as you wish."

I looked over at Ostin and Taylor. They both had fear in their eyes. "I'll be back," I said. I staggered out and the door automatically closed behind me. Halfway down the hall Hatch turned to me and said, "I sincerely hope you won't be back to that place."

"I belong with my friends."

"Then the question is, will your friends still be there? And that is completely up to you." The elevator door opened. "After you."

"Where are we going?"

Hatch pushed a button on the elevator. "I want to talk. But first, there are tests to be run."

PART FOUR

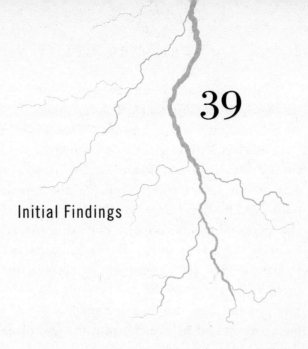

39

Initial Findings

Later that afternoon, Hatch was in his office talking to Quentin when Dr. Parker knocked on his door.

"Come in," he said gruffly.

She opened the door. "Good evening, Dr. Hatch. Quentin."

"Quentin was just leaving," Hatch said.

Quentin immediately stood. "Yes, sir. Thank you, sir."

He walked out of the office and Hatch motioned to the same chair Quentin had occupied. "Take a seat." Before she could speak Hatch asked, "How's our boy?"

"I've never seen anyone like him."

"Explain."

"I've confirmed your initial findings. His el-waves are extremely high. Except they've grown since your first encounter."

"So he *is* becoming more powerful," Hatch said.

"So it would appear. But even more curious is that he seems to handle electricity differently than the others."

Hatch slightly leaned forward. "What do you mean?"

"His electricity seems to be circulating within his body, either through his bone marrow or central nervous system, which may account for some rather surprising phenomena. I administered a mild shock to him to see how he'd respond and his el-waves actually increased by one percent. I was so intrigued by this result that I upped the power to nearly five hundred joules. At that level I thought he'd probably jump out of his seat, but instead he just sat there. His body told a different story, however. His el-waves spiked fifty percent, then dropped and maintained at an increased seventeen percent and held there until the end of our examination. He still might be elevated."

Hatch leaned forward in his chair. "You're saying he can absorb electricity from other sources?"

"It would appear so."

"Like Nichelle?"

"Except that Nichelle doesn't retain power; she's simply a conduit to its dissemination. Vey seems to capture it."

Hatch rubbed his chin in fascination. "How is hoarding all that electricity affecting his health?"

"If it's hurting him, it's not manifesting. He's perfectly healthy. With the exception of his Tourette's syndrome."

"He has Tourette's?"

"Yes. That's why he has the facial tics."

"I thought he was just anxious." Hatch rubbed his palms together the way he always did when he was excited. "Could his Tourette's have something to do with why he's different than the other children?"

"I don't know. We don't even know enough about Tourette's to know what causes it. We know it's a neurological disorder, but not a whole lot more than that."

"But it's possible?"

"It's possible."

"I want this information kept in strictest confidentiality."

"Of course. All research is confidential."

"I don't even want your assistants to know. This is between you and me."

"Very well."

"If he'll cooperate, Mr. Vey could be the model of the Glows 2.0."

"And if he won't?"

"Then we'll have to fix that. How was his attitude?"

"He was quite defiant."

"Of that I'm sure. But there's one thing I'm equally certain of."

"What's that?"

"The boy loves his mother."

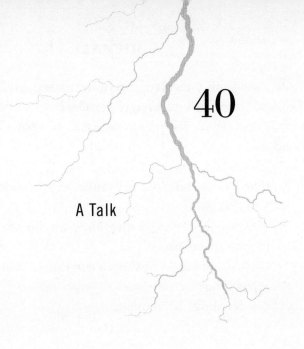

40

A Talk

The Elgen guards all looked the same to me. They were all nearly the same height and build and wore the same uniform: a black beret, dark glasses, and black jumpsuits that appeared to have been made from a rubberized material. They all had communication radios hanging from their ears and jaws, and they carried an array of weapons on a utility belt—a knife, a canister of Mace, two different types of revolvers, resin handcuffs, a smoke grenade, a concussion grenade, and a long wooden truncheon.

I was sitting on the floor looking through a shelf of books when I heard the lock on my door slide. I looked up to see the door open.

"Sorry to disturb you, Mr. Vey," a guard said. "But Dr. Hatch is ready to meet with you."

I thought he sounded unusually polite for a prison guard. Of course prisoners aren't usually given a room with a plasma TV, surround-sound audio, and Monet prints on the wall. My room seemed more like a luxury suite than a prison cell, but if there's no doorknob on the inside, you're still a prisoner.

"All right." I stood as the door opened fully. There was a second guard standing a few feet behind him in the hall. The second guard didn't say a word. I noticed that they both had their hands on their Mace. I guessed they had been ordered to be pleasant.

"This way, sir," the guard said. We took the elevator down one level to the second floor.

They led me down a marble-floored corridor to the end of the hall and into a large reception area, where a secretary sat at a large wooden desk with several monitors. Directly behind her was a glass wall, partially obstructing another door. In front of the receptionist's desk was another guard sitting behind a tall, circular podium with a Plexiglas shield.

The receptionist, a thin woman about my mother's age and wearing narrow reading glasses, looked up as we entered.

"We have Michael Vey," the first guard said, though it was evident she was expecting us.

"I'll inform Dr. Hatch," she said. She pushed a button, then spoke into her phone. She nodded, then pushed a button beneath her desk. There was a loud buzz and the door slid open. "Dr. Hatch would like you to go on in."

The second guard motioned for me to go first, so I walked ahead of them through the open door. I stepped inside while they stopped at the door's threshold. I was ticking like crazy.

Hatch's office reminded me of the ones I had seen on the TV lawyer shows, with bronze statues and busts and cases of books I wondered if anyone ever read. Television screens took up an entire wall. Hatch was sitting at his desk. He wasn't wearing his sunglasses. Nichelle sat in a chair at the side of the room. I didn't look at her. I couldn't stand her.

Hatch motioned to a leather chair in front of his desk. "Hello, Michael," he said. "Please, take a seat."

I walked up to the chair and sat down, looking around the office. On the wall behind Hatch was a picture of Dr. Hatch shaking hands with the president of the United States. He noticed that I was looking at the picture.

"It's not hard to get to the president," Hatch said. "If you have money."

"Where's my mother?" I asked.

His eyes narrowed into thin slits. "To the point. I like that. After all, that's why you made this futile little trip, isn't it?"

"Where are you keeping my mother?"

"We'll get to that. But first, there's something you need to understand. More important than where *she* is, is where *you* are. And who you are." His voice dropped. "Do you even know?"

"Of course I know who I am."

"Yes, I know you think you do. But you don't really know." His gaze softened. "Who are you? You're a victim, Michael. A victim of your environment. You have been brainwashed, your thoughts contaminated by the human Petri dish your mind has been cultured in.

"For instance, you've been told that all men are created equal, but anyone who isn't stupid or ignorant can see that that just isn't true. Some are rich, some are poor. Some are smart and some are fools. No, no one is born equal. Especially you.

"You're not even equal to the other electric children. You handle electricity in a different way. And you seem to be getting more powerful. I compared your el-waves from now to when I first met you in Idaho. They've risen. It's very impressive." He leaned forward. "Do you know what we do here, Michael?"

"Kill babies with your machine?"

Hatch chuckled. "What an interesting take you have on this. That's the one thing I've learned about working with youth—if you think you know what they're thinking, you're mistaken." He straightened his tie. "You're right, you know. At least partially. It is about the machine. The MEI we call it. The MEI may have been a failure as an imaging device, but it led to the discovery of something more important. Much more important.

"If you think about it, Michael, there's a marvelous fate to all this. Many of the world's greatest discoveries are results of accidents. The MEI was one of those happy accidents. We set out to take pictures of the human body and instead we improved the human body. We invented superhumans. We invented the electric children.

"We've spent the last dozen years tracking them down. There were seventeen of you who survived. Seventeen very special children. Sadly, there are only thirteen of you left—four of you died before the age of seven."

"Died of what?"

"Cancer. No doubt attributable to the excessive electricity coursing through your cells. We can't be certain, of course, but there's a chance that unless we find a cure for your condition, that may be all of your fates."

I sat back in my chair. I had never considered that what I had was a disease.

"But I digress. I was saying that we had found all the survivors except two: you and Miss Ridley. Miss Ridley was adopted out-of-state and you know how inefficient government bureaucracy is. Her records got lost in the process. And you, well, we tracked you for a while, all throughout California.

"You don't know it, but we've been more a part of your life than you realize. If you look through your family picture album, say on that trip you took to Disneyland when you were seven, you're likely to find a picture of one of our agents in the background. Then, right after your father's death, your mother pulled a fast one and disappeared. We lost you.

"Actually, it's quite impressive how she eluded us, seeing that you didn't even know you were being followed. So we set some traps and hoped that you would someday come looking for us. And you did. Actually, it was Miss Ridley who did. But we never dreamed that we'd be so fortunate that she'd lead us to you. In this matter, fate was truly generous."

Fate sucks, I thought. "What do you want from us?"

Hatch stood and walked around to the front of his desk, leaning back against it. "We're scientists, Michael. We want what all scientists want. Truth. The truth about you. The truth about how you do what you do. We want to know why you lived when so many others died."

"No matter what you call yourself, you're just a bunch of murderers," I said.

"So much anger in you, Michael," Hatch said coolly. "But boys in glass houses shouldn't throw stones, should they?"

"What do you mean?"

"Don't play stupid, Michael. We know all about it."

I looked at him blankly. "About what?"

"Are you telling me that you really don't know why you left California?"

The way he asked the question frightened me. "We left because my mother was trying to protect me."

He laughed. "Protect you from what?"

I couldn't answer. He walked closer to my chair. "So you really don't know." Hatch rubbed his chin. "I think, deep inside, you do. You must. No child, not even an eight-year-old, could forget something that traumatic. Your mother wasn't protecting you, Michael. She was protecting others *from you*." His eyes leveled on me in a piercing gaze. I was ticking like crazy, both blinking and gulping.

Hatch leaned back against his desk. "I knew your father. I knew him well. Maybe even better than you did."

My chest constricted.

"Do you even know where your father worked?" Hatch asked.

"He worked at a hospital," I blurted out angrily.

Hatch just looked at me for a moment, then the corners of his mouth rose in a subtle smile. "Good. So your mother didn't hide everything from you. He did indeed work at a hospital. Your father was the head of radiology at Pasadena General." Hatch slightly leaned forward. "He helped us test the MEI."

His words hit me like a bucket of ice water. "No!" I shouted. "He wouldn't do that. He was a good man."

Hatch nodded. "You're right, he was a good man. He was a

visionary. And, like me, he never intended to hurt anyone. He wanted to advance science and save lives. He wanted to make the world a better place." Hatch's voice fell. "Unfortunately, he never got that chance." Hatch exhaled slowly. "I know what happened to your father, Michael." Hatch turned around and lifted a folder from his desk, extracting from it a single paper. "I've been saving this for some time now, haven't I, Nichelle?"

I had forgotten that she was in the room. "Yes, sir," Nichelle said. "Years."

Hatch held up a paper with a gold border around it. "Michael, have you ever seen a death certificate?"

I shook my head.

"I didn't think so." He turned the paper back around. "Let me read the important parts. State of California, County of Los Angeles . . . Carl T. Vey died at 7:56 p.m. in Los Angeles County on the fifth day of October, 2004 . . . Cause of death: Cardiac arrest from an electric shock." He set down the paper. "It's about time you owned up to the truth about your father's death." His eyes turned dark. "You stopped your father's heart."

At that moment, I had a flashback. I was sitting on my father's lap. My father was grasping his chest, his eyes wide and panicked. Then flashing red and blue lights illuminated our kitchen drapes, and sirens wailed in chorus with my mother crying. It was true. That's what my mother was hiding from me. I had killed my own father. Darkness filled my heart and mind.

"I was barely eight!" I shouted. "I didn't know how to control my electricity."

Hatch just stared at me. "Isn't that interesting. We wanted to save lives, so we created a machine that could do that. Like you, we didn't know better. Yet you condemn us—" His voice rose and he pointed at me. "How dare you call me, or your father, a murderer. You're no different than us, not one iota." He walked behind his desk and sat down. He looked calmer and his voice was gentle again. "But you can atone for this, Michael. Just as we are trying to atone for our mistake. We're trying to do the right thing."

"That's why you're torturing Taylor?"

The loud screech went through my head and I fell forward, grabbing my temples. "Aaah."

Hatch spun around to Nichelle. "Stop it!"

The pain stopped.

"Get her out of here," I said.

"I can't do that," Hatch said. "I don't fully trust you yet."

"You don't trust *me*?"

"You're still brainwashed from the outside world. Until you see clearly, I can only trust you to behave like a human."

"I just want my mother."

"Of course you do. Which, of course, is precisely why we took her. And whether you see her again depends entirely upon you. If you comply with my instructions, your mother will be set free. We'll fly her here to see you, joyful reunion and all that. If not . . ." His expression fell. "If not, sadly, I cannot guarantee her safety. Even if I wanted to."

I looked at him quietly. "What are your 'instructions'?"

"Simple, really. Let's call them demonstrations of loyalty."

"What kind of demonstrations?"

"I trust you remember Clyde. You met him in the parking lot and you spoke with him in the jail, didn't you?"

"How did you know that?"

Hatch smiled but didn't answer me. "Clyde is, or should I say, was, what we call a GP. It's a nickname we give our human guinea pigs."

"Guinea pigs?" I suddenly understood why Clyde had reacted with such fear and hostility toward me.

"GPs are inconsequential—the coffee grounds of humanity. They are America's untouchables, criminals and losers, none of them worth the carbon their bodies are made of. So, from time to time, we use them for the advancement of our scientific pursuits."

I was horrified by what he was telling me. "Where do you get them?" I asked.

"From all over. Sometimes we pull them off the streets or from homeless shelters. Sometimes we find them engaged in some kind of criminal activity. In fact we brought in two new ones just today. Would you like to meet them?"

"No," I said.

"These, I think you will." He pushed a button on his desk. "Bring GPs Seven Sixty-Four and Seven Sixty-Five to my office immediately."

I looked at him incredulously. "You kidnap people and use them for experiments?"

"Well, the word *people* might be a bit strong but the rest of what you said is accurate." He looked at me with a grim smile. "We're doing them a favor, really. Out in society they would only self-destruct. Most of them already had. This way we preserve their lives a little longer, improve their standard of living, and give meaning to their pathetic existences. They are actually contributing to society instead of just staining it."

A moment later one of the guards opened Hatch's door. "They're here, sir."

"Bring them in."

The guard signaled to someone outside the door and two other guards brought in the shackled GPs. I couldn't believe what I saw. Jack and Wade. They looked terrified, especially Wade, who was trembling so hard his chains were rattling. They were both barefoot and dressed in Day-Glo orange jumpsuits. In addition to the shackles and chains on their legs and wrists they had large plastic and stainless steel collars fastened around their necks. The collars had green flashing lights. The sight of them bound made me sick to my stomach.

"I'm sorry," I said to them, shaking my head. "I'm so sorry."

Jack and Wade just looked at me with fearful eyes. I didn't understand why they didn't say anything.

I turned back to Hatch. "What are those things around their necks?" I asked angrily.

"Simple devices to ensure they don't decide to leave us," Hatch said. "It's based on the invisible fence theory." He looked at me. "Are you familiar with that?"

"No."

"That's right, you had neither a dog nor a yard. Some dog owners put special electric shock collars on their pets that will administer a mild shock to their dog when it crosses an invisible boundary. It trains the dog to not leave the yard. These collars your associates are sporting operate on the same principle. If your friends leave this building they will be shocked.

"The collar also monitors their vocal cords. If they attempt to shout or even speak they will be shocked. But I'm afraid it's a bit more potent than that painful little wake-up call a dog gets. The charge these collars generate is quite a bit more lively and will completely incapacitate them." His eyes moved back and forth between Jack and Wade. "Maybe even kill them."

"You need to let them go," I said. "They're not part of this."

"You're quite wrong about that, Michael. The moment they chose to help you they became a part of this." His voice rose and he looked at Jack and Wade with disdain. "The moment they violated our academy they became a part of this."

"What are you going to do with them?"

"The same thing we do with all our GPs—whatever furthers our cause." He looked at the guard. "Take them back to their cells."

"You heard him," the guard said to Jack and Wade. They turned and shuffled out of the room.

"How many prisoners do you have here?" I asked.

"Only a few dozen. Our Pasadena facility is quite small compared to the others. In fact, now that we have you and Miss Ridley, we'll be shutting down this facility and moving elsewhere. Someplace where we have a little more . . . flexibility."

"Flexibility to do what?"

He looked at me gravely. "We're scientists, Michael. And we have a vision. We've been trying to create the perfect Glow. And we're getting close. You and Miss Ridley are very much a part of our plans.

"We've tested thousands of DNA samples. We've run thousands of blood tests, searching for the one link that all you survivors have in common. We've even been testing diets and nutritional supplements to gauge how eating affects your powers. We've discovered that with a nonsugar diet high in potassium we can actually increase electrical flow.

"But you, Michael, are something else. Even without our help, you've been increasing your electrical capacity nearly two percent a day. At that rate you'll be doubling in power just about every two months. In a year you may be the most powerful Glow of all—if your electricity doesn't kill you first."

"What do you mean, 'kill me first'?"

"Like I told you before, we've already lost four of you to cancer. That's why I sent you in for the checkup. You're going to need our help. The doctors out there can't help you; they've never seen anyone like you before. There are no medical books on your condition. If you want to live to manhood, you had better stay close to us."

His words filled me with even greater fear. What had they found in my exam? Was I really dying? It was too big to think about and I pushed it from my mind. "Why did you take my mother instead of me?"

"Trust me, your mother would rather it had been her than you. Mothers are like that. Actually we tried to take you both, but your chubby friend ruined that when he showed up with all those people around. We only had time to take one of you and, frankly, better her than you."

"But I'm the one with the power."

"Yes, but as you well know, power, undirected, is worthless—an engine without wheels. It's the old saying, isn't it? You can lead a horse to water but you can't make him drink. Unless you happen to have your horse's mother locked away in a cage somewhere. Having collateral will make you much more . . . malleable.

"Take your fellow Glow, Tanner. He has an amazing power. He can bring down an airplane from the ground. The first time I told him to crash a 747 he refused. Until we let him see his little brother getting nearly electrocuted by one of your peers. It only took ten minutes of his screams before he was quite eager to help out.

"You know how it goes, Michael. The first time you resist. The second time you relent. The third time you volunteer. It's that easy. Today, I tell Tanner to bring down a commercial flight and he says, 'which plane?'" He looked into my eyes. "We're creating an army, Michael. And you are a natural leader. You would make a very good general."

"An army to fight who?"

"Whomever we need to fight. Whoever stands in our way as we reach for our destiny. Just think of the powers at our disposal. Just consider Tanner. He can bring down a jet airliner without a bomb, missile, or security risk. There's no tracking, there's no preventing. Sudden and complete mechanical failure and the plane drops out of the sky. Do you have any idea what his talent is worth? Terrorists would pay tens of millions. Governments would pay hundreds of millions. Or billions. Especially if that plane were carrying a nuclear weapon—or the president of the United States.

"And that's just one of many of your graduating class's talents. We just need more of you. A lot more of you."

"What makes you think anyone will follow you?"

"They will and they do. Most of them have, at least. It's amazing what you can do to a young mind before the rest of the world contaminates it. It's you older kids, the brainwashed, who are the problem. Like poor, misguided Miss Ridley. I offered her the world and she spat it back in my face."

"Taylor's a good person," I said, my right eye twitching.

"That depends entirely on what you mean by 'good.' If, by 'good' you mean shortsighted, ungrateful, and small-minded, then you're right."

He stood and his expression relaxed. "That's enough for today. I'm going to let you stay in one of the guest suites tonight. You'll be much more comfortable there. Unfortunately, for now, you will still be assigned a guard. Don't get me wrong, Michael. I trust you. I really do. I just don't trust the world you come from. Too much of it is still in your head. But we'll work on it.

"In the meantime, if you have any seditious schemes, remember, your mother will pay severely for your mistakes. You shock someone, she'll be shocked twice. You hurt someone, well, you get the picture. It's beautifully ironic. For centuries the sins of the parents have been

answered on the heads of their children. Now the opposite is true."
He walked to the door. "It's time for you to go."

I stood and also walked to the door, followed a few yards back by
Nichelle.

"I'm giving you forty-eight hours to consider your predicament.
I urge you to seriously do so. Lives are at stake here. You've already
killed your father. Will you kill your mother too?"

His words cut like razor blades.

"And then there are your friends. If you choose to disregard my
offer, Jack and Wade will be the first to go. Then Ostin and finally
Taylor. It's your call. They're all counting on you to do the right
thing. If you don't, they'll disappear one by one. Think carefully now.
Are you going to lose a few of them before you change your mind?
Or will you do the right thing the first time?

"As you grow older, Michael, you'll learn an important lesson—
that most people spend their entire lives wishing for a second chance
to do what they should have done right the first time. Don't be like
them, Michael." He smiled at me, placing his hand on my shoulder,
which made me feel sick inside. "I believe in you. I know you think
you're doing the right thing by resisting, but it's because your point
of view is skewed. All you have to do is walk across the aisle and see
it from our side. And as your reward, I'm offering you everything
you've dreamed of. You'll be the head of the electric children. You'll
have a life a rock star would envy. And you'll have your Taylor." He
smiled. "Yes, I know how you feel about Taylor. And she'll be all
yours. Your little friend, Ostin, will be allowed to go home to his
mommy and daddy. And your mother will be set free. And some day
you'll have the adoration of millions. All around the world, children
will want to be you.

"Remember, history is made by those willing to tear up the last
mapmaker's map. Make history, Michael. You have two days to
decide whether or not to join us. I dare say that these are the two
most important days of your life. I know your heart may not entirely
be in it at first; I don't expect it to be. There's too much brainwash-
ing in there. I just want to see that you're willing to commit. That's

all I ask. And for that simple commitment I offer you the world." He turned and nodded to the guard. "Have a good night, Michael."

"Let's go," a guard said to me.

Nichelle and the guards took me to a suite on the third floor. I sat on the bed and the door locked behind me. My head was spinning like a top. My entire world had been turned upside down.

For the next two days I was left alone in my room. Under different circumstances I would have thought I'd died and gone to heaven. The suite had a refrigerator and cabinet that were full of drinks and candies from all around the world. I tried some Japanese candy, Chocoballs and Hi-Chews, which were some of the best candy I'd ever eaten. Four meals were brought in daily, on plates that looked like my mom's best china. There were menus for entertainment as well as food. The first day an Asian woman came to my room and offered me a massage, which I didn't accept.

There were shelves of video games. The newest on the market, some not yet on the market, and some I'd only dreamed of. I thought of how excited Ostin would be to see them. I only wished that he were there to play them with me.

In spite of all the distractions, all I could think about was my impending decision. What did Hatch mean by "demonstrations of loyalty"? What would he require of me? Something told me that his "simple commitment" was anything but simple.

My second night, as I lay in bed, I made my decision. If they would let my mother and my friends go, I would stay. There was no other choice to be made.

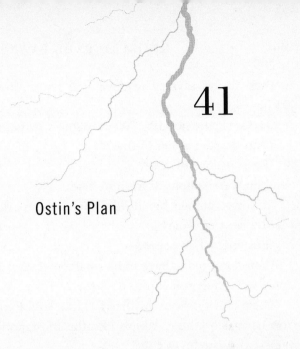

41

Ostin's Plan

Ostin was miserable. His stomach was growling and he was homesick. Taylor came and sat by him. "Are you okay?" she asked softly.

"No."

"Are you afraid?"

"Yeah."

"Me too." She put her arm around him. "I wanted to tell you that I'm sorry that I wasn't very nice to you back in Idaho."

"I thought you were nice. Except at that party when you kept threatening to reboot me."

Taylor looked down. "Maddie's party. That seems like a million years ago. It's funny how the things that were so important back then don't matter anymore. Maybe Hatch is right: We have been brainwashed."

"Hatch isn't right," Ostin said. "Hatch is a devil. It's like my mother always says, 'The devil will tell a thousand truths to sell one lie.'"

Taylor slowly nodded. "Want to know something?"

Ostin looked at her. "What?"

"I was jealous of you."

"You were jealous of me?" he said.

Taylor scratched her head. "You're so smart. I've always wished that I were that smart."

"But you get good grades."

"You don't really have to be smart to get good grades. Just good at doing what they tell you to do."

Ostin slowly shook his head. "How could you be jealous of me? You have everything. You're like the most popular girl in the universe. Everyone loves you."

"Not everyone. Being popular isn't always easy. You make enemies. And they're usually people who pretend to be your friend. Frenemies."

"I never thought of that."

"So maybe I do know something you don't." She sighed. "It all just seems so stupid now. What am I going to wear to Emily's party, what if Megan wears the same thing, who is Chase going to ask to the prom? It's all so meaningless."

Ostin put his head down. "I wish those were still our problems."

Taylor said, "Me too. What do you think they're going to do to Michael?"

"They'll try to break him."

"It's my fault he's here."

"No, it's not. I mean, he would have come after you, but he would have come anyway. They have his mother. He's got a great mother." Ostin touched her arm. "It's not your fault."

She smiled sadly. "Thanks."

"Besides, even if it were, we're a club, right? All for one and one for all."

"Yeah. I'd just rather be the one for all instead of the all for one."

Ostin sat back and breathed out heavily. "You know, there's

something about all this I don't understand. Why have they kept these kids here for so long?"

"What do you mean?"

"Ian, Abigail, McKenna. They clearly aren't going to convert. So why don't they just"—he hesitated—"you know, get rid of them?"

"I don't know."

Suddenly Ostin's eyes widened. "The only reason you keep something around is because it's valuable. That's it."

"What?"

"If they're valuable, they'll protect them." His whole face animated. "I have an idea how to get out of here. But I'll need everyone's help."

Taylor's eyes lit with hope. "Let's go talk to them."

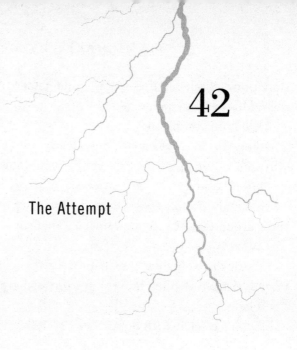

42

The Attempt

In the darkness of the cell, Ian looked like a ghost, the pale glow of his skin rising a half foot taller than Ostin. He stood with his arms crossed at his chest, staring down at Ostin. "That's the stupidest idea I've ever heard."

"Keep your voice down," Ostin said. "They'll hear us."

"You don't tell me what to do. In here, I'm in charge."

"You're not in charge of me."

"Yes, I am. This is my turf."

"No, you're not my boss."

"Are you dissing me?"

"I'll diss you if I want. I'm not afraid of you, bat boy."

Ian got in Ostin's face. "What did you call me?"

"You two knock it off," Taylor said. "He was just trying to help."

"Keep out of it," McKenna said.

There was an audible whirr as three of the five video cameras panned across the room.

"Don't tell me what to do," Taylor said. "I'll fry your brain."

"Try it," McKenna said, her skin beginning to brighten. "I'll cook you."

"You'll never get a chance, lightbulb."

"Will you all stop it?" Abigail said. "It's bad enough we have them hating us."

Ian growled, "So, chunky soup here is dissing me for being blind?"

"Chunky soup?" Ostin said, "Take it back."

Ian uncrossed his arms. "Make me."

"I will."

"I'd like to see you try, doughboy. The only exercise you get is unwrapping Twinkies. I'll roll you out like pizza dough."

"You're going to pay for that."

"Ooh, scary," Ian said.

Ostin rushed at him and knocked him over by the door. Ian groaned as he hit the ground.

"What the . . . McKenna!" Ian shouted. "Taylor's doing something to me. She's messing with my brain."

A harsh voice came over the speaker system. "Occupants of Cell B, stop what you're doing, immediately."

Ian began screaming. "Abi, McKenna, stop the new girl! Stop her."

"That does it," McKenna said. "You're going to pay."

"Bring it on, Day-Glo," Taylor said. "I can take both of you."

The girls surrounded Taylor. Ian and Ostin were locked in combat when the door clicked and opened. Two guards ran into the room.

"Now!" Ostin said.

McKenna suddenly burst into a brilliant light, temporarily blinding the guards. Taylor turned and focused on the two men as Ian charged at them, knocking them both over. Abigail and McKenna quickly jumped on the men, pulling their Mace from their belts and spraying them in the face with it. Taylor kept rebooting them over and over and the men flailed about confused and gasping from the Mace.

"Ostin," Ian said, "come help me." They rolled the first guard over and handcuffed his hands behind his back, then dragged him inside;

next they handcuffed and dragged in the second one and stuffed both of their mouths with toilet paper. Ostin pulled their magnetic keys from their pockets.

"Got the keys?" Ian asked.

Ostin held them up. "Got 'em."

"Let's go," Ian said.

"Give us some light, McKenna," Ostin said.

"On it."

The four of them followed Ian out into the hallway, pulling the cell door shut behind them.

"Which way?" Ostin asked.

"The guards came from this direction," Ian said.

"How can you tell?" Taylor asked.

"I'm an electric hound dog," Ian said. "People leave electronic imprints when they move."

They ran down the hall toward a service elevator. "Oh, oh," Ian said. "They're coming." Suddenly an alarm went off.

"Monkey butts," Ostin said.

"Here, give me the key." Ian opened the elevator and they all rushed in.

"Go to the second floor. That's the administration level. They won't expect that."

Taylor hit the button. The door shut and the elevator began to move. The elevator hit the second floor and paused but the door didn't open. Suddenly it began moving up again.

"What's it doing?" Abigail asked.

"I don't think we're controlling it anymore," Ostin said.

The elevator climbed all the way to the fourth floor and froze. Ian's head dropped. "We're dead."

"What do you see?" Taylor asked.

"Trouble," Ian said.

The door opened. There were at least fifteen guards standing in front of them with guns drawn. "On your knees!" one shouted. "And put your hands behind your head."

"Taylor?" Ostin asked.

Taylor squinted. "There're too many of them."

Ian sighed and knelt down. The rest followed.

"You are smart," Ian said to Ostin. "That's the closest to freedom anyone here has ever got."

Ostin sighed. "Close only counts in horseshoes and nuclear weapons."

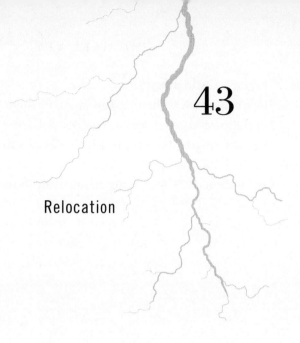

43

Relocation

On the second floor Hatch had been watching the escape attempt unfold on the screens in front of him.

After the teens had been handcuffed and separated, the chief of security reported to Hatch. "The prisoners have been subdued, sir."

"Well done, Mr. Welch," he said. "Return them to their cell. Put the human boy in solitary confinement."

"Yes, sir. Thank you, sir."

Then Hatch's secretary's voice came over his phone. "Your call, sir."

"Thank you." He pushed the button again. "This is Hatch."

The British voice sounded annoyed. "What do you need?"

"The BA money has made it into all the accounts. We're filtering it through Switzerland and the Cayman Islands. Our Glow has been withdrawn from Dubai and relocated to our Italian compound. We're ready to commence evacuation of the Pasadena facility."

"What is the status of the Vey boy?"

"I've given him two days to pick a side. He's got eighteen hours left."

"And what side will he pick?" The voice was monotone but still managed to convey the intended threat.

"He'll be with us. He has too much to lose."

"I hope you're right. About the relocation, the board is rightfully concerned that you follow protocol. We want no attention drawn to our move."

"Of course. We'll evacuate the children first, then we'll drug and transport the GPs to our Lima facility. Our 727 will be sufficient for that. We'll destroy all records and quietly renovate the building. We already have the city building permits, and our leasing company has legitimate tenants ready to occupy the facility—a private school."

"Very well. Then I'll see you in Rome in a few months."

"I look forward to it. After the last month, it will be nice to relax a few days."

"Just don't plan on too much of it. We're ready to launch phase two."

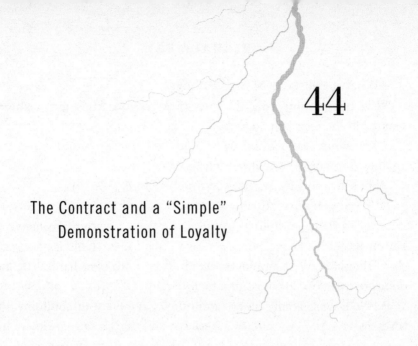

44

The Contract and a "Simple"
Demonstration of Loyalty

It was evening of my second day in captivity when two guards came to my room. I was lying on my bed playing a video game when the door opened and they stepped inside, followed by Nichelle. I hated seeing her. Actually, I hated her. She always made me tic.

"Time to go," the first guard said, not as politely as the last time they'd come for me.

"Where are we going?" I asked.

"Dr. Hatch has requested your presence."

"Let me get my shoes on." I put on my shoes, then walked out of my room with one guard in front and one in back, with Nichelle walking at the rear guard's side. They walked right past Hatch's secretary and into his office. Hatch was at his desk. He stood as I entered.

"How are you, Michael?" he asked.

"Tired," I said.

"I would imagine. You've had enough on your mind to cause anyone insomnia." He turned to the guards. "You may go."

"Yes, sir," the guards said in unison.

To my surprise he said to Nichelle, "You too."

Nichelle looked at me. "Just try something," she said.

"Nichelle, that's really not necessary."

She glared at me before following the guards out of the room. Hatch shook his head. "Sorry about that. What Nichelle lacks in tact she makes up for in unpleasantness." His expression hardened. "So, down to business. Have you come to a decision?"

My tics were acting up and I tried not to blink but couldn't help it. "Yes, sir."

"And that is?"

"If you'll free my mother and my friends, I'll join you."

He just stared at me until the silence became uncomfortable. "You know I can't release Taylor," he finally said. "She's too dangerous. She knows too much."

"But that was our deal."

"No, you'll recall that our deal was that I'm giving her to you. A much better scenario, I'd say."

I just looked at him. That *was* what he'd said.

"I'm not trying to be difficult, Michael. But Taylor brought this on herself—and you. She'll have to live with the consequences. But, with you joining us, I think she'll come around and before too long she'll join us back in the house. And, she'll be yours."

I couldn't help but wonder how he planned to ensure that.

"But, of course, your mother will be set free immediately, as will Ostin and Jack. We'll fuel up Jack's car, give him some traveling money, and he can drive back home."

"What proof do I have of that?"

"What proof would you have? Ostin can call you as soon as they're on the road. And we'll let you talk to your mother." He leaned forward, extending his hand. "Do we have an agreement?"

I slightly hesitated, then stepped forward and took his hand. "Yes, sir." We shook. Then he sat back in his chair.

"Very well." He pushed a piece of paper toward me. "I'd like you to sign this document, to convey your resolve."

I leaned over the desk and looked at the form.

I, Michael Vey, do hereby enroll and subscribe as a full member of the Elgen Academy and promise to do whatever is required of me to promote and advance the academy's work, mission, and objectives as long as my services are required.

X

I thought it was peculiar that he wanted me to sign something. It's not like anything signed by a fifteen-year-old would be legally binding.

"You may use my pen." Hatch held out to me a beautiful, gold-plated pen inset with rubies. I read the statement again, then signed beneath it. I pushed the document back to him with the pen.

"Keep the pen," he said. "A memento of a very special occasion."

He leaned back and examined the document. "'I, Michael Vey, do hereby enroll and subscribe as a full member of the Elgen Academy and promise to do whatever is required of me to promote and advance the academy's work, mission, and objectives as long as my services are required.' That's quite a commitment you've just made." He set it back down and looked into my eyes. "Quite a promise. Unfortunately, promises are broken all the time. Like you, I need some proof. I need to see what's behind your commitment."

"What proof would you have?" I asked, using his words back at him.

"Simple. We're going to take a little test. Fortunately, unlike Mr. Poulsen's biology class, this is one you don't have to study for." He stood and walked around his desk. "This way, please."

I followed him out of his office. The guards saluted him, then fell back to my side, Nichelle trailing behind all of us. My mind was reeling. *What kind of test would this be?*

We went to the service elevator near the back of the building and all five of us entered. One of the guards pushed the button for D. I frowned. We were going back down to the level where I had found Taylor. The elevator stopped and the door opened. Hatch stepped out and I followed him. We walked down the hall to the end of the corridor, past the cell with Ian and the girls. We turned left, then left again, and walked on to a metal door at the end of the hall. A sign above the door read BLOCK H. There was another guard standing by the door and he pulled open the door as we approached, exposing a long, cavernous room with bare white walls. I followed Hatch inside.

In the center of the room was a chair bolted to the floor with a man in an orange GP jumpsuit sitting in it. The man's arms and legs were clamped to the chair by metal straps, like an electric chair, and a metal brace circled around his neck below his electric vocal collar, holding him erect. He couldn't move if he wanted to. The man in the chair had a hood over his head that fell to his chin.

"So, Michael, you've told me that you're now one of us and you've promised, as a full member of the academy, to do whatever is required to promote and advance the cause of our revolution. Here's your opportunity to show me that you mean what you say." He gestured toward the man. "Here's your test."

I looked at the man, then back at Hatch. "I don't understand. What's my test?"

Hatch walked up to the bound man and pulled off his hood. The man in the chair was not a man at all—it was Wade. "Simple, Michael. Electrocute him."

I looked at Wade as his eyes grew wide with fright. Suddenly he screamed out, "Please, no!" His outburst was followed by a scream of pain as blue-yellow electricity arced from his collar. Hatch shook his head in disgust. "Unless he decides to do it to himself."

I stared at Hatch, blinking like crazy. "How does killing Wade advance the work of the academy?"

"That is not yours to question," he said. "You committed to obey, now do as you're told. As you promised."

"I won't do it," I said.

Hatch sighed. "Michael, let me explain this better." He motioned to a large screen that hung down from the corner of the room like a stalactite. "Clark, turn on the monitor please. Set it to channel 788." The guard pushed several buttons and the monitor lit up. Hatch took the remote from the guard and turned to me. "For your amusement, we'll call this the Mommy Channel."

An image materialized on the screen of a frail, beaten-looking woman, huddled in the corner of a cell. It took me a moment to recognize who it was. My heart raced.

"Mom!"

She looked up at the screen as if she could hear me.

"Mom, it's me, Michael!" I shouted.

"She can't hear you," Hatch said. "Or see you." He stepped closer to Wade, lightly jostling the remote in his hand. "You have a choice, Michael. I was very clear about that choice. It's time you learned this important life lesson: You do as you promise or those you love suffer.

"See the silver box on the far end of the cell? It is connected to this remote in my hand." He pushed a button on the remote and a light on the silver box began blinking. "I have just armed the capacitor. If I push this button right here, it will release about a thousand amps into the cage. Enough to kill your mother." He looked into my eyes, weighing the effect his words had on me. "Or maybe not. It might just prove remarkably painful. As you know, the human body can be so unpredictable. Whether we discover its lethality is up to you. So, right now, you can punish GP Seven Sixty-Five or punish your mother. It's your choice."

I stood there looking at the screen, my body trembling. Through the corner of my eye I could see Wade shaking as well. "It's not my choice," I said. "It's not my choice to decide who lives or dies."

"It might not be a fair choice, but it most certainly is your choice."

I just stood there.

"Michael," Hatch said gently, "you said you were with us. You signed a binding document that confirmed your commitment. Were you lying to me?"

"You didn't say I'd have to kill someone."

"No, I didn't. In fact, I wasn't specific at all, was I? And that's the point. I demanded your allegiance, whatever that requires. And right now, this is what your allegiance requires." He folded his arms at his chest. "Or shall I push the button?"

I looked down at Wade. Sweat was beading on his forehead and his underarms were soaked through all the way down his sides. I walked to his side, then put my hand on his shoulder. He shuddered at my touch.

Hatch nodded. "Good choice, Michael. Now give him everything. That would be the merciful thing."

I looked down. Tears were welling up in Wade's eyes. I still stood there, frozen.

After a minute Hatch looked at his watch. "We haven't all day. You have thirty seconds before I make the choice for you. Who will live? A good, loving mother or a juvenile delinquent who will never amount to beans? What would your mother say?"

Something about what Hatch said resonated through me. I looked back up at the monitor, at my mother lying there alone and scared, then at Hatch, the man who had put her there.

"What would my mother say?" I said. My eyes narrowed. "My mother would say that she'd rather die than see her son become a murderer." I took my hand off Wade, then lunged at Hatch. Pain seared through my entire body, buckling my knees. I fell to the ground screaming.

Hatch took a deep breath to regain his composure. He kicked me, then walked to the door. "Thank you, Nichelle. Buy yourself a new bauble."

"Thank you," she said.

From the doorway Hatch looked back at me. "I'm so disappointed in you, Michael. You are a liar and an oath breaker." He turned to the guards. "Take him to Cell 25. Then have Tara report to my office." He looked back at me. "Unlike you, Mr. Vey, I don't break my promises. But I will break you. And here's my promise. You will never disobey me again. By the time I'm done with you, you'll beg for the privilege of electrocuting your own mother." He turned to the guard. "Take him."

My heart filled with fear. When Hatch was gone I asked, "What's Cell 25?"

Nichelle smiled. "Terror."

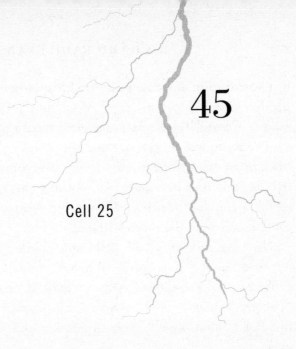

45

Cell 25

Cell 25 was located at the end of the first corridor of the GP prison, the first floor below ground and one floor above level D, where Hatch had taken me for my "test." Even from the outside the cell looked different than the rest. The door was gray-black and broader than the others with a large, hydraulic latch. There were peculiar hatches and hinges and a panel of flashing lights.

The guards opened the door with a key, pushed me inside, and the thick, metal door sealed the world shut behind me. The room was completely dark except for my own soft glow. There was no sound but my heart pounding in my ears. I wondered what Nichelle had meant by "terror." I found out soon enough.

It was maybe an hour after they'd thrown me in the cell that I was suddenly filled with fear like I had never felt before. Something evil was crawling around in the cell. Even though I couldn't see it, I was sure of it. Something frightening beyond words. I was so paralyzed with fear I struggled to inhale the dry, hot air. *Venomous snakes? Spiders? Thousands of spiders?* "What's in here?" I shouted.

The room was dead space and there was no sound, not even the trace of an echo from my screaming. Trembling, I reached out and felt the cell wall but there was nothing there, just smooth, warm metal. I couldn't see or hear anything, but somehow I just knew something was in the room with me.

"Let me out of here!" I screamed, pounding on the walls. I screamed until I was hoarse. When I couldn't stand it anymore, I probed a corner of the cell with my foot. "It's nothing," I told myself. "There's nothing's here." I slowly slunk down in the corner, my arms huddled around myself. "There's nothing here," I repeated over and over.

I tried to force my mind to think of other things but the fear was too powerful. I began screaming again. *Black widow spiders. Crocodiles. No, sharks. Great whites.* "No, that's impossible," I told myself. "I'm not in water." And yet the absurd was somehow believable. What was going on in my head?

Peculiarly, about an hour after my panic had begun, the feelings vanished as suddenly as they had come, as if I'd suddenly awoken from a nightmare. Not all my fear was gone, of course, but the extreme aspect of it had vanished.

After a few minutes I slowly stood, venturing out of my corner. I felt my way around the cell. There was no bed or even a mat, just a slick concrete floor and a porcelain toilet in one corner of the room. I went back to the same corner and sat down again. I wondered how long I would survive.

The next few days (or what I thought were days, since I was quickly losing track of time) passed in pain and discomfort. The cell's temperature was usually high enough that I was covered with my own sweat, then it would abruptly drop until I was shivering with cold.

Food, when I got it, was also served sporadically. The food came to me through a hatch door that did not allow light into the cell, as the door on my side only opened after the outer door was sealed. I guessed that my feeding schedule was irregular to throw off my body's natural sense of timing. The food stunk, literally, and the first time I ate it I spit it out. I don't know what it was, I couldn't see it, but the texture and smell reminded me of canned dog food. I was given no water and as I began to thirst I realized that my only option was to drink from the toilet, which I'm sure was their intent from the beginning.

Then there was the sound—a consistent, loud, electronic beep that began shortly after my first panic attack and chirped every thirty seconds without cease. The sound began to occupy my sleep and dreams and eventually became incredibly painful as it filled my every thought. I had read about tortures like this before, like the water torture, where a single drop of water falls consistently on a bound man's head. They say that after a while the tiny drop begins to feel like a sledgehammer. I believed it. After several days of the sound my head felt like it might explode.

What made it even more unbearable was the uncertainty of it all. I was kept in the dark, figuratively as well as literally. Were they ever going to release me? Would it be minutes or days or years? I had no idea. I thought of Hatch's "promise." *You will never disobey me again. By the time I'm done with you, you'll beg for the privilege of electrocuting your own mother.* I wondered if he was right. Could one be so physically and emotionally broken that he no longer cared about anyone or anything except survival? I didn't want to find out.

Intermingled with my terror and pain were thoughts of my mother. On the screen she had looked so small and frail. I doubted that she could have survived the shock if Hatch had followed through with his threat. Had he pushed the button or not? The thought of it filled me with both hate and guilt. I wished that he had just killed me instead. Didn't he say that I was dying anyway?

I realized that the panic attacks I was having seemed to be on a type of schedule and I wondered if it was possible that Hatch and his scientists had actually perfected a process to generate fear.

Thirteen meals had passed. (That's how I kept track of time.) My fear attack had just ended and I lay on the ground, drenched in sweat and trembling. I heard myself mumbling, "I can't do it anymore. You win, I can't do it anymore." I felt the watch on my arm, the one my mother had given me. I couldn't read the words in the dark but I didn't have to. I'm sure Hatch had let me keep the watch to keep my mind on my mother. Nothing Hatch did was by accident and it certainly wasn't out of kindness. I began to cry. "I'm sorry I failed you, Mom."

I had lost weight and it felt as if every cell of my body ached. If they meant to break me, they knew exactly what they were doing. Of course they did. They were scientists.

As I lay on the ground, I noticed something very peculiar. In the corner of the room there was a dim light. The metal pipe that ran from the wall to the toilet began to lightly glow, not consistently, but intermittently. *It's happening*, I thought. *I'm losing my mind. I'm hallucinating.* I looked away. A moment later I looked back. The pipe was still glowing, though slightly brighter now. I crawled over to the toilet and cautiously put out my hand to touch it. The moment I touched it, it went dark. Then a feeling came over me that cannot be accurately described to anyone who hasn't felt it. I felt pure peace. It felt as if some power were pulsing through my body, pushing out the fear and hurt and replacing it with perfect tranquility. I felt as comfortable as if I were lying on my own bed at home listening to my music. Even the constant chirp sounded pleasant.

I let go of the pipe and my pain, exhaustion, and fear instantly returned. I quickly grabbed it again. Maybe I was losing my mind, but if holding on to a toilet pipe could make me feel good, I was going to hold on to that pipe.

Suddenly I understood. The cell with Taylor, Ian, Abigail, and McKenna was somewhere on the floor below mine. Abigail could take away pain. Abigail must be touching a pipe that ran between the two cells, conducting her power to me, much the same way I had shocked Cody Applebaum in school detention. But how would she even know I was here?

She didn't. Ian did. Ian had probably been watching me all along.

He knew I was here. Was it possible that he, Abigail, and McKenna were working together to save me? They didn't even know me. Yet it made sense. McKenna could have made the pipe glow to lead me to it. My eyes watered and I began to cry. It was not the first time since I'd been placed in the cell—but the first time that I had cried for something other than pain. For the first time in days I had hope that I might survive.

From that point on, whenever things got bad, I went to the pipe and grasped it and immediately the pain ceased. During the "terror sessions" my invisible friends were always waiting. I deduced that Ian must be able to see when and how they were torturing me.

I was filled with gratitude for my unseen friends and I learned that harboring an emotion as powerful as gratitude has power of its own. My greatest fear was that they might be discovered and moved to a different cell. I knew Hatch and his guards were watching me, so I was discreet in how I held to the pipe. I usually pretended to be throwing up or drinking.

Actually, their discovery was my second-greatest fear. My greatest fear was that my mother was dead. Not even Abigail's power could take that pain from my heart.

46

Lack of Trust

I felt as if I'd been in Cell 25 for weeks when I heard the inner tumblings of the lock on the door. There was a slide of metal and the door opened and I saw the first light since I'd been incarcerated. As usual, I was lying on the ground, and I instinctively pushed myself way away from the door, covering my face from the harsh light. "Stay away," I mumbled.

Nichelle walked into the cell escorted by two of the guards. "It reeks in here. It smells like the giraffe house at the zoo." She started laughing. "He smells as bad as Zeus." One of the guards laughed.

She took a few more steps toward me and looked down at me. "Hatch wants you. Get up."

Hatch. His name alone filled me with terror. I rolled over to my knees and elbows and tried to stand but I couldn't.

"I said get up!" she shouted.

"I can't," I replied, my forehead pressed to the ground.

After a moment Nichelle nodded to one of the guards and he walked over to lift me. He stopped before he touched me and looked at Nichelle.

Nichelle squatted down in front of me. "If you shock him, we'll keep you in here for the rest of your short, miserable life. Do you understand?"

"I won't shock him."

"Why would I believe you? You're a liar."

"Liar or not, I can't stand up."

She looked at me for a moment, then said to the guard, "Help him."

The guard put his hands under my armpits and easily lifted me. When I was on my feet he let go of me and I collapsed back to the ground, crying out with pain. Nichelle rolled her eyes. "Carry him."

The guard lifted me again and this time he put his arm around me, carrying more of my weight than I was, as I staggered down the hall to the elevator. As we walked I sucked in the cool air, breathing it in like water. In spite of my pain, I can't tell you how luxurious it felt.

In the elevator I noticed Nichelle pushed the D button and I silently groaned. Hatch was back in the dungeon. *Another test*, I thought. *If he asked me again to electrocute Wade would I do it?*

I tried to think of better possibilities. Perhaps I was being reassigned to the dungeon. Maybe with Ian and the two girls. I wanted to see them badly. I wanted to hug them and thank them. The dungeon would be a Caribbean vacation compared to Cell 25.

My hope dissipated as we walked past their cell, back to the room at the end of the hall. Back to block H, the room where Wade had been bound and where I had "failed" my test. The room's light was on and the door was partially open. The guard carried me inside.

There were three chairs in the room and Taylor and Ostin were strapped into two of them. *Please, not them*, I thought.

I don't know what I looked like. In Cell 25 it was too dark to even see my reflection in the toilet, but, based on Taylor's reaction, I must have looked pretty awful. She gasped when she saw me.

"Michael," she said.

"Oh, buddy," Ostin said. "What have they done to you?"

"Shut up," Nichelle said. "Save your pity for yourselves."

The guard dropped me in a plastic chair and then fastened my hands and feet with plastic ties. A large plastic belt was drawn around my waist and fastened in back. It was overkill. I couldn't have even stood up under my own power. Only my tics seemed strong.

"What's going on?" I asked.

"Shut up," Nichelle said. "No talking."

"You're a toad-face," Ostin said.

Nichelle immediately tried to reach him with her powers, forgetting that she had no effect on him. She walked over and smacked him on the head. "You're fat."

"Yeah, well you're ugly, and I can lose weight."

She sneered and slapped him on the side of the head again.

"Ow," Ostin said.

"Keep your mouth shut, butterball."

About five minutes later Hatch walked into the room. He said to me darkly, "I trust your accommodations were to your satisfaction."

My head felt like it weighed a ton and I just sat there, staring at my feet.

"Look at me when I'm talking to you!" he shouted.

It took effort, but I raised my head and looked into his eyes. Hatch wore his dark glasses and a strange-looking helmet. I turned my head to one side and my neck cracked. I looked back at Hatch, "What did you do to my mother?"

"Twenty-six days in Cell 25 and still defiant. If I wasn't so disappointed in you I'd be impressed. Be assured that she's paid dearly for your choices, but she survived the shock, if that's what you're getting at. And I'm pleased. I didn't want to discard my best card yet. Though, as you see, even without her, the deck is stacked in my favor."

He turned and looked at Taylor. "Don't waste your time trying to reboot me, Miss Ridley. You have little enough of it left." He tapped his helmet. "Those electric waves of yours won't make it through this very special helmet your sister helped us create." He smiled at her smugly. "Perhaps you're wondering how we came up with this."

"I don't care," Taylor said.

"You should, it's quite interesting. When I was in my early twenties I did some work for the NSA—the National Security Agency. The NSA building in Maryland is completely wrapped in copper. It keeps prying spy satellites from listening inside. This helmet employs the same principle."

"Still not interested," Taylor said.

"On the other hand, for Mr. Vey, this copper helmet is the worst thing I could be wearing." He leaned close to me. "If he could get his little hands on this he could fry my head like a Sunday roast. That's why we have him strapped down to a plastic chair." He smiled at me. "I do hope you're comfortable."

"What are you going to do?" I asked. "Kill us?"

"Just some of you. Let me be clear about this. I want you, Michael. I want you to join us. I want to understand your power. But you're not cooperating." He stepped away from me. "Like you, during your vacation in Cell 25, I've had a lot of time to think about things. I've decided that our problem here is really just a matter of credibility. You, Michael, won't cooperate because you lack trust. Trust that I will do what I have threatened to do. I'd like to show you otherwise. Like they say in the old movies, I need to show you that *I mean business.*

"So we're going to have a demonstration with a couple of your friends. Proof of what I'll do to your mother if you choose not to cooperate." He took a step toward the door. "You may come in now." He turned back to me. "Michael, I think you remember our friend Zeus."

Zeus walked into the room. His long, oily blond hair was partially concealed beneath a copper helmet similar to the one Hatch wore. The last time I saw him he'd shocked my mother. I desperately wanted to get my hands on him.

"You creep," I said.

"The name is Zeus," he said.

"Your name is Zeus," Taylor said. "Like the Greek god?" She rolled her eyes. "Puhleeeeeze."

I could see Taylor trying to get to him but she couldn't.

"I told you, Miss Ridley, you can't get through our helmets," Hatch said. "And as far as the name, that's not the only similarity my boy here has with his Greek counterpart, is it Michael? Michael's seen a demonstration of his gift. Like the Greek god, Zeus also throws lightning bolts." He smiled at us. "So, Michael, to put it bluntly, Zeus is going to fry your friends."

"You won't do that," I said.

"There you go," Hatch said, flourishing his hand. "Lack of trust. You've just proved my point. Yes, I will do that."

"But you need them."

"Wrong again. The truth is I'm only annoyed by your chubby little friend and, frankly, Miss Ridley isn't really of as much value to us alive as we thought she'd be. Fortunately, we have a carbon copy of her, so she is quite expendable. Our research team thinks an autopsy will prove most valuable. We've never dissected a Glow before; it could help the cause immensely." He turned to Taylor. "Did you ever dissect a frog in science class?" He smiled. "Of course you did. Now you're the frog and some parts of you will be kept in little jars."

Taylor looked pale, like she might throw up.

"I'll give you whatever you want," I said.

Hatch looked at me, his eyes narrowed with contempt. "You had that chance twenty-six days ago. Maybe now you'll learn that, unlike you, I am a man of my word. We'll discuss a new deal after my demonstration."

He walked toward the door. "So, if you'll pardon me, I think I'll leave." He looked at Ostin. "I hate the smell of burnt butter."

"You're a psycho!" Ostin shouted at Hatch.

Hatch grunted. "Little man, do you really think you could say anything that I would find remotely hurtful? It's like being insulted by a slug. You are a donkey among thoroughbreds. How sad that there is nothing even vaguely special about you. You're just so . . . average."

"No he's not," Taylor said. "He's brilliant. He's a member of the Electroclan."

Hatch grinned. "The Electroclan. That's almost comical." His expression darkened. "Too bad you got in the way of the big boys, Ostin, or you could still be home with mummy and daddy eating pizza. Good-bye."

Hatch turned to Zeus. "When you're done cooking our friends, call the guards and have Vey returned to Cell 25 to contemplate the consequences of his choices." He looked at the guards. "You might want to wait outside. Zeus is very powerful but not always accurate. Come with me, Nichelle."

Nichelle smiled darkly at Taylor. "I'll miss you so much," she said sarcastically, then she followed Hatch out. The guards followed her and shut the door behind them, leaving the four of us alone. A wicked smile crossed Zeus's face. "All right, kiddies, it's playtime."

Taylor said, "Why are you doing this? You're one of us."

"I'm not one of you."

"You could be," I said. "You could join the Electroclan."

"What's that," he said laughing. "Your club? That's like booking a ticket on the *Titanic* after it hit the iceberg."

"What's your real name?" Taylor asked.

He turned to her. "Zeus."

"What's your first name?"

"Zeus."

"Your last name?"

"It's Zeus, Zeus, Zeus. First, last, middle, that's it."

"You really think you're going to kill us?" Ostin said. "Dude, you're like fifteen."

"Shut up," he said.

"No," I said. "He's right. Think about it."

"Yeah, think about this." He raised his hands and a quick burst of blue electricity arced between them. He stepped toward me. "Like that, electric boy?"

It was obvious that his electricity was different than mine. Mine came from within my body, while his seemed confined to the out-side. I wondered how much he had to give. I, on the other hand, couldn't even stand under my own power.

He turned back around. "So who wants to go first? It's usually ladies before gentlemen, or maybe that doesn't apply to executions." He walked over to Taylor. "Does it?"

"Go ahead," Taylor said.

He touched her cheek. "It's a shame you didn't decide to join us. We could have had some fun. We're going to rule the world, you know."

"Why would you want to do that?" Ostin asked.

"I thought you were supposed to be smart," Zeus said. "Oh, you have no powers at all. Except eating." He laughed.

"Hey," Ostin said. "Before you fry me, tell me something. I mean, unless they don't trust you with the scientific stuff."

Zeus looked annoyed. "What?"

"I can't figure out how Hatch made that helmet work. I mean, the science of it doesn't make sense. Why doesn't the copper actually conduct the electricity and amplify Taylor's electromagnetic waves? Is there like a radio converter inside it?"

"It's just a helmet, doughboy."

"No, there's got to be something inside it. You probably just don't know that much about electricity."

Zeus's face turned red. "I'm made of electricity, idiot. It's just a stupid helmet."

"It couldn't be. You must not have examined it. There's got to be a little electric converter inside, maybe a little black pad with some circuit board. Did you notice some wires?"

"There's not a stupid black pad inside—there's no wires! It's just a copper helmet, like a football helmet made of metal. Look, chubster." He started to pull off his helmet but noticed Taylor, who was looking a little too eager. He stopped. "Oh, I see. Well played, fat boy. You almost got me. You're not as dumb as you look. Now prepare to fry." He lifted his hands.

"You surprise me, Zeus," Taylor said. "You're obviously really powerful. More powerful than any of us."

He turned to her. "You said it."

"You're named after a god. You could be, like, the ruler of the world."

He dropped his hands to his side. "What's your point?"

She shrugged. "Nothing. I'm just surprised that you're taking orders from Hatch. He should be taking orders from you. He tells you to kill us, you obey like a dog."

Zeus looked confused. "Enough talking." He turned back to Ostin. "You're a nobody. You go first." He again raised his hands.

"Hey, Zits," I shouted. "What kind of electro*wimp* picks on kids without powers?"

He turned back to me. "What did you call me?"

"Zits," I said. "Z-I-T-S. Actually, I don't think you even need electric bolts. You could just breathe on us." I looked him in the eyes and smiled. "Seriously, dude, when was the last time you brushed your teeth?"

"Shut up!"

"No, really. Did you eat a diaper?"

"Shut up!" he shouted. He squinted. "Do you know how much I enjoyed guarding your mother? I shocked her at least a dozen times just to watch her squeal."

"Yeah, well you could have just sat next to her and let her smell you. That would have been much worse. I've had hamsters with better hygiene."

"Enough! Don't think I won't electrocute you, Vey!"

Taylor looked at me as if I'd lost my mind. "It's his Tourette's, he can't help it."

"I'm scared, Zits," I said. "You know Hatch would have your head if you did. But here's my promise: after I'm in charge, my first command is to make you my shoeshine boy. You'll be following me around with a towel."

"You'll never be in charge."

"No, that's what Hatch said. You heard him. He wants my power. I'm not kidding, Zits. When Hatch was trying to get me to join you guys, he promised me that you would be my servant."

Zeus looked at me with a worried expression. After a moment he shouted, "Shut up! And stop calling me Zits!"

"I don't think I will. In fact, it's going to be the first rule I make. I'm going to have everyone else call you that."

"I don't care what Hatch says. I'm gonna fry you, Vey."

"Oooh, now I'm really shaking. You don't have enough juice in you to light a flashlight."

"Michael!" Taylor shouted. "Stop it. He's got a temper. I've seen it."

"You should listen to the cheerleader, Vey." He stepped toward me. "You think you're so cool. But you can't shoot electricity like me, can you? You're just a flesh-covered battery."

"And you're a flesh-covered outhouse. You should tie a couple hundred of those car air fresheners around your neck."

"Last warning!" Zeus shouted.

"I'm not kidding, Zits. There are porta-potties with better aromas. Would a little deodorant kill you? What was the last year you took a bath?"

"That's it!" He lifted his arms in front of himself and electricity arced between his fingers. "You're gonna die!"

He pointed his hands toward me, letting loose a storm of crackling blue-white electricity. I surged at that precise moment and the sound of his electricity hitting the field of my electricity was like the crash of two cymbals. The room lit up as bright as a welder's lamp.

To my surprise, I felt absolutely fine. Not only was my surge protecting me, but it wasn't going away either. The longest I had ever held a surge was ten or fifteen seconds, but I wasn't tiring at all. In fact, I was growing stronger. I was absorbing Zeus's electricity. Even the weakness I felt from before was leaving me.

There was so much electricity in the room that all of our hair was standing straight up. I looked over at Taylor. She stared at me in disbelief.

It's not hurting me, I thought.

She nodded.

Can you read my mind?

She nodded again. The electricity in the room had created some kind of bridge.

I can, I heard her say, even though her lips didn't move. Now I could read her thoughts as well.

Zeus could see that his electricity wasn't hurting me and he was getting angrier. He looked like a crazy man, his hands raised and moving. "Burn, Energizer!"

The foul stench of burning plastic filled the room. I looked down to see that my chair was melting. The plastic ties that the guard used to bind my wrists and legs had melted through and the vinyl band around my waist had melted as well. I was free.

I looked back up and smiled at Zeus. Rage burned in his eyes. He clenched his teeth and intensified his assault. But the force of his electricity only added to mine. I was getting stronger, and, from his appearance, he was growing weaker. Sweat was beading on his forehead and his breathing was heavy.

My skin began to glow a pale white, growing brighter and brighter until I was lit up like an incandescent lightbulb.

"Aaaargh!" he shouted in exhaustion, and the electricity stopped. He flicked his hands as if his fingers had been burned. "Okay, then I'll burn her!"

He turned toward Taylor.

"No you won't," I said, standing up. He turned back to look at me. I was now glowing brighter than the overhead lights. I lifted my arms and held my palms out toward Zeus. "Try this." I pulsed. A bright flash of light burst from me like a shock wave and Zeus screamed out as he was thrown against the wall. Taylor's and Ostin's chairs also flipped sideways. Zeus slid to the floor unconscious.

I ran to Taylor's side. "Are you okay?"

It took her a moment to answer. "I think so. I can't get loose."

I grabbed the plastic ties on her hands and surged and they melted in my hands. She reached down and unfastened her legs. Then I ran to Ostin. He was lying still. I knelt down by him. "Ostin?"

He wasn't breathing.

"Buddy!" I put my head to his chest. His heart had stopped.

"Ostin!" I shouted. I burned off his bands and began to administer CPR. "His heart stopped," I shouted.

Taylor came to my side.

"Come on, Ostin," she said.

I put my ear to his chest. Nothing. Tears began to fill my eyes. "You can't die, buddy. You can't."

I continued pressing his chest but nothing I did seemed to have any effect.

Then Taylor said, "Shock him."

"What?"

"Shock his heart. That's what doctors do when a heart stops."

I put my hand over his heart and pulsed. His whole body shook. I put my head to his chest, but there was nothing. "Ostin, buddy. Hang in there."

I put my hand on his heart again. "Surge." His body shook again. Suddenly his body trembled. I put my head on his chest. "His heart's beating!"

"Yeah!" Taylor said.

A moment later Ostin groaned and his eyes opened. He looked at me, then said, "That hurt."

I exhaled in relief. "Oh, man, that was close. Don't ever scare us like that again."

"Don't ever shock me like that again."

Zeus started to come to, groaning lightly. Taylor walked over and pulled off his helmet, throwing it behind her. He looked up at her. "Where am I?"

"You're on the ground," she said. He began to lift his head but Taylor squinted and knocked him back down. "Don't even think about it. And you better behave or Michael's going to finish you."

Ostin sat up, rubbing his chest. "How did you create a shock wave?"

"I'm not sure," I said. "I think Zeus's electricity made me stronger."

Ostin smiled. "Just like I was theorizing, you can absorb electricity."

Taylor pointed to a camera. "Hey, guys, whatever we're doing, we better hurry. We're being watched."

"No," Ostin said. "The light's off. Michael must have blown the camera with his surge."

"Still, Taylor's right," I said. "We've got to move fast. There are guards outside the door."

"What should we do with him?" Taylor asked, looking at Zeus.

Zeus looked up at me fearfully. *Don't hurt me.*

I heard his voice clearly but his mouth hadn't moved. There was still enough electricity in the room that I could read minds without touching.

"Please don't hurt me," he said aloud.

"Why shouldn't I?" I asked.

He just stared at me, unable to come up with a reason.

I leaned close to him. "I'll tell you why. Because I'm not you and I'm not Hatch." I leaned in closer. "Think of a number between one and a million."

He looked at me. "What?"

"Think of a number," I said.

Five hundred twenty-six thousand and twelve, he thought.

"Five hundred twenty-six thousand and twelve," I said.

He looked at me in astonishment. "How did you do that?"

"I can read your mind, Zeus. And if you so much as think of shocking one of us, I'll fry you like a chicken nugget. Do you understand?"

He nodded.

"Why are you loyal to Hatch?" I asked.

He didn't answer in his thoughts or otherwise. I guess he didn't know.

"He's worthless," Ostin said. "We can't trust him."

I am worthless, Zeus thought.

Taylor looked at me. *Did you hear that?* she thought.

I nodded. *What has he done?*

Let's find out, Taylor thought. *I'm going in deep.*

Taylor knelt down next to Zeus and put her head against his. We watched as she went through him, like she was reading a book. After several minutes, her expression changed and she sat back up. "I see."

"What is it?" Ostin asked.

Taylor said to Zeus, "When you were a child, did you kill your family in a swimming pool?"

The statement seemed to hit him as powerfully as my shock wave. He began trembling and he covered his face with his hands. "Yes."

"Are you sure about that?" she asked.

He peered up at her. "What do you mean?"

Taylor looked at me and then back at Zeus. "I looked through your memories but I couldn't find a memory of the swimming pool. *Any* swimming pool. I only found what Hatch told you when you were little."

"That's the way Hatch works," I said to Taylor. "He makes people think they're bad so they'll do bad things. Zeus thinks he's evil so he's acting the part. Can you do anything with it?"

Taylor looked at me. "What do you mean?"

"Can you . . . change his mind?"

A smile came to her face. "I've never tried."

Zeus looked back and forth between us. "What are you going to do?"

"You didn't kill your family, Zeus," Taylor said. "I'm guessing that Hatch did, then convinced you that you had done it. Are you willing to let me erase those lies?"

"Can you?"

"I've never done this before, but I'll try." She put her head against his. After about two minutes she moaned a little, then fell back.

"What happened?"

"I think I did it."

Zeus lay there with his eyes closed.

I said, "Zeus, have you ever gone swimming?"

"No."

"Never?"

He shook his head. "I can't. I shock myself in water."

"What happened to your family?"

He looked down. "I'm not sure." His eyes welled up with tears. "Something bad happened to them."

I looked at Taylor. "Good job."

"I don't know why I tried to hurt you," Zeus said.

"It's because Hatch was controlling you," I replied. "But he can't anymore."

He sat there looking confused. "What do I do now?"

"Join the Electroclan. Help us bring this place down."

He looked at me for a moment. Then I heard his thoughts. *I'm with you.* "I'm with you," he said, his voice echoing his thoughts. "What do you want me to do?"

"You were with my mother when they took her. Do you know where she is?"

Zeus shook his head. "They took her to one of the other compounds."

"There are other places like this?" Ostin asked.

"At least four that I know of. They're in other countries and they're bigger."

"Do you know where they are?" I asked.

"There's an office in Rome and a compound in the jungles of Peru. There's at least one in Taiwan." He frowned. "Sorry. That's all I know."

My heart ached. My mother had never seemed so far away. "Who runs the other compounds?" I asked.

"Hatch," Zeus said. "He's like the president. But he answers to the board."

"Then Hatch will have records of the other compounds," Ostin said.

Taylor said, "I don't think Hatch will be eager to share."

"No," I said. "We'll have to take them. But first, we've got to free the others."

Just then the cell door swung all the way open and three guards ran into the room holding machine guns. "Everyone on the ground," the first guard shouted. "Move your—" He stopped mid-sentence. "Move . . . uh."

All three of the guards lowered their guns and looked at each

other as if they'd suddenly forgotten why they had come in. I smiled at
Taylor.

"Zeus," I said.

"No problem."

Electricity arced from Zeus to all three guards. They dropped to
the floor.

"Good job," I said. "Let's tie them up."

We quickly cuffed two of the guards' hands behind their backs.
As I was trying to get the handcuffs on the biggest of the guards, he
suddenly turned on me. He jumped up, lifting me above his head. I
pulsed and he screamed out, dropping me on top of him.

"You okay?" Ostin asked.

"Yeah," I said, climbing off the guard. "He's not." I locked the
guard's hands in cuffs.

Ostin took their utility belts with concussion and smoke grenades
and fastened one of them around his waist.

"We've got to figure out how to get everyone out of here," I said.
"Let's start with Ian and the girls, then we'll get Jack and Wade."

"What about Nichelle?" Taylor asked.

"Ostin, you're the only one she can't affect."

He patted his weapons belt. "I'll take care of her."

"Zeus, while Ostin and I free Ian and the girls, you and Taylor go
to the end of the hallway and make sure no one sneaks up on us."

"What about the cameras in the hall?" Taylor asked.

"We've got to take them out," I said.

"I know how to do it," Zeus said. "When I was eight I was fooling
around and blew one out. Hatch grounded me for an entire week."

"Well, start with that one," I said, pointing to a camera right
outside our door. Zeus reached up and electricity jumped from his
fingers to the camera. The camera's light went off and the camera
froze.

"Nice shootin', Tex," Ostin said.

"Thanks."

"Okay, let's go," I said. "I'll go first. Zeus, you and Taylor behind
me, Ostin, lock the cell then come up behind us."

"On it," he said.

We ran single-file down the hall to Ian and the girls' cell door. Zeus blew out another three cameras as he and Taylor crept to the end of the hallway. Taylor cautiously peered around the corner. "It's clear," she said.

I pounded on the cell door. "Ian. Can you hear me?"

I heard a faint pounding back.

"He sees us."

"How are we going to open it?" Taylor asked.

"Zeus, can you concentrate your electricity and cut through it?"

"No. That's Bryan's gig."

"I know how to open it," Ostin said, winded from running back to us. "You can use your electricity."

"But Ian said it's an air lock," I said. "It doesn't work by electricity."

Ostin smiled. "That's the flaw in their design. The lock is air, but how does the lock get its air?"

I shrugged. "An air tank?"

"Yes, with an electronic valve. While I was locked inside I asked Ian to follow where the hose went. There's an electronic valve above each cell door. If my calculations are right, all you have to do is blow the switch and the air pressure drops."

"He's good," Taylor said.

"Where's the valve?" I asked.

Ostin pointed above the door. "Right about there. A strong enough pulse should knock it out."

It was at least four feet above me. "I need a lift," I said.

"On it." Ostin got down on all fours.

"You sure?" I asked.

"Just do it."

I stepped on his back and reached as high as I could but it still wasn't high enough. "This isn't going to work."

"Wait," Taylor said. "We do this in cheerleading. Come here, Ostin."

Ostin stood.

"Take my hand like this." They locked hands. "Now, Michael, step right there and we'll lift you up."

"You sure you can lift me?"

"Oh yeah, this is how we make our pyramids in cheer."

I stepped on their arms.

"Lift!" Taylor said.

I rose higher than the door. "Awesome." I put my hand flat against the wall above the doorjamb. "Here, Ostin?"

"That's about right."

"Here it goes." I pulsed with all I had. The light next to me flickered.

"Now what?"

"Wait for it," Ostin said.

Suddenly we heard the hiss of escaping air. The door clicked.

"We did it," Ostin said.

Taylor and Ostin let me down and I pushed open the door. Ian, McKenna, and Abigail were standing in the middle of the room waiting for us. Seeing them filled me with strong emotion. I ran up to Abigail and put my arms around her, then McKenna and Ian.

"You guys saved my life," I said.

"You were very brave," Ian said. "Amazingly brave. I don't think I could have survived what you went through."

"We're proud of you," McKenna said. Abigail nodded.

"Thank you. How can I ever repay you?"

"I think you just did," Ian said, looking at the open door.

In the hallway an alarm went off, a bright red strobe accompanied by a deafening, shrill siren. Everyone covered their ears.

"Taylor, Ostin!" I shouted. "Give me another lift!"

They lifted me again. I reached up, grabbed the alarm, and pulsed. The alarm wound down with a sound like a sick cow.

"Thank goodness," Taylor said. "That was annoying."

"Okay, let's make a plan," I said.

As we were talking, Ian was frantically looking around, up and down the ceiling then to the walls. "The guards are collecting," he whispered. "There are two coming down the front hall toward us right now."

"Where?" I asked.

He pointed toward the far wall, moving his finger along with them. "Right there, on the other side of the wall."

"Ian, keep telling us where they are. Taylor, when they get close, reboot them. Zeus, the second you see their gun barrels, blast them with electricity."

"You got it, chief."

I walked out into the corridor with Ian. He was now facing the far cell wall, following the guards' movement. "They're about at the corner," Ian whispered. "Now."

Zeus and I backed against the wall, just at the corner. I saw the glint of metal from two gun barrels and Zeus shot electricity from both hands. Both guards dropped to the ground. "You got 'em," Ian said. "Two guards down."

"Are there any more down here?" I asked.

"Not yet. But there are some moving down the stairwell."

"Let's take care of these two," I said. Zeus and I dragged the two guards into the farthest part of the cell and handcuffed them together to the toilet, then gathered again outside the cell. "We've got to free Jack and Wade and the rest of the GPs."

"There's a problem with that," McKenna said. "They control all the collars from the command center. They could just set them all off and kill everyone."

"Where's the command center?" Ostin asked.

"Fourth floor," Ian said. "Next to the guards' barracks."

"Oh, great," Ostin said. "We've been there."

Ian smiled. "C'mon, Ostin. You didn't want it to be too easy, did you? The honey's always in the center of the hive."

"So we're headed to the fourth floor," I said.

Ostin said, "Trust me, don't take the elevator."

"Then the only way out is the stairwell."

"Which," Ian said, "they're covering."

"Do you know how many guards there are?" I asked.

Ian nodded. "I counted this afternoon and there were twenty-seven. Usually there are thirteen on duty during the day, and the other fourteen are split up between the other two shifts. But they all live here and right now they're all on alert."

"How do you know all this?" Ostin asked.

"I watch everything in the building. It's kept me sane for three years."

Just then the entire floor went black. We could see nothing but the glow of each other.

"They must have cut the power," Ostin said. "That's going to hurt them."

"They have night-vision goggles," Zeus said. "I've seen them run drills."

"Oh," Ostin said. "Then it's going to hurt us."

"No problem," McKenna said. She immediately began to glow, lighting up the corridor.

"That's so cool," Ostin said. "Do you have a boyfriend?"

McKenna smiled.

Taylor rolled her eyes. "Not now, Ostin."

"Sorry. Back to business. There were twenty-seven guards, we've taken out five, so there's twenty-two left," Ostin said. "I'll keep count."

"Ian," I said, "what's going on?"

"Six guards are covering the stairwell. There are three above us; the others are gathering on the second and fourth floor by the elevators."

"Which elevators?"

"Front and back. They might be getting ready to stage another attack. Or they might be waiting for us."

"What about the other electric children?" I asked.

"Hatch has them gathered on two."

"What powers do they have?"

"Quentin can produce a small EMP."

"What's that?" I asked.

"Electromagnetic pulse," Ostin blurted out. "It can knock out radios and stuff."

"Bryan can burn through things. Tara can manipulate emotions . . ."

"Wait," I said. "Can she create fear?"

Ian nodded. "Unfortunately."

"She's the one who was torturing you," Abigail said.

"She's as bad as Nichelle," I said.

Taylor looked at me but said nothing.

"Speaking of which, where is Nichelle?" I asked.

"She's on level two next to Hatch." Ian looked straight up. "Two men just went up top. I think they're getting the helicopter ready."

"I bet Hatch is going to run," I said. "How big is the helicopter?"

"It's pretty big. It will hold Hatch and all the kids. If things go bad, Hatch will probably take them with him."

"Well, things are going to go bad for them," I said. "Let's go." We turned the corner and ran down the next length of hall to the stairwell. Zeus continued down the hallway past the stairwell, blowing out five more cameras, which he could see from their glowing red diodes.

With McKenna's light we could see both elevators from where we stood, one in front of us, the other at the end of the hall—the same elevator Ostin and I had come through when we first entered the building. I could see under the door that the stairwell was still lit and as I opened the door bullets immediately began to fly. I jumped back and I could hear bullets ricocheting inside.

"Where exactly are they?" I asked Ian.

Ian looked up and down. "They're on floors one, two, and four. There are six of them."

"What are they doing? I mean, what are their positions?"

"Two of them are coming down the stairs. The rest are leaning over the railings with guns."

"Taylor, do you think you could reboot them all at once?"

"I'll try."

"I'll open the door," Abigail said.

"Ready?" I asked.

Taylor nodded. She put her hands on her temples. "Go."

Abigail pulled open the door and this time there was no gunfire. I slid my hand inside and grabbed the railing and pulsed with all of my power. There was a loud chorus of screams, and I could hear guns and men falling down the stairs.

"You got four of them," Ian said. "One of them crawled out of the well onto the second floor, and the other ran back out on the fourth."

"How bad are the four?"

"They're not moving."

"Eighteen left," Ostin said.

"Let's move," Zeus said.

"How many are on the next floor up?"

Ian looked back and forth. "Three."

"Near the stairwell?"

"No. That's the GP level; they're guarding the prisoners." He cocked his head. "Wait, there's some motion on the third floor."

"The kids?" Taylor asked.

"Maybe. I'm having trouble seeing through them. Nichelle must be near."

"Let's move up to the next floor." We all started to climb the stairwell. Suddenly I stopped. *It's hopeless.* I thought. *You're leading them to their deaths. Surrender now.*

"What are you doing?" Zeus asked.

"It's no good," I said. "This isn't going to work."

"What?" Taylor said.

"We can't make it," I said. "We'll never make it out of here. They're going to kill us."

"Stop talking that way," Taylor said.

"No, he's right," Zeus said. "It's hopeless."

Taylor's eyes flashed. "No," she said, "it's Tara." She looked back. "Abigail, take Michael's and Zeus's hands. Quick."

Abigail ran up half a flight. The instant she touched my hand the fear left. "What happened?" I asked.

"It was Tara," Taylor said. "My sister."

"Tara's your sister?" I asked.

"She's my twin. I'll tell you about it later."

"You have a twin?" Ostin asked.

"I can handle her," Taylor said. She put her hands on her temples and concentrated. A scream echoed down the stairwell. "Stop it, Taylor!" Tara shouted.

"You stop it!" Taylor shouted back. "Leave my friends alone."

"Your friends are going to die."

"No they're not. Why are you helping Hatch? You're better than that."

"Dr. Hatch is better. He's doing the right thing."

"Hatch is evil. He killed your parents."

"They weren't really my parents."

"You don't really believe that. Think for yourself, Tara."

"You can't change the world without casualties."

"You're saying everything he's brainwashed you with. What do you believe?"

"You're the brainwashed one."

"Hatch told you that too, didn't he?"

Tara didn't answer.

"C'mon, Tara. You're better than that. Join us."

"I'm not one of you. I'm special. I have special abilities."

"You do, Tara. And you used those special abilities to hurt that man on the motorcycle. What good have you ever used them for?"

"That man on the motorcycle was just human."

"I'm human, Tara. And so are you. Would you kill me if Hatch told you to?"

She didn't answer.

"Would you?"

"You can keep pecking in the dirt, Taylor. But I'm not a chicken. I'm an eagle."

Then there was silence.

"She went back inside," Ian said.

I touched Taylor's shoulder. "I didn't know that you had a sister."

Taylor's face bent in anger. "I don't."

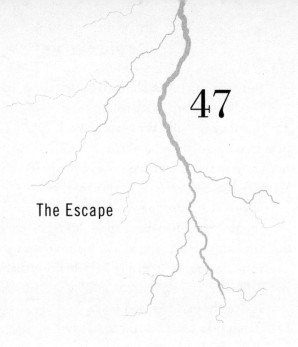

47

The Escape

We cautiously crept up to the GP level: me and Zeus in front, followed by Ostin, Ian, and Taylor, with McKenna and Abigail bringing up the rear. The cameras inside the stairwell were panning back and forth like animals, heads up, watching for danger.

"Zeus, take those things out," I whispered.

"On it."

One by one Zeus blasted the cameras. Their blinking red lights went dark and they drooped, as if hanging their heads in defeat. Then the stairwell itself went dark.

"I think they're trying to make this difficult," Zeus said.

"No problem," McKenna said. She began to glow again.

"McKenna," I said, "stay close to the wall. You make an easy target."

She pressed back against the wall.

"Ian, where are they?" I whispered.

"Three guards on GP, two guards on level one and six on two—three guarding the doors and three with Hatch and the children. They've abandoned the third floor. There are seven guards on four and three scientists. It looks like they're preparing for a battle on the fourth floor."

"They must have guessed that's where we're going," I said.

As we came up to the first level, I whispered to Ian, "How close to the door are they?"

"One's touching it, the other's standing by the elevator."

I put my hand on the door and pulsed. We could hear the guard's gun hit the floor.

"Seventeen," Ostin said.

Suddenly Ian shouted, "Move, move!"

We scattered. Bullets started ripping through the door.

When the gunfire paused, Zeus asked Ian, "Where is he?"

Ian pointed. Zeus shoved his finger through one of the holes and fired back with a bolt of electricity.

"Got him," Ian said. "You are good."

"Thanks," Zeus said.

"Sixteen," Ostin said. "We're forty percent there."

We approached the door to the second floor cautiously. Hatch was on level two and there were the electric children and six guards. Fortunately, with the stairwell cameras dead, they were blind to our movement.

On our way up to the third floor we had to step over the bodies of two of the guards from our first battle. They were still unconscious. McKenna and Abigail put on the guards' bulletproof vests, even though they hung to the girl's knees. Then Ostin and I handcuffed the guards and stripped them of their weapons. Ostin added one of their knives to his utility belt, which looked like a small sword on him. I took one of the rifles and jammed it between the door and the railing to keep the door from being opened behind us.

With each step, Ian looked from side to side as he kept track of everything going on in the building. My biggest fear was that Hatch would attack with Nichelle and the electric children, but with the exception of Tara, they kept their distance.

"He can't risk them," Zeus said to me. "The kids are too valuable. The guards are dispensable."

We stopped on the stairwell between levels three and four. There was another guard's body on the stairs. We stripped the guard of his weapons. We now had more than we could carry, so we dropped them down the stairwell. Ostin put on the guard's bulletproof vest.

Ian groaned. "We've got a problem."

"What?" I said.

"On level four they're setting up inside the door with a flame-thrower."

"A flamethrower?" Ostin asked. "If we open the door that will fill the whole stairwell."

"It's worse, they've even armed the scientists. Superman couldn't make it through that door alive."

I looked back down the stairwell. "I've got an idea. How many guards on three?"

"None, they've abandoned the floor."

"You're sure?"

He looked again. "Yes."

"Ostin, how much smoke does one of these smoke grenades make?"

"Well, if they're like the ones on the Discovery Channel, they'll each produce forty thousand cubic feet of smoke in about thirty-five seconds."

"How many cubic feet is the fourth floor?"

Ostin loved questions like that. "I estimate this place is about forty-four hundred square feet per floor, the ceiling's about eight feet high, so, if my calculations are accurate that's thirty-five thousand, two hundred cubic feet of space per floor."

I grinned. "So twelve smoke grenades would cover it."

"The smoke will be so thick they could chew it like bubble gum. But how do we get the smoke grenades up there?"

"No problem," I said. "Follow me."

We climbed back down to the third level—the floor of the electric children suites. Knowing that the cameras were still live, Zeus went inside alone to take out the cameras, while I explained the plan to everyone else. A minute later Zeus opened the stairwell door on three. "All clear. The cameras are dead."

We all went inside.

Abigail and McKenna each called an elevator. When the elevators arrived they pushed the button for the fourth floor, then stepped back out and held the elevator doors open.

"Everyone ready?" I asked.

"Let's roll," Zeus said.

The elevators began to beep from being detained.

"Ostin?"

"Ready," he shouted from the stairwell.

"Now!"

At my signal Ostin leaned out the stairwell door and threw a concussion grenade up to the fourth floor, while Abigail and McKenna pulled the pins on their smoke grenades, six apiece, threw them into the elevators, and let the elevators go. A half-minute later Ian started to laugh. "It's working." Smoke was filling the fourth level.

"Taylor, now!" I shouted.

Taylor began concentrating, trying to create as much general confusion as she could.

We could hear the guards and scientists above us in a state of panic.

"They're running around like a bunch of chickens with their heads cut off," Ian said. "They're climbing out the windows."

Within five minutes the guards and scientists had completely vacated the floor. We went back to the stairwell. Smoke from our grenades had seeped into the stairwell and Ostin was covering his mouth and nose with his shirt, which he had pulled up through his vest.

"They're all gone," I said.

"Nine guards left," Ostin said.

"How's the smoke?" I asked Ian.

"It's dissipating. Give it a few more minutes."

I climbed past Ostin and tried the door. "It's bolted shut," I said. "Any ideas, Ostin?"

Suddenly the bolt slid and the door opened. Abigail and McKenna were standing there.

I looked at them curiously. "How'd you get up here?"

McKenna smiled. "We took the elevator."

We covered our noses and walked into the room. The smoke had mostly dissipated but its odor hadn't, leaving the room bathed in a pungent, sulfurous smell. Ostin stopped to look at the mounted guns they had facing the door. "Whoa. That's a Barrett M182 anti-matériel rifle retrofitted with a M2A1-7 flamethrower."

"How do you know that?" I asked.

"Internet."

"That's one nasty gun," Ian said, scratching his head.

"Ian, I'm going to release the prisoners," I said. "Will you keep watch?"

"Sure thing."

The command center was located at the front end of the floor, opposite from the stairwell we'd just come through. The room was open with large glass panels so that inside we could still see the stairwell and the rest of our group. There were two large consoles, each about the size of a car's hood, and as loaded with buttons and switches as a jet cockpit.

"Man, this is cool," Ostin said. "I need one of these in my room."

The first console had fourteen small screens stacked on top of each other in five levels, the numbers corresponding with each level of the building except for the GP level, which was missing. The images on these screens, each numbered, were constantly changing, switching between more than a hundred security cameras. However, thanks to Zeus's handiwork, only the first, second, and fourth floor monitors were completely live. Next to the screens was a long row of buttons allowing the operator to select and control any camera on the grounds.

"These are all the building's security cameras," I said to Ostin, pointing to a monitor. "See, there's the main hall, the yard, and the students' suites."

"The students' suites?" Zeus asked, walking into the room. "I completely took the third floor camera out."

"Not all of them. There are still the ones in the bedrooms."

"There are cameras in the bedrooms?" Zeus asked, looking surprised. "I didn't know we were being watched all the time. That's kind of . . . embarrassing."

Unfortunately we had taken out all the cameras in the stairwell, which would have been useful to us now.

Taylor joined us in the command center.

The second console was entirely dedicated to the GP level. There was a bank of twenty-five small screens, each with a number, all surrounding one large, central monitor. On the small screens we could see the GPs. There was little movement in the cells; the prisoners were either lying on their beds or sitting on them. In one room a few were on the ground playing cards.

"Interesting," Ostin said, watching them. "They've created their own sign language."

All but two of the cells were full and most had more than one occupant, some as many as four.

On the main console there were twenty-five panels, each with three buttons, a toggle switch, a sliding switch, and two green diodes. In the center of the console was a microphone.

"Ostin, help me figure this out," I said.

Ostin walked up behind me and looked over the console. "Each screen and panel corresponds with a cell and if you push the red button"—he reached over and pushed the red button on Cell 5 and the video image of two GPs playing cards on the small screen appeared on the central monitor—"you can enlarge the view of a single cell." He pushed the button again and the image zoomed in still more. He did it until we could actually read the cards one of the prisoners held in his hand.

"That's one way to cheat at cards," Zeus said.

"And this toggle switch moves the camera." Ostin pushed the button to the right and the camera panned right. "Man, I wish I had one of these."

He looked at the buttons on the panels below the red one. They were labeled VOX, PL, and EC. EC had a sliding button beneath it. "VOX, of course, is the intercom system. PL . . ." Ostin rubbed his chin as he thought. "Pneumatic locks. The green light tells you that it's locked. And EC would be electric collars. I'm guessing that the sliding button below them would intensify the severity of the shock; the green light signals that it's on."

"Look around for Jack," I said.

"Is that him in 9?" Taylor said, pointing to a small screen. The man in the cell was lying on his back looking up at the ceiling.

I pushed the red button on 9 and the picture came up on the central monitor.

"Push it again," Ostin said.

I pushed the button twice until the man's face took half the screen. "That's him," Taylor said.

"I didn't recognize him with the beard," I said.

"Where's Wade?" Ostin asked. "They're not together?"

I honestly didn't know if Wade was still alive. I hadn't had the chance to tell them anything about what had happened to us. "Keep looking," I said.

"There he is," Ostin said. "In 11."

I pushed the button on 11 and the image filled the screen. Wade wasn't alone. There was another man in the same room.

"He's almost across the hall from Jack," I said.

I pushed the button on 9 again and the picture of Jack came back up on the center screen. I pushed the VOX button on the 9 panel. "Jack."

He suddenly looked up toward the corner of the room.

"Jack, can you hear me?"

He looked around, as if trying to figure out where the voice had come from.

"Jack, it's me, Michael. Are you okay?"

This time he nodded.

"I can't hear anything," I said to Ostin.

"He's not speaking. He still has the electric collar on."

"Right." I looked down at the panel. "Which way should I push it to deactivate it?"

"Try pushing it to the right," Taylor said.

I started to slide the switch to the right. Jack immediately grabbed his collar.

"Stop! Stop!" Ostin shouted.

"Sorry. My bad," Taylor said into the microphone.

"Rules out the right," I said.

I slid the switch to the left. The green light on the panel went off.

"I think you did it," Ostin said.

"Jack," I said into the microphone, "I think we've disarmed your collar. Try speaking."

He looked nervous. "Michael," he said in a raspy voice. A look of relief came across his face. "Thanks. Where are you?"

"We've escaped. We've taken control of the main command center. We're going to unlock all the doors in the prison, but there are still three guards on your floor. We want you to get Wade and help us."

"I don't know where Wade is," Jack said.

"He's close. He's in Cell 11. That's directly across the hall, one cell to the right. I'm going to unlock your door, but don't open it until I tell you to. Taylor, where are the guards?"

"There's one coming down the hall toward 9."

"Hold tight, Jack. Ostin, on my word, unlock Wade's cell."

"Got it."

"He's turning back," Taylor said.

"Okay, Jack, be sure to shut your door so they don't suspect anything."

"Got it."

"Ready. Go." I pushed the PL button and a light on the panel turned green.

"Wait," Jack said, "there's no handle on the inside of the door. I can't open it."

"I got an idea," Ostin said. He walked over to the other console, looked around for a moment, then pushed a button.

"The door just opened a little," Jack said.

"What did you do?" I asked.

"I turned on the hall air conditioner and created negative air—"

"That was smart," Taylor said, cutting him off.

"Thanks."

"Okay, where's the guard, Taylor?"

"Still on the other end of the hall."

"Ostin, open Cell 11."

"Got it."

"Okay, Jack. Go. Fast."

Jack pried open his cell door, stepped out into the corridor, pulled his door shut, then pushed in the door at Cell 11. I hit the red button on 11 and the image took full screen. We watched the reunion. Wade stood as Jack entered and the other inmate just stared anxiously. "Ostin, shut off their collars. To the left."

"Got it. Done."

I pushed the VOX. "Jack, shut the door. We turned off the collars, but keep your voices down."

Wade looked around, afraid to speak.

"It's okay, you can talk," Jack said.

"Who is that?" Wade asked.

"It's Michael," Jack said. "They've escaped."

He looked at the camera. "You're the man, Michael."

"Can you take your collars off?"

"Yeah, they're just buckled like a seat belt. Are you sure they're turned off? Because the collars are programmed to go off on full if we try to take them off."

"They're off," Ostin said, then turned to me and shrugged. "I think," he said to me.

The three of them quickly removed their collars.

"Guys, here comes the guard," Taylor said.

"Ostin, can you figure out how to shut off the lights on the floor?"

He went over to the other console. "Just a minute." He quickly scanned the board. "I think this is it."

"Jack, the guard is coming. When he passes your cell we're going to shut off the lights. Can you and Wade jump him and drag him back into your cell?"

"My pleasure. Wade, you hit low, I'll take his arms."

"Count me in," the other inmate said.

"We have night vision here," I said, "so wait for our command."

"Got it."

"He's nearing the cell," Taylor said. "Okay, he's past the cell."

"Ostin, now," I said.

The GP level screens all went dark. Suddenly the images on them changed from black to pale green, ghostlike images.

I whispered. "Jack, can you see anything?"

"No."

"The guard is three feet to your right, directly in front of your old cell. He's facing Cell 9. Open your door."

He opened the door. The guard must have heard my voice and started to turn back.

"Now!"

The three of them blindly charged the guard. Wade hit first, wrapping his arms around the guard's legs, while Jack knocked him over. The other inmate grabbed the guard around the neck. The guard was flailing around but had no idea who or what had hit him.

Truthfully, the attack didn't look a whole lot different than back when Jack and his posse tried to pants me. The three of them dragged the guard back into their cell.

"Eight guards," Ostin said.

"Lights on," I said.

The lights came back on. The two remaining guards just looked around, confused by what had happened.

"Shut the door," I said.

Wade pushed the door shut. The third inmate still had the guard by the throat, and Jack pinned his arms behind his back as Wade handcuffed him. Then Jack pulled off all the guard's weapons, taking a rifle, Taser, and concussion grenade. He handed a pistol and a smoke grenade to Wade and the truncheon and Mace to the other inmate. The inmate immediately sprayed the Mace in the guard's face. "Feels good, don't it?"

The guard gasped and sputtered. "Don't kill me."

"Keep your mouth shut," Jack said to the guard. "You call for help and it will be the last thing you do."

"Put a collar on him," Ostin said into the microphone, "and we'll reactivate it at full."

"Gladly," Jack said. He fastened one of the collars around the guard's neck.

I slid the switch. "Reactivated," I said.

"Welcome to the other side," Jack said. He turned to the other inmate and put out his hand. "What's your name?"

"Salvatore."

"You did well, Salvatore."

"Grazie."

Zeus said, "If you can manually control the elevators, I can take out the front guard, while Jack takes out the other guard. Then we can start bringing the prisoners up here, bypassing the guards on two."

"Brilliant. Except you better have Ian go with you, so you don't walk into an ambush. Ostin, you're in charge of the elevators. Abigail and McKenna, keep watch on the monitors."

"What about me?" Taylor asked.

"Stay close to me," I said. "I'm going to need your help."

I got back on the speaker. "Jack, there are only eight guards left, and Hatch and six electric children. We're going to start transporting all the prisoners up to the fourth floor and arm them. We've got a whole weapons depot up here. What will happen if I unlock all the doors?"

"They're pretty keyed up," he said. "Prison riot. Could turn ugly."

"That's what I was afraid of."

"There're a few guys who could really help us, though."

"How many?"

"Half dozen."

"Okay, this is the plan. There are two guards still on your floor, one in each corridor. Ian and Zeus are going to come down the front elevator and take out the first guard. There's a guard at the end of the corridor to your left. You're going to have to keep him from helping out the other guard."

Jack took out his grenade. "No problem."

"When you've secured the floor, tell us where your friends are. Give the weapons you capture to the ones you trust and then start bringing them up here six at a time. I need you and Wade up here with us. Hatch may launch a counterattack up the stairwell."

"Got it."

Zeus and Ian walked over to the elevator. "We're ready."

"On it," Ostin said. He opened the elevator door. "Level GL. I'm going to cut the lights again. Ian, when you get there tell Zeus where to fire. And stay away from the elevator door. The guard is still armed; he may just fire at the sound of the doors opening."

"Got it."

They stepped into the elevator. Ostin shut the door and sent them down. Then he again cut the lights on that level. We could see the guards on our screens freeze in their positions.

"Look!" Abigail said. "The stairwell door."

Fire and sparks began shooting through the stairwell door. "Someone's cutting their way in here," I said.

"It must be Bryan," McKenna said. "He can do that."

"Taylor!" I shouted. "See what you can do to stop him!"

Taylor walked closer to the stairwell and focused her attention on the door. "Nothing's happening."

Ostin was still staring at his monitor. "Zeus and Ian have reached ground level," he said.

There was a bright flash of lightning on the screen. "Seven guards," Ostin shouted. "What's Ian doing?"

On the monitor, Ian looked frantic. He ran down the hall toward Cell 11.

Already a full line had been cut through the door. "Michael!" Taylor shouted. "I can't stop them!

"Ostin, who's out there?"

"I can't tell. Zeus shot out the cameras."

I turned back to the console. "Ostin, lights up on GL." I pushed the master VOX. "Jack, one of our guys, Ian, is about to come around the corner behind you. Don't shoot him. Can you take the other guard out?"

Jack raised a hand. "On it. Do it, Wade."

Wade threw a smoke grenade down to the end of the hall. The guard vanished behind a cloud of smoke.

"We've got you surrounded, man!" Jack shouted. "You're the only one left. Surrender your weapon now or we start shooting."

The choking guard threw his gun out ahead of him. "Don't shoot. I surrender."

"Get on your knees and put your hands behind your back." Jack turned back to Wade. "Get a collar."

"Six guards left!" Ostin shouted.

Ian rounded the corner and pushed open the cell door. He was out of breath, "Michael, can you hear me?"

"I'm here," I said.

He gasped out his warning. "It's Bryan . . . he's cutting through the . . . stairwell wall."

"We can see the sparks. Is he wearing a helmet?"

"Yes."

I looked at Taylor. "Get away from there. You can't help."

Just then Zeus walked into the cell behind Ian, carrying the guard's weapons. "What's going on?"

"Michael," Ian said. "Bryan's with Hatch and three guards. And he has Nichelle with him. They're coming for you."

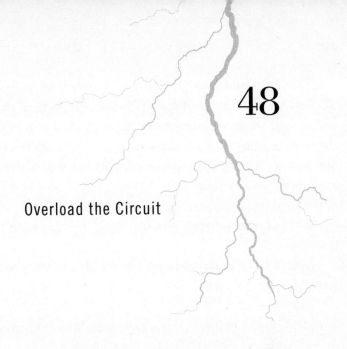

48

Overload the Circuit

earing that Nichelle was on
the other side of the wall sent chills through me.

"Michael, we've got to get out of here," Taylor said.

"I need to finish. Hatch could still kill all the prisoners. Abigail,
McKenna, get out of here."

"We're not leaving you," they said simultaneously.

Sparks bounced off the floor as Bryan completed the second cut.

"He's halfway through," Taylor said.

"I'm not going out without a fight," Ostin said. He ran from the
console over to the flamethrower.

"Ostin, I need you back here," I said. "I need you to unlock all the
prison doors and turn off all the collars."

He turned to me. "We've got to stop them."

Taylor went to the flamethrower. "You go, I'll do it." She crouched
down next to the machine as Ostin ran back to the console and
started hitting switches.

I hit the central VOX button. "Attention, prisoners. This is Michael Vey. We are freeing you. We're unlocking all the doors. Your collars will soon be deactivated. As soon as the light goes off, take them off as quickly as you can. We're under attack, so we don't have much time. Ian, Jack, and Zeus will help get you out of the building. Do exactly as they say."

"How does this work?" Taylor said.

"Just pull the top trigger," Ostin said. "But not now. It will set the floor on fire."

"Michael!" Jack shouted over the intercom. "We're coming up the stairwell to rescue you!"

"Just be careful."

"Hey!" Ostin shouted. "Zeus is coming back up the elevator."

I looked over. "What? Tell him to turn back."

"I can't. There's no intercom in there."

The cutting had started again and Bryan completed another line in the wall.

"He's almost through!" Taylor yelled.

"Ostin, are you done?"

"Just about."

"Ian, all the collars are just about off. I don't know how long we can hold the floor, so use the elevators with caution."

"Got it, Michael."

The front elevator door opened and Zeus walked out.

"What are you doing here?" I shouted to him.

"I need to face Hatch," Zeus said.

"Send him an e-mail. Nichelle's with him. Take the girls and get out of here."

"We're not leaving," McKenna said again.

Taylor looked back at me and shook her head. "I'm not leaving you alone."

"McKenna, Taylor, these are Hatch's personal guards. They'll kill you. They'll kill all of us. Just get out. Please."

Just then Bryan completed the last cut and the thick plated metal fell forward, crashing onto the floor. A concussion grenade flew through the hole at us, exploding in the middle of the room. Taylor screamed, falling to the floor behind the flamethrower.

"Put down your weapons," Hatch shouted, "or we'll throw in real grenades!"

"They have those?" Ostin asked.

"I don't want to find out," I said. "Okay!" I yelled. "Taylor, back away from the flamethrower."

A moment later a guard stuck his head through the hole in the door. He looked around, then stepped inside. He was wearing a different uniform than I'd seen before—a bright green, rubberized suit with a helmet and bulletproof vest. He pointed his gun at us, as if daring one of us to engage him. Then Hatch, wearing the copper helmet, stepped through the hole behind him, closely followed by Nichelle and two other guards. Hatch looked around the room and said to me, "Quite a mess you've made of things, Vey."

"I did my best," I said.

Zeus was standing in the middle of the hall, halfway between Hatch at the stairwell and me at the console. Hatch looked at Zeus and his face twisted in a scowl. "Well, Frank, you turned out to be quite a disappointment."

"My name's not Frank," Zeus said.

"You're right. It's Leonard. Leonard Frank Smith. That's all you are now. What a pity. I made you into a god and you chose to be Frank. I'd laugh if it wasn't so pathetic."

"You gave me a title so you could make me your slave. You lied to me. You lied to all of us."

"Who told you that, Frank? The liar Vey?" He looked at me, then back to Zeus. "It's not too late for you, Frank. Take out Taylor, Abigail, and McKenna right now and I'll let you back into the family."

The girls looked at him anxiously.

"Really?" Zeus said. "You'll let me be your minion again? What a deal."

"Nichelle," Hatch said.

Suddenly the worst pain I'd felt yet pierced my skull. Nichelle had always claimed that Hatch made her hold back but now, for the first time, I believed her. Taylor, McKenna, Abigail, Zeus, and I all screamed out.

At the same time the pop and spray of gunfire echoed in the stairwell and a concussion grenade exploded behind Hatch and the guards. One of the guards emerged from the stairwell. "Dr. Hatch, the GPs are attacking from below. We can't hold them long. There's at least two dozen of them."

"Help them," Hatch said to his guards. They climbed back through the hole into the stairwell. Hatch turned back to us. "Poor, misguided Zeus. You picked the wrong curtain. I gave you power and privilege. I gave you identity. Michael Vey gave you this . . ."

"Michael gave me freedom. You've done nothing for me that wasn't in your best interest. That's all this is about—absolute obedience to you. That's what you want from the whole world. But you're nothing, Hatch."

Hatch's expression turned fierce. "Nichelle, show Frank what nothing truly is. Show no mercy."

She smiled, then looked at Zeus, who immediately fell to his knees, grabbing his temples and screaming.

Then she turned it on all of us. "You insignificant little cretins," Nichelle said. "I told you that I could squash you all like mosquitoes."

Taylor, McKenna, Abigail, and Taylor simultaneously crouched over in pain. My knees buckled and I fell to the ground behind the console. As I writhed in agony, Ostin looked at me helplessly, then crawled past me under one of the consoles and pulled the cord out of the wall. He took the knife from his utility belt and cut the end of the cord and handed me the frayed end.

"Put this in your mouth," Ostin whispered.

I looked at him but did nothing. I was in too much pain to speak, and everything seemed to be spinning around me. I was on the verge of passing out. Ostin put the cord in my hand.

"Just do it!" he said.

I lifted the end of the cord to my mouth as he plugged it back into the wall. Electricity sparked in my mouth and a surge of power hit my body. Immediately, the dizziness left me and I felt normal again. Actually, I felt better than normal. I felt stronger.

Ostin crawled closer to me and whispered. "Michael, listen to me. I think I know how to stop Nichelle. Overload the circuit."

I pulled the cord from my mouth; the power was still flowing into my hand. "What?"

"Don't hold back, give her everything at once. Like blowing a breaker at home."

"Are you crazy?"

"Trust me."

I looked at him for a moment, then I heard Taylor scream out in pain. "Stop, please, stop! Michael!"

"Get behind me, Ostin." I forced myself to one knee, then to my feet.

Nichelle was now focusing her attention on Taylor, who was writhing in agony.

"Hey, Nichelle!" I shouted.

She turned and looked at me.

"You want my electricity? Take it!" I spread out my arms and surged with everything.

Nichelle suddenly started shaking and her expression changed from cruelty to fear. "What are you doing?"

"Keep it up!" Ostin shouted.

Hatch looked at me, then back at Nichelle. "Nichelle, stop him! That's an order!"

I continued to surge.

"What are you doing?" Nichelle repeated, her voice now trembling. "Stop it! That hurts! Stop!"

"I don't think so," I said.

Taylor, Zeus, and the girls all stopped shaking. Nichelle had released them.

"Stop it!" Nichelle screamed again, then she began convulsing as if she were having a seizure.

"What's going on?!" Hatch shouted. "Answer me!"

Nichelle fell to her knees, doubling over in agony. "Stop! Please, stop!"

Hatch turned to me, his jaw clenched, his face red with anger. Sweat beaded on his forehead. For a second we just stared at each other.

Then a guard shouted to Hatch from the stairwell. "Sir, they're on us! You've got to get out now!"

Hatch pulled a revolver from beneath his jacket and pointed it at me. "You did this, Vey. Now pay." He pulled the trigger.

As the gun erupted, lightning flashed across the room and hit the bullet just inches in front of me, blowing it into nothing. Then Zeus turned and hit the gun itself. Hatch screamed out in pain, throwing his gun in the air.

"My name is *Zeus*!"

There was another explosion in the stairwell. "Sir, we've got to go *now*!" the guard shouted, grabbing Hatch's shoulder.

"Help me!" Nichelle cried.

Hatch was holding his arm and glanced down at her. "You're no use to me anymore."

"But I'm your friend."

"You betrayed your own kind, Nichelle. No one likes a traitor. Even those they serve."

Hatch looked at me once more, his face twisted in hatred, then he ducked back out into the stairwell and climbed up to the roof.

"Zero guards," Ostin shouted as he stood up from behind the console.

Nichelle was on her knees, looking at me fearfully. I surged once more. She let out a yelp, then collapsed to the ground in an unconscious heap. A faint wisp of smoke rose from her body.

I let go of the electric cord and fell to one knee, exhausted.

The battle continued to rage in the stairwell as Jack and the prisoners pushed past our floor to the roof.

Ostin looked at me, then Zeus, then back at me. "That was the coolest thing I've ever seen," he said. "A bullet travels at a mile a second, lightning travels at a hundred and eighty-six thousand miles per second. That rocked."

Ostin looked around. Smoke was still wafting through the room and we all seemed frozen in place, like survivors of a natural disaster. He walked over to Nichelle and pushed her with his foot.

"Is she dead?" Taylor asked.

Ostin knelt down and put his hand on her neck. "Unfortunately not."

Just then Ian climbed through the stairwell into the room. "Michael, Hatch is gone. He escaped in the helicopter."

"With all the kids?"

"That I could see."

I sat down on the floor and raked my hand back through my hair. Then I looked over at Ostin. I'm sure it was the release of tension, but I suddenly started to laugh.

Taylor looked at me like I'd gone crazy. "What's so funny?"

"Ostin," I said, slowly shaking my head. "Ostin is. 'Overload the circuit.' Where in the world did you get that idea?"

Ostin said defensively, "Nichelle gave it to me. When she called you all mosquitoes."

"What?" Taylor said.

"Have you ever had a mosquito on your arm, but rather than swat it, just squeezed the skin around where it's sucking?"

"You had a strange, sick childhood," Taylor said.

"No, really, it's cool. The mosquito can't disengage, so it just fills up with blood until it explodes. I figured that since your natural reaction to Nichelle was always to resist, that she had probably just been dragging your powers out of you a little at a time, like sucking out of a straw. I figured if you just gave it to her all at once, she wouldn't be able to handle it."

"Brilliant," I said. "Brilliant." I looked over at Zeus. He was standing quietly, leaning against the wall, his head bowed. "Hey, Zeus," I said.

He slowly turned around. "Frank," he said. "I'm just Frank."

I shook my head. "No, dude, you're definitely Zeus."

He smiled.

"He's right," Taylor said. "You're Zeus." She walked up to him and kissed him on the cheek. "You were awesome. You were more than awesome—you were a hero."

"Thanks." He touched his cheek. "You're the first girl who's ever kissed me."

Taylor smiled. "You deserved it."

Just then Jack and Wade climbed in through the hole in the door. Jack opened his arms to me. "Michael, my man," he said, walking up to me. "Stand up, Vey, I'm going in for the bromance."

I stood and Jack embraced me, almost knocking me over. Then he stepped back and announced, "First time I ever hugged a dude I didn't have a choke hold on."

Wade stood a few yards behind Jack, staring at me. "You saved my life, man."

"And you returned the favor," I said. "We're even."

"Not even close," Wade said. "Not even close."

"So now what?" Taylor asked.

I looked down at my watch. The crystal was broken and its silver band was now scratched, but it was still there. It had come through the battle, just like me. "There's a phone back here," I said. "You better call your parents. They're worried sick about you. You too, Ostin."

Ostin started to the phone but stopped. "But what about your mom?"

"I'm going to find her," I said.

"*We're* going to find her," Jack said. "And bring her home."

I looked at Jack and shook my head. "Thanks, but I've already gotten you guys in enough trouble. I can't take that chance again."

"Trouble?" Jack said. "You can't buy this kind of excitement."

"I'm in," Wade said. "You risked your mom's life for me, I'll risk mine for hers. Besides, even that prison wasn't as bad as living with my granny." He looked at Jack. "The food was better."

"The guards were nicer too," Jack said.

I looked down and smiled. "Well, I could use a ride."

"I'm in too," Zeus said. "I helped capture her. I'll help free her." He looked at me. "What else am I going to do? Can't stay here."

"Count me in," Ian said, stepping forward. "I can't speak for the girls, but last I checked, my schedule was wide open." He looked at Abigail and McKenna. "How about you guys?"

"I'm in," McKenna said.

Abigail just looked down. She furtively wiped a tear from her cheek. "I'm sorry. I just want to go home."

McKenna walked over and put her arm around her.

I looked at Abigail affectionately. "Go home, Abi. You've done enough. But I'll forever be indebted to you."

"As will I," Taylor said.

"We all will," Ian said. "We love you, Abi."

Taylor walked over to the phone and picked up the receiver. She dialed three numbers, then stopped and looked back at me, smiling. Then she set down the phone and walked over and took my hand.

"You, Michael Vey, are a freaking rock star."

My eyes started twitching. "Thanks."

She grinned. "Oh, now you start blinking. You had bombs blowing up around you, bullets shot at you, and two dozen armed bad guys trying to kill you and you're a steely-eyed ninja, and now, when I hold your hand, you're nervous?"

I shrugged. "I can't help it."

She smiled. "I like that." She leaned forward and kissed me on the lips. Then she wrapped her arms around me and we kissed again. Out of the corner of my eye I saw Ostin giving me a thumbs-up. I could practically hear him. I knew what he was thinking without my powers. *Told you so, dude.*

The rest of the clan was smiling as well. When we parted, Taylor said, "Now let's go get your mother."

I leaned back. "Wait, Taylor. You can't come."

She put her hands on her hips. "If you think I'm going to let my boyfriend run off without me, you don't know me."

"But what about your parents?"

"I'll call them."

"What about cheerleading?"

She looked at me incredulously. "You're joking, right? Save the world or shake pom-poms. How shallow do you think I am?"

I started to laugh. It was a pretty stupid thing to say.

Suddenly, McKenna shouted out, "Michael, watch out!"

I spun around. No one had seen her enter. A girl I had never seen before was standing just fifteen feet from me. Zeus surged, knocking her back against the wall. She slid to the ground holding her arm. She cowered, her eyes averted. "Please don't hurt me."

I stepped toward her. "Who are you?"

"She's Grace," Ian said. "She's one of the seventeen."

"You're one of Hatch's kids," I said. "What are you doing here?"

"I ran away from Hatch."

"Careful," Ostin said. "She could be a plant."

"We'll know soon enough. Taylor, see if it's true."

Taylor walked over and put her hands on the girl's temples. Then she turned back to us. "It's true. She hates Hatch."

"I want to come with you," she said.

"Come with me? Where do you think I'm going?"

"To find your mother. I know where she is."

I looked over at Zeus. "What does she do?"

"No one was really sure," Zeus said. "Something with computers."

"I'm like a human flash drive," Grace said. "I can download computers. I broke into the academy's mainframe and downloaded all the information they had before they destroyed it all. You're going to need it to finish what you started."

I looked at her. "What do you mean, 'what I've started'?"

Grace was still holding her arm as she stood. "This is just the beginning. The Elgen have built compounds all around the world. They're already trying to create new electric children. If we don't work together and stop them, they'll hunt us all down individually and then they'll take over."

"It's true," Ian said. "None of us will be safe alone." He turned to Abigail and frowned. "Even you, Abi."

Abigail looked down. McKenna rubbed her back.

"Hatch never forgives and he never forgets," Zeus said. "He's like an elephant with anger management issues."

In the center of the hallway Nichelle groaned.

"Whoa! That's Nichelle," Grace said, her voice tinged with fear.

"Sure is," I said.

Taylor walked over to Nichelle's side. "So what do we do with sunny delight?"

Nichelle's eyes opened. For a moment she looked around the room, then the screeching and pain hit all of us. I immediately surged and Nichelle screamed out, "Okay, I'll stop!"

"Ugh!" Taylor groaned, rubbing her forehead. "Girl, you are one bad apple. Rotten to the core."

"I'd like to fry her like a corn dog," Zeus said. "And be done with her."

Nichelle looked up at me fearfully as I walked over to her. "No, I have something more fitting in mind. Something much worse."

"Worse than lightning?" Taylor asked.

I nodded, looking in Nichelle's face. "Look at her. She has nothing left. Her powers are now worthless, her so-called friends have abandoned her, and we're not going to let her take a single thing from this place." I crouched down and took the diamond collar off her neck. "We'll let her go back to the real world and live the rest of her life as a nobody."

As the reality of my words sunk in her expression turned. "No," she said. "Don't do this. Shock me, Vey!"

I shook my head as I stood. "No. You're on your own."

Taylor walked over and took my hand.

Nichelle turned to Zeus. "Zeus, think of all the times I punished you! Finish me!"

Zeus folded his arms. "I'm done taking orders from you, Nichelle."

"It's time for you to leave, Nichelle," I said. "Jack, would you escort her out? Make sure she doesn't take anything with her."

"Gladly." He walked over and lifted Nichelle by her arm. She struggled futilely against his grasp.

"Let go of me, you creep! I hate you. I hate you all!"

Jack just grinned. "Come on, Wade. Let's show Little Miss Sunshine the real world."

"Hurry back," I said as they waited for the elevator. "We have plans to make."

Jack smiled, raising his fist in the air in a power salute. "Go Electroclan."

As the elevator door closed behind them, a large grin blanketed Ostin's face. "Wow."

"What?" I said.

"We're buddies with Jack and Wade, we just freed an entire prison, and"—he glanced at Taylor—"Taylor Ridley's your girlfriend . . ."

Taylor smiled.

"We're definitely not in Idaho anymore."

"That's for sure," I said.

He held out his hand. "Bones, dude."

I held out my hand and this time it was without hesitation. "Bones."

Taylor smiled and, for the first time, she held her hand out as well. "Bones."

Ostin looked at Taylor and me, then around the room at each of our new friends. His smile grew wider. "You know what we have here, don't you?"

"What?" I asked.

"It's the rise of the Electroclan."

Don't miss the next electrifying book in the Michael Vey series!

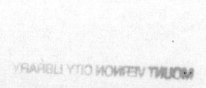